**Laura Roslin Stared Down the Barrel of the Gun**

that was aimed at her, and in a heartbeat two options ripped through her mind. The first was that she would scream in panic, drop behind the podium, try to get away, in an effort to save her life. If Sharon Valerii was really there—if they were all really Cylons—then it wouldn't matter. She was going to die no matter what. But if Valerii wasn't there, if this was all an illusion, then the people of the Colonies would see broadcasts of their president scrambling away from nothing, like a woman possessed. What sort of inspiration would that provide? How could they possibly draw any hope for their future from that?

The second option was that she stand there, staring at her death about to be spat at her from the barrel of a gun. Either she would die bravely, or not at all.

In that instant, she realized that, all things considered, there was only one option.

She stared into the eyes of Sharon Valerii with complete defiance and said nothing.

Valerii fired off three rounds at point-blank range.

---

**Praise for Battlestar Galactica™**

"Much, much better than you can possibly imagine."

—*Salon*

"The toughest, smartest show on television."

—*Rolling Stone*

## Battlestar Galactica™ Novels from Tor Books

*Battlestar Galactica* by Jeffrey A. Carver*
*The Cylons' Secret* by Craig Shaw Gardner*
*Sagittarius Is Bleeding* by Peter David*
*Unity* by Steven Harper*

## Original Fiction by Peter David

*Howling Mad*
*Darkness of the Light**

## King Arthur Trilogy

*Knight Life*
*One Knight Only*
*Fall of Knight*

## Sir Apropos of Nothing Series

#1: *Sir Apropos of Nothing*
#2: *The Woad to Wuin*
#3: *Tong Lashing*

## Star Trek: The New Frontier

## Nonfiction

*Writing for Comics with Peter David*

*A Tor Book

# SAGITTARIUS IS BLEEDING

*A Battlestar Galactica™ novel by*

PETER DAVID

*based on the Sci Fi Channel series created by*

RONALD D. MOORE

*based on a teleplay by*

GLEN A. LARSON

TOR®

A TOM DOHERTY ASSOCIATES BOOK
NEW YORK

This is a work of fiction. All the characters and events portrayed in this novel are either fictitious or are used fictitiously.

SAGITTARIUS IS BLEEDING



Edited by James Frenkel

A Tor Book
Published by Tom Doherty Associates, LLC
175 Fifth Avenue
New York, NY 10010

www.tor.com

Tor® is a registered trademark of Tom Doherty Associates, LLC.

ISBN-13: 978-0-7653-5518-8
ISBN-10: 0-7653-5518-3

First Edition: October 2006
First Mass Market Edition: July 2007

Printed in the United States of America

0 9 8 7 6 5 4 3 2 1

# SAGITTARIUS IS BLEEDING

# CHAPTER 1

*Laura Roslin is having the strangest feeling of déjà vu.*

*She is standing in the middle of a field, and there is a collection of what appear to be obelisks encircling her. There is a firm wind wafting her long brown hair, and she looks down to see that she is wearing a nightgown. This is rather odd, since she is the president of the Twelve Colonies and is not one to go wandering about in her sleepwear under any circumstances.*

*She is not in pain. This is no small thing to her, for there has been a long period of her life where she literally forgot what it was like not to be aching. It is a terrible thing to have one's body turn against one. Yes, if one is attentive enough, one can sense the everyday aches and pains as one's body dies, molecule by molecule, over the standard wear and tear of its lifetime. But what Laura has been experiencing is hardly anything that is remotely typical for a body's daily wear. This has been her body in open revolt, as if she had somehow been inconsiderate of its needs or harsh in her dealings with it.*

*What anger, what venom there must be, for a body to feel that the soul of the person inhabiting it must be pun-*

*ished in the way her body was punishing her. Constant agony as uncontrolled cell replication literally ate her breasts alive. She wondered every so often—not true, she wondered all the time—what in the world she ever did to deserve this. Did it attack her breasts as a symbolic message that she had been a bad woman? Did it attack her at all as a specific message that she had led a bad life? Certainly there must have been some sort of reason. It wasn't possible that the gods could be so randomly cruel.*

*Could they?*

*Perhaps they could. After all, look at the millions upon millions of people who had died thanks to the Cylon attack. What had humans ever done to deserve that?*

*Well . . . there are possible explanations for that, aren't there. Explanations she does not like to dwell upon, since they do not exactly cast humanity in the best light.*

*Better to enjoy the here and now of where she is . . . wherever that may be.*

*Yes . . . yes, she recognizes it now. It is strange that she would have forgotten it, or had the slightest unfamiliarity with it, even for an instant.*

*She is on Kobol, the birthplace of humanity. Kobol, the home of the temple of Athena, which is destined to guide them to their goal: the planet Earth, their salvation, a haven from the Cylons that pursue them.*

*Except she is not on Kobol . . . not exactly. It is difficult to determine whether she is on Kobol, but that which surrounds her is an illusion . . . or if she has somehow been miraculously transported, through means she could not begin to guess, to the destination she has been seeking. Be it illusion or miracle, either way the result is the same: She is standing on the planet Earth. She and the others have . . .*

*The others.*

*She looks around and says, "Where are the others?" Her mouth moves, but no sound is emerging. She cannot determine whether she has been struck dumb or if she has suddenly gone deaf. Even if she did know which condition had afflicted her—or rather, which additional affliction she had just acquired—it would not have answered the question as to where the others had gotten off to.*

*Commander William Adama had been there. Yes, that's right, this had already happened. She had been there and Bill Adama had been right nearby, which was fortunate since a pragmatist such as he might well not have believed it if it had merely been described to him. He would have had to see it for himself. But now, faced with the indisputable reality of ancient prophecy given form, he stared in wonderment at the skies, at the constellations that gave crucial clues to the way home. For the scriptures had said specifically that when the thirteenth tribe landed on Earth, they looked up in the heavens and saw their twelve brothers. This, right here, is (was) the ultimate religious experience and leap of faith for one as rooted in matters of military necessity as the commander of the last of the Battlestars.*

*With him was his son, Lee Adama, a Viper pilot who went by the name "Apollo." Lee, who had become an advisor to her on military matters, and had a relationship with his father that was, to say the least, complicated. Also present was Kara Thrace, another Viper pilot who had served under Lee. She was nicknamed "Starbuck," and it was she who had recovered the sacred arrow of Apollo, the relic which has made this amazing journey possible.*

*They are all there.*

*They are not.*

*They should be there, and Laura Roslin should be dressed in normal civilian clothes. But they are not there, and Laura remains in her nightgown and is alone.*

*She does not know how this could possibly be. Has she somehow made a return to Kobol for some additional knowledge of Earth? But when did this happen? She doesn't remember experiencing any sort of adventure that would have brought her to this pass. She racks her brain, thinking and thinking, and suddenly she laughs (still with no sound emerging). Obvious. So obvious. She has no recollection of anything that brought her here because nothing happened to bring her. She is dreaming. Yes. So simple, oh so simple. She is dreaming, reliving that amazing moment without any of her companions.*

*Again, though . . . why? Well, at least this wasn't something over which one could question the motivations of the gods. This was a product of the sleeping mind, and certainly no one could hope to comprehend whatever scenarios the sleeping mind might throw together.*

*She finds it curious, though, as if she's watching from outside herself. Typically one doesn't realize one is dreaming while it's happening. She would think that the sudden comprehension would be enough to kick her out of the dream entirely. But it does not. It seems to be of no relevance whether she understands or not. Rather it's as if she is a spectator at some sort of film that will be unspooled if she is watching or no.*

*The obelisks. She remembers them so clearly, constructs of abstract faith brought to rock-hard reality. Each made of stone, each one bearing an engraving of one of the symbols of the Twelve Colonies, studded with jewels that are twinkling in the night. Each of the symbols representing the colonies back when they were called by their original names: Aries, Taurus, Gemini, and so on. They ring the perimeter of the meadow where Laura is standing, as the stars of home beckon to her above, pointing the way to their destination.*

*Except . . . she has already been here. Why is she here again? The vagaries of dreams, certainly, but . . .*

*Something doesn't look right. Something is different from the last time.*

*It takes her long moments to notice something on one of the obelisks that was not there before. Some sort of darkness, dripping from the pointed arrow, nocked into the bow of Sagittarius the archer.*

*Laura Roslin approaches it slowly, the hem of her nightgown swirling around her legs. She reaches out toward the dark stain on the Sagittarius obelisk and touches it tentatively with one extended finger. She looks at her hand closely, rubbing her fingers together to get a feel of the liquid's consistency.*

*The color is red, dark red.*

*The liquid is blood.*

*Sagittarius is bleeding.*

*Uncaring of what it will do to the fabric, Laura uses the sleeve of her nightgown to wipe the blood away. It's gone for only a moment, and then wells back up. Blood is dripping steadily from the arrow, and then she notices that the twins, Gemini, are bleeding from their chests as if they've been wounded. She takes a step toward them, and then her head snaps around as Aquarius, the water bearer, sees the water in the top of his jug transform to blood as well.*

*She cries out in alarm without hearing her voice doing so, and starts to back up, putting one hand to her chest. It's on fire once more. She calls for help, but none hear, including herself. They're all bleeding now, blood seeping from the edges of the engravings. The stones are all running red with blood. She looks and sees that there is blood on her hands as well, and she's not sure if it's there because she was touching the bleeding obelisks and got some on her, or if it started generating there spontaneously.*

*And then, slowly, Sagittarius starts to fall forward. It is coming right toward her, and she backs up even further. It seems to be growing, casting a vast shadow over her, and she is running and running and it is becoming impossibly larger and longer, as if it is growing for the specific purpose of catching up with her. Laura Roslin throws herself forward in a desperate effort to escape, and is rewarded with hearing the obelisk thud to the ground behind her. It is the only noise she has heard in this eerie silence.*

*She rolls over onto her back, clutching her chest and watching in goggle-eyed amazement as, one after the next, each of the obelisks collapses. They fall upon each other from all angles, ponderously slow, and the ground beneath her trembles every time another one collapses. Within moments they are piled up, a stack of stones like so many cards. Then great cracks start appearing in them, as if in delayed reaction to their crashing one atop the other. They begin to break apart, slowly first and then faster and faster, and the chunks in turn transform into dust. A strong wind picks up and, minutes later, the obelisks representing the Twelve Colonies have completely blown away, traveling in different directions and scattering to the four winds.*

*Laura Roslin is alone.*

*She wants so much to cry, to sob deeply over what she has just seen. But Laura has always prided herself on her strength, and tears will not—never do—serve any purpose. She creeps forward on her hands and knees, for she does not feel as if she has the strength to stand. There are some small piles of dust and rubble still there, and she picks one up. She stares at it for a long moment, and then allows it to slip through her fingers. The granules twinkle like stars as they fall through.*

*She remembers stars twinkling. She has become deeply nostalgic for that. When she was at home and looked at the stars in the sky, naturally they twinkled as their light passed through the atmosphere.*

*Now when she looks out the window of her ship,* Colonial One, *the stars never twinkle.*

*It is the little things you miss. The little things that pile up on you, one by one, until you are crushed beneath their weight.*

*Crushed. Beneath weight.*

*Laura's head whips around. There is something be-*

*hind her, something she was unaware of until just this second.*

*There is a thirteenth obelisk. It is right behind her, falling toward her.*

*There is a carving upon it. It almost looks like a cross of some kind, but it is upside down and it is not quite a cross. She realizes what it is: a crude representation of a war hammer.*

*That is all she has time to notice before the obelisk slams upon her and she lets out a scream, and this one she hears because*

Laura Roslin screamed.

She sat up in bed in her room, gasping for air, her nightgown plastered to her skin, and she swore she could hear her own outcry echoing in her ears. Her breath came in ragged gasps, and her hair was hanging down and blocking her eyes. She shoved it out of her face, fully expecting to see crumbled obelisks everywhere, but there was nothing except the darkness of her own bed chamber. That, and a loud thumping which she first mistook for the pounding of her heart, but then she slowly realized was someone thudding the door with his fist. "His" was an easy deduction to make because she heard the alarmed voice of her aide, Billy Keikeya, shouting, "Madame President! What's wrong! Are you under attack? Should I call the—"

Her voice sounded slightly raspy as she spoke, and she realized she'd irritated her vocal cords when she'd screamed. Plus she was still gasping for breath, so she sounded as if she'd been running a marathon as she called back, "It's all right, Billy. I'm fine. Everything's fine."

"No one's holding you at gunpoint?"

"No. No one is."

There was a pause, and then from the other side of the door Billy said, "With all respect, Madame President, if someone *were* holding you at gunpoint, they could be making you say that."

Despite the circumstances . . . despite the horrific images that were as vivid to her waking mind as her sleeping one . . . she smiled slightly. "Damn, Billy. You're too clever by half." Even as she spoke, she slipped her feet out from under the covers, lowered them to the floor, got up and walked over to the closet. She pulled her robe on and continued, "It's all right, come in."

"Are you decent?"

Now she actually laughed. "No, I'm stark naked and have three lovers in here. Come on in and join the party."

There was a slightly audible gulp. "You know, out here is actually perfectly all right if—"

"Billy, I'm alone, I'm decent, come in and put your mind at ease."

The door opened and a very tentative Keikeya poked his head in, squinting and trying to make out shapes in the darkness. "Ah. All right. So . . . no security breach here, then . . ."

"None whatsoever." She paused and tilted her head in a slightly quizzical fashion. "How did you hear me?"

"Pardon?"

"I said," she repeated patiently, "how did you hear me?"

"Well . . . you screamed, and it was fairly loud, so . . ."

"Yes, I understand that part," she said. "But it's not as if your quarters are right next door. And the walls are fairly soundproof." Her eyes narrowed. "You don't have a listening device in here or something, do you . . . ?"

"No, ma'am, of course not." Billy was fully dressed, save that he wasn't wearing a necktie. His hand automatically smoothed down the nonexistent tie. "I just don't require all that much sleep. Three, four hours and I'm good as new."

"That's impressive," said Laura. "But it doesn't really answer my question. What, are you lurking outside my door all night?"

"Not . . . lurking exactly."

"Then what exactly? Billy . . . ?"

He rolled his eyes and leaned back against the wall. "It's just . . . you've been through a lot, Madame President. Being thrust into the presidency, being arrested, fighting cancer, winning . . . I mean, gods, that was like a miracle being handed to you."

"A miracle that could benefit a lot more people than me, Billy," she reminded him. "The blood resulting from Shar . . . from the lieutena . . ." She paused and then said, ". . . from the Cylon's pregnancy has astounding healing properties"

She felt a bit guilty, tripping over her referring to Sharon Valerii, the Viper pilot nicknamed "Boomer." A woman who had, several times, served as a source of salvation for *Galactica* and the struggling remnants of humanity . . . but whose home consisted of a prison cell because she could never, ever be trusted. Because she was the enemy. Because she was a Cylon. But fetal blood culled from the . . . the whatever-it-was that was gestating in her stomach . . . had sent Laura's cancer into complete remission. To say nothing of the fact that Sharon's cooperation with *Galactica* command had staved off the Cylons on at least one occasion. Laura felt as if she should be thankful. She felt as if they should be rewarding Sharon Valerii somehow. Give her a medal of honor, a congratulatory basket of something, anything.

Instead she sat in her cell and her baby—which Laura Roslin had been ready to order aborted—continued to grow in her belly, and Laura still struggled with the idea of thinking of Sharon as anything other than a thing. A thing to which the last survivors of the human race in general, and Laura Roslin in particular, owed their lives. Hardly the gratitude one would expect for someone who had done so much.

Well . . . she'd been allowed to keep her child, at least for the time being. Considering a creature who had looked like Sharon—who had *been* her—had gunned down Commander William Adama at point-blank range, perhaps that was as much generosity as one could possibly anticipate.

Her mind was drifting. It annoyed her. She preferred to stay on track in all her dealings. "So anyway . . . what's your point, Billy?"

"The point is, I just feel as if anything could go wrong at any time. And if that happens, someone should be on top of it."

"So you . . . what? Wander the halls and check on me? Listen for any signs of distress? Drop by every hour?"

"No, ma'am."

"No?"

He winced as if caught out in some dirty little secret. "More like every half hour."

She stared at him in the dimness of her quarters, her eyes round in surprise. Then she waggled her finger, indicating that he should come near. He did so, his face a question, and she pulled his head forward and kissed him gently on the top of it. "You," she said, "are a very sweet man. If Dualla lets you slip through her fingers, she would be a foolish young woman, mark my words."

"Ma'am . . ."

"Listen to me, Billy," and she rested her hands on his shoulders. "You'll do me no good if you worry yourself into exhaustion. At least now I understand why it looks like you're fighting to stay awake during press conferences. You need more than three hours' sleep, and not getting it because you're literally wandering the halls watching out for me is unacceptable."

"But—"

"Un . . . acceptable," she repeated firmly. "Besides, I have security personnel who are on duty."

"Which, under ordinary circumstances, would be perfectly fine," said Billy. "But these are dangerous times, Madame President, and besides, we never know who might be a Cylon and who might not be. So I figure that the more eyes watching out for things, the better."

"Mm-hmm. And what if you're a Cylon, Billy?" He started to laugh, but she continued, "After all, supposedly Valerii didn't know of her own nature for the longest time. How do you know you aren't actually patrolling the halls, waiting for the perfect time to do mischief?"

He stared at her, no longer laughing. "You want me to get more sleep and then you tell me something guaranteed to keep me awake all night? Besides, Doctor Baltar's Cylon detection test confirmed I was human. Unless," he suddenly said, "Doctor Baltar is also a Cylon, or under Cylon influence, in which case—"

Laura sighed. "Good night, Billy. Get more sleep and stop worrying about me. That's a presidential directive."

"Yes, ma'am. Thank you, Madame President." He bowed ever so slightly, which naturally wasn't remotely necessary but he likely couldn't help it, and started to exit her chambers. Then he paused, turned and asked, "By the way . . . why *did* you scream, Madame President?"

"Nothing. It was nothing. I had a bad dream."

"About what?"

"About this conversation and its refusal to end. Good night, William," she said with a touch of pointed formality.

Taking the hint, Billy said, "Good night, ma'am," and exited, closing the door behind himself.

Shaking her head, Laura sent the lights back from dim to darkness, removed her robe, and climbed back into bed.

And there she lay, for hour after hour, her mind suddenly alive with concerns. Concerns over the dream, concerns over everyone and his brother being a Cylon. She remembered a conversation she'd once had with Adama in which she'd said, "If you're a Cylon, I'd like to know." To which Adama had quite accurately replied, "If I'm a Cylon, you're really screwed."

She was convinced by now that Adama was not a Cylon.

But as she recalled the bleeding archer, the precursor of their own colony of Sagittaron—and the subsequent collapsing of all the obelisks, which had a symbolism that even a blind man could have seen—she wasn't entirely convinced that they weren't still really screwed.

# CHAPTER 2

In the Viper pilots' lounge, Kara Thrace threw down her cards as her lips twisted in disgust. She fixed her opponent with a fearsome stare and said far more loudly than was necessary, to everyone who was seated at the table, "Who told this bum he could sit in? Huh?"

"You did," Gaius Baltar reminded her coolly.

Kara glanced around the table and saw an array of heads bobbing in agreement. "And you people *let* me? Knowing what you know about me? Knowing what an idiot I am, you were that dumb as to listen to me? Okay, fine." She tilted back in her chair and took a deep swallow of her drink, which sent a pleasant burning sensation down her throat. "In that case, I wash my hands of you. You brought it on yourselves."

Deckhand Callista Henderson, nicknamed Cally, cast a weary *you*-talk-to-her glance at Viper Pilot Lee Adama. Lee, however, refused to rise to it, and instead simply shook his head in resignation.

Meanwhile the target of Kara's ire was leaning forward and raking in his chips. "It's no big deal, Kara. It was just luck," said Boxey, who had to stand on his toes to reach the pot.

"Kara. He's calling me Kara, like we're . . . like we're friends or something," Kara said in mock indignation. "Punk kid! Remember who the grown-ups are around here."

"Admittedly, it's not always easy to tell," Baltar said pointedly.

"A little respect, is all I'm asking."

Lee Adama leaned forward and told the boy, "Personally, I'd give her as little as possible." Kara reached over and thumped Lee in the upper arm, which garnered a laugh followed by a loud "Ow!" as the pain caught up with him.

"How about Starbuck. Should I just call you Starbuck?" asked Boxey.

"Yeah, whatever," said Kara, who was accustomed to responding to the name that was her call handle. Sometimes she even wondered whether Starbuck was her real name, and Kara Thrace was simply this nice, good-girl name that she put on to hide her true persona.

"Are you really upset with me?" The thirteen-year-old boy looked genuinely concerned. "For winning so much money, I mean."

Kara, who was feeling a little bleary-minded with the combination of the lateness of the hour and the alcohol she'd consumed, smiled wanly and chucked Boxey under the chin. "Nah. Not really. You shouldn't worry about my feelings."

"I wasn't," Boxey replied. "I just wanted to figure out if you were gonna jump me once the game was over and try to get the money back."

This prompted guffaws from everyone else, and an archly fierce scowl from Kara.

Lee leaned forward and said, "If you ask me . . ."

"Which nobody did," Kara quickly told him.

". . . you've gotten a lot better at your game, kid. You been taking lessons? Hanging out with a bad crowd?"

"Worse than this one?" asked Baltar. "The mind positively boggles."

"I've met some guys, yeah," Boxey said guardedly.

He paused, and the adults looked at each other with knowing smiles. Cally poked him in the ribs and said in a sing-song voice, "There's a girrrrrrrl . . ."

"Is not!"

"Is too."

"Is not!"

"Is too."

"I can feel my IQ spiraling into the abyss the longer this conversation continues," said Baltar. "Is anyone planning to deal a new hand so I can win some money back from the human chip-vacuum over here?"

"Not happening anytime soon, Mr. Vice President," Boxey assured him.

"Oh, great! *He* gets Mr. Vice President, *I* get Kara! Why is that?"

"Just a thought," suggested Baltar, "but could it possibly have anything to do with the fact that your name is Kara and mine isn't?"

"Frak you," said Kara.

"Been there, done that," Lee muttered a bit too loudly, which drew him a lethal glance from Starbuck.

Boxey looked up in confusion. "What?"

"Nothing," every adult at the table echoed.

With that bewildering consensus, another round of play passed, and once again, Boxey won. By this point everyone was throwing down their cards in disgust. "I want to meet this girl," Cally said loudly as she watched the last of her chips get swept away into Boxey's pile. "Whoever she is. I want to see what she's been teaching you."

"Just how to be a better card player," Boxey said defensively.

"No one's this good a card player."

"I am," Baltar pointed out.

"Couldn't tell it from what we're seeing here."

"Everyone has an off night."

"Well," Cally continued, "like I said, I want to meet her. You ask me, she's probably not even human if she taught you to play that well. Probably a Cylon."

*"That's not funny!"*

Boxey's outburst was so unexpected that the adults were startled into silence. Immediately chagrined at his reaction, Boxey looked down and said sullenly, "Sorry. I shouldn't have . . . I'm sorry."

"No, I am," said Cally, and she reached over and placed a hand atop his. "I mean, you lost your whole family to the Cylon attack on Caprica. I should have . . ."

"It's not that."

Kara raised an eyebrow in mild surprise. "It's not?"

"Well, it is a little," Boxey corrected himself. "But I'm not the only one. Millions and millions of people died, and the ones who didn't, almost no whole families made it. So I've got lots of, you know, company in trying to deal with all that."

"Then what . . . ?" Kara was still confused, and then she saw Lee mouth a name to her that she instantly recognized. "Oh."

Baltar had also worked it out, but he was less subtle than Lee. "You're referring to Sharon Valerii," he said.

Boxey nodded. "Do you ever get creeped out about it?" he asked Baltar.

" 'Creeped out'?"

"Well, she piloted the ship that brought the both of us off Caprica."

"Ah, yes. You know . . . since then, there's been so much going on, I haven't had the opportunity to give it much thought."

"Wish I could say that," said Boxey. He had completely forgotten about the deck that was in front of him, even though it was his turn to shuffle. "Sometimes I have dreams about her. I see her there, and she's at the helm of the ship, and suddenly she goes nuts like she did on Adama. Except in my dream, she doesn't shoot anyone. Instead she pilots the ship down, straight into the planet. And we die. Or at least we're going to die, except I wake up at the last second."

"Oh, thank the gods for that. Can we play cards?" Baltar said irritably.

Starbuck said, "Shut up, Gaius," silencing the vice president. "Boxey, you've got to remember something: The Sharon Valerii who flew that ship from Caprica and saved you, the one who shot Adama . . . she's gone."

"I know. She was shot and killed. Except she's in a cell, isn't she?"

"Well . . . yes."

"See, that's the thing I don't understand."

"I'm not sure any of us understands it any better, except perhaps for Doctor Baltar," said Lee, indicating the vice president. "He's as close as we have to an expert on Cylons."

"I suppose that much is true," Baltar said, shifting uncomfortably in his chair. "Even so, there's still a good deal about them that we don't understand."

"Okay, well . . . Boomer's locked up in a cell right now, right?"

Kara winced slightly at the familiar call name being used to refer to the thing in the brig. "That's right."

"But she's not the one who shot the commander . . . I mean, the admiral," he amended, acknowledging Adama's recent promotion.

"No, she's not," Baltar confirmed.

"So . . . what did she do that was wrong? I mean, if you get locked in the brig, it's because you're being punished for something. So what did she do?"

Now it was Lee's turn to look uncomfortable. "Specifically . . . nothing. She herself has done nothing wrong. But the other Sharon shot my father, so . . ."

"So it has to do with that Admiral Adama is your father?"

"No, it has to do with that the Sharon who is in the

cell is just like the Sharon who tried to kill the admiral. If one Sharon did that, then this one might try it."

"But she might not try anything."

"There . . . is that possibility, yes."

"And she hasn't so far."

"Again, yes, but—"

"Here's what I don't get," said Boxey. "If you," and he pointed at Kara, "had a twin sister, and she did something really, really wrong, and you hadn't done anything, and they told you they were going to lock you in a cell because you might do something even though you hadn't yet . . . would that be, y'know . . . fair?"

"No, that wouldn't be fair," said Kara as she took back the card deck and started shuffling. "But it's not the same thing."

"How come?"

"Because it's not."

"But I don't see why . . ."

"Because she's *not human*!" Kara said. "Okay? She's a machine. She's a toaster. If I had a twin sister, she'd be human like me. But Sharon isn't human and she never was. She's . . . a frakking . . . toaster. Understand?" She started riffling the cards from one hand to the other.

"I guess."

"Good."

He paused, frowning, and then asked, "I just never saw a toaster that could get pregnant."

The cards flew out of Kara's hands, spraying all over the table.

"Yeah, that was a new one on us," Lee deadpanned.

Suddenly an alarm slammed through the ready room. Kara Thrace, who had been slightly wobbly from her alcohol intake, was immediately on her feet. So were Lee and Cally, all of them scrambling toward the flight deck, leaving Baltar and Boxey staring at each other.

"Cylons," said Lee with certainty as they ran.

"Good," Kara said. "With a choice of robots trying to kill me or this conversation, I'll take the robots."

Seconds after the pilots had left the table, one of Baltar's personal guards—tasked with attending to the safety of the vice president—came in and took Baltar firmly by the arm, pulling him to his feet before Baltar could even react. "Come sir," he said, "we're under attack. Regulations state that I have to get you to a secure location."

"Well, thank the gods," said Baltar. "And just where would be 'secure' exactly? I thought our entire problem was that no place was secure."

"Sir, we're under attack. Regulations state—"

"Yes, yes, yes." Baltar turned and tried to scoop up the remains of his chips, but the agent wouldn't be delayed any longer. As he pulled Baltar away, the vice president called to Boxey, *"Don't you dare touch my stack!"*

Boxey watched him go, then walked over to Baltar's unimpressively small stack of chips and touched them repeatedly in a mutinous display of defiance that no one saw.

Then he sank back into his chair and thought about Sharon Valerii, who had saved his life, sitting alone and scared in a cell, except it wasn't her, except it was.

He wondered if she remembered him, or even had the slightest idea who he was.

Baltar hurried down the hallways, the agent making sure to keep him moving quickly. His mind was an enforced blank, as it always was at such times when his life was at risk. Suddenly a familiar voice said to him low, suggestively, almost right in his ear, "Where are you running to, Gaius?"

He almost skidded to a halt as he looked to his right and saw, no longer the agent, but the statuesque blond Cylon that he'd come to know as Number Six. Even as he nearly stopped, though, Number Six pulled him forward so that he continued to move. He tried to respond, but his voice was paralyzed in his throat. She was right there . . . *right there*. The woman who had been his lover, his salvation, who had given him something other than machinery and research to live for and had horrifically turned it into a means of destroying the human race. What the hell kind of man was he, that he could only have happiness at the cost of genocide?

He swore he could smell her perfect scent, and his heart raced—not from fear, but from hopeless longing for a woman, a time, an innocence and naiveté long gone.

"I don't know," said Baltar, and he was speaking of so much that he didn't know—his destination, what would happen next, whether they would survive another minute, why he even deserved to live considering so many people had died because of his stupidity—that the three simple words spoke volumes of his character.

They meant nothing, however, to the agent, who simply replied, "There's nothing you need to know right now, sir, except that you need to keep moving." The agent's voice snapped Baltar back to reality and he struggled to keep up with him while, at the same time, he swore he could hear the faint, mocking laughter of Number Six in his head.

Boxey had been modest when he spoke of how he had picked up tips on quality card playing since making some new acquaintances. He had, in fact, acquired—in a remarkably short time—some other skills as well.

Actually, "acquired" might not have been the best way to put it. "Honed" would be more accurate. Boxey had always been an exceptional hide-and-seek player in his youth. Many was the time that his parents recounted incidents where Boxey seemed to have literally disappeared into thin air. They would enter his room, calling his name, and there would be no sign of him. With weary cries of "Not again!" they would wind up tearing the house apart before Boxey was inevitably betrayed by his laughing—no, chortling—with glee that he had driven his parents crazy once more.

All of that was long ago and far away, or at least so it seemed. Boxey's tendency to laugh aloud at his own cleverness was gone. So was the life. It seemed to Boxey that the memories he had might as well have come from someone else entirely, for all the relevance they had to his current life.

Nevertheless, one of the skills that had not disappeared with his aging into adolescence had been the ability to be sneaky. To make himself not be seen, to blend into the background. He had said nothing to Starbuck or Apollo or any of the others about it, but he had acquired quite the nimble set of fingers. It had been more out of profound boredom than anything else that he had taken up petty thievery on the *Peacemaker*, the civilian transport ship to which he'd been assigned. It was one of the larger transports, and it was extremely easy to slip into and out of the throngs of people who seemed constantly to be milling about in the corridors, looking for something to do to occupy their time. The truth of the matter was that they were as bored as he was; he was just being aggressive about killing the boredom.

It was after he had lifted the wallet of one particularly officious gentleman that he had turned around, prepared to blend in with the shadows, only to discover himself face to face with a smiling red-haired girl. She had freckles, which initially struck Boxey as odd until he remembered that, yes, not all that long ago, the sun had shone on people's faces and done things to their skin. Freckles were gradually beginning to disappear these days, as were all hints of tans, but this girl still sported them. Her face was round, and she had deep brown eyes and small ears that poked out from copious straight hair that hung down to her shoulders.

Boxey braced himself, waiting for her to sound the alarm. Instead all she did was say, "You call *that* blending in with the shadows?" and she rolled her eyes in impatience over this Obviously Dumb Boy's ham-handed attempt at thievery.

Her name was Minerva, Minerva Greenwald, and as she gave Boxey handy hints in making himself scarce, his young heart thudded with the poundings of his first crush.

Boxey still continued to make his way over to the *Galactica* every chance he got, snagging a ride on any shuttle that was going from the *Peacemaker* to the *Galactica* for some reason or other. All the pilots knew Boxey by that point, and were perfectly happy to bring him over with a nod and a wink to the regulations that said they weren't supposed to give anybody lifts. Boxey, nimble-fingered as he was, had also become deft at acquiring hard-to-come-by items from the black market. No one questioned too closely when Boxey was able to provide some particularly rare fruit, or a cigar, or a bottle of fine brandy. Boxey didn't believe in buying friendship, but there was nothing wrong with renting it or bribing it into existence for periods of time.

With all of those questionable talents at Boxey's command, it was small wonder that, while everyone was scrambling to the flight deck and leaping into their Vipers, and the ship was in a state of high alert, Boxey was able to slip into the brig. There were guards at the front, yes, but they were busy talking to each other, speculating about how the frakking Cylons had found them yet *again*, and when the hell was this going to let up already, and what if it never did, and what if sooner or later the luck of the last remains of humanity finally gave out. With all of that going on, it was not all that much trouble for Boxey to secure himself in a corner, wait until the proper moment presented itself, and ease himself behind the guards and through the main door without their even noticing he was there.

The cell area was cramped, as was pretty much everything else on *Galactica*. It wasn't particularly surprising; it was a battleship, after all. There was very little in the military mindset that made room for comfort. Functionality was valued above everything, and if the designers of *Galactica* didn't hesitate to cram the ship's military personnel into as incommodious quarters as possible, certainly they weren't going to go out of their way to provide luxurious accommodations for prisoners.

It was darker in the cell area than outside, and Boxey paused a few moments to let his eyes adjust.

He spotted her at the far end of the brig. Her cell didn't look to be much bigger than five by ten feet, and Boxey tried to imagine what it would be like to have his entire life confined to such a narrow area. The brig didn't have bars the way that other cells did. Instead it had walls that consisted of metal grid screens which appeared to be welded tightly together, reinforced by Plexiglas.

Sharon was in her cot, lying on her back, her arms flopped over her head. It was difficult for Boxey to determine if she was awake or not, although the steadiness of her breathing seemed to indicate that she was asleep. He also couldn't help but notice the developing bulge in her stomach. It wasn't especially large, but it bore the distinctive shape that separated the belly of a pregnant woman from one who was just getting fat . . . a distinction that Boxey had learned, but not before inadvertently insulting quite a few overweight women.

He approached her slowly, moving on the balls of his feet, applying everything he had ever known or had come to know about the art of stealth. She continued not to move. He couldn't see her face clearly, and for some reason that brought him a measure of comfort. He knew Sharon Valerii's face as well as he knew his own, if not better. He had stared at her the entire time that she had flown him from beleaguered Caprica to the relative safety of *Galactica*. So as long as he didn't see Boomer sitting in that cell, well, then . . . somehow the entire business of her being connected to the Cylons—of her being a Cylon herself—was far more ephemeral and easy to deny.

And then, while Boxey was still a short distance away, Sharon abruptly sat up.

Boxey was crouched low and she didn't see him at first, but the sharp intake of his breath—involuntary since he was startled—seemed to make her ears prick up. He suspected she hadn't heard him so much as just sensed that someone had entered. "Who's here?" she demanded, looking concerned. Her voice was muffled by the thickness of the walls; Boxey had to strain to hear her. Her hand drifted toward her stomach in a gesture that could only be considered protective. What a human thing for her to do, to react in such an instinctive manner when she thought her unborn child might be threatened. She glanced around suspiciously, undoubtedly nervous but trying valiantly not to look it. "I said who's here? If you're going to try and attack me, I'm warning you . . . I'll defend myself."

He hesitated, briefly considering the idea of scooting back out the way he'd come and abandoning this entire ill-conceived notion. But then he called to her, as softly as he could so as not to make her even more skittish than she was, "It's me."

"Me?" Her brow furrowed, as she clearly recognized the voice, but wasn't sure from where. Then something clicked in her mind. "Boxey?" she called. "Is that you?"

It was odd. He didn't know whether to feel relief . . . or unease. He stood, smoothing down his shirt. "Yeah. It's me," he said uncertainly.

Sharon let out a sigh of relief and sagged back against the cell wall. "I can barely hear . . ." Then she stopped and pointed at a phone situated on the outside of the cell, matching up with an identical phone on the inside. Boxey went to it, picked it up, and put it to his ear as Sharon did the same on the inside. "What are you doing here?" she asked, her voice coming through loud and clear over the receiver. Then she seemed to get more tense again. "What *are* you doing here? Who sent you?"

"Nobody sent me," he said. "I just . . . I wanted to see you. I wanted to see if . . ." His voice trailed off.

"See if what?" she asked.

"If you remembered me."

"Of course I remember you. Why wouldn't I . . ."

"Because they say it wasn't you."

It was her turn to become quiet. "Oh. Right. Of course." She gave a short, bitter laugh. "Because the Sharon Valerii who rescued you from Caprica . . . the Sharon who you used to hang out here with, share meals with, the one who called you her unofficial little brother . . ."

"She's dead."

"Yes."

"Because she shot Commander Adama, and so Cally shot her."

"How is Cally?" Sharon asked with a trace of humor.

Boxey shrugged. "She's okay. I just beat her ass at cards."

"Good. Good for you."

There was another prolonged silence, and then Boxey said, "So . . . are you her? The one who died?"

"It's . . . complicated."

"That's what everybody keeps saying. I dunno. Sounds like a simple enough question to me."

"It is. It's the answer that's compli . . ." She sighed. "It comes down to this: I have . . . echoes . . . of you. Not the actual memories. Those will go to another . . . me. To me, you're like . . . a vague dream." She smiled and added, "But a nice dream, I assure you."

"Okay." He hesitated, and then said, "Did she know . . . did you know . . . that you were a Cylon when you took me off Caprica?"

"No."

"Because it . . ." He cleared his throat, betraying yet again his nervousness. "I just get worried that maybe the whole thing was . . . you know . . ."

"A Cylon plot?" she asked. "You want to know if my

taking you off Caprica is somehow related to a vast Cylon conspiracy?" Despite the seriousness of the situation, there was a hint of humor in her voice. "Boxey, don't take this wrong, but in the grand scheme of things, you're not that important."

"My father was."

That brought her up short. She looked down, unwilling to meet his eyes. "Yes. He was."

"He was assigned to the Armistice Station," Boxey continued, and there was growing anger in his voice. "He got sent there every year to meet with one of the Cylons, except they never came. And then one of them, or more of them, I guess, showed up, and they blew up the station, and they blew up him. My dad. The first one to die in the new war."

"Yes, he was," Sharon said again, tonelessly, as if she were reciting a particularly unmemorable verse of poetry.

"Were you there for that, too? Did you kill him, like you tried to kill Commander Adama?"

"No, I wasn't. That wasn't my . . . my model. That wasn't me."

"But if you'd been ordered to do it, you'd have done it, 'cause you're a machine."

"But I wasn't, and I didn't. And being a machine has nothing to do with it," she said, sounding a little heated. "Plenty of perfectly human soldiers are given orders they don't like, but they go out and get the job done. That's their responsibility. It's . . ." She stopped, took a deep breath as if trying to calm herself. Then, her gaze fixed on Boxey, she said, "You know what no one considers, kid? That there's as many similarities between our two sides as differences."

"We're not machines."

"Of course you are," Sharon said reasonably. "What else is a human body *but* a machine? You have moving parts . . . you require fuel . . . you break down and need to be repaired by someone—call them 'doctor' or 'mechanic,' it's the same thing—and eventually when the machine gets hopelessly broken, it's junked. The only difference is that when our bodies get broken, we live on. Face it, kiddo . . . you don't hate us because we're machines. You hate us because we're better machines than you are."

"We hate you because you're trying to wipe us out," Boxey replied icily.

"Considering humanity's history of war, it's perfectly possible that—left to your own devices—you might well have wiped yourselves out. Personally, I think it's fairly likely."

"And so you're just getting the job done for us?"

She shrugged. "That's one way to look at it, I guess."

"What other way is there?"

"There's always other ways, Boxey," Sharon told him. "You'd be amazed. You'd be stunned, how a thousand people can look at the exact same event and come away with a thousand different interpretations."

"I'm an orphan because of your race. How many ways can *that* be interpreted?"

She tried to respond to that, but instead she lowered her eyes, as if she were suddenly ashamed. "Why are you here, Boxey? Really? I mean, are you here to yell at me? Because if that's what you want, go ahead. I could just hang up the phone and turn my back, but you'll still have all this anger and no one to unload it on. So you might as well unload it on me, the face of the enemy."

"Don't you do that," he said heatedly. "Don't you start being nice and sacrificing and all that stuff now."

"What do you want me to be? Do you have *any* clue?"

He was about to snap off an answer, but then he paused and realized that he didn't have one.

"I'm sorry if you hate me," she said.

"I don't hate you."

Now she looked up, and there was bemusement on her face. "You don't. Well, you could have fooled me.

Actually, strike that: You did fool me. If you don't hate me, then what . . . ?"

"I miss you. Okay?" he admitted. "I miss hanging out with you. I miss knowing that you were my friend. I miss having the world be nice and easy and black and white, where you knew who was the good guy and who was the bad guy and everything was simple."

Despite the tension of the situation, Sharon couldn't help but smile. "Boxey," she said with great sadness, "I really hate to break it to you . . . but the world was never like that. Not ever. The best spouse in the world can still cheat on their mate, and the worst villain in the world is still capable of pulling a small child out of the way of a speeding car. There's no absolute heroes and no absolute villains. Everything is shades of gray. By the time you were an adult, you'd probably have figured that out. Unfortunately, you learned the lesson earlier than you should have."

"Because of you."

"Because of the Cylons, yes," she told him. "But not me. It may be hard for you to believe or understand . . . but I've never hurt anybody in my life."

"In this life."

"Yes," she admitted. "In a manner of speaking, yes. In this life."

"*Hey!*"

Boxey was startled by the angry shout, and turned to see that one of the guards from outside was standing in the doorway, glaring at him. "What the frak are you doing in here?"

"We were just talking . . ."

"And how do we know that?" demanded the guard as he stalked quickly across the room. "For all I know, you were taking orders from her."

"*What?*" The startled exclamation came from both Boxey and Sharon, the latter hearing the guard's muted voice through the phone.

"She's a Cylon and you sneak in here to have private

time with her. She may be giving you instructions for a new plan to sabotage us. You could be a Cylon, just like her."

"That's stupid!" Boxey protested. "A Cylon just like her . . . ? That's nuts!"

"And why do you say that?" demanded the guard.

"Because . . . well . . ." He gestured haplessly at her. "For starters, she's a girl. How can I be just like that?"

"That's it," said the marine, and he grabbed Boxey by the back of the shirt and hauled him away. The receiver slipped out of Boxey's grasp, swung down on the cord, and smacked up against the side of the cell.

Curiously, Sharon stood there long after Boxey was gone, the phone still in her hand even though there was no one on the other end. Then, very slowly, she hung up the phone, settled down on her cot, and rubbed her stomach absently.

# CHAPTER 3

*It never gets easier.*

Admiral William Adama and Colonel Saul Tigh were polar opposites whenever the *Galactica* was under assault. Tigh, the executive officer, prowled the CIC, studying the screens from every possible angle, moving from station to station like a panther stalking its prey. Adama, by contrast, usually remained immobile unless he was directly summoned by one of his officers. A calm and cool eye to Tigh's hurricane, Adama watched the battle unfold, taking in reports that came at him fast and furious from all directions. His expression typically could have been carved from stone as he assessed the inevitable see-sawing nature of any battle.

*It never gets easier.*

Adama had gotten very, very skilled at making it look easy. One would have thought that he was sending strangers into combat. One would further have thought that there was no doubt in his mind that they would all make it back to the barn without a scratch, as if their lives were charmed and the notion that they might not return in one piece—or at all—was simply too laughable to contemplate.

Except he did contemplate it. Every single damned time that the Vipers launched into combat, there went Lee Adama, Apollo, his son. There went Kara Thrace, Starbuck, who had been the true love of his late son, Zack, and was like a daughter to him. Every single one of the other pilots, even though he didn't have the same depth of emotional bond to them, were members of his extended family. Adama lived and died with each encounter and every shot from a Cylon raider that came flying their way.

Each time his Vipers flew into combat, he waited for it to get easier. He waited for some sort of distance to creep into his heart that would enable him to endure this with less effort.

But it never happened. In fact, it seemed to him that during battles, he literally forgot to breathe. That it wasn't until they were safely away from the latest Cylon assault that he would exhale a breath he didn't even realize he was holding. He was surprised by it every single time.

*It never gets easier.*

The truth of that continued to echo through his brain, and he did what he always did in these situations: He compartmentalized his mind. The concerns that if he had to mourn the loss of his remaining son, he might crack completely . . . the notion that, sooner or later, Apollo and Starbuck's luck would have to run out, they simply could not go on beating the odds forever . . . all of this he tucked away in one little chamber of his brain, a small compartment with a door on it that he would slam, turn the key in, lock, and then go on about his business. His fears and terrors could make as much noise from within their imprisonment as they wanted, but it was all muffled and meaningless. And his face never reflected an instant of it.

"Lieutenant Gaeta, ETA on the Jump, please," called out Adama.

Felix Gaeta scanned the readouts as he worked on programming the next Jump into the ship's computer. It wasn't as if he had to do the Faster Than Light calculations from scratch every time. He routinely updated them so that he would be ready to Jump the fleet to a safe location as quickly as possible. Nevertheless, there had to be systems, procedures followed and double-checks made, lest a miscalculation send the *Galactica,* the *Pegasus,* and the entire civilian fleet leaping directly into a planetary body. Certainly that would solve the problem of constantly being pursued by the Cylons, but it was an unacceptably terminal means of addressing it.

"Three minutes, twenty seconds, Admiral," Gaeta called out, his voice calm and level and not sounding the least bit rushed despite the fact that a fleet of robots was trying to kill them. He realized he was scratching his right hand and forced himself to stop. It was a nervous condition he'd recently developed, a response to the constant stress. It was starting to give him a rash, so he was forcing himself to deal with it.

"See if you can shave a few seconds off that," Tigh said, stepping around to Gaeta's station. "Every single one counts."

Adama winced a bit inwardly. He knew it was Tigh's way to be brusque, to demand the best and more than the best from his officers. But he didn't feel there was anything remotely constructive in what Tigh had just said. Certainly Gaeta knew that every second counted. This wasn't a news flash or an observation that had just come to Tigh's attention. However he wasn't about to remonstrate his XO in the midst of a battle situation. The depressing thing was that he knew that, even if he scolded Tigh about it in the privacy of his quarters, it still wouldn't make a damned bit of difference. Tigh would either apologize and say he would try to do better, or he would say that Gaeta had in fact looked at him sideways two days earlier and he was letting him know who was boss. Either way, nothing was going to change anytime soon. Adama was beginning to think that he had seen it all.

"Never seen that before," Starbuck muttered.

Her words, even though they were spoken to herself, sounded in the ear piece of Lee Adama, who was in the midst of engaging a Cylon raider that was coming right at him. "Starbuck, this is Apollo, I didn't copy that!" he said, firing at the raider that deftly angled away from him.

Starbuck didn't answer immediately. She was studying the battlefield before her. At least there were fewer raiders this time. The number of Cylons assailing them seemed to have dwindled since they had blown up the *Resurrection* ship, the vessel that had functioned to "resurrect" Cylon agents after they were killed. She strongly suspected there was a connection, although she wasn't sure what it was . . .

*Head in the game, Starbuck, get your head in the game.*

She barrel rolled and swung around toward a Cylon raider who was coming at her, guns blazing. Except . . .

Except . . .

"They're shooting wide!" she said as deep space was filled with Vipers going up against Cylon raiders. "I'm not even dodging the frakking things! It's like they're not even shooting at me!"

"Of course not, they're shooting at *Galactica*! Or the fleet!"

"Negative, I say again, negative, Apollo," Starbuck insisted. "I'm tracking trajectory! They're shooting at . . . at nothing!"

"Why the frak would they be doing that?" said Apollo. "Trouble with target lock?"

"There aren't people in those things shooting their guns, Apollo! Those ships *are* Cylons, remember? It's like saying their whole fleet has a giant head cold and can't see straight!"

Even as she spoke, she continued to press the attack. And now Apollo saw what Starbuck was talking about as the Cylons essentially did everything they could to stay out of the Vipers' way while returning fire that was woefully off target. Apollo hadn't been tagged even once.

"Not hitting them? Are you sure?" asked Adama.

Petty Officer Second Class Anastasia Dualla said, "Reconfirming it, Admiral. Starbuck first noticed it, then Apollo, and now Hotdog and Kat are saying so as well. Either the Cylons have forgotten how to shoot, or they're deliberately aiming wide of our people. And they're not drawing appreciably closer to *Galactica*."

"Admiral," Gaeta informed him, "we're ready to make the Jump."

"Shall I recall the Vipers, Admiral?" asked Dualla, leaning toward her communications board in that slightly hunched manner she had when they were in the midst of a battle.

Adama's mind was racing. He had come to know the clockwork repetition of the Cylon mind, or at least he thought he had. Why in the world would they start changing tactics now? Something seemed wrong.

"Admiral . . ." Dualla prompted.

"He heard you, Dualla," Tigh said sharply, and Adama realized that Tigh was standing near his shoulder. The decisive sound of his voice and defiant look of his posture would never have betrayed the confusion in his eyes over Adama's hesitation. "He'll give the order when he's ready." Then, in a low voice that only Adama could hear, Tigh murmured, "Which will be anytime now, right?"

"Tell the Vipers to buy us more time. Make sure the Cylons keep their distance," said Adama said in a calm, almost detached voice. Then he continued, "Colonel . . . scramble a raptor for immediate launch. Lieutenant

Gaeta, relay the Jump coordinates to the raptor. Tell them I need a recon mission stat. In and out. If they linger at the Jump point even one second, that's one second too long."

Neither Tigh nor Gaeta nor any of the rest of the crew in CIC even pretended to understand, but fortunately enough, understanding an order wasn't necessary for following it.

So it was that a raptor, under the guidance of Lieutenant Kathleen "Puppeteer" Shay (so called for her compulsion to have her hands in so many things), hurled itself into the ether while the Vipers continued to fight a delaying action against the Cylons.

The call that came through seconds later from the *Pegasus* didn't especially surprise Adama. He picked up the phone and said into it, "*Pegasus,* this is *Galactica* actual."

"Galactica, *this is* Pegasus *actual,*" came the voice of Commander Barry Garner. The former engineering chief had been pressed into service as commander of Battlestar *Pegasus* after the assassination of Admiral Cain by a Cylon operative, followed by the scandalous murder of Commander Jack Fisk, who had had deep ties with the black market trade. Garner, who very likely had never figured to serve as his vessel's CO, nevertheless did his best to be up to the challenge. If he ever felt overwhelmed by what was expected of him, he never let it show, a technique of which Adama approved. "*Admiral, all due respect, what are we waiting for? Our Vipers are battling the Cylons right alongside yours, but it's not as if we need an extended workout.*"

"We're investigating something," Adama said cautiously. Under the circumstances, it was never safe to assume that the Cylons hadn't found a way of listening in on their communications. In fact, it was probably safer to assume they *had* found a way and to act with appropriate caution. "Stand by."

"*Stand by?*"

"Yes, *Commander,* stand by," said Adama with particular emphasis on rank, a not-so-subtle reminder of exactly who was in charge.

There was only the slightest pause, and then Garner replied, *"Standing by, aye."*

Puppeteer, handling the controls with the vast confidence she always displayed in such situations, folded space around herself and leaped to the coordinates that Gaeta had conveyed to her. She had never quite adjusted to the sensation. It wasn't enough of a reaction that it hampered her ability to handle a raptor or get her job done. It was just a second or two of nausea that swept through her, and then she was able to mentally right herself and get on with whatever her mission was.

This time was no exception. Puppeteer braced herself as the FTL drive kicked in and propelled her to the new destination that was intended to be safe haven—albeit temporary, of course, thanks to the damned Cylons constantly nipping at their heels. Not for the first time, Puppeteer wondered if there was ever going to be a time when humanity could just take a long, deep breath of relief and go about its business without worrying about the damned toasters leaping on them like jackals on lions.

Space twisted around her in half a heartbeat, using technology and scientific theory that she couldn't have explained if someone had put a gun to her head. Still, it was like walking into a room and flipping a light switch. As long as the light illuminated the room, who gave a damn how it worked.

She was never actually able to perceive the Jump while she was in transition. It wasn't as if some vast vortex of stars swirled around her in a hypnotic haze, providing a tunnel through which her ship hurtled. She was simply in one place, then she was in another, with a slight sense of having been stretched like a rubber band and then having snapped back almost instantaneously.

The FTL drive spat her out into the new coordinates,

and she felt that same typical instant of nausea, which she pushed away from her.

Then space around her seemed to explode.

Acting completely on reflex and survival instinct, she jammed the raptor's stick and sent the ship spiraling backwards. Even as she did so, her eye had just enough time to catch sight of something, and it took her brain another second or so to process what she was seeing.

*"Frak me!"* she shouted as she reactivated the FTL drive. Blasts continued to erupt around her. The ship jolted and she felt a moment of panic—not just from the prospect of dying, but from doing so without being able to get back to *Galactica* with her mission completed. She'd been hit—only a glancing blow. But they were zeroing in on her, and she couldn't count on her luck to hold up. The FTL roared to life once more as she slammed the ship forward, and suddenly there was a blinding explosion dead in front of her, and everything went black.

"How much longer do we wait?" Tigh said. There was nothing in his tone that suggested he was challenging Adama's authority, but he was clearly getting a bit apprehensive about the delay.

"Just long enough," replied Adama. He had actually calculated exactly how long he intended to wait for a report from the raptor, balancing that against the apparently questionable Cylon assault. He was certain there would come a point where the Cylons would drop the miss-on-purpose assault and start firing for real, and he factored that in to a mental countdown that was running rapidly toward zero. But he didn't feel the need to say all that to Tigh, and Tigh—being the officer he was with the long history that he and Adama shared—would never consider pushing harder on the question.

*Ten,* the mental clock ticked down in Adama's head, *nine, eight, seven . . .*

Dualla suddenly turned and said, "Admiral! Raptor One is back! She's reporting . . ." Dualla's eyes widened.

"Dualla," Adama prompted, time running out.

"Sir, Puppeteer says the Jump point is swarming with Cylons! She says it was like space was alive with them! She can't even begin to guess how many there were!"

Colonel Tigh paled slightly upon hearing the news, and there was a moment of stunned shock in the CIC. Gaeta's hand had been poised over the FTL controls the entire time. Now, as if all feeling had fled from his fingers, he slowly lowered it while staring in astonishment at Adama.

*It never gets easier.*

"An ambush," growled Adama. "They're trying to herd us right into it." He paused and then said, "Dualla . . . get the horses back into the barn."

"All Vipers, return to *Galactica* immediately."

Knowing that he was about to order his officer to roll the dice with the last survivors of humanity, Adama said, "Lieutenant, plot a blind Jump. Best guess. Get us out of here."

Gaeta visibly gulped, but it wasn't as if the order was a complete surprise to him. It wasn't the first time that he'd been required to do such a thing. He'd accomplished it successfully before, but it was always a white-knuckle maneuver. Acting as the thorough professional that Adama expected him to be, Gaeta said, "Aye, sir," and number crunched as fast as he could. By the time the last of the Vipers had returned to the bay, he had coordinates transmitted to the rest of the fleet . . . prompting an immediate, albeit not unanticipated, communiqué from Garner on the *Pegasus*. *"Are these coordinates right, Admiral?"* he asked. *"They're different from—"*

"I know that, Chief. The previous coordinates are unusable. This is our best guess."

There was the briefest hesitation, and then Garner said coolly, *"Well, then, this should be fairly interesting."*

"Yes." Adama hung up the phone, then turned to Gaeta. Gaeta was staring right at him, waiting for confirmation. All Adama had to do was nod, and then Gaeta keyed in the final coordinates.

"FTL engines on line," Gaeta said. He glanced just once at his own hand, feeling that the entirety of humanity was residing in it, waiting to see what he was going to do. Then the FTL drive kicked in and the fleet vanished from the site, hurtling into the complete unknown.

A split instant later, they reemerged into normal space.

A blazing star hung directly in front of them.

"*Frak!*" exploded from Gaeta's lips.

"*Full reverse thrust! All ships!*" shouted Adama, and the order was instantly relayed. It wasn't entirely necessary, considering that when one is hurtling right into a star, it doesn't take much to realize that the best direction to be heading at that moment is anywhere other than forward.

They were still thousands of miles away from the star, but distances in space could be eaten up very quickly, especially by ships that were dropping out of light speed. Furthermore, the *Galactica* wasn't built for maneuverability. It didn't corner worth a damn, and it wasn't designed to stop on a mark. Objects in motion tend to stay in motion unless acted upon by another force. With no friction in space, the only force to halt the *Galactica* was the reverse thrusters. Unfortunately, they were already being acted upon by another force entirely: the star's gravity field. It was just beginning to act on them and Adama had no desire to pit the strength of his ship's engines against the pulling power of billions of tons of blazing gas. Worst-case scenario, they would be yanked in and toasted in a matter of seconds. Best-case scenario, the *Galactica* would be ripped in half. Neither was an appealing prospect.

The smaller ships were able to halt themselves easily, but then they madly scrambled to get out of the way, for the *Pegasus*—bringing up the rear—wasn't slowing any easier than the *Galactica.* The civilian transports cut right, left, up, down and sideways, any direction they could go relative to the aft Battlestar that would easily smash them to bits if it collided with them.

The prospect of being rear-ended by the *Pegasus* occurred to Adama, but he had to deal with one crisis at a time. Although he might have been imagining it, he thought he could hear the hull of the mighty warship screaming in protest as the engines labored to halt the ship's forward progress. No . . . he wasn't imagining it. Above all the sounds of reports and orders being relayed and confirmed, people were looking around in response to what sounded like groaning, as if the ship were a senior citizen being forced to run laps. It wasn't the first time that Adama was being reminded that the *Galactica* had been scheduled for retirement, to be transformed into a museum due to its age. *You and me both, we could use the rest,* he thought grimly.

The *Galactica* hurtled toward a collision with the star, and the screens adjusted automatically to dim the blinding brightness so the crew's retinas wouldn't be burned away from looking at it. Adama had several seconds to ponder the irony of that: that they wouldn't go blind while they were exploding in the nuclear heart of a celestial furnace.

The entire vessel trembled even more violently, and it was slowing and slowing, but it was going to be too close. And then, ever so gradually, the ship slowed to a halt and then stopped. Seconds later, the full force of the reverse thrusters finally accomplished the job, and the *Galactica* started to move backwards.

*"Pegasus hasn't stopped yet! She's coming right at us!"* Gaeta called out.

*"Cut thrusters! Brace for impact!"* shouted Adama. He gripped the nearest railings. He saw others closing their eyes involuntarily, although not looking at the screens certainly wasn't going to ward off disaster.

The *Pegasus* was approaching them like some vast harbinger of doom, and suddenly they saw the vehicle cutting hard to port. It was going to be an unspeakably near thing.

"Come on, come on, turn," growled Tigh.

And then, as if in response to Tigh's imploring, the vast battleship moved sharply to port even as *Galactica*'s own reverse thrusters hauled them away. The nose of the ship angled downward in relation to the *Galactica*, and even as the *Pegasus* seemed gargantuan in their screens, it then dropped straight down and away from them. Adama could have sworn he'd seen the terrified faces of people on the *Pegasus*, their faces pressed against viewing ports, watching the two behemoths narrowly avoid each other.

A long, tense silence filled the CIC, punctuated only by the many sounds that the various instruments in the command center routinely made. And then Adama turned to Gaeta, who looked as if all the blood had drained from his face and was somewhere down around his shoes, and said as calmly as could be, "You trying to make things exciting, Lieutenant?"

"Not that exciting, no sir," Gaeta said, and there was a slight gasp in his voice indicating he'd been holding his breath . . . a tendency Adama could certainly relate to.

"Well . . . if they say any landing you can walk away from is a good one, the same can be said of a light-speed Jump. Well done, Mr. Gaeta."

"Thank you sir," sighed Gaeta, and there was ragged clapping and cheers from the others in the CIC.

But it was quickly silenced by a look from Adama. "Now that we narrowly survived, we need to give top priority to figuring out how the Cylons knew where we were going to be leaping to. If we have a bug or virus in our computer . . . if we have a security leak . . . we need to find it and plug it."

"Aye, sir, I'm on it," Gaeta said firmly.

Adama nodded and turned away, mostly so that no one else would see the visible relief flooding through him. Tigh stepped in close to him and said, "Good instincts on your decision, Admiral. About suspecting it might be a trap."

"It doesn't make sense, though," said Adama. "Even if they were trying to get us to leap into an ambush . . . why shoot wide of our people? All it did was raise our suspicions. They could just have easily engaged us for real, we activate the FTL engines with the coordinates they already know, and bam, we're in their trap. Why alert us to the possibility . . . ?"

"Perhaps the Cylons aren't as clever as we give them credit for," suggested Tigh.

Adama glanced sidelong at him. "If I'm given a choice between overestimating an enemy or underestimating . . . I'll go with the former."

"Me, I'm just glad the *Pegasus* was only a near miss instead of a disaster."

Smiling ever so slightly in amusement, Adama noted, "People always say that. A 'near miss.' It wasn't a near miss. It was a complete miss. It was a near hit."

"As long as we didn't take it up the aft, I'm satisfied with whatever it was."

Adama nodded wearily at that.

Tigh turned away, intending to go and hover nearby Gaeta as he began running checks on his navigation system. But he paused long enough to say, "It never gets easier, does it."

Staring at him blandly, Adama let the statement hang there for what seemed like forever, and then said, "I hadn't noticed."

On *Colonial One*, Laura Roslin was receiving an update from Adama over the phone of what had transpired. Her blood chilled as he described to her the horrific ambush that would have been awaiting them if they had been foolish enough to go leaping through space to the planned coordinates.

"Well done, Admiral," Roslin commended him. "In this day and age, when it's so easy to second-guess every decision people make about everything, it's nice to know that this decision of yours was completely valid. No 'down side,' as it were."

"As it were," agreed Adama. He was willing to admit to himself that there had been a time when he literally couldn't stand the sound of Roslin's voice. He had been certain she was using the cloak of government to thrust humans into situations where their very existence was jeopardized. But over the past weeks, be it because of receiving deft and canny political advice from Roslin, or because of working with Baltar and that damned Cylon Sharon of all people (he'd been convinced he'd had a knife in his stomach the entire time he was speaking with her, due to the extreme belly aches he'd been enduring), he'd come to respect Laura Roslin greatly. Perhaps even . . . feel more than just respect. Not that this was something he intended to bring up to her, or even completely acknowledge himself. They both simply had too many responsibilities to risk entanglements of any sort. At least, that was what he kept telling himself.

"And you're trying to determine how the Cylons knew where we were going to Jump to?"

"It's being investigated even as we speak."

"That's a relief. The last thing we need is them working their way into our systems once more." She added thoughtfully, "What about the *Pegasus*? My understanding is that their computer system would be far more susceptible to Cylon tinkering, since all their computers are linked." The fact that *Galactica*'s computers were not linked one to another had been the ship's salvation, since it meant that the Cylons could not readily infiltrate the computer network.

"You're absolutely right, Madame President," Adama agreed. "That is being investigated as well."

"Good. Please keep close tabs on that, Admiral. I'm not entirely sure I trust Chief Garner to get the job done . . . or trust him at all, really."

This comment surprised Adama. "Why not, Madame President? Do you have information I'm lacking? Is there reason to doubt his capability as an officer?"

"No to both," she admitted. "But considering that we wound up almost assassinating Commander Cain, and considering Commander Fisk was fronting a black market operation, you'll understand if I don't exactly have the highest hopes for the *Pegasus* command squad."

"Understood."

She imagined that Adama was smiling as he said that. He had the loveliest smile.

Then an image hammered its way back into her memory. She jumped into the pause that had crept into their conversation to ask, "Admiral . . . I have a rather odd question for you."

"It's been an odd day, so it fits right in."

"If I told you that Sagittarius was bleeding, what would that suggest to you?"

He didn't reply immediately, except to laugh low in his throat and say, "Well, the question certainly lived up to the advance billing." He considered it for a short time, and then said, "Given that Sagittarius is the ancient name for the colony Sagittaron . . ."

"Yes?"

"I'd say if anyone was going to cause any sort of bleeding in connection with Sagittaron, I'd probably look no further than Tom Zarek to be the cause."

Laura Roslin could have hit herself in the side of the head in frustration. "Of course," she said. "After all, he's the representative to the Quorum of Twelve for Sagittaron, gods know why."

"I'm only wondering why it is that we're talking in symbolism and metaphor."

"It . . ." She waited a moment, not wanting simply to spill everything that was going through her mind at

Adama's feet. She had her own problems, and she had to deal with them. "I was just . . . wondering . . . what the image might suggest. That's all."

"That's *all*?"

"Yes, Admiral," she said calmly, almost with an air of indifference. "That's all."

She could picture him shrugging as he said, "Very well. That's all, then. *Galactica* actual over and out."

There was a click as he hung up the phone, and yet Laura Roslin stared at the disconnected receiver for a good long time, wondering if Adama had a point and Tom Zarek was somehow up to trouble again.

# CHAPTER 4

Tom Zarek—freedom fighter, untrustworthy schemer, hero, villain, all depending upon whom one talked to—had continued to make his home on the *Astral Queen*, despite the fact that as the representative of the Quorum of Twelve, he was entitled to far more luxurious accommodations. He chose not to avail himself of them, for he felt it vital to keep as much of his connection to the "common man" as he possibly could.

On the other hand, he wasn't stupid. He had far outgrown the small, confined cell that had been his home ever since he had been elevated from mere prisoner to his colony's (or, more correctly, what remained of his colony's) most prominent figure. So he had taken for his office and quarters what had been the lodgings of the warden/captain of the *Astral Queen*. Since the events of the prisoner uprising, the administrators had decided that the best idea would be for them to make themselves as scarce as possible.

This left something of a power void in the day-to-day affairs of the prisoners themselves. Naturally they had turned to Zarek to make certain that some degree of order was kept in their existence, and Zarek had obliged them. Much of his time was spent on overseeing disputes. Not as a judge, certainly: Zarek was far too rebellious by nature to allow himself to become so authoritarian. He was, instead, a mediator. He always managed to find a common ground, and his method of bargaining was rapidly become legendary. If one of the parties didn't like the compromise that Zarek proposed, then his sergeant-at-arms would break the complainer's kneecaps. If they both complained, both parties got their kneecaps broken. Zarek had announced this policy and, at first, the prisoners had thought he was joking. They were disabused of that notion the first time two moaning disputees were seen crawling out Zarek's door. Their agony drove home the point with far greater force than anything Zarek could have said.

There was some minor rumbling about trying to take down Zarek rather than submit to such a means of oversight. But that notion went away once the residents of the *Astral Queen* came to the realization that Zarek's death would create a power vacuum, and if that happened, the bodies would start stacking up like cordwood in the subsequent struggle for dominance. One might despise the way a dam is constructed, but no one is stupid enough to shoot the guy who's got his finger in it preventing the water from flooding through.

So it was that Zarek's position and status were perfectly safe by dint of the fact that, although they didn't one hundred percent trust him, they distrusted each other far more.

At least, that was the status until the day that the civilian fleet had yet another narrow escape from the Cylons.

Although the ships were spread out, it was still hard to keep secrets, especially when something unusual happened. And certainly the *Galactica* nearly plunging into the heart of a star fell into the category of "unusual." The fact that the civilians had come extremely close to losing their best means of protection against an implacable enemy had not gone unnoticed, and a number of Zarek's "constituents" were demanding to know just what the frak had happened.

Zarek was moving quickly down a corridor, accompanied by Cortez, his sergeant at arms, and a handful of petty functionaries. This, in and of itself, was not unusual. There were several people following Zarek as well, constituents peppering him with their concerns. This was also not unusual. What was unusual was the volume and vociferousness with which they were speaking.

The largest and loudest of them was a man Zarek had known for some time, a bear of a man named Luther Paine, who seemed bound and determined to live up to his last name. Zarek kept walking, since it had been his experience that—if he stopped—it made it much harder for him to extricate himself. So he was walking and talking at the same time. "I hear what you're saying, Luther."

"I don't give a damn that you're hearing what I'm saying," Paine told him sharply. "I want you to listen to what I'm saying! I want you to find out what in the name of the gods happened with this latest invasion!"

"I already know what happened, and so do you," Zarek said. "We were attacked, we escaped. End of story."

"End of story! We almost saw the *Galactica* go up in a ball of flame, and then the *Pegasus* almost collided!"

Violating his own determination to keep moving in the face of hostility, Zarek turned and faced Paine. He wanted to try and end this quickly, before it began to spiral out of control. Paine was someone to whom the prisoners listened, and he didn't need this idiot running all over the place, stirring things up. "The key word there is 'almost.' Almost doesn't mean a thing. It's results that count, and the result was that we got away. If you don't like the way we did it, feel free to pop over to the *Galactica* and tell Adama yourself."

"I shouldn't have to! You're our frakking representative! You should be the one who tells him! Or are you afraid to?"

This last comment riled Cortez, and he took a step forward with his fists tightly clenched. The two men were built about the same, and it was anybody's guess who would come out on top if they came to blows. Zarek put a hand out in either direction, wanting to keep the men apart. "I'm not afraid of Adama. You know that," he said tightly to Paine.

"Oh yeah? And how, 'zactly, am I supposed to know that?" Paine's tone remained defiant, and he kept tossing glances at Cortez as if to verify just where Cortez was in relation to himself.

"If I haven't been afraid of entire governments . . . if I haven't been afraid to be jailed for my beliefs . . . what makes you think I'm afraid now?"

Paine's jaw twitched back and forth a couple of times. He didn't drop his gaze, but he amended, "Maybe not afraid, then. Maybe just too damned comfortable."

Zarek rolled his eyes and started walking again, and Paine followed behind. "You," said Zarek, "have no idea what you're talking about."

"Oh, don't I? Pretty cushy status you've got for yourself now, huh, Zarek? Member of the Quorum. Gone all legitimate now. Angling for the presidency. Maybe you and Adama have something worked out. You stay out of his business, he stays out of yours. Maybe you figure it's not smart to make too much of a ruckus now because you're trying to climb up the ladder. Leave the guys on the lower rungs behind while trying not to piss off the ones standing at the top."

"Yeah, that's it, you've got me all figured out," said Zarek with obvious exasperation. "Look, Luther, I've listened to you, I'm considering what you're saying. My guess is, the Quorum of Twelve is going to have some of the same questions as you. I don't need to go running off on my own. I'll have eleven other representatives, and we'll get a lot more done and a lot more answers if we operate as one instead of all of us flying off in all different directions. There will probably be an inquiry, and we'll find out at that point what went wrong, and make sure it doesn't happen again. Will that do it for you?"

Luther Paine sounded as if he wanted to say something else, but instead simply replied, "Yeah. Yeah, that does it for me fine."

"Good. Now if you'll excuse me, I have a meeting scheduled with . . ."

His main office, used for conferences and meeting with various dignitaries, was just ahead. Cortez stepped forward, preparing to open the door for him, and that was when an explosion—sounding all the louder because it was within a confined space—went off just a few feet away from Zarek. He was nearly deafened from the noise. He was stunned to see Cortez drop, clutching at his right shoulder, blood welling up between his fingers. The others who had been walking along with him scattered as quickly as they could.

"On second thought, it's not fine," snapped Paine.

His eyes were wide and he had a crazed look on his face. Zarek didn't know what the hell had gotten into him. It wasn't as if Zarek didn't have the respect of every man on the *Astral Queen.* The only thing that occurred to him was that this was some sort of bizarre power play. That Paine was hoping to move up in power and prestige by taking down the guy who was one of the top players. If Zarek was dead, Paine could make up anything he wanted in terms of an excuse for doing it. Who knew if Paine perhaps represented some sort of growing belief that Zarek really was becoming too much of the "establishment"?

That, however, was a consideration for a future time, presuming there was one.

"Where did you get that gun?" Zarek demanded, deciding that the best thing to do was act as if he was totally in command of the situation.

Paine looked slightly taken aback that Zarek wasn't daunted by having a weapon pointed at his face. "Black market," he snapped. "Not that it's any of your business."

"If you're waving it in my direction, that makes it my business." He looked down at Cortez. "You all right?"

"I'll live," growled Cortez, looking daggers at Paine.

"You go right on telling yourself that," Paine snapped back.

That was when the door to Zarek's office opened and a man emerged from it. And emerged. And emerged.

That, at least, was what it seemed like to Zarek. The man was gargantuan, as large an individual as he had ever seen. His shoulders were half again as broad as Paine's, and his bare arms had muscles that looked as big as Zarek's skull. He had a head of red hair and a bristling red beard that was a slightly darker hue. His simple white shirt was having a difficult time, strained as it was covering his massive chest, although his dark green trousers hung loosely. He seemed to radiate confidence, as if he were certain there was no challenge he could not undertake. More: that if he undertook it, he would succeed in whatever the endeavor was.

"Is there a problem here?" he asked, his voice rumbling like thunder.

Zarek could not recall a time in his life when he had been at a loss for words, but there was a first time for everything, and this was it.

Even Luther Paine seemed daunted. Rallying quickly, he said fiercely, "This isn't your concern."

"Oh," was all the man said. "All right." For half a heartbeat, he turned as if he were about to walk away. Then his arm reached across the distance between him and Paine before Paine had even registered that the behemoth was moving toward him. His huge hand enfolded Paine's as if it was an adult's hand firmly grasping a child's, and then he squeezed. His expression never changed. There was an audible *crack* that was partly muffled by the giant's hand, and Paine let out an ear-splitting scream.

"Pardon me," said the giant, easing past Zarek. Very carefully, he pried Paine's now broken fingers from the gun, one digit at a time. Paine clutched his hand, his eyes wide, and whimpered in shock and pain. The giant held the gun carefully between his thumb and forefinger and passed it over to Zarek, who wordlessly received it. "I don't think," said the behemoth, "that he'll be firing this anytime soon."

Zarek tried not to look as stunned as he felt. Several of the followers who had fled were now slowly returning. Having heard the scream, their curiosity had overwhelmed their sense of self-preservation. Taking control of the situation, Zarek said, "Take them to the infirmary." He paused, and then added, "Get Cortez down there sooner. Feel free to take your own sweet time with Luther. Cortez . . . keep your hands off him, as tempting as it may be to do otherwise."

Luther Paine could only manage a whimper in response as he and Cortez were helped away toward the lower-deck infirmary. The way that Cortez kept firing furious looks at Paine, Zarek was only willing to give fifty-fifty odds that Cortez would heed his instructions. At that moment, he didn't care all that much; his attention was focused instead on the formidable individual who had staved off disaster.

"We had an appointment," said the giant, his soft voice a stark contrast to his appearance.

"Of course, yes. Come in . . . or rather, come back in." And he gestured toward his office. The giant stepped through the door, ducking slightly to avoid striking his head on the overhang. Zarek followed him in and blinked in surprise upon seeing an attractive young woman leaning against the desk. She smiled a dazzling smile that made Zarek feel twenty years younger. She was tall and slender, although her hips were nicely rounded. Her face was oval, her eyes twinkled with amusement, and her long flowing hair was the exact same shade as the giant's. This told Zarek two things: First, that she was very likely the giant's daughter, and second, that Zarek would be well advised to keep reminding himself that this girl's father could break him in half if he looked at her wrong. So he quickly gave a perfunctory nod and turned his attention back to the new arrival. "You're . . . Wolf Gunderson . . . ?"

"Gunnerson," he corrected, and extended his hand to shake Zarek's. Zarek looked at the formidable paw with not unreasonable concern. Noticing Zarek's hesitation, Gunnerson didn't seem offended. If anything, there was amusement on his face. Noticing this, Zarek overcame his trepidation and shook Gunnerson's hand. He could tell the giant was taking care not to squeeze too hard . . . or at all. "And this," he gestured toward the girl, "is my daughter, Freya."

"A pleasure, Mr. Zarek," she said, her voice musical. "I've read a great deal about you."

"Really."

"Yes. In history books."

Zarek forced a smile. She had spoken in a perfectly straightforward manner, and naturally had not intended to make Zarek feel as if he was some sort of modern-day relic. He took no offense at it, but suddenly he was feeling arthritic pain in every joint. Imagined, no doubt, but still, it reminded him that when he was her age, she was an egg residing in her mother's uterus, awaiting the call to action.

"I thank you for taking the time to see me," her father said.

"Well, obviously I'm the one who should be thanking you," said Zarek. He gestured toward a chair. "Please, won't you sit down . . ."

Gunnerson looked dubiously at the chair Zarek was offering and said, "I think I'll stand, if it's all the same to you. Freya?" And he gestured toward it. She nodded and took the seat, crossing her legs. Her long blue skirt was slit up the side, and some of the cloth fell away to reveal one of the most stunning female legs Zarek had gazed upon in a while. He assumed the companion leg was equally compelling. He cleared his throat loudly, walked aound the desk and took a seat. "Your timing certainly couldn't have been better."

"My followers and I have always been fortunate in that regard."

"Your followers," echoed Zarek. "Yes, when you asked for this meeting, you mentioned a group that you were representing . . . ?"

"That's correct. The Midguardians. Perhaps you've heard of us . . . ?"

Zarek shook his head, looking regretful. "I'm afraid not, no. But there's quite a few independent political action groups, and it's so hard to keep track . . ."

"Oh, we're not a political action group," said Freya. "We're a colony."

That brought Zarek up short. He shook his head in polite confusion. "I . . . don't understand. There are twelve known colonies . . . and the lost thirteenth. You're saying you're the lost thirteenth . . . ?"

Gunnerson shook his head. "I am saying we are a separate colony entirely. We have embraced sections of the Sacred Scrolls that were rejected by the religious establishment. We believe these sections to be far closer to the truths of the universe than anything that the church of the Lords of Kobol would have us believe."

"You don't believe in the Lords of Kobol?" This was now sounding familiar to Zarek. He was starting to think that he had heard of these people: religious fanatics whose beliefs positioned them far outside mainstream society.

"No," Wolf Gunnerson said firmly. He cocked an eyebrow. "You're shocked."

"What? Oh, no. No." And Zarek forced a laugh. "No, it takes a good deal to shock me. Simply having a different belief system isn't going to do that. Hell, I'm more or less used to being out on my own when it comes to beliefs."

"Indeed you are," Freya spoke up approvingly. "You're not afraid to use violence for the purpose of social change. You're not a man who shrinks from doing what is necessary to accomplish his ends."

Obviously the history books were generous to him. "I do what needs to be done," he said, trying to sound modest and only partly succeeding.

"As do the Midguardians," said Wolf. "As do I." He leaned forward, resting his huge hands on Zarek's desk and looking for all the world as if he could easily smash the furniture apart. "That is why I have come to you in seeking out representation."

"How," asked Zarek, "do you mean? What sort of representation?"

"Our people resided on Sagittaron, the same as you," said Gunnerson. "Ours was an ancient order, but it was only in the last twenty years . . . during the time of your incarceration . . . that we began to make our presence known."

"Why only recently?"

"Isn't it obvious?" When Zarek shook his head, Gunnerson gestured toward him. "Your shining example, of course. Your refusal to accept the repression of Sagittarons. We had been guarding our beliefs, our history and heritage, afraid to come into the light. But you," and he pointed at Zarek, "made us realize that we were little more than cowards. That we had to take a stand if we were to call ourselves true sons and daughters of Woten."

"Of Woten?"

"The head of our Pantheon," Freya said helpfully, "just as Zeus is of yours. I'm named for his wife."

"I myself lean more toward the teachings of his son, Thorr. I am told"—Wolf smiled—"that I bear a resemblance to him."

"If you say so," said Zarek. "But I'm still not entirely

certain what it is you expect from me . . . although naturally I'm flattered that you consider me such an inspiration. Although, then again, considering where my beliefs landed me, maybe I'm not the best person to follow."

"It's very simple, Mr. Zarek," Gunnerson said. "When millions of people resided on the world of Sagittaron, we were a hopeless minority. Barely five hundred of us. Asking for representation in the Council, asking for our beliefs in the book of Edda—"

"The . . . book of Edda?"

Gunnerson nodded. "The book that was stricken from the Sacred Scrolls. The one that has the entire history of our gods, from their birth to their deaths."

"Your gods are all dead?"

"Not yet. But we know how they will end."

"As part of a prophecy? But certainly your gods are powerful enough that they're not held sway to prophecy. Their fates aren't determined . . ."

"Of course they are. As are ours, and yours."

"You don't believe that man controls his own destiny?"

Gunnerson looked at him skeptically. "Mr. Zarek . . . we're on the run from killer robots who harry our every step, with no world to call our own, and not even fifty thousand of us left alive. Does it *sound* as if we're in control of our destiny at the moment?"

"A valid observation," admitted Zarek.

"The point is," Gunnerson continued, "it was difficult enough—hopeless, even—to have our beliefs, the rights of our individual ethnicity, to be taken seriously when there were millions of Sagittarons in existence. Now, however, there are . . . what? Barely over five thousand?"

"Five thousand, two hundred and fifty one, last I checked."

"And virtually all of our number remain intact," said Freya. "There were five hundred of us before, and the five hundred remain."

Zarek was dumbfounded at that. "All the practitioners of your . . . your faith . . . made it onto a ship?"

"Yes. Our fleet ship, the *Bifrost,* had been prepared for just this eventuality. Because the Edda warned us, and it warned of exactly what did occur. It's all part of our writings, just as accurate—if not more so—than any predictions Pythia may have presented. Imagine if the religious establishment, and the government, had been willing to give us our due. Far more might well have survived. My point is that five hundred is a much higher percentage of twenty five hundred than it is of millions. As such, our presence as part of the Sagittaron colony—to which our ship is registered—is much more significant than it was. Based on the percentage of our population, we deserve a seat on the Quorum of Twelve, and a say in what happens to us. We want our voice to be heard."

"And what is that voice intending to say, if I might ask?" inquired Zarek.

"That we alone know the truth of what is supposed to happen to humanity. We will be happy to share this knowledge with all others, so they will no longer be surprised by what happens to them. That way they will no longer be wandering in the dark, as we did for so long. We will share the benefit of the wisdom given us by our ancients, who were inspired—not by any mere mortal such as Pythia—but insights provided by the Lord Woten himself. After all, our people were saved. If our teachings are embraced, who knows? The remainder of humanity might be as well."

"And if the Quorum doesn't see fit to give you a place in it?"

"Well, then," Wolf Gunnerson said with a shrug, "it is best for all not to consider such things."

Tom Zarek definitely did not like the sound of that.

# CHAPTER 5

Number Six had Baltar's back up against the wall. Literally.

The vice president of the Colonies and the foremost living expert on Cylons had come to the conclusion that he had the most complicated love life in . . . well, in the history of love lives.

Ever since the obliteration of much of humanity on Caprica . . . ever since he had come to *Galactica* as a refugee . . . he'd had Cylons on the brain. More accurately, one Cylon: a mental representation of the gorgeous blonde who had bewitched him and caused him to betray—however inadvertently—the whole of humanity. Day after day she stood before him, or draped herself around him, or yanked him around like a lap dog, looking every bit as real as she had back in Caprica. She had rejoiced in her control of him, and in the fact that she was so near and yet so far.

Then had come the day when her hold on him had slipped ever so slightly. It was the day that he had been brought over to the newly arrived *Pegasus* and discovered his dream girl in the flesh. Her name was Gina and she was a prisoner aboard that other Battlestar. Nearly comatose, desiring nothing but to die, Baltar had brought her back from that dark precipice while the blonde Cylon called Number Six glowered from the back of his mind. She had become her own worst enemy. Her power over Baltar was that she represented that which he could never truly have again, and thus he would follow her about like a lovesick puppy in perpetual frustration. A physical incarnation of her, if she and Baltar came together, would take that power away.

At least that was how Baltar had seen it. And he had made the mistake of saying it to Six's face.

He had been working in his lab when she had shown up with her typical litany of smirking, superior comments, like a prison warden who knew that her subject could never escape. But Baltar's thoughts were filled with Gina, who had escaped her imprisonment and had joined a group of rebels lobbying for making peace with the Cylons (not that any of the rebels knew her true nature). So when Number Six disturbed his concentration while he was running an experiment, he was disinclined to allow her mock advances to pass without rebuttal.

"Is it my imagination," Baltar had asked her, sitting on a lab stool and turning to face her, "or do you seem a tad more desperate than you used to? It seems to me that you're . . . oh, what's the best way to put it . . . that you're trying too hard. Yes, that's it. As if you're worried that your influence over me may be waning." Her face was frozen, which was even more encouraging to him, and he stepped toward her with a contemptuous grin on his face. "And who knows? Perhaps you're right. Perhaps, with the reality of Gina in the picture, the mere image of you can only stand by and smolder." He spoke the last words with an almost fiendish delight. He had adored this mental link to his past life with obsessive fervor, but he had also been aware that she had used him, abused him, both in his previous life and now. It was the purest example of a love/hate relationship there was, and at this moment the hate aspect was in ascendance.

Number Six stared at him for a long moment. Inwardly he felt his nerve shriveling before her, but he fought to keep a look of smug triumph. Suddenly she stepped forward, shoved him back against the wall and kissed him passionately. She seemed to be radiating heat. He tried to push her away, but she brought her knee up into his crotch—not quickly and painfully, but instead slow, kneading it gently. He gasped into her mouth, and her tongue darted quickly in and out. He felt his pulse racing. It felt as if there were too much blood in his body, and he had to think that if he dropped dead from a heart attack right then, they'd never be able to figure out what the hell had happened.

"You're thinking about her, aren't you," she said, taking a quick break from kissing him to whisper in his ear. Her soft breaths caressing his ears sent chills down his spine.

"No . . . no, I swear . . ."

"She can't give you what I can . . ."

Her knee started to move up and down, and Baltar automatically began responding, his body moving along with it. He was finding it hard to breathe, hard to think of anything beyond what she was doing to him. His mind was spinning away, completely out of control . . .

"Doctor Baltar?"

Baltar froze in place. Number Six was gone. Standing in the open doorway was a Colonial marine, Corporal Venner. He was staring at Baltar, not sure what he was seeing. "I, um . . . I was knocking, and you weren't answering . . . are you okay? You were moaning or something . . . I wasn't sure if you were having some kinda attack . . ."

"Fine. Fine, I'm . . . fine," Baltar said, and quickly started moving his back up and down again. "Just . . . coping with an extremely nagging itch. Ahhhhhh." He let out his breath slowly as if an irritation were being dealt with. "Yesssss, that's . . . that's doing the job." Once he felt he'd carried on the pathetic charade long enough, he stepped away from the wall and clapped his hands together briskly. "Right. Feeling much better. How"—he cleared his throat—"how can I be of service?"

"Well, Doctor . . ." Venner paused. "Or should I be calling you Mr. Vice President?"

"I answer to either. I suppose here, in my lab, 'Doctor' is perfectly serviceable. Certainly I'm more accustomed to it."

"All right, then, Doctor." And he pulled someone forward from behind him. It was a young boy, and Baltar recognized him instantly.

"Boxey . . . isn't it?" asked Baltar.

"Hey, Doc," Boxey replied.

The marine looked from the boy to the scientist. "You know each other?"

Something about the situation made Baltar think that minimizing his connection to the boy was preferable. "We were rescued from Caprica at the same time," Baltar answered him. "Shared a vessel. Is there a problem . . . ?"

"Yeah, there's a problem." He clamped a firm hand on Boxey's shoulder, as if the boy posed a flight risk. "We need you to jump him to the front of the line for that Cylon test of yours."

*"What?"* Baltar's eyebrows almost bumped up against the top of his head. "Breeding them a little young, wouldn't you say?"

"Could be."

"Corporal," said Baltar, "this is preposterous. That boy is no more a Cylon than I am."

He heard a sharp, female laugh. His head snapped around. There was no sign of Number Six, but he was certain he'd heard her voice.

"Doctor . . . ?" Venner sounded curious, even a bit suspicious.

"Just a little nervous tic," Baltar said quickly. "Happens sometimes when Cylons are being discussed. Oops . . . there it goes again." And he snapped his head once more in response to nothing at all. "So . . . may I ask just what in the world makes you think that a thirteen-year-old boy is a Cylon agent?"

"He snuck into the holding cell where the known Cylon agent is being held. He was caught conferring with her."

"The known Cylon agent? Sharon Valerii, you mean?"

"Yes, sir."

Baltar tilted his head questioningly. "Isn't she guarded?"

"He slipped past the guards while they were distracted during the recent Cylon raid."

Baltar made a *harrumph* sound deep in his throat. "A single boy eluded the notice of armed guards, and you think the boy should be tested? If you ask me, you might want to have the guards assessed if they allowed that to happen."

Venner's scowl darkened. "Doctor, if you're not willing to—"

"Yes, yes, of course I'm willing. I think it's a waste of everyone's time, but I'll attend to it. Wait outside, please."

"I'm not supposed to leave him unattended."

"He's not unattended, he's with me. There's only one door out of here and you'll be standing in front of it. Unless you think he can elude you as well."

"No sir, but—"

"You say 'but' to an instruction issued you by the vice president of the Colonies?"

There was a dare in Baltar's tone, and Venner wisely didn't challenge it. Automatically snapping to attention, Venner said briskly, "I'll be just on the other side of the door if you need anything, sir."

"That's very comforting."

Venner exited the room. Baltar turned to Boxey,

pointed at a stool, and said, "Sit there." Boxey did as he was told and watched as Baltar prepared a syringe to draw blood. "So what were you doing speaking to the Cylon?" asked Baltar.

"She saved my life. Yours too," Boxey replied. "I just wanted to see her."

"Technically, she didn't save your life. Another Sharon Valerii did that."

"Yeah, I kind of have trouble understanding that part."

"It's very simple," said Baltar, gesturing for Boxey to roll up his sleeve. Boxey did so. "One model of Cylon dies, and her memories are transferred into the next one, like a computer downloading information one to the next." He tapped Boxey's exposed forearm, found a vein he liked, and proceeded to draw blood from it. Boxey made a slight sound of pain at first, but then he decided to remain stiff-lipped and did not cry out.

"But . . . when you're talking about computers, you know that one's different from the other," said Boxey. "Are the Sharons the same person?"

"For all intents and purposes, yes," said Baltar as he drew the blood.

"Is that the same as a regular yes?"

Baltar was beginning to lose his patience. "Yes," he said as he withdrew the syringe from Boxey's arm and set the vial of blood in a stand. "Why is this all so important to you?"

"Because I don't know why she saved us," said Boxey. "If she's evil, why did she do something that helped us? That helped anybody?"

"It wasn't time for her to act on her programming," said Baltar. "There was a certain point when it kicked in, and that was when she shot Admiral Adama."

"And that's what made her evil?"

"I'm not entirely certain that label applies, but for the sake of argument, yes."

"So what if she never had done that? Would she have been good?"

"I . . . suppose so, yes. She would have been 'good,' to use your phrasing, but with the potential for evildoing. Which, on further reflection," he admitted, "more or less describes just about anyone."

"But not 'just about anyone' is that way. Just her."

Letting his impatience rattle him, Baltar snapped, "Are you going somewhere with this? I mean, let's get to it, shall we? Is there some particularly cogent observation that you want to make about the entire subject? Some dazzling insight you wish to offer that you and only you have discerned?"

Boxey looked taken aback by the outburst. "I just . . ."

"You just *what*?"

"I just didn't think she looked evil, is all."

Baltar was about to fire off a reply, but instead he sat there a moment with his mouth open. Then he closed it and looked askance at the boy. "You didn't think she looked evil."

"Yeah." Boxey shrugged. "That's all."

"And what, pray, does evil look like?"

Boxey considered it a moment, and then said, "You."

*"Me?"*

"Yeah. I'm not saying you are," Boxey hurriedly added. "You're probably not . . ."

"Probably. Well, I like *that*!"

"It's just that . . . well . . . you're not a beautiful woman, first of all. It's hard to think a beautiful woman like Sharon is evil . . ."

"Trust me: Some of the most evil people I've known are beautiful women," said Baltar. In his mind's eye, he could envision Number Six taking a deep bow.

"And also, you're . . ."

"I'm what?"

"You're all twitchy."

That drew an even more confused reaction from Baltar. *"Twitchy?"*

"Jumpy. Your eyes keep moving from side to side. Even back when we left Caprica, I first noticed it. You act like . . . like you're afraid that someone's watching you, all the time. Like you're up to something and you're concerned that you're going to get caught at it. Someone who looks worried all the time that he's going to be caught at something . . . it makes it seem like you're evil, because only someone evil would have that much to be nervous about."

"Well, I appreciate that dazzling bit of character analysis," Baltar said sarcastically. "But I'll have you know I'm not evil."

"How do you know?"

"Because," said Baltar, "I've done nothing wrong." This time Number Six was doubled over in laughter. He forced himself to ignore it.

"Neither has Sharon. At least, the Sharon who's locked up. I just wanted to—"

"You know what?" Baltar snapped. "You'll understand when you're grown up." He knew it wasn't true, of course. The only thing growing up guaranteed was that parts of you were going to start hurting that had never hurt before. Other than that, nothing else was assured.

"Grown up." Boxey laughed bitterly.

"What's so funny?"

He fixed Baltar with a gaze and said, "Doctor . . . almost everybody is dead. Dead. And we're being chased by killer robots, and some of them can look so much like us that we can't tell them apart without blood tests." And he indicated the vial. "Grow up? You really, really think I'm going to get to grow up? Part of me thinks I won't even live to see my next birthday."

Baltar was about to make a sarcastic reply, but then he saw the quiet certainty in the boy's face. At first he didn't know what to say. Then he heard himself replying, "That's no way for someone your age to be thinking. You should be thinking about meeting girls and going to parties and your first kiss and the curve of a girl's neck and what your profession is going to be and all sorts of things, none of which have a damned thing to do with dying. Youth is always the hope for the future. Always. If young people believe that they have no future, then what's the point of any of this?"

Boxey considered that a moment and then said, "Survival?"

"There's more to life than survival. There has to be. There's the quality of the life you're surviving for."

"I . . . I guess . . ."

"Don't guess," Baltar told him firmly. "Guessing is an appalling habit. It shows laziness of mind. One either knows or doesn't know. If you know, speak of a certainty. If you don't know, be man enough to say you don't know, and then research the question until you do know. Anything else is unacceptable. Understand?"

"I gue—" He caught himself and then nodded. "Yes. I understand."

"Good. Now go out to the nice Colonial marine and tell him I'll have the results to him in a day or so."

"A day . . . ?"

"It's a very complicated test and takes a good long while to administer. Plus it's not as if guaranteeing the fleet's safety from you is the only thing I have on my docket. It will be finished when it's finished."

"Okay." Boxey started to head for the door, then paused and said, "Doctor . . . ?"

"Yes?" Baltar said, trying to keep the impatience from his voice and not entirely succeeding.

"Sorry about the whole thing about saying you're twitchy and jumpy. I know you're not evil."

"Thank you for the vote of confidence," Baltar said with a graciousness he didn't feel.

Boxey left the lab, and Baltar sat there and stared at the blood sample. When Number Six rested her hands on his shoulders and her chin atop his head, he didn't react. "Pity your test doesn't really work. That you've told everyone you can distinguish human from Cylon when you, in fact, cannot."

"Yes. A terrible pity."

"You know what you should do . . ."

There was a mischief in her voice that he really didn't like. Nevertheless he asked out of morbid curiosity, "What should I do?"

"You should tell them that his test came back positive. That he's a Cylon."

The very notion was appalling to him. "Why in the name of the gods would I want to do that?"

"Do you know what they'd do to him if you said that?"

"I honestly don't, no."

"Well then," she said challengingly, "isn't that all the reason you need to do it? You said it yourself: If you don't know something, you find out. It would be an interesting test of just how much veracity you have, and how willing they are to believe what you say. Oh, come on, Gaius," she prompted when he still seemed reluctant. "Don't you want to watch them eat their young?"

"Why did you laugh before?"

"Before?" She was walking around the lab, her long legs in a sure, measured stride. "When did I laugh before?"

"When I said that he was no more a Cylon than I was. What are you hiding?"

"Nothing, Gaius, I swear. I was just amused by the—"

"By the what? By the suggestion of my not being a Cylon? Is there . . ." He gulped. He was having trouble catching his breath, as if it had become far too hot in there. "Is there something I should know?"

"I just find it interesting that you've dismissed the idea out of hand," she said. "After all, back on Caprica you crouched behind me and thus survived a nuclear explosion. That doesn't strike you as odd? Your house blew apart around you. I was destroyed right in front of you. Yet you survived? Isn't it far more likely that we were both destroyed, and your memories were simply transferred to a new body?"

Baltar felt as if he'd been hit in the face by a crossbeam. The fact that her casual explanation of his survival . . . or perhaps nonsurvival . . . made perfect sense wasn't what horrified him. Or, more correctly, it wasn't what horrified him the most. What horrified him the most was that it hadn't occurred to him before. He was a man of science, and as such it was part of his very nature to question, to probe, to seek answers not only for questions that already existed, but questions that others hadn't thought to ask. For someone of that mindset never to consider something as possible as that . . . it was such a shocking omission that it almost made him wonder if . . .

What?

He'd been designed never to wonder about it? Preprogrammed?

Baltar shook his head, his mouth moving but no words emerging.

Number Six walked over to him and, extending a finger, ran it along the line of his jaw. "Poor Gaius," she sighed. "You know so much about so many things. The resident expert on Cylons. And yet you don't even know yourself."

"It . . . makes no sense," he said sharply, rallying against the unthinkable. "If I were a . . . what you say . . . you wouldn't have had to seduce me and trick me into betraying humanity. I would have just done it."

She kissed his cheek. "Tell them the test has come back positive. Tell them the boy is one of us. For that matter, how do you know he's not? Maybe I'm trying to help you out."

"Why . . ." He paused, trying to gather his scattered thoughts. "Why would you do that? What possible reason would you have for turning over one of your own?"

"Perhaps I'm feeling generous. Or perhaps—since our god made us in his own image—perhaps we, like He does, move in mysterious ways."

"You weren't made by any deities. You were made by

humans. Humans are not gods by any stretch of the imagination."

"And perhaps, ultimately, that's the difference between us. You can never be any more than you already are. Our possibilities are unlimited."

"Is that why you try to destroy us?" he asked grimly. "Because in the event of your 'ascent' to divinity, you want to make certain that no one exists who remembers you when you were nothing but pretentious vacuum cleaners?"

She blew softly in his ear and, despite himself, he shuddered. "You keep right on doing that, Gaius. Keep right on asking questions. You do it so well. It's the main reason that I love you so much."

He closed his eyes, giving in to the pleasure of her touch. He moaned softly, and then he looked around. There was no sign of Number Six. She had vanished back into the recesses of his lust, or his guilt, or his programming, or wherever it was she came from.

Baltar turned and stared at the tube of blood that he had just drawn, and wondered what to do.

# CHAPTER 6

Laura Roslin never would have imagined that she would be able to handle press conferences. One would have thought that, given her history as a teacher, she would have had no trepidation about getting up in front of crowds and fielding questions. To a degree, that was true . . . when it was a roomful of students who, more often than not, were perfectly happy to accept whatever she said as a given. That was a far cry from dealing with a roomful of hard-nosed reporters who challenged her on everything she said, and would come back with question upon question upon question. The way in which they regarded her shifted so frequently that she often found it difficult to get herself on any sort of firm footing with them . . . which, for all Laura knew, was exactly the way they preferred it.

When she had first been thrust into the position of president . . . an eventuality that someone as low in the pecking order as Secretary of Education could not have considered a possibility . . . the press had been all over her. She was an unproven commodity, thrust to the forefront of leadership in a time of war. How in the gods' name could someone who was often dismissed out of hand as "the schoolteacher" (a nickname she suspected had originated with Adama, not her biggest fan at the time) be expected to enable the remnants of mankind to survive? Some of the reporters had adopted a wait-and-see attitude, and a few supported her out of a sense of obligation: If people didn't rally around their president, whoever that might be, then surely all was lost. But others had been merciless: She had been described as Laura the Lame, Laura the Borer, President Laura the Last. Contempt practically oozed from the screens and write-ups.

But then came the military coup that had thrown her out of office, and as one the press rallied behind her. It was self-serving, to be sure. The thinking was simple: If Commander Adama could sweep in and oust the representative of the people, certainly there was nothing to stop him from annihilating freedom of the press for all time. He had the military might: He could round up every single journalist, stick them on a freighter and shoot them off in the opposite direction from whichever way the fleet was going. It wasn't widely believed that he would, but it wasn't widely believed that he would not. Laura Roslin was transformed overnight into a martyr, a political prisoner in the hands of an out-of-control military.

Then came her escape, her quest to the Temple of Athena . . . a quest that had been predicted in ancient writings, which she fulfilled, giving them a guide toward Earth . . . and just like that, she was a religious symbol. A savior. Gods above, they were actually worshipping her. (And the wag who had dubbed her "Laura the Borer" had now renamed her, after her determined expedition to the Temple of Athena, "Laura the Explorer.")

And then she almost succumbed to breast cancer, a disease so pernicious and so far gone that it would have claimed anyone else. Except an amazing discovery had been handed her in the form of fetal blood from the unborn child of Sharon Valerii . . . or the creature passing for human that called itself Sharon Valerii . . . a discovery that had cured her. But the press and general public hadn't known about Sharon. So instead, the attitude was behold, she was risen: Laura Roslin, the walking miracle.

As she prepared for her morning press conference, finishing up in the bathroom and checking her makeup before going out to face the cameras and reporters, Laura wondered when in hell she was going to be regarded simply as Laura Roslin, the woman. That was all. A woman, no more and no less than any other woman, trying to overcome odds that more generous gods would never have thought to heap upon her. No matter her outward appearance, no matter what the façade she displayed for the world and what the world chose to call her in turn, inwardly she was still simply Laura Roslin. Laura Roslin, with all the fears and uncertainties and frailties that the human condition was heir to. Yet she gamely soldiered forward, trying to be all things to all people, and often felt as if she were being torn in a dozen directions at once.

Her people needed her. They needed her to be whatever it was they were describing her as this week. There were times when she absolutely detested them for it, and wanted to go off into a corner, clap her hands over her ears, and make them all vanish. And when those times arose, she would just sit down somewhere, preferably in a darkened room, lower her head and take a series of long, cleansing breaths until it all went away.

She straightened her back, forced a smile onto her face, and walked into the press room.

They were waiting for her, just as she knew they would be. The moment she set foot in the room, she sensed that something was wrong, but she couldn't tell for certain what it was. She saw that Admiral William Adama was standing nearby the podium. He'd been speaking to the press, but the moment she entered the room, he immediately fell silent. He appeared to toss a conspiratorial glance toward the press, and even more strangely, they nodded almost as one. It was as if there had been some sort of mutual decision made between Adama and the reporters, and Laura didn't have any idea what that decision might be.

She chose not to press the matter. Instead she moved to the podium, nodded quickly to acknowledge the reporters, and said, "Very briefly: Admiral Adama has been investigating the circumstances under which the Cylons apparently knew exactly where we were going to Jump to, and were lying in wait to ambush us. Admiral Adama, would you care to . . . ?" She gestured to the podium and the assorted microphones that were poised on the edge of it, like metal flowers.

Adama smiled, stepped forward, and said into the microphone, "I've got nothing." He turned, bobbed his head to her as if this were a wholly satisfactory way of handling the matter, and stepped back.

Laura Roslin stared at him, and had to make a specific effort to close her mouth again rather than leaving it dangling open in astonishment. "Yes, well," she said cheerily, "if there are any questions, now would be an excellent time to put them forward."

All hands shot up, and she picked one almost at random. The reporter stood up and said, "Who?"

"I'm sorry . . . I don't understand," said Laura. "Could you elaborate on that question slightly?"

The reporter nodded, and said, "What?"

"I said," Laura told him, feeling her patience beginning to unravel, "I would prefer it if you could elaborate . . . ?"

Another reporter jumped to his feet. "When?" he said.

Then there was another reporter, standing up and saying, "Where?" followed by another who asked with even greater intensity, "Why?"

"This . . . this is absurd, that you . . ."

"How?"

None of the regular reporters had spoken. It was a female voice that Laura felt as if she should recognize, but she didn't. Her gaze swept the throng in the room, but didn't pick anyone out.

Then someone stepped forward and Laura stifled a scream in her throat.

It was Sharon Valerii.

The crowd of reporters spread wordlessly to either side, allowing Sharon to approach Laura unimpeded. It seemed as if she were moving in slow motion, each step slow and deliberate, her body following suit. She was dressed in the garb of a colonial pilot, but her belly was swollen with her child.

Sharon held a gun lazily in one hand, and now she swept her arm up so that it was pointed directly at Laura Roslin. She spoke, and it was as if the words coming from her mouth were just slightly out of synch with the movement of her lips. Yet Laura heard her, and the words were familiar, even if she didn't understand them.

"Sagittarius is bleeding," said Sharon.

Laura tried to run, but a strong hand grabbed her by the arm, anchoring her to the spot. It was Adama. Laura swung a fist and hit him in the side of the head, but Adama didn't seem to notice. He winced slightly, but that was all, and didn't ease up on his grip. Instead, he said, in that measured, contemplative, normally very comforting tone, "It's better this way."

"You're insane!" she screamed, and she tried to pull loose from him. It didn't help. He was too strong, and now Adama was holding Roslin so that she was across his body like a human shield.

"Wrong. I'm the only sane one here," he told her between gritted teeth.

Sharon had her gun leveled at Laura. And now Laura was hearing something: a heartbeat. A human heartbeat, and it seemed to fill the air, fill everything. She had no clue where it was coming from, but the sound of it was rapidly becoming deafening.

"Sagittarius is bleeding," Sharon said again, and standing just behind her, looking not at all concerned, was Tom Zarek. Before Laura could ask her what the hell that was supposed to mean, Sharon's finger closed on the trigger, and Laura . . .

. . . jerked awake.

She was in her office, seated upright in her chair, having decided to try and catch a fast sleep before the press conference. She was tired . . . no. She was exhausted. She spent her days worried about the next Cylon attack and her nights having bizarre dreams like this that kept waking her up. "It's not fair," she moaned, rubbing her eyes with the balls of her hands. "When am I supposed to . . . ?" She left the question unfinished, stifling a yawn, and then Billy came knocking at her door. "Yes?"

"Madame President," he said in that formal tone he occasionally adopted, probably without even thinking about it. "It's time for the press conference."

She glanced right and left, not entirely sure how to respond. Was this another dream? The same dream? Was she wide awake? She gripped the skin of her right hand and squeezed as hard as she could. "Ow!" she cried out.

Billy was staring at her in bewilderment. "Why did you do that?"

"Just . . . checking something," she said. She stood and smoothed her skirt, trying to pull herself together.

"Are you all—?"

"I'm fine, Billy, I'm fine. Gods, you don't have to mother hen me, all right?"

"Yes, ma'am," he said quickly.

She hesitated and then, feeling a bit sheepish, said, "Sorry about the 'mother hen' comment."

"No . . . no, you're right. Sometimes I make too much of a fuss over you."

She smiled at that. Patting him on the shoulder, she

said, "It's all right. I don't have a mom and I don't have kids. It's nice to know that someone is worried about me."

"Don't sell yourself short, Madame President. There's more people worried about you than you can possibly believe." He paused, frowned at that and then said, "That actually sounded much better in my head than it came out."

"I'd almost think it would have to," said Laura, but there was laughter on her lips. "All right, so . . . let's press on, shall we?" Receiving a sympathetic nod from Billy, she pushed open the door and entered the press room. Instantly everyone who was sitting came to their feet in order to show the proper respect.

"Thank you, please, take your seats," she said, gesturing for them to do so. She turned and it was all she could do to not let her surprise sound in her voice.

Admiral Adama was standing there, looking at her in a mildly quizzical manner, just as he had been in her dream. There was a brief surge of panic in her heart: What if she was losing the ability to discern if she was asleep or awake? What if the line between reality and fantasy was blurring to such a degree that . . . ?

"Madame President?" Adama's voice was soft, concerned, and she instantly remembered that he was there because she had asked him to be there, for gods' sake. After all, the mishap involving the Jump was on everyone's mind, and there was no one more authoritative to field questions about such a matter than Adama.

She drew herself up and her voice had its customary, no-nonsense tone. She had to pull herself together. She knew she felt vulnerable since the breast cancer had nearly taken her life and she had escaped through a miraculous medical intervention. After all, she had prepared herself for death, gone through all the common stages of being faced with her imminent demise and had finally accepted it. Naturally she was grateful that her dismal fate had been averted. It wasn't as if she'd wanted to die, just because she was prepared for it. But she was still feeling somewhat disoriented over the entire thing. The fact that she wasn't getting any sleep—or, more correctly—that her sleep was constantly being interrupted and disrupted by various dreams, was not making matters any easier for her to deal with.

But that was what she had to do. She had to deal with it.

"Thank you for coming, Admiral," she said briskly. He nodded in response, his suspicions mollified by her apparently clear-headed attitude. "I assume that everyone's mind is on the same thing. If you'd care to address it?" and she gestured toward the podium. Adama nodded and moved toward it as she stepped back to make room for him.

"The recent mishap," said Adama with the easy confidence of one who was intimidated by nothing, "involving our escape from the Cylons resulted from a computer malfunction compelling us to engage in a blind Jump. We are currently in the process of investigating precisely what caused the mishap so that we can ensure there is no repeat."

Immediately hands shot up. "Madame President," called out one reporter, "doesn't it lessen your confidence in the *Galactica*, knowing that such accidents can occur?"

"Accidents can always occur," replied Roslin easily. "That's why they're called accidents. Obviously such FTL maneuvers are inherently hazardous, but I think we can all agree that being at the mercy of Cylon raiders is far more hazardous. I believe it is a testament to the professionalism of the officers and staff of *Galactica* that they were able to pull off such a difficult endeavor and enable us to live to tell the tale. That is the aspect of this incident upon which I personally would prefer to focus."

"There are rumors that the Cylons knew where we were going to be Jumping to, and that was the reason for the blind Jump," said another reporter. "Have the Cylons managed to penetrate the *Galactica*'s computer system again?"

Laura saw Adama's jaw twitch slightly. It was a small unconscious tell she'd picked up on that he gave whenever a reporter asked a question that hit too close to home. She was exceptional at reading body language, a talent courtesy of her "wastrel" youth when she'd spent way too many late nights playing cards. Adama had already confided in her what had really happened, and they'd both agreed there was no point in letting the general public know what had transpired.

Yet obviously there was a leak somewhere. It was understandable: Humans remained humans, and they loved to talk even when they shouldn't. Stray words had a habit of being overheard by nearby ears that weren't supposed to be there, and somehow such comments always managed to find their way to reporters. Adama, naturally, wanted to keep everything under wraps. That was the military way: total control. It was always entertaining to see Adama come face to face with situations that he couldn't dominate with a few orders or tossing someone in the brig, and the free flow of information was definitely one of those situations.

"My understanding," Adama said tightly, "was that, as reporters, you were interested in reporting facts, not rumors. The military holds itself to a high standard of conduct . . . one that you might want to consider emulating."

*Great. Lecture the press. That always works well,* thought Laura. "The Admiral has assured me that there is no evidence—none—that there is any Cylon influence on, or infestation of, the *Galactica*'s computer system. Correct, Admiral?"

"Yes," he said tersely.

"Moving on, then," she said . . . and then the next words she was to speak froze in her throat.

Tom Zarek was standing toward the back of the room, watching her with a level, unreadable gaze. That alone was startling enough. What in gods' name was Zarek doing there?

But that paled in comparison to the fact that Sharon Valerii was standing next to him.

Laura stood there, paralyzed. She . . . *it* . . . was right there! What the hell had Zarek done, what sort of scam had he pulled, that he'd gotten her sprung from confinement! She was the most dangerous creature on two legs in the Colonial fleet. She was staring at Laura Roslin with as much pure hatred as Laura had ever seen in another creature.

*I'm dreaming, this has to be a dream, but I'm awake, I know I'm awake, I think I'm awake, gods, what if I don't know anymore . . .*

Laura pointed a finger at the Cylon, which she noted—as if she were looking at someone else's arm—was trembling violently. "What are you doing here? Who let you in?"

Zarek looked behind himself, deftly feigning confusion. The reporters seemed equally bewildered.

"They stuck a needle in my baby for you," snarled Valerii. "They exploited her blood in order to save you, who wanted to kill her. You didn't deserve to be saved. You don't deserve to live."

She started toward Laura, moving as if she were in slow motion, and she was pulling her weapon from its holster.

Laura started to back up, and a firm hand lit on her shoulder. "Madame President . . . ?" said Adama, concern etched on his face.

She looked from Adama back to Sharon, who was advancing with her weapon out and aimed straight at her.

*She's not here. That's all there is to it, she's not here. Adama wouldn't just stand here and not react to it . . . unless, what if he's a Cylon, too, and Zarek, what if they're all Cylons? What if there's only Cylons left, no humans at all, I'm the last one, and they're about to finish their genocide with my death . . .*

Laura Roslin stared down the barrel of the gun that was aimed at her, and in a heartbeat two options ripped through her mind. The first was that she would scream in panic, drop behind the podium, try to get away, in an effort to save her life. If Sharon Valerii was really there—if they were all really Cylons—then it wouldn't matter. She was going to die no matter what. But if Valerii wasn't there, if this was all an illusion, then the people of the Colonies would see broadcasts of their president scrambling away from nothing like a woman possessed. What sort of inspiration would that provide? How could they possibly draw any hope for their future from that?

The second option was that she stand there, staring at her death about to be spat at her from the barrel of a gun. Either she would die bravely, or not at all.

In that instant, she realized that, all things considered, there was only one option after all.

She stared into the eyes of Sharon Valerii with complete defiance and said nothing.

Valerii fired off three rounds at point-blank range. Laura flinched involuntarily, closed her eyes while anticipating the impact. None came. She opened her eyes and, although Zarek was still there, there was no sign of Sharon Valerii.

Everyone was still staring at her. There was dead silence in the room. Adama was looking at her with concern, while Zarek regarded her as if she'd grown a second head.

Laura cleared her throat and, her nerves shot, her mind fraught with uncertainty, didn't let any of that come through in her voice. "Councilman Zarek . . . there are . . . procedures to be followed. You should have made an appointment with my aide rather than just . . . show up out of nowhere."

Zarek was caught off guard, unable to understand the seeming see-saw nature of her reaction. One moment she'd seemed alarmed; the next she was . . . what?

Carping over procedure not being followed? He realized everyone was now looking at him rather than her. "I was . . . hoping that you could clear some time in your schedule," he said, the picture of courtesy. "And furthermore, Madame President, I have to think that you wouldn't have such a violent reaction to any other Quorum member who sought some of your valuable time. I'm honored that you'd single me out for such treatment."

Laura was still feeling more rattled than she cared to let on, and was concerned that, the longer this went on, the more difficulty she'd have covering that fact. "Speak with my aide. He will attend to your request. Ladies and gentlemen, I'm afraid I have to cut this conference short. There are other matters that require my attention."

She turned quickly and exited the room, leaving behind her a chorus of "But Madame President!" "President Roslin!"

Beating a retreat to her private study, Laura leaned forward on her desk, resting on her hands with palms flat. There was a fast knock at the door and Adama entered without preamble. "It's customary," Laura said wryly, "to wait until the person inside the room actually says 'come in' before entering."

Adama stared at her as if she hadn't spoken. "Do you want to tell me what's going on?"

"No, Admiral, I don't. And as it so happens, since I'm president, I don't have to."

"But you admit there is something going on."

"I admit nothing."

He took a step toward her and there was none of the military officiousness in him that she had used to think constituted his entire persona. "Laura . . . I'm not an admiral asking a president now. I'm asking as a friend. Someone who's concerned about you. Something is wrong. Is it something relating to your cancer? Or its treatment?"

*I don't know, I don't know what's going on, I can't trust my own senses anymore . . .*

She wanted to say all that and more, but she did not. "As much as you might want to pretend otherwise, Bill . . . you are an admiral. And I am the president. And those simple truths can't be set aside merely because we declare them to be so."

"Have you been to Doctor Cottle . . . ?"

"That would be my business, Admiral. Yours is *Galactica*. I believe you're running an investigation, are you not?"

"Yes," he said.

"Then you'd best get back to it. We both have expectations being made of us. Oh," she added as an afterthought, "were I you . . . I'd pay particular attention to Vice President Baltar."

Adama didn't look at all surprised, merely interested. "Do you have reason to believe he was involved somehow?"

She wasn't certain what to tell him. Yes, she had reason to believe it . . . but it wasn't something she could convincingly convey, not to Adama, and not even entirely to herself.

*My life was flashing before my eyes, just as they always say it does, on the cusp of death . . . and I was there on Caprica, and I saw Baltar . . . I saw him . . . and he was with this woman. They were nuzzling each other, and I haven't thought about it since that day because gods know I had other things to worry about. I saw it, I thought, "She's gorgeous, the lucky bastard," and then it dropped out of my mind like a stone. That'll happen when the Cylons try to annihilate your entire race and you wind up on the run. But I've seen that woman since. She's a Cylon operative. I saw Baltar locked in a passionate embrace with a Cylon operative. Except I don't know that that's what I saw. The mind is a tricky thing, and memory even more elusive. It's possible that in what I thought were the last hours of my life, everything became muddled together. That the beautiful woman whom I saw with Baltar was someone else entirely, and that I had just "inserted" the face of the known Cylon operative onto the woman.*

*But why would I do that?*

*Impossible to know. Who can possibly understand the depths of the human mind? I never quite trusted Doctor Baltar, for reasons I couldn't quite put my finger on. So wouldn't it make perfect sense for me to associate him with another figure of distrust, a Cylon? Wouldn't that be the simplest answer?*

*And yet . . .*

"I . . . have no concrete reason, Admiral. Just a hunch. Just . . . instincts."

Adama considered that, then nodded. "In our time together, Madame President . . . I've learned to trust your instincts. On occasion they're more reliable than my own." He paused, then added with just a trace of dry humor, "On rare occasion."

"All right then."

He nodded. Then he spoke once more, and she couldn't be sure, but it almost sounded as if there was a hint of hurt feelings in his tone. Only a hint, since Adama was far too stoic to allow whatever he was feeling to rise to the surface. The only time she could recall seeing pure, unadulterated emotions bubble over from Adama was when he finally caught up with Roslin and company on Kobol and had unabashedly hugged his wayward offspring in as pure a display of affection as she had ever seen a father provide a son.

"I had thought," he said gravely, "that we had been through enough . . . that you could find it within yourself to be honest with me."

She kept her face a neutral mask, wanting to tell him what was going on, but reluctant to because . . . she had no idea why.

Yes. Yes, she did.

Because she didn't want to seem weak. Bad enough

that she had been prey to the frailties of her body. Now, if her mind was going . . . that was even worse.

Until she had a clearer idea of what was going on, she simply couldn't bring herself to tell Adama what was happening. How could she? She didn't fully understand it herself.

"Thank you for your time, Admiral," was all she said.

Adama studied her for a moment with a gaze that she felt could bore into the back of her head. Then he simply replied, "Thank you, Madame President," gave the slightest of formal bows, and walked out of the room.

Laura Roslin, with a heavy sigh, slid back in her chair, rolled her eyes toward the ceiling, and prayed to whatever gods would listen to her that she was not, in fact, going completely out of her mind. It was at that point that she realized that, even if she was, she might well not be fully aware of it, and that was hardly a comforting insight.

# CHAPTER 7

Whenever William Adama stopped by his lab, Gaius Baltar always felt a deep chill at the base of his spine. He became particularly concerned over the uncontrolled appearances of Number Six during such times. He might be able to cover up his occasional slips or comments to her when he was in the presence of others. But Adama had that penetrating way about him that peeled away Baltar's defenses like the layers of an onion. He had to keep reminding himself that he was a genius. One of the most brilliant minds in all of humanity, pre- or post-destruction. Adama was a glorified grunt, nothing more. In the end, despite the fact that sometimes Baltar felt as if his upper lip was sweating profusely in Adama's presence, there was ultimately no way that Adama could really see through him.

"So are you seeing a Cylon, Doctor?" asked Adama calmly.

Baltar almost knocked over an array of test tubes nearby him as he twisted around violently to face Adama. The ship's commander had arrived a minute or so ago and made polite conversation with Baltar over meaningless political issues. The sudden change in topic—and the question he'd posed—had caught Baltar off guard. In spite of himself, he had reflexively looked around to see if Number Six was standing there. He had no idea what he would do if suddenly, magically, Adama could see her as well. Or, worse, knew not only of Baltar's connection to her, but all that he had done—unwillingly and willingly—for the Cylon cause.

Baltar forced himself to maintain his composure, which was not an easy task considering the baleful look that Adama was giving him. "I . . . don't quite understand your meaning, Admiral."

Adama slowly walked the perimeter of the lab, but he never took his gaze from Baltar. "My people inform me that you're running tests on a young man—Andrew Boxman, also known as Boxey—to determine whether or not he's a Cylon."

"He knows, Gaius."

Her timing, as always, could not have been worse. Number Six was following in Adama's footsteps. Baltar couldn't be sure, but she actually appeared concerned. That alone was enough to alarm him, because most of the time Number Six delighted in whatever problems were being thrown Baltar's way. She was conscience and tormentor rolled into one, enjoying watching him writhe in the throes of his guilty conscience and his perpetual fear of being found out. Now, though, in Adama's presence, she didn't seem to be taking any joy in it at all. Which meant . . . what? That Adama was close to finding something out?

"You need to throw him off the track," she insisted. "Tell him that the boy tested positive. Tell him he's a Cylon. You don't want him sniffing too close to you, do you."

"That's true enough," Baltar said, addressing both Number Six and Adama with the same comment.

"Are the test results finalized?"

"Yes, as a matter of fact, they are."

"Good. You see, Doctor," and Adama ceased his pacing, "we have to remain ever vigilant to any threats in our midst. *Any* threats. And any such threats must be thoroughly investigated, if you understand what I'm saying."

"Perfectly," Baltar replied, but inwardly he was trying not to panic.

Number Six's observations weren't helping in the least. "What do you want him to do, Gaius? Sing it for you? He suspects you. He doesn't know what he suspects you of, but it's something. The best thing you can do right now is throw suspicion elsewhere, and the boy is the most useful target. You'd be an absolute fool not to take advantage of the opportunity that's been handed you on a silver platter."

"He's . . . just a boy," Baltar managed to say between gritted teeth.

"Yes. He is," Adama agreed. "A boy who, by all accounts, is quite popular with my pilots. They've taken him under their wing, so to speak. He comes and goes freely here. So if he's a Cylon agent, then that means he's playing my people for fools, and that is not something I take lightly." He paused and then added, "Nor do I appreciate being played for a fool. So . . . let's have it, Doctor. Is he? Or isn't he?"

Baltar felt paralyzed by uncertainty. With every fiber of his being, he wanted to lie to Adama's face. Do as Number Six suggested. Throw Adama off the scent. Except the man looked as if he could sniff out deceit with one nostril tied behind his back. If Baltar were simply trying to cover his own ass, that would be one thing. He'd lie as quickly and smoothly as he could and risk everything in order to assure his own survival. But this . . . the deliberate incrimination of an innocent boy, just for the purpose of providing some distractions for Adama and his crew of busybodies . . . despite Number Six's urgings, it was too much. Besides, there was always the concern that Adama would see right through the lie, and that would leave Baltar in an even deeper world of trouble . . .

"Don't you pass it up, Gaius," Number Six urged him. She was hanging on his shoulder. "Don't pass up the opportunity. They're always looking for scapegoats, and this is the perfect—"

"You misunderstood me, Admiral," Baltar almost shouted. He realized belatedly that he was, in fact, raising his voice, to speak above the urgings of Number Six whom Adama couldn't hear. Seeing Adama's expression in reaction to his volume, he instantly ratcheted it back down as he continued, "When I said he's just a boy, I meant . . . he's just a boy. He is not, as near as I can determine, anything more sinister than that. Although I admit that young boys can be, indeed . . . rather sinister creatures." He forced a laugh that felt as weak as it sounded.

*"You're being an idiot!"* Number Six practically shouted at him.

"I know," Baltar told her, then turned quickly to face Adama and continued, "I know you were hoping to find another of the Cylon models so you could put another face to the enemy. I feel as if, by getting a negative result, I've made your job harder."

Adama barely shrugged. "Then it's harder. The difficulty of a job doesn't mean it's not worth doing."

"I feel exactly the same way."

"Do you." He arched a single eyebrow. "Would you like to know how you've always struck me, Doctor?"

"I'd be fascinated to know that, Admiral," said Baltar with a thin smile that reflected no trace of amusement.

"As someone who always seems daunted by any job that he's faced with, and would rather simply fly below the radar at any given moment, rather than stepping up to what's expected of him."

"Really." Baltar's smile remained fixed, although his tone was cold. "An interesting assessment of a man who saved the life of the president when no one else could."

"Yes. Yes, you did, for which you have the thanks of a grateful citizenry . . . not the least among which is myself. And yet . . ." he added, almost as an afterthought.

"And yet?" prompted Baltar.

"What remarkable timing that was. In one stroke, you not only avoided having to take over as president . . . but you saved the life of a Cylon half-breed."

Baltar's instinct was to run in the other direction. To sprint out the door and put as much distance between himself and Adama as possible. Instead he walked straight toward Adama until he was standing less than a foot away, practically nose-to-nose with the admiral. "And if the president had passed away . . . and dear Doctor Cottle subsequently discovered somehow that the fetus's blood had the restorative power to save her . . . you'd be standing right here accusing me of holding back knowledge that could have preserved the life of Laura Roslin. You'd be questioning my allegiances, my knowledge as a Cylon expert, and quite possibly whether my parents were married at the time of my birth. Isn't that true?"

Adama studied him and then said, "Possibly."

"Possibly," echoed Baltar. "So what with this being a case of damned if I do, damned if I don't . . . then I might as well 'do,' save Roslin's life, and endure your scrutiny, your suspicions and your veiled insults. But don't worry about it, Admiral. I've been insulted by the best." His gazed flickered toward Number Six, who was standing off to the side. She was no longer fuming. Although her disappointment was palpable, she seemed mildly amused by Baltar's standing up to Adama.

But Adama didn't seem the least bit daunted in his apparent conviction that there was something Baltar wasn't telling him. Baltar couldn't help but wonder what the hell Roslin had said to him . . . and it had to have come from Roslin. He was certain of that, although he wasn't quite sure why.

"Thank you," Adama said levelly, "for your efforts in clearing the boy . . . and for saving Laura Roslin. In appreciation of that, I will give you advance warning: I'm watching you."

"I don't blame you," Baltar replied. "I hear there's so little on broadcast these days that's remotely interesting. Find your entertainment where you can, Admiral, by all means."

Adama said nothing at that, but instead turned and walked out of the lab. The moment he was gone, Baltar let out a long sigh and shriveled like a balloon.

"I'm impressed, Gaius," said Number Six. "I've never seen such a simultaneous display of sheer nerve and sheer stupidity."

"Glad I could accommodate you."

"Don't be."

He closed his eyes, rubbed the bridge of his nose, and opened his eyes again. Number Six was gone. Baltar couldn't recall the last time he'd been quite that glad not to see her someplace.

Boxey had had no idea what to think when Corporal Venner had shown up at the secure area where he was being held. He was slightly more buoyed, however, when he saw that Kara Thrace was with him. Boxey was relieved to see the friendly face, although he wasn't certain exactly what to expect from it.

She winked at him. "You're sprung, kid."

He let out a huge sigh and sagged back in the chair he'd been seated on. "That's a relief," he admitted.

Venner, eyes narrowed in suspicion, was quick to pounce. "Why? Were you worried that the results were going to prove you're a Cylon?"

"Well . . . sure," said Boxey.

This prompted a startled reaction from both Venner and Kara. "You were?" she asked.

"Isn't that the whole thing with Cylons who look like

people? That sometimes they don't know? Sharon didn't know, right? I mean, that's what you guys told me."

Kara looked at Venner and shrugged. "He's right. We were all talking about that. How Sharon—the one who shot the admiral—that she said she didn't know. That she didn't know it before and she didn't know she was going to shoot the Old Man, and even after, she didn't remember it."

"Oh, of course," Venner said sarcastically. "And naturally you're gonna believe everything that a Cylon says."

"Because humans are *so* much more trustworthy," shot back Kara. "Gods, when I think of the number of guys who told me they loved me just to get a piece of . . ." She stopped and glanced back at Boxey, and then cleared her throat and forced a smile. "You, uh . . . you didn't hear that."

"Hear what?" asked Boxey, who really hadn't heard it because Kara had been saying it so fast.

"Good lad," Kara replied in approval, leaving Boxey no more clear on what was being discussed than before, but at least Starbuck was happy with him.

Boxey's spirits were rising for the first time in what seemed like ages. "So what're we up to, huh? Another poker game? Just hanging out in the—?"

"Boxey," Kara interrupted him, and she looked a bit pained when she spoke. "You're, uh . . . well, you're going back to the *Peacemaker*, actually."

"But I thought that—"

"No buts, kid," Venner said.

Kara rounded on him with obvious annoyance. "Do you think that maybe, just maybe, you could give us some frakking space, huh? In fact, I have a better idea. I'll take it from here. You can go on about your duties."

"I have my orders . . ."

"Awww," said Kara, "and what a pity I don't outrank you . . . oh! Wait! I do! Now scram!"

Venner drew himself up and said darkly, "I'll be forced to report this to Colonel Tigh."

"Yeah, you do that, because the threat of being reported to Colonel Tigh is really gonna leave me trembling."

Scowling once more, Venner walked away, although he kept glancing over his shoulder as if he thought that Boxey was going to produce a gun from within his mouth and open fire.

Kara strolled over to a bench, sat, and patted the empty space next to her. Boxey sat where she indicated. "Look," she said, "you just need to keep your distance for a little while until things cool down."

"I didn't do anything wrong!"

"You snuck into the brig and spoke at length with an enemy of the Colonies," she reminded him. "If we were going by the book, then you'd be guilty of consorting with the enemy and that carries with it a year's sentence. You'd have plenty of time to chat with Sharon Valerii if you were in a cell next to her, wouldn't'cha."

He suddenly became very interested in the tops of his shoes. "I guess," he muttered.

"You guess." She chuckled despite the seriousness of the situation. "Bottom line, Boxey, you have no idea how damned lucky you are. You really could wind up doing serious jail time. You are clueless as to how seriously things get taken around here. This is a military vessel, for gods' sake. It's not a playground."

"I wasn't playing . . ."

"You sure as hell were," Kara told him firmly in a no-nonsense voice. "You sure treated it like a game. Showing off just so everybody could know how clever you were."

"What, and you never do that?"

"All the time."

"Then what's the difference?"

"The difference is, I blow Cylons out of space better than any other motherfrakker in the fleet, that's what," Kara said, making no attempt to hide her sense of smug accomplishment. "And that includes the CAG. So when trouble hits, they don't want my ass in a cell; they want it in a Viper where it belongs. And even with that going for me," she added, shaking her head, "I have no doubt that if Tigh could find a way to put me away for good, he wouldn't hesitate. And he's the one pushing to get you off *Galactica*. Venner and the other marines did a full write-up on you, and Tigh's whole thing is security. He sees you as a risk that has no business being on a military vessel, no matter how much we may like you."

"So . . ." Boxey felt a girlish urge to cry, and managed through sheer force of will to keep the tears from welling in his eyes. "So I can't come here and hang out with you guys anymore?"

" 'Anymore' is a long time. Just until things cool down, at least. Give it some time, and then I'll work the circuit: I'll talk to the CAG, and he'll talk to the Old Man, and the Old Man will lean on Tigh, and we'll have you back here. But there's one thing you've got to understand," and her voice dropped to a severe tone that fully commanded his attention. "You've got to keep your lip zipped about the Cylon we have locked up here. Do you get that? You can't just go running around, telling the other kids about what goes on here."

"I haven't," Boxey protested. "You told me not to, weeks ago. I knew it was important then . . ."

"Yeah, but now it's even more important. The admiral, Tigh . . . they're worried that if word gets out to the fleet, all hell is going to break loose. That people won't understand that she's . . . that it's . . ." She corrected herself, scowling. "A military asset. There's a lot of jumpy people out there who never, ever expected to find themselves in the middle of a space-going war zone, and they don't know how to take it. They'd kill the Cylon as soon as look at it, and gods only know what they would do in order to make that happen. We'd rather not find out. You get what I'm saying, Boxey? This isn't just me talking. This is coming straight from the admiral, and if I'm not convinced that you understand it, then things could get nasty. So I've got to know that you do understand."

"I understand."

"Say it again." And her gaze was like a laser penetrating his mind.

"I. Understand," he said with as much conviction as he could muster.

She studied him for a time, and he felt as if the admiral were looking at him through her eyes. Then she finally relaxed slightly and said, "Good. Plus, hey . . . remember . . . once we find Earth, we'll all be together on the same planet anyway." She ruffled his hair. "That'll be our happily ever after. Won't that be great?"

"Yeah. Great," Boxey said hollowly.

Kara tried to jolly Boxey out of his doldrums over being exiled from the *Galactica*, but ultimately there wasn't much that she could do. The boy dragged his heels all the way over to the transport dock, where one of the frequent shuttle vessels that moved constantly from one ship to the next picked him up for passage back to the *Peacemaker*. He never once looked away as he watched the *Galactica* dwindle in the aft viewing window. The battle vessel remained huge; it wasn't as if Boxey was going all *that* far. Nevertheless, it was far enough to make him feel very distanced and very much alone.

When he disembarked at the *Peacemaker*, he was surprised to find that a familiar face was waiting for him. Yet somehow he wasn't actually all that surprised. Upon reflection, it seemed quite inevitable.

"How did you know?" he asked.

"I didn't," replied Freya Gunnerson. "I've just been checking in on any ship making a run from *Galactica*. I figured that, sooner or later, you'd be on it. You were making me nervous, though. Where've you been?" Teasingly she added, "Minerva Greenwald's been asking about you, you little heartbreaker."

He started walking and she fell into step alongside him. "I don't wanna talk about it."

She laughed at that. "You know what I've learned? That people who say they don't want to talk about something usually do. Come on, Boxey." And she nudged him in the shoulder. "You're my unofficial kid brother. You know I've liked you ever since we met, when I was put in charge of finding shelter for orphaned refugees. Haven't I said so?"

"Yeah, well . . . adults are really good at saying things and not so good at seeing 'em through."

"What's that supposed to mean?"

Boxey didn't want to tell her. Everything that Starbuck had said weighed heavily upon him.

Then again, he'd insisted that he hadn't told any other kids, and he hadn't. But Freya was different. She was the best adult friend he had outside of people on *Galactica*. And even more than the others, she'd always had a ready ear for him and whatever problems he had at any given time. Still . . .

"I can't," he said. "It's . . . it's secret . . ."

"So what?" said Freya. "Boxey, I'm a lawyer. That's all we do, is keep secrets."

He looked at her with interest. "Really?"

"Really. It's part of our job. It's drilled into us. In fact, any lawyer who blabs a secret winds up losing her job because of it. That's how seriously we take it. So anything you tell me goes no further. Guaranteed."

That seemed more than reasonable to Boxey, who was chafing under the yoke of torn loyalties. This was a way to balance both. It all came spilling out of him. Freya listened, her eyes widening as he finished bringing her up to date on everything that had happened to him.

"That's just wrong," she finally said. They had stopped walking, having arrived in a central mall area where residents of the *Peacemaker* were interacting in a casual social setting. There were a few small trees that someone had uprooted while they were fleeing their home world; it's amazing what some people will risk their lives for. The trees had now become the centerpiece of the mall, with special lights arranged to simulate the long-lost sunlight that the trees might never experience again. They sat under the trees and Freya continued, "They shouldn't have held you like that. You should have contacted me."

"I didn't think about it. I was kind of embarrassed about the whole thing. I thought you might be mad at me."

"Why in the world would I be mad at you?"

"Kara was," Boxey said. "And I bet the others were, too. I mean, she didn't shout at me or anything. But she said I shouldn't really have been on *Galactica* in the first place, and that I couldn't go back there for a long time." Boxey knew he wasn't being entirely fair in his description of the way Starbuck had interacted with him. But he was frustrated and vulnerable, and at that moment felt as if he'd lost an entire coterie of friends that had been his only constant since the Cylon attack. He was loath to risk losing any more, and if it meant slightly exaggerating the way of things to Freya, well, he was willing to do that. "Plus, I was kind of scared. I mean . . . what if I *was* a Cylon?"

"Even if you were, that doesn't mean you automatically have no rights."

He looked at her in confusion. "I thought it kind of does."

"Not necessarily."

Boxey snorted in disbelief. "Well, Sharon Valerii sure has no rights. They keep her locked up in that cell."

"For how long?"

He shrugged. "Forever, I guess. She's pregnant and everything, and they keep her caged in there like an animal."

Freya leaned back, stroking her chin thoughtfully. It was a mannerism she'd unconsciously picked up from her father; the absence of beard didn't deter her. "Pregnant and everything. Caged up." She shook her head.

"Yes, they certainly are treating her as if she has no rights. But treating someone that way doesn't automatically make it so. I think we may have to do something about that."

"We?"

She had been looking inward, but now she turned her attention to Boxey. "Boxey . . . do you like it here? I mean, really like it here on the *Peacemaker*?"

"It's . . ." He was noncommittal. "It's okay, I guess. I like hanging out with Minerva . . ."

"Okay you guess. See, I happen to think that people are entitled to a lifestyle that's slightly better than 'Okay you guess.' How would you like to come and live on the *Bifrost*?"

"What's there?" Although Boxey was very fond of Freya, he didn't know all that much about her background or anything about where she resided when she wasn't working with the homeless.

"My people. The Midguardians."

"You have your own ship?"

She nodded. "We do. Because we knew that the human race was going to be assaulted. We knew that end times would come, and these are them. And we prepared for it. If you'd like, you can live with us, and you can study our ancient writings, and you'll know things that are happening, too. You'll be prepared, as we were."

"If my father had been one of you . . . would he have known about what the Cylons were going to do? Would he . . ." He hesitated, the wound still fresh in his heart even after all these weeks. "Would he still be alive?"

Freya looked at him tenderly. "I won't lie to you, Boxey. I don't know for sure. It's not as if we have a day-by-day calendar. But I'll tell you this: He certainly would have had a better chance if he had attended to the prophecies of the Edda than depending on the Lords of Kobol to protect him. They didn't do an especially good job, did they."

"No. They sure didn't." He took a deep breath, then let it out. "Sure. Why not? Let's go to your ship."

"Excellent," she said, patting him on the back as they both rose. "We'll get you over there . . . we'll get you settled in . . . and then," she added with determination, "we'll see what we can do about Sharon Valerii."

# CHAPTER 8

"*Nothing?*"

William Adama was in his quarters, staring at Saul Tigh with a combination of incredulity and frustration. These weren't emotions that he relished having there. His quarters were traditionally his place of retreat from the day-to-day, and even night-to-night, stress of commanding the *Galactica* and feeling the weight of humanity's survival on his shoulders. Everything there was designed to be as soothing and supportive as possible. It was his "womb," his comfort zone. Whenever Tigh came there to talk about something, Adama inevitably braced himself mentally, knowing that it was probably going to be disruptive of his hard-fought-for stability. This evening was obviously not going to be an exception. "The investigation's turned up nothing?"

"Not so far," Tigh admitted. He had loosened his jacket, which he routinely did when he was off duty. He sat across from Adama and shook his head, looking discouraged. "Gaeta seems ready to tear his hair out. It's certainly giving him a nervous condition; poor bastard keeps scratching the back of his hand like he wants to peel the skin off. He's practically taken apart the entire CNP and Dradis piece by piece and put it back together again, and can't find a damned thing to indicate how the Cylons could possibly have tapped into it to determine where we were going to be Jumping to."

"So what are you saying?" asked Adama. "That we're completely screwed? That we live with the idea of blind Jumps for the rest of our lives?"

"I sure as hell hope not," Tigh said grimly. "Because frankly, I'm not sure how long those lives will be. Our luck is going to run out sooner or later, and I'm betting sooner."

"As am I." Adama leaned back in his chair and rubbed the bridge of his nose. "I was less than candid with you earlier, by the way."

Tigh raised an eyebrow. "Oh?"

"I have noticed: It's not getting easier."

Tigh laughed at that, a moment of needed levity. Then he added, "By the way, the business with the boy has been sorted out."

"The boy?" Adama wasn't following at first, but then he remembered. "Oh, the youngster. Boxey. We really thought he might be a Cylon?" Adama sounded openly skeptical.

Tigh shrugged in a what-can-you-do? manner. "We can't be too careful," he said.

"Historically, I think it's been proven that we can," replied Adama. Tigh naturally knew to what he was referring: the time that a simple military tribunal had gotten completely out of hand, casting suspicion on everyone and anyone until Adama had been forced to shut the thing down.

"Maybe so," Tigh agreed reluctantly, "but that still leaves us with the same problem. Gaeta and his best people are still looking into the matter, but it might be that we have to look in a different direction."

Adama looked as if he were studying the words that

Tigh had just spoken, hanging there in the air. "Are you suggesting . . . ?"

"I'm suggesting," said Tigh, leaping into it since he had put it out there, "that we may have a Cylon operative in the CIC. Someone right under our very noses."

"You really think that one of our own people . . ."

"I'm trying not to think, frankly." And then he hastened to add, "And please, no comments about how I must have a lot of practice at that."

"Wasn't even considering it," said Adama, who had indeed been considering it and had simply thought better of it.

"What I mean is, if you start to think too hard about things like this, you eliminate possibilities because . . . well . . ."

"They're unthinkable."

"Right. And we can't afford to do that."

"So what's the solution?"

Tigh leaned forward, his fingers interlaced and hands resting on Adama's desk. "Listening devices."

"What do you mean?"

"I mean listening devices. We bug the quarters of everyone in CIC."

"Without their knowledge."

"Well, that's certainly the only way it would yield us any information," Tigh said reasonably.

Adama felt as if he were lost in a vast morass of impenetrable moral conundrums. His face, as always, displayed no sign of his inner frustration. "You're suggesting we bug our own people. Listen in on their private lives, even though they're not actually suspects of any crime."

"Of course they're suspects, Bill, and don't make me out to be the bad guy here," said Tigh, sounding defensive.

"It's completely contrary to military protocol . . ."

"That's true. Here's the thing: All the guys who wrote the rules of military protocol? They're all dead. They were blown to bits by the Cylons, and now we're out here trying to hold things together through events that the framers of those protocols could never have conceived. Bill . . . we're dealing with an enemy who looks just like us."

"It's been my experience," Adama said slowly, "that the enemy usually looks like us. Most of the time . . . the enemy *is* us."

"Fair enough. But—"

"What are you proposing, Saul? We listen in on anything and everything for an indefinite period of time? What right do we have to spy on our own people?"

"The right to do everything in our power to keep them safe. Let's be reasonable, Bill: If the Cylons are talking to any humans, I want to know about it. And I very much suspect you want to as well."

Adama didn't say anything for a time, drumming his fingers on the desk. "The whole thing stinks," he said finally.

"No argument on that, Admiral," replied Tigh, his face set and determined. "But I've waded through so much crap in my life that my nostrils died ages ago. Which is why I'm offering to attend to this so that you don't have to know anything about it."

"You're concerned about my sense of smell."

"Something like that."

"Are you going to bug yourself? And me?"

Tigh blinked at that. "I . . . don't see the point. We know we're not Cylons. And since we'd know about the bugs, we wouldn't say or do anything incriminating anyway."

"What about your wife?"

The colonel clearly couldn't quite believe what he was saying. "My wife? Ellen?"

"Do you have more than one wife?"

"No . . ."

"Then that would be her."

"You're inferring she's a Cylon . . . ?"

"No," corrected Adama, "I'm *implying* she could be. That is what the whole purpose of this eavesdropping plan is, isn't it? To weed out possible agents in command positions?"

"She's not in a command position!"

"She sleeps next to my first officer. Have you never considered the dangers of pillow talk? For that matter, what if you're muttering classified information in your sleep and she's sitting there jotting down notes?"

"That's absolutely ridiculous!"

"Ridiculous it may be," Adama said with no hint of rancor. "But absolutely? I don't think so."

*"She's my wife!"*

"Does that make her above suspicion?"

"You bet it . . ." And then Tigh stopped, and Adama could see that Tigh was really starting to think about it. Adama had long ago realized that this was Tigh's way: to react to something with pure gut instinct. Given time, he would often consider the consequences of what he was saying and doing. The problem was that, if he didn't have the time, the decision he went with wasn't always the most prudent. Adama didn't hold it against him; everyone had their failings. Still, it was something that was never far from his thoughts. Tigh lowered his gaze and continued reluctantly, "It . . . doesn't make her above suspicion."

"No. It doesn't. I figured the way to make you understand the enormity of what you're proposing is to make it hit closer to home."

"Understood." Tigh rose. "I apologize for suggesting the—"

"Do you have the know-how to do it?"

This brought Tigh up short. He blinked repeatedly, as if someone were shining a flashlight directly in his face. "Pardon?"

"Do you personally have the know-how to install the sort of bugs we're talking about?"

"Well . . . yes. I did some surveillance work early in

my career. We have the necessary equipment in ship's stores . . ."

"Do it," Adama said quietly. "It stays between you and me. And this is not a fishing expedition. If we hear two officers conspiring to assemble a still or find out that someone likes to spend their free time reciting lewd poetry with our names in it . . . we don't give a damn about it. No recriminations, no black marks. We're looking for evidence of Cylons or Cylon allies only. Is that understood?"

"Perfectly."

"Oh, and Saul . . ." Adama paused and then continued, "If you can manage it . . . monitor the vice president as well."

Tigh nodded.

Adama sat and stared at nothing for a long time after Tigh left. He despised the notion of being in a situation that seemed to have no graceful way out. It wasn't just the prospect of eavesdropping on his own people. It was that he was combating potential spying with actual spying. He had thought that the most cataclysmic problem he was ever going to have to deal with was that the Cylons were becoming indistinguishable from humans. What worried him far more was the possibility that humans were—not all at once, because these things don't happen overnight, but very slowly—becoming indistinguishable from Cylons.

# CHAPTER 9

Laura Roslin had become an enforced insomniac.

Prophetic dreams were nothing new for her. She had had them enough times while she'd been under the influence of the cancer medication, extract of Chamalla. But they had seemed helpful to her. Prophetic, guiding dreams that were admittedly sometimes violent. But they ultimately had a purpose, and that purpose appeared to be to help her in particular and humanity in general. No matter what she had experienced, she had never felt threatened by them.

But this was a very different circumstance. As she lay in her bed and stared up at the ceiling, she felt as if she were under constant threat. As if something had just crawled into her mind and was lying there, festering and trying to undermine her belief in herself and her strength of character.

*She's being paranoid. There is no one out to get her. All right, that isn't true: There's an entire mechanized race that's out to get her. Her and everyone else. But that has nothing to do with what's going on in her head. This is all just spillover from dodging death. That's all. All the things that prey on her during the day are haunting her at night. And since she knows that's what was happening she can control it. She is stronger than simple night terrors. Stronger and better.*

*But why Sagittaron? Or Sagittarius, as the ancient name was phrased. Why did that figure so prominently? And Sharon Valerii?*

*Well, Valerii was obvious, of course. She represented the face of the enemy . . . and yet she was also responsible, however indirectly, for Laura's new lease on life. So naturally she would feel conflicted about Valerii . . . about it . . . and that was what dreams were, after all. A place for the mind to work out conflicts.*

*As for Sagittaron . . . well, that was where Tom Zarek hailed from. Laura was of the firm conviction that, short of the Cylons, Tom Zarek continued to represent the single greatest threat to humanity's continued existence. It was the nature of those such as Zarek to instigate unrest, to foment hostility by attempting to change the status quo—not through diplomacy or thought or consideration—but through violent action. There was enough violence threatening humankind from without; they certainly didn't need it from within.*

*Perhaps that was where the image of blood was coming from as well. Blood was life. Blood was cleansing. She was charged with maintaining the very life blood of humans, to keep it flowing in a cold and uncaring galaxy against an implacable foe that sought to annihilate them.*

*Symbolism. That's what dreams were all about. The more she thought about it, the less daunted by the dreams she was becoming. If she only thought of them as a barrage of frightening images, then it was no wonder she would feel overwhelmed by what was going on inside her skull. But if she broke them down to individual concepts and did all she could to understand what they symbolized, why . . . it wasn't a problem at all.*

*Knowledge was the key to understanding.*

*Knowledge—as Laura Roslin the teacher knew very well—was power. To have knowledge of what her dreams meant gave her the power to be undaunted by them.*

At that moment, her alarm clock went off. Laura was slightly jolted by the noise, and it was just enough to make her realize that she had indeed drifted off to sleep at some point in her musings. But it had been a peaceful, dreamless sleep—the first one in an age, it felt like. That knowledge buoyed her spirits. She felt as if she were on the mend, as if she had taken the first step on a road back to recapturing her equilibrium.

It couldn't have come at a better time. Her performance at the press conference had been nothing short of a fiasco. Billy had done some brilliant spinning when reporters had subsequently asked him if Laura hadn't seemed a bit erratic during the conference, and he smoothly chalked it up to the residue of some heavy-duty medication she'd been taking during her recent illness. He expressed full confidence that the medicines would have worked their way out of her body in short order, and she would be back to her smiling, confident self, ready to put her near-death experience behind her and serve the needs of the people. Everyone had nodded and smiled approvingly, even with relief. As much as reporters enjoyed challenging the status quo, at heart they were as eager for stability and constancy as anyone else. Laura represented that, far more so than the brusque, occasionally distant, and often inscrutable Admiral Adama.

At least, that was the general perception of him.

But she had come to know him in a very different way. Had come to respect him, even admire him. Even . . .

"Best not to go there," Laura said aloud and was slightly startled at the sound of her own voice. She shook it off and slid her legs out from under the covers.

Reflexively she glanced toward the window, and then mentally and sadly scolded herself. She had still not gotten used to the lack of sun. In the old days (only a few months gone, but funny how they had become "the old days") she had never required an alarm since she had readily awoken to the first rays of the morning sun. Ever since she'd been a little girl, that was all that she had required. It was a regular part of her routine, something that she had simply taken for granted. That was one of the most humbling things about her current situation, about the situation that faced all of them: Nothing could be taken for granted anymore. If one couldn't count on the sun to always be there for them, what could one count on?

"Yourself," she said aloud to her unspoken question. She smiled at that. She liked the confident sound of it. In every respect, inside and out, she was beginning to feel and sound more and more like her old self.

*Maybe you're still dreaming this. Maybe you only think you're awake, but you're not, and bad things are going to happen . . .*

She shook the doubts off like a dog divesting itself of water.

She walked into the bathroom and attended to the normal, mundane aspects of morning ablution. As she brushed her teeth, she considered all she had to do today, and was pleased by the degree of clear-headedness that she was displaying. In every way, she was starting to feel like her old self. Her pre-cancer self. The one who not only believed that mankind had a great and glorious destiny, but that she was going to be around to be a part of it. She realized that she had missed that Laura Roslin almost as much as she now missed the sun.

Removing her nightgown, she stepped into the shower, mindful of the need to keep it as brief as possible. The fleet had already had to cope once with the loss of water that had put them into crisis mode. She wasn't about to forget that and endlessly squander a precious resource. Get in, get cleaned off, get out.

She remembered with amusement Billy's suggestion that they mount a campaign centered around "Save water; shower with a friend." Involuntarily her thoughts turned once more to Adama . . .

*Don't. Go. There.*

"Boy," she muttered, soaping her hair, "you really are a glutton for punish—"

Something felt wrong.

She lowered her hands and looked at them.

She assumed she was looking at thick residue from brown water. Not that long ago some sort of rust build-up had caused the water to acquire a distinctly coppery tint. But a man from maintenance had come in, done some work on the pipes, and declared them to be rust-free. He'd been right; from that moment on, the water had been fine. So initially her instinct was to think that she was faced with a recurrence of that problem.

Then she realized that it was a distinctly different tint.

Her hands were red. Dark red. Blood red.

At first she thought there was something wrong with the shampoo. Then she looked down. Her eyes widened in horror. Blood was pouring down her body, cascading down her torso and legs and swirling down the drain.

She jumped back, slamming against the far wall of the shower, and looked up, a scream strangling unvoiced in her throat.

Blood was gushing from the showerhead.

She slipped and stumbled out of the shower. She hit the floor, landing hard on her elbows and sending jolts of pain running up and down her arms. She barely felt it. She felt as if her mind was being shredded by what was happening.

She half-stumbled, half-crawled out of the bathroom, and something splattered upon her from overhead. She looked up, terrified at what she was going to see.

A gigantic red spot had formed upon the ceiling, and blood was dripping from overhead . . . a few drops at first, but then a steady trickle and then a gush, cascading down upon her bed, soaking it through.

Laura finally screamed in full voice, grabbing at her

bathrobe and throwing it on even as she bolted for the door. She slammed into it as her bloodied hand slipped off the knob, failing to open it. Then she found traction, pulled the door opened and stumbled into the hallway, shouting for help.

Billy was there in an instant, as if materializing from thin air. All endeavors to maintain professional demeanor, to adhere to proper titles such as "Madame President," evaporated. "Laura!" he yelled, trying to make himself heard over Laura's inarticulate shouts. "Laura, what's wrong?!"

"*Blood! Blood! It's everywhere! It's—*"

"What are you *talking* about!?"

"Look at me!" She held up her hands. "I'm covered in—"

"There's nothing!"

"The blood, it was coming out of the shower, the ceiling, it's everywhere—"

"There's no blood! I don't know what you're talking about! There's nothing!"

Billy's words penetrated her own hysteria, and she fought it down enough to look at her hands herself. They were clean. There was nothing on them except residual dampness from the water.

"This . . . this can't be," she muttered, shaking her head. She ran her fingers through her hair. There was no stickiness as one would imagine from a head covered in blood, and her fingers came away clean. She held up her arms. The loose folds of the sleeves of her robe fell away and she saw that her arms were clean as well. "Can't be . . . the ceiling . . . the shower . . ."

"Show me," Billy said firmly.

She nodded, feeling disconnected from the moment, even from her own body. She turned and pointed wordlessly at her quarters. Billy stepped past her and stuck his head in. She waited for some reaction from him, but he turned back to her and simply stared at her, his face a question mark.

Laura walked over, pushed past him, and looked in, looked up at the ceiling.

Dry. Normal. No sign of anything untoward.

She pointed with a quavering hand and said, "The bathroom . . ." But before Billy could step past to check it out, she forced her feet to move. She ignored his attempt to hold her back as she walked quickly across the room and looked into the bathroom.

Nothing.

Water was still pouring out of the showerhead. It was pure and clean and not the slightest bit sanguine. Feeling as if she were sleepwalking while awake, Laura reached in and shut off the water.

"It could have been that plumbing thing . . ." Billy started, but his voice trailed off since he knew that he was not only failing to convince Laura, but himself as well. Slowly Laura walked back into her bedroom and sat down on the edge of the bed. Automatically she rearranged the folds of the robe to cover her legs, and she just sat there and stared off into space.

Billy stood in front of her and then crouched so that he was at eye level with her. "Laura," he said, gently but firmly, sounding less like an aide and more like a concerned uncle, "you've got to tell me what's going on. I can't help you if you—"

"You can't help me," Laura said softly. "I'm going crazy. That's all there is to it."

"You're not going crazy."

"How do you know?"

"Because people who are really going crazy don't have the presence of mind to question it. They just accept the reality that's handed them. Or maybe the 'perceived reality' would be a better way to put it."

She put her face in her hands, trying to compose herself. Billy said nothing; he just crouched there and waited.

She told him. She told him about the series of bizarre dreams, with the recurring theme of blood. She told him about Sharon and Zarek figuring into them, and the symbolism of Sagittarius seeping blood. She told him how she had not been sleeping, and how when she did sleep she woke up, and how when she was awake she was beginning to lose track of whether she was awake or asleep. She told him how the lines between dream imagery and reality were beginning to blur, perhaps irreparably.

"Maybe . . ." she began to say, and then stopped.

"Maybe what?"

"Maybe . . . I should take a leave of absence. Even resign my duties . . ."

Billy shook his head. "No. No, I believe in you. You can work your way through this."

She said nothing for a long moment. "Madame President . . ." Billy began.

But she put up a hand and cut him off. Amazingly, despite everything that had just transpired, she forced a wry smile. "This is the beginning of a pep talk, isn't it."

"Well . . ." Billy hesitated. "I don't know that I would have . . . yeah, okay, yes. It was."

"I appreciate that. But I'm starting to think this is a situation that requires more than just a pep talk. I think someone is out to get me." When she saw his look, she continued, "I know how that sounds."

"Well, they always say that it's not paranoia if someone really is out to get you. If you think that's what's happening, then we should speak to Admiral Adama. We should . . ."

"No."

"But . . ."

"I said no. What's the first thing on the agenda?"

He was about to offer more of a protest, but then he saw the firm expression on her face and discarded the idea. "Well . . . actually, I don't think it's going to be something that makes you feel any better."

"Billy, anything short of Tom Zarek is going to be perfectly fine, I assure you." Then she saw the look on his face and said, with the resigned sigh of the damned, "It's Zarek, isn't it."

"You told him to meet with me to make an appointment. He did, I did. I figured doing it in the morning would get it out of the way quickly."

"Good thinking, Billy."

He stood. "I'll cancel . . ."

"No, you won't. I'll attend to it."

"Are you sure?"

She fixed him with a determined stare. "Billy . . . either this is happening due to outside influence, or my mind is turning against me. I won't be beaten by someone else, and I certainly won't be beaten by my own brain. I will be keeping up with my schedule, and that's all."

Billy nodded and said simply, "Thank you, Madame President." He walked out of the room, and it wasn't until he was gone that Laura Roslin started to tremble uncontrollably, and did so until the shakes finally passed.

"Madame President. You're looking well."

Laura, looking utterly self-possessed and not at all like someone who felt as if reality and fantasy were bleeding hopelessly together, pulled up the chair behind her desk and said, "Thank you, Councilman. What's on your mind?"

Zarek, sitting across the desk from her, smiled in amusement. "Getting right to the point, Madame President?"

She returned the smile, but there was no warmth in it, nor did she pretend there was. "I have a schedule to keep."

"And perhaps you want to minimize the amount of time you have to look at me?"

"You said it, Councilman, not I."

"Well," he said, sitting back in his chair and folding

his arms. "I guess that's the difference between us. I say what I think."

"But you didn't do that, did you, Councilman. You said what I think. Or at least what you believe I was thinking. I don't need people to speak on my behalf, and I certainly don't appreciate it when people try to read my mind."

Putting his hands up in a gesture of surrender, Zarek never lost his lopsided grin. Laura had no doubt that he was getting some sort of perverse enjoyment out of this. "Point taken, Madame President. I'll get to it, then. Have you heard of the Midguardians?"

"Of course," she said promptly.

He was visibly surprised. "You have?"

"I wouldn't be much of a president if I didn't have at least some passing knowledge of every major group represented in the fleet. I'd actually been under the impression that the practitioners of their ancient religion had died out."

"As it turns out, no. But not for lack of trying on the part of others. I've been reading up on them, and the persecution of these people is one of the darker times in our history."

"May I ask," she said, curious in spite of herself, "why you've taken a sudden interest in the Midguardians?"

"Because they've approached me about the prospect of being officially recognized."

"As what?"

"As a colony, with equal rights and privileges to any of the others."

Laura laughed in that way someone does when they can't quite believe the person they're talking to is serious. When she saw that Zarek's expression wasn't changing; she realized that he did, indeed, mean what he was saying. "Why in the world would we want to do that? They're a religion, not a colony."

"They are a race. A people with their own heritage and history. They are deserving of recognition as such."

"Councilman," said Laura, still having trouble believing that they were having this conversation at all, "I'm not entirely certain why you're even approaching me on this. I can't simply wave my hand and change the basic structure of government. I'm the president, not the king."

"I know that," said Zarek, not showing the least sign of flagging in his determination. "But every member of the Quorum has one thing in common: They respect you."

"Every member?"

The unspoken challenge was there, and Zarek rose to it. "Every member. Including me. And my coming to you is my way of acknowledging that they will listen to you before they listen to me. If you recommend this—"

"Why would I do that?"

"Because," he said as if it were the most obvious thing in the world, "it's the right thing to do."

Laura wasn't entirely certain how to react to that. But, as always, whatever inner questions she had weren't reflected in her demeanor. Instead she peered over the tops of her glasses as if studying a new form of bacteria. "That's it? That's your whole argument? Because it's the right thing to do?"

"I'd like to think that would be enough."

"And do you think employing violence to get your way is also the right thing to do?"

"You don't see me employing violence here, do you?" he pointed out. "I didn't come in here threatening you. No one's putting a gun to your head. I've no blackmail. No way to force you into anything."

*What about what you're doing to my head? What about the terrorist tactics you're pulling that have made it so I can't sleep, and that are starting to seep into my every waking moment? Are you doing it in order to tear me down? Undermine my leadership? Make me easy to manipulate, get me to agree to something out of exhaustion that I wouldn't ordinarily have even considered?*

She briefly contemplated hurling such questions at him, but she dismissed the notion. There was no advantage to confronting him in that manner. First of all, she still wasn't completely certain there was an entity behind what was happening to her. Second, even if she was certain, she didn't know for sure it was Zarek. Third, even if she was certain, there was no way to prove it. It wasn't as if a cool customer like Zarek was going to break down and admit to anything just from a few probing questions being offered by her. Fourth—and the greatest consideration of all—she didn't want to chance admitting any weakness to someone as untrustworthy and scheming as Tom Zarek. If he wasn't behind it, he'd think she was losing her mind, and if he was behind it, he'd take satisfaction in knowing that he was getting to her.

"No. You're not doing anything like that," she allowed. "But, given our history, I find it difficult to believe you'd think that I would simply take your recommendation on faith—"

"I'm not asking you to do any such thing," he said immediately. He jumped on this so quickly, in fact, that Laura mentally kicked herself, certain that she had just walked into something. "All I'm asking is that you meet with one of their representatives. One Wolf Gunnerson. He's a very impressive, and very charismatic, individual."

"Why didn't he simply come to me directly?"

"Because he believes in following a chain of command. He doesn't feel it's his place to go straight to the president. That his representative should do that instead. And since he and his people are from Sagittaron . . ."

"That representative would be you."

"Exactly."

Laura's gut reaction was to say no. Except . . . based on what, really? She was the president of the Colonies. She represented all the people. If one of them felt they had a genuine grievance, fairness and conscience demanded that she make herself available to hear it. How could she reasonably refuse to meet with this Gunnerson person based entirely on her antipathy toward Zarek?

"Very well."

As if she hadn't spoken, Zarek said, "I think if you give any consideration to fairness, Madame President, I . . ."

For all that Zarek annoyed the hell out of her—for all that she found it aggravating to be in the same room with him—she had to admit to herself that she would always treasure the look on his face when his brain finally processed what she had just said. His voice trailed off for a moment and then he said, " 'Very well'?"

"My aide will set up a time to meet."

Zarek's face changed, and she realized that the patronizing, barely tolerant smile had been inadvertently replaced by a genuine one. It surprised her to see that he actually had a rather pleasant face when he wasn't looking at her like a fox sizing up a prospective meal. "Well, that's . . . thank you, Madame President. That was very unexpected."

"Unexpected?" she said pleasantly. "Why so?"

"Candidly . . . I expected much more of an argument."

She shrugged as if it were no big deal . . . which, stripped of her animosity and distrust for Tom Zarek, it really wasn't . . . and said, "One of my citizens wants to speak with me. I'm the president of all the people, Councilman Zarek . . . even the people with whom I disagree. Even my enemies."

Zarek's smile once again remained in place, but the warmth evaporated from it. "I certainly hope you're not referring to me, Madame President. I'm only the enemy of those who would repress others. I'd hate to think you'd count yourself among such individuals."

"I was merely speaking in generalities, Councilman," she purred. "Whether you feel what I said applied to you . . . well, that's certainly your decision to make, not mine."

"Understood," Zarek said coolly as he stood. Laura did likewise. He extended his hand and she shook it firmly. "A pleasure as always."

As she watched him leave, her eyes narrowed, and she considered the fact that meeting with Zarek was "always" something, all right . . . but "a pleasure" wasn't what she would have termed it.

# CHAPTER 10

William Adama had thought he had heard it all. But when Colonel Tigh told him who had shown up out of nowhere, requesting to meet with the admiral as soon as possible, it still took him a few moments to cut through the sheer incredulity that seized him.

"She's claiming to be her what?" he asked for what might have been the third time. All eyes in CIC had turned to watch with interest, and it was obvious that they were sharing Adama's disbelief.

From Tigh's expression, it was clear that he was not relishing being the bearer of this particular news. "She says," Tigh repeated, looking as if he was ready to strangle whoever the "she" was that was the subject of his communiqué, "that she's her lawyer."

Adama wanted to laugh. But he'd never laughed in front of his crew and didn't feel inclined to set precedent. "Her lawyer," he echoed.

"Yes."

"Motherfrakker," came a murmured comment from Dualla.

Adama fired a glance at her and she quickly fell

silent. He stepped closer in toward Tigh and said in a low, angry voice, "How did she even find out the Cylon is on board?"

"She said 'sources.' You ask me, it's that kid, Boxey."

"We don't know that for sure," said Adama, who privately thought Tigh was probably right. "What's this woman's name?"

"Gunnerson. Freya Gunnerson. From the *Bifrost*. I ran a fast check on her and she is a genuine attorney." Tigh shook his head. "If the frakking Cylons had to destroy the bulk of humanity, you'd think at least they could have done us the favor of making sure to take out all the lawyers."

Adama considered the comment to be in poor taste at best, but he let it pass. "Does she have any known affiliation to any terrorist groups or any Cylon sympathizers?"

"Maybe, but nothing that a preliminary background check turned up. She's a Midguardian, though."

"Yes, everyone on the *Bifrost* is." Adama knew the ship was one of the few privately owned vessels in the fleet. "They may be heathens, but they're not especially enamored of the Cylons in any way that I know of. So where in the world is this coming from? Why would she be showing up here and claiming she's Valerii's attorney?"

"Free publicity. She's trying to make a name for herself. Get famous fast."

"Sharon Valerii is a member of the race that's trying to obliterate us," Adama pointed out. "Allying with her is a fast track to infamy, not fame."

"For some people, that's enough." When Adama didn't respond, Tigh said, "I'll send her packing . . ."

"Bring her to meeting room A."

Tigh's eyes widened. His surprise was mirrored in the faces of the CIC crew. "Seriously?"

"Seriously."

Tigh turned to a nearby functionary and said, "Please have the woman who's in the holding area escorted to meeting room A." The moment the functionary was out the door, he turned back to Adama and said, "I'm coming with you, then." He saw the look in Adama's face, the understated surprise that Tigh would dare to issue flat fiats to him. But Tigh didn't back down. "She's a Cylon sympathizer. Perhaps a Cylon herself. For all we know, she wants a one-on-one with you so she can . . ." He didn't want to complete the sentence, still sensitive—even now—to the bullets that had ripped open Adama's chest and nearly killed him.

"I was taking it for granted she's been screened for weapons," Adama said mildly.

"Of course. But who ever knows what we're dealing with? What if she has some sort of bomb that she's got built into herself, and she can blow herself up? If she's a toaster, anything is possible."

"If she's a toaster and she blows herself up, do you really think the best strategy is to put the ship's commander and second in command in the same room with her?"

Tigh started to reply, and realized that he didn't have a ready answer to that.

"I'll be back shortly," Adama assured him, and headed to the meeting room.

Before he left, though, Tigh called after him, "Admiral. Be careful. They can be incredibly evil bastards."

"Cylons?"

"Lawyers."

Adama hadn't been certain what to look forward to when meeting Freya Gunnerson, briefcase in her hand and determination in her face. Horns, perhaps, or a large single red eye strobing from one side of her head to the other. He certainly hadn't anticipated the tall, impressive-looking woman who was waiting for him. She didn't seem especially devious. Of course, she wouldn't have been especially devious if she'd looked that way, now, would she. She had been sitting, but she rose and extended her hand. "Admiral. This is an honor," she said. Her voice was musical, and she genuinely did sound as if she was honored to meet him. None of which served to put Adama off his guard, but it certainly ran contrary to his expectations. "I'm Freya Gunnerson."

He shook her hand firmly. "William Adama."

"Yes, I know. The military genius who's kept us alive in the face of adversity."

"I've had some help. Please sit."

She did so, placing a briefcase on the table. She snapped the latches open and saw Adama's cautious expression. "Your people have already thoroughly inspected this, I assure you."

There had been no question in Adama's mind that was true. The caution had been automatic after a lifetime of military experience. Nevertheless, he tilted his head slightly in acknowledgment. She opened the briefcase and removed a notepad and a file folder, which she placed on the table and proceeded to flip through. "I assume," she said, "that your XO told you why I'm here."

"I prefer to hear it with my own ears."

"I am here," she said patiently, "to represent the interests of Sharon Valerii."

"In what sense?"

"In the sense that I would like to know what crime she's committed."

Adama stared at her gravely. "What *crime*?"

"Yes, Admiral. What crime has she committed that warrants her being held indefinitely?"

"Attempted murder."

"I assume you're referring to yourself as the attempted victim." Adama's nod was barely perceptible, but she went on as if he had readily bobbed his head. "My understanding—and correct me if I have the facts wrong—is that the person you are holding indefinitely was, in fact, on Caprica at the time of the assault."

"*It* is not a person."

"Really." She seemed genuinely interested in his opinion. "And on what do you base that assessment?"

"She is a Cylon. Are you disputing that?"

"Not at all. I'm simply asking on what basis you declare that she's not a person."

Adama could scarcely believe he was having the conversation. "The Cylons," he said very slowly, as if addressing someone who was having trouble understanding him, "are machines. We created them."

"Humans routinely create other humans. Does that make them machines?" Before he could answer, she leaned forward and continued, "I am simply a person of conscience, Admiral. I see someone's rights being trampled upon, and I feel the need to step in and see that those rights are restored."

"I'm not interested in fencing with you, Counselor," Adama said in an icy tone. "Sharon Valarii is one of an identical series of creations, transferring all her knowledge from one to the next to the next. She was constructed for that purpose. Cylons are not humans. Sharon Valerii is not a person. Sharon Valerii is not human. Sharon Valerii has no more rights than the chair you're sitting in."

"Really." The edges of her mouth turned up. "And how many pregnant chairs have you encountered?"

"That's a ridiculous comparison."

"Actually," said Freya, "it's a perfectly valid comparison. In case you never got around to taking basic biology in school, Admiral, one of the determinations of whether two beings are part of the same genus is their ability to reproduce. I will grant you that Sharon Valerii may be a different species from humans . . . but certainly she's part of the same genus. Otherwise how else can she be pregnant by your lieutenant . . ." She glanced at one of the sheets of paper, "Agathon, I believe?"

"Yes," he growled.

"My contention is that she is at the very least of the same genus, and quite possibly of the same species. Or at least near enough to be indistinguishable from humans. And if she's indistinguishable from a human, on what basis can we contend that she's not?"

"On the basis that she presents a security risk to this fleet."

"An assertion you base on what aspect of her behavior, exactly? I'm not asking about her lookalikes. I'm asking you what specific crimes the woman in that cell has herself committed."

Adama took a deep breath and let it out slowly. "None that I'm aware of," he admitted. "But that doesn't mean she doesn't present a threat. Counselor, if we're done here . . ."

"We are if you say we are," she acknowledged. "This is your boat, after all. It's just that I was given to believe that you were a man of honor."

Adama's face could have been carved of stone. "Are you questioning my honor?"

"I'm questioning what sort of man takes someone who has committed no crime—who has served the needs of humanity every time she was asked to—and treats her as if she is the most vile of criminals."

"She. Isn't. Human."

She chuckled at that, but there was a sadness in her voice. "Isn't that how one group always justifies mistreating another group? By pretending they're not human, despite all evidence to the contrary? And because of that, they're not deserving of rights."

"My heart bleeds, counselor, considering the Cylons obviously think of us as animals to be slaughtered."

"And we thought of them as slaves before they turned on us. No one's hands are clean in this one, Admiral. But certainly part of their determination to exterminate us stems from the notion that they don't think we're deserving of the right to live free . . . just as you judge Sharon Valerii the same way. How are we to judge ourselves any better than the Cylons, if that's the way we think?"

"And you can't treat a Cylon like Sharon Valerii as if she is a human with the same rights as a human."

"Convince me that she's not human," Freya said challengingly. "Her memories 'transfer'? There are studies documenting humans functioning with highly developed versions of ESP. So the Cylons have simply improved upon that which was already a part of them. Cylons kill humans? As if humans don't kill humans."

"I don't have to convince you of anything."

Her face hardened. "Actually, Admiral, you do. See, our criminal justice system doesn't allow for people to be held indefinitely, with no charges brought against them, while they're pumped for information over alleged terrorist activities. No civilized society would allow such behavior, I'd like to think. In order to deprive someone of their fundamental right to liberty, the burden of proof is upon her accusers to prove that she has, in fact, done something worth being incarcerated for. You've admitted to my face that Sharon Valerii has done nothing. She's being held for no damned good reason."

"She is a military asset."

"So are you, Admiral. But you're not under armed guard and you can go wherever you wish. The fact remains that by every measurable standard, Sharon Valerii is a person. And all people within the Colonies have equal rights; that's built right into the charter of the Twelve Colonies. Your imprisonment of Sharon Valerii is unconstitutional."

"And you expect me to release her on the basis of this . . . specious claim?" said Adama incredulously.

"No. Getting her released is my fight, to be taken up with others. But at the very least, I should think that—in the interest of simple human decency—you would allow me to meet with her."

" 'Others' can't know about her. I don't even want to think what would happen if the general populace learns that she's here."

"If you think she's going to remain under wraps forever, you're deluding yourself. I'll wager at least several people in the Quorum probably know by now. Or whatever marines you've got guarding her have told their loved ones about it, sworn of course to strictest secrecy. But secrets have a way of getting out, and in case you haven't noticed, governments stink at keeping them. A casual slip of the tongue. A few too many drinks resulting in the wrong words said within earshot of the wrong ear. Next thing you know, this whole thing explodes in your face." She eased back, sounding less confrontational but no less determined. "Look . . . Admiral . . . if you allow me to meet with her, then anything I know about her—including her existence—becomes a matter of attorney/client privilege. I'll keep everything to myself. You turn me away, shut me out . . . there's no reason at all for me not to discuss whatever I know with whomever will listen."

"Are you blackmailing me?" asked Adama, his tone fraught with danger.

"No, Admiral. That would be illegal. I'm simply explaining what will happen if you do the right thing . . . and the wrong thing. This isn't blackmail. It's simply endeavoring to give you an informed opinion."

Adama's instinct was to kick her off the ship. This woman hadn't been there. She didn't understand. She hadn't seen the look that came over Sharon Valerii's face as she leveled her gun at Adama's chest and shot him at point-blank range. If Freya Gunnerson had seen that, she wouldn't be sitting here today claiming that the thing down in the brig was entitled to be treated like any other human. In fact, if she had seen Sharon Valerii coming her way, she'd probably have run in the other direction.

Plus, on a practical level, Adama couldn't see any way in which Sharon could be released, if for no other reason than that it would be a death sentence for her. Her predecessor had been gunned down. The odds were sensational that she would meet the same fate. The only way she would avoid it would be if she was assigned quarters and hid there for the rest of her life. What was really the difference between that and residing in a cell?

But what kept niggling in the back of Adama's brain was that, for all that he was still unconvinced that Valerii was entitled to the same rights as a human . . . there were small shreds of truth creeping into what Freya was saying. Valerii was part of a life form so indistinguishable from humans that she was capable of bearing a human's child. And the only way to tell humans from Cylons was via a complicated blood test that he still wasn't one hundred percent sure was reliable, although that might stem from his fundamental distrust of Gaius Baltar.

There was one thing that William Adama was very aware of, that any military man was aware of. And that was that there was no inherent danger in simply talking with someone. Indeed, just about every war in humanity's history had stemmed from two or more sides being unable to talk to each other. So instead they had blown the living crap out of each other until finally they had enough, at which point they wound up talking . . . which, if they'd only done that in the first place, would have spared countless lives.

Of even more recent vintage, and always fresh in Adama's memory, was the breakdown in communication between him and Laura Roslin that had resulted in complete chaos, the shattering of the fleet, a military invasion that had turned his own son against him. It was a situation that he, Adama, had instigated with military thinking, and that he, Adama, had finally settled when he had opened himself to genuinely listening to what Roslin had to say. Laura Roslin had far too much class to say something as infantile as "I told you so," and no one else would have dared to. But Adama had been saying it to himself most every day since then.

Freya Gunnerson wanted to talk to Sharon Valerii. She was doing so in the interest of justice. If he stood in the way of that, what did that make him?

"All right," he said. Surprise registered on her face, and she tried quickly to cover it as he continued, "You may meet with her. You will remain on the other side of the enclosure, speak to her via phone only. Furthermore, one of my officers will be there at all times."

"Admiral, as I mentioned, there is such a thing as lawyer/client confidentiality."

He wasn't about to argue the fine points of it. "Take or leave it," he told her.

Freya looked as if she were about to argue the point further, but obviously thought better of it. "I'll take it."

"Remain here and I'll have it arranged."

He rose to leave, and she automatically stood as well. Again she extended her hand and he shook it firmly. "You're making the right decision, Admiral. Allowing people to talk is never a bad thing. Just imagine: If enough people talk about the right subjects, we could actually have peace in our time."

"We can only hope," replied Adama.

Adama recognized the look of astonishment on Lee's face; it very likely mirrored the one that had been on his own when Tigh had first told him about their new arrival.

"You want me to sit in on a lawyer meeting with Sharon?"

Adama, walking down a hallway next to Lee, nodded. "They're down waiting at the brig for you. I need you to head down there now."

Lee stopped in his tracks and Adama turned, his face impassive. "Problem?" inquired Adama.

"It's crazy. She's a Cylon. Cylons don't have lawyers."

"Apparently they do now."

"Why me?"

"Because I want someone with a different perspective than my own watching the two of them interact."

"A Cylon who looked just like the one we have

locked up shot my father," Lee reminded him unnecessarily. "What makes you think your perspective is going to be any different than mine?"

"Because it often has been in the past. And because you're not the one who was shot. Now head down to the brig." When Lee, looking conflicted, didn't immediately move, Adama said, "That was not intended as a request."

With an irritated why-me sigh, Lee said, "Yes, sir," turned away, and headed off to do as he'd been instructed.

Sharon Valerii was lying on her bunk, slowly rubbing her hand across her swollen belly. She'd felt the baby stirring recently. The first time she'd felt it move, there had been the thrill of amazement that any pregnant woman feels whenever there are the first stirrings of life within her, fluttering like the wings of a butterfly. She felt a flare of jealousy, or at least envy, for other women who were able to share such moments of discovery and excitement with their husbands or lovers. Who was she going to tell? The men standing guard outside?

There was no one to care for her.

She hadn't even told Helo, the father of her child. The poor bastard had gotten into so much trouble over her. When that bastard officer from *Pegasus* had tried to rape her, both Helo and the chief had intervened on her behalf, and that intervention had almost cost them their lives. Since then . . . well, she hadn't been trying to distance herself from Helo. But she wasn't doing anything to play upon his emotions either. She cared for him far too much to continue pouring fuel onto the raging fire that represented his divided loyalties. Whenever he did stop by, she saw the torment in his eyes every time he looked at her: She was the woman he loved, and yet she was a complete stranger to him. Why make it harder on him, just because it would make it easier on her?

She would have laughed if she hadn't felt like crying.

She knew what the others thought of her. They believed her to be a soulless machine. She wondered what they would make of it if they knew that she was beating herself up in an attempt to spare the feelings of others.

There was a sudden noise at the door and, as she always did, she started ever so slightly, and her hand reflexively covered her belly protectively. Sharon never knew what was going to be coming through that door: something as innocuous as food, or as dangerous as someone who was going to try and beat information out of her or—even worse—take her baby from her. In the first days of her imprisonment, she had thought she was going to lose her mind with constantly being on edge. Eventually she had learned to tolerate it. The human ability to adapt to circumstances, no matter how bizarre, was . . .

*Human ability.*

The Cylons firmly believed that they were far superior to humans. She knew that some of the other models regarded her as weak because she didn't believe that to be true. She believed that going around thinking you're superior is an inherently weak attitude to have. She tolerated their contempt. She told herself that everything she was enduring, all the misery that arose from her sustained exposure to humans, was worth it. Perhaps if she kept telling herself that long enough, she'd even come to believe it.

The door opened and she braced herself. The first person in was Lee Adama, which piqued her curiosity. She hadn't seen Lee all that much since her incarceration, but believed him to be a bit more open minded of an individual than his father. But she was sure she'd never be able to consider him a friend or ally ever again, because whenever he looked at her he would see the face of the woman who tried to kill his father. It hadn't been her, but in the end, it didn't matter. She was still going to carry that stigma to her dying day . . . which might come at any time, and none save Helo and Chief Tyrol, her former lover, would mourn her.

She didn't recognize the next person, though. It was some woman, and she actually seemed pleased to see Sharon. In fact, there was even a look of triumph glittering in her eye. She went straight to the phone, sat down, picked up the receiver, and gestured for Sharon to do the same. Sharon stared at her, still not knowing what was going on, but then she shrugged and did as she was bidden.

"Sharon Valerii?" The woman's voice came through the phone.

It seemed a pretty silly question. Who the hell else would she be? "Yes," Sharon said cautiously.

"I'm Freya Gunnerson, and if you're interested, I'd like to offer my services as your attorney."

Sharon laughed. Then she saw that this Freya person wasn't laughing along with her. Sharon turned her attention to Lee. "Did you put her up to this?"

Lee took the phone and she repeated the question. "She came here to see you," Lee informed her.

"Does the Old Man know about this?"

"Admiral Adama approved it, yes," he said. She noted the cold use of the full name and rank of William Adama, as opposed to the familiar and loving nickname of "the Old Man" that Sharon had just employed. The message was clear: Don't pretend to a familiarity that you're no longer entitled to employ.

"Why did he approve it?"

"I'm not in the habit of questioning the admiral's thinking."

Sharon laughed again. Twice in as many minutes. "Since when? Since before or after he declared you an enemy to the fleet and you took sides against him?"

He was about to reply, but Freya took the phone back.

"If it's all the same to you, Lieutenant," Freya said crisply, "I think it would be advisable if you addressed all your comments to, and through, me from now on."

Sharon stopped laughing and looked at Freya as if seeing her for the first time. "Why would I do that?"

"Because he's not your friend, Sharon. As much as you would like to believe he is . . . he isn't. None of them are. They see you as a machine. They see you as subhuman and a threat. They all think they're better than you are, and they only feel comfortable when you're behind bars. They don't have your best interests at heart."

"Nice to see that you know us so well," Lee snapped, "considering you only met me two minutes ago, and you haven't met anyone else."

"I hear you complaining about my opinions, Captain, but I don't hear you disagreeing." Freya lowered the phone, stood, and fixed a level gaze on him. "But perhaps I missed a meeting somewhere. Would you care to detail for me your history of strident advocacy for granting Sharon Valerii the freedom that your father has deprived her of?" She waited a moment and then said, "Anytime, Captain. Dazzle me with your track record."

Lee said nothing, but merely glowered at her. Nodding in apparent satisfaction, Freya sat once more and turned her attention back to Sharon, who was intrigued by this point. "Who are you again?"

"Freya Gunnerson," she said with no trace of impatience, as if she were accustomed to having people repeatedly ask her who she was. "I told you: If you desire my services, then I'm your attorney."

"And if I don't?"

Freya shrugged. "Then I leave. It's as simple as that. But before I do, I would like to ask you one question: Why would you be opposed to having someone on your side?"

"What 'side' is that?"

"The side that believes you should be allowed to live your life as you see fit," Freya said, pouncing on the question like a lion on a deer. "The side that believes your child shouldn't have to be born imprisoned. And that's another thing, while I'm at it. The constitution of the Colonies clearly states that anyone who is born on a particular colony becomes a citizen of that colony, with that citizenship then extended back to the mother."

"The Colonies were destroyed," Lee Adama spoke up, and added with a glance at Sharon, "by *her* kind."

"They may have been destroyed in fact, but they continue in spirit, as the ongoing existence of the Quorum of Twelve certainly indicates," Freya replied without hesitation. "I don't see the Quorum voting to dissolve itself simply because the worlds upon which they settled were depopulated by the Cylons. As long as the Quorum exists, the spirit of the constitution exists. Which means when the child is born, it becomes a citizen, with the full rights that any citizen has. And the child's mother will have those same rights, so all the nice discussions about whether Sharon Valerii is human or not human and whether she deserves the rights of a human . . . they all become moot."

"You're saying you think I have rights?" asked Sharon.

"I'm saying your incarceration here is a war crime. I'm saying they don't have one damned good reason not to let you walk out of here. That the longer you remain here, the better civil suit you have against them for wrongful imprisonment. You've done nothing to deserve this, nothing to warrant this sort of treatment. And if you allow me to, I'm going to make sure everyone knows it, and that you are accorded your full rights under the law."

"But . . . what if . . ." She looked nervously at Lee and then back to Freya. "But what if you make that argument about my baby and they just take that as an excuse to kill it, like they tried to before."

Freya shook her head and there was a satisfied smirk on her face. "They wouldn't dare. My understanding through my sources is that your baby's blood performed the miraculous healing of the president. What if she relapses? What if someone else becomes drastically ill? How would Lee Adama feel about it if . . . oh, I don't know . . . Kara Thrace, one of his top pilots, suddenly discovered she had breast cancer?"

"You leave her the frak out of this," Lee snapped.

Freya's smirk grew wider. Clearly she was pleased that she had gotten under Lee's skin so quickly. Sharon felt badly for Lee's discomfort . . . and suddenly wondered why she did. After all, he was out there and she was in here. He was allied with those who wanted to keep Sharon locked up forever. When the soldiers had come to try and abort her pregnancy, it had been Helo who stood in their way, not Lee Adama. *He is not your friend . . .*

She found herself looking at Freya with new eyes. "The point is," the lawyer was continuing, "they don't dare do anything to your baby now. They might need it for something. But if you have any interest in making sure that your child is something other than a lab rat . . ."

Sharon put up a hand, her mind racing, and Freya immediately lapsed into silence. "What's in this for you?" she asked.

Freya laughed softly. "People keep asking me that. Lieutenant . . . sometimes people just do things because they feel it's the right thing to do. I think you knew that, once upon a time. It could be that you've simply forgotten that. I wouldn't blame you, considering everything you've been put through."

"Everything *she's* been put through?" Lee seemed astounded. "How about everything she's put everyone else through?"

"My understanding, Captain, is that you're here to observe the proceedings, not contribute," Freya reminded him. "If you would kindly adhere to what's expected of you, this would all go much faster and much more smoothly." When Lee didn't reply, she tilted her head as if that settled it and once again returned her attention to Sharon. "In any event, Lieutenant . . . believe it or not, I'm just doing this because I feel it's right."

"I'm not entirely sure I believe you," Sharon said.

"You don't have to. I'm perfectly happy to let my actions prove my worth."

"And what would those actions be? What's the best-case scenario?"

"The best-case scenario," Freya said, looking pleased to be discussing the specifics of the case, "is that they throw open the door and you walk out."

Sharon ignored the amused snort from Lee. "If they do that . . . I'm a dead woman walking," Sharon said, unaware that she was saying aloud what had been going through Adama's mind earlier. "You'll be able to measure my life expectancy in microns."

"Not necessarily," Freya told her. "The residents of the *Bifrost,* where I live, would offer you sanctuary."

"I should have known," Lee said with a roll of his eyes. "Religious extremists."

"I can't say I appreciate the slander of my people or my beliefs."

Sharon looked from one to the other in puzzlement. "Extremists? What is he—?"

Freya was about to respond, but Lee did it for her. "They don't believe what everyone else believes," he called to Sharon loudly enough so that his voice carried over the phone. "They don't even believe in the gods. In the Lords of Kobol."

"Neither do I," Sharon said.

Lee blinked in surprise. For a moment, it was as if he'd forgotten he was staring into the face of the enemy. "You don't?"

"Cylons believe in one god, Lee. Not many."

"You're kidding. Why?"

"I don't think this is truly the time for a deep theological discussion," Freya interrupted. "You have to understand, Lieutenant . . . may I call you Sharon . . . ?" When Sharon nodded, she went on, "You have to understand that people such as Captain Adama tend to see things in extremes. Either you're with him or against him. There's not much tolerance for simple differing opinions. We are not extremists. We simply believe other than what Captain Adama and his friends believe . . ."

"My 'friends' in that instance being almost everyone else in the Colonies," Lee said.

"That's as may be. But we're not extremists. And since we've historically been in the minority, we tend to be more accepting of other minorities. We have a live-and-let-live approach. I assure you, you would be safe from harm in the *Bifrost*. You and your child would be allowed to live free, as the gods . . . or god," she included with a nod of her head toward Sharon, "intended you to."

"I . . . I don't know," Sharon said uncertainly.

"I think you do know," Freya replied. She appeared sympathetic, but there was a look of steel in her eye. "I think you already realize that I'm your first, best chance for getting out of here. The difficult thing for you," she added sympathetically, "is letting go of your fading hopes that any of your old ties to these . . . individuals . . . are going to do you any good. They are your past, Sharon. I'm your future. Are you going to live in your past . . . or embrace your future?"

"Can . . ." Sharon hesitated, glancing once more at Lee, and then said, "Can I have some time to think it over?"

"Of course," said Freya. She stood and said, "Take all the time you want. I mean . . . it's not as if you're going anywhere."

With that, she headed out, Lee Adama right behind her. He cast a glimpse at Sharon over his shoulder, but she didn't meet his eye. Instead she was staring off into space, lost in thought, with her hand unconsciously rubbing her belly.

# CHAPTER 11

*Laura feels at peace, for the first time in a long time. She feels at peace because there is no question in her mind this time. The line between fantasy and reality is clearly demarcated. She has no doubt that she is dreaming now. With that knowledge brings peace of a kind. The recent press conference where figments of her innermost fears were strolling around in the objective light of day was a bit much for her. But this . . . this is definitely within her comfort level.*

*Yet what she is experiencing is simultaneously comforting and disconcerting.*

*She hears a heartbeat. It is steady and rhythmic, as a heartbeat should be. It's difficult for her to place where it's originating from, because everything around her is so dark. She strains to find a light source, but none is forthcoming. She tries to hold her hands up in front of her face, but she's having trouble determining whether she's actually moving them or not. She doesn't quite understand why. It's as if her mind is completely disconnected from her body. Still, she's not upset over the lack of light. She's not upset about anything. Instead she feels completely calm and content. Although all her problems are still present in her mind, she nevertheless feels as if she hasn't a care in the world. She is calmer than at any other time that she can recall, and not only that, but she feels totally protected, as if nothing out in the world can possibly hurt her while she floats blissfully in . . .*

*Oh . . . you have to be kidding . . .*

*The words echo in her mind and she tries to say them aloud, but her mouth won't form the words.*

*This can't be happening . . .*

*Seized with a determination to shake off a dream that had abruptly become far too strange for her to continue, she starts twisting about violently. She is suddenly relieved that she can't see her own body since she isn't sure she could tolerate the bizarreness of what she is now certain she will experience. She feels completely constricted, even though there are no ropes or any other sort of bonds around her.*

*Then the environment in which she is floating begins to respond to her struggles. There is trembling and violent vibration, and she perceives that there are walls surrounding her, starting to close in, and pushing her down, down through the liquid that is enveloping her . . .*

*Too weird . . . too weird . . . make it stop, gods, please . . .*

*But as much as she is repulsed by the reality of what is happening to her, or at least what she thinks is happening to her, there is nothing that she can do to prevent it. She tries to get a sense of herself within the context of the dream, but she cannot. She doesn't know whether this is something that is supposed to be happening to her . . . or to someone else.*

*She is shoved forward, the walls contracting around her, forcing her against her will. She seeks purchase and finds none. She continues to struggle but it means nothing. She is leaving the warmth behind, and suddenly coldness strikes her in the face. Laura opens her mouth, but nothing except a pathetic mewl escapes her lips.*

*"Her eyes are open," says a voice, and it's a terribly familiar one. The world is shifting at odd angles around her, and she is looking up into the familiar face of Gaius Baltar. She recognizes him even though he is wearing a surgical mask over the lower half of his face. "Amazing. It's like she's looking right at me."*

*"It's a girl," the voice of Sharon Valerii moans, "I knew it would be a girl . . . God . . . she's covered in blood."*

*"We'll clean her off," says Baltar. "Nurse. Come here." He turns and, holding Laura carefully in his blood-covered hands, he extends her to the waiting figure of a Cylon soldier, all gleaming metal and a single, glowing red eye. Laura screams even louder, and it's still emerging as a babyish cry.*

*The Cylon takes her from Baltar. Its metal hands are cold, and Laura is shivering from the chill and from the fear. He turns around and walks away. Baltar is shouting for him to come back, and Sharon, who Laura can now see is lying flat on a table with her legs splayed, is reaching out desperately and crying for the Cylon to return her. The Cylon ignores her, walking out of the room, and now they are outside, the Cylon striding away from a small building, its feet clanking steadily. She is looking up at the night sky, and she recognizes the constellations. She has seen them before. She is on Earth. She is home.*

*Behind her the building explodes in a fireball of sound and flame . . .*

She woke up and found that the Cylon warrior's face had been replaced with that of Billy.

She started involuntarily and realized that she was sitting in her office chair, which made perfect sense since she was in her office. For a heartbeat she thought she was still dreaming—again—for how in the world had she gotten from her bedroom to her office? Then, in that disorienting way that always occurs when one wakes up in an unexpected place, she remembered that she had, in fact, already gotten up that morning, and had come to work. She had leaned back in her chair and closed her eyes for just a moment to rest them . . .

. . . at least, she thought that was what she had done. What if she was wrong? What if her memory was playing tricks on her and actually she really was still asleep? Maybe she was even in a coma, and all that was going to happen now was that she was going to keep dreaming about waking up and waking up—

"Madame President . . ."

Billy's voice, filled with unmistakeable concern that was cloaked with a veil of professionalism, said, "Your next appointment is here. Mr. Gunnerson . . ."

"Yes. Yes, of course." She straightened her short jacket and sat forward in as businesslike a manner as she could, doing her best to indicate that she was raring to go. "Bring him in," she said in her most no-nonsense voice.

Billy looked as if he were about to say something, but then thought better of it and simply inclined his head. "Yes, Madame President."

He went out and, moments later, came back in with what appeared to be a walking land mass. Laura kept her face neutral as she rose to greet him, but inwardly she was astounded at the size of the man. He had to bend over slightly to pass through the door, and when he reached out to shake her hand, her hand literally disappeared into his. "Wolf Gunnerson, Madame President. It's an honor."

"A pleasure to meet you, sir," she said, gesturing toward the chair opposite her. He sat, albeit not without effort, as she sat back down in her own chair. She glanced behind him and saw only Billy. "For some reason I was under the impression Councilman Zarek would be joining you to help make your case."

"Councilman Zarek told me he thought it'd be better if I came in on my own. He said"—and Gunnerson raised a bushy, quizzical eyebrow—"that you would probably feel more at ease if he were not here."

She smiled slightly. "Councilman Zarek overestimates his ability to discomfort me. He would have been welcome to join you, but . . ." She shrugged as if it were of little consequence. "So . . . I understand you feel your people should be recognized as . . . what? A thirteenth colony?"

"A fourteenth," he reminded her, "if we count the long-lost colony that may or may not have wound up on our destination of Earth."

"Fair enough."

"For that matter, thirteen has never been the luckiest of numbers. Perhaps increasing the number of colonies—here and gone—to fourteen will change some of the luck we've been having lately."

Laura allowed a small laugh. In spite of herself, she was actually finding the fellow pleasant enough. She hadn't known what she was going to be confronted with: some sort of wild-eyed religious fanatic, perhaps. But this soft-spoken behemoth didn't match her preconceptions.

"I'll take that under advisement," she said evenly. "Somehow, though, I doubt that that will be the sort of convincing argument the Quorum would consider."

"Yes, I know that," he laughed. It was a deep, rumbling laugh that sounded like the beginnings of a ground quake. Then he grew serious and continued, "I'm not naïve, Madame President. I know the way things work. Most of the time, when a decision is to be made about something, the consideration isn't what is right . . . or what's just . . . or what's fair. It's 'What's in it for me?' "

"That's a less-than-charitable view of the world."

"But not less than realistic."

"If you're trying to focus on the realistic," said Laura, "then certainly you have to acknowledge that my voice is merely that: a voice. As I made clear to the councilman, the question of statehood—which is really what you're asking for—is not something that lies within the province of this office. That's in the hands of the Quroum, and the Quorum doesn't answer to me."

"No. But they listen to you. And if you put forward our case, that would carry weight."

"And why would I . . ." She stopped and now they were both smiling. "All right . . . I suppose, yes, I'm saying what's in it for me? Or, more specifically, for the members of the Quorum. I don't dispute that the Midguardians have been treated less than charitably in the past. But that persecution was a long time ago . . ."

"A long time ago in the minds of you and yours. But a mere eye blink to me and mine. And even now, my people remain marginalized because of our beliefs. Dismissed as heretics and unbelievers. We've no active involvement or say in the destiny of humanity. That's not right."

"I don't dispute that," said Laura. "But, despite what you may have read in some of the more enthusiastic publications . . . I am not a god. I don't get to wave my hand and have everyone fall into line. There's—dare I say it—politics involved. And whether we like it or not, that aspect has to be addressed."

"Have you heard," he said, unexpectedly switching topics, "of the book of Edda?"

"Yes. It's your book of history."

"Correct. History of the past . . . and the present . . . and the future. The lifetime of mankind, covered in our verses, with greater accuracy and detail than is to be found in any of your prophecies."

"Well," Laura said, not exactly convinced despite the obvious fervency of his belief. "That's easy for you to say. But having never read it myself, or had access to it . . ."

"That's because the leaders of the 'accepted' religion have done everything within their ability to make certain no one does. After all," and he leaned back, the chair creaking beneath his weight, "if it's learned that someone other than the accepted oracles are able to know what's to come, that would certainly diminish the miracles that support the current belief system. Wouldn't you say?"

"I would say," she said slowly, "that it's easy to complain of so-called conspiracies where none was intended."

"It is indeed . . . just as it's difficult sometimes to convince others that such conspiracies exist. That's what the conspirators typically count upon: disbelief. It's the single greatest weapon at their command."

"Mr. Gunnerson," she said, striving to keep the fatigue from her voice, "with all respect, I feel as if we're going in circles here, and I don't have the time—"

Gunnerson reached into his inner jacket pocket and pulled out a small leather case. Placing it on her desk, he opened it with unmistakeable reverence. There was a small book inside. He removed it, held it up, and said with a touch of pride, "The Edda." He flipped through it with the confidence of someone who knew what was contained on every page and found what he was looking for. He turned to a page toward the back. Then he cleared his throat and said to her, "Understand that I'm not only translating on the fly, but it's supposed to be sung. But I figure you don't need my abysmal attempts at vocalizing, particularly this early in the morning, so . . ."

She gestured for him to proceed, intrigued in spite of herself.

He held up the book and began to read. Although he was, indeed, not singing it, his voice still went up and down in places as if it were meant to be chanted and he couldn't help himself.

*"The day would come, when the prodigal sons*
*A gleam in metal, crimson of eye*
*Would rain destruction down upon their fathers*
*From the tinted sky*
*The fathers would run, fleeing from the wrath*
*Of sons, accompanied by daughters*
*Their eyes would turn toward far-off home*

*With verdant land and chill blue waters*
*Two ships would guide them, one at first*
*The galaxy would be its name*
*Accompanied by flying horse*
*Very different, much the same . . ."*

Her eyes widened, astonishment rippling through her. Gunnerson didn't see it since he was looking down at his book, and when he closed it she had already managed to regain her composure. "There's more," he said quietly. "It describes individuals in the grand scheme of things who match up rather closely to you, Admiral Adama, some others."

"It's . . . impressive," Laura Roslin admitted, but she was not about to simply swallow everything that was being handed her. "On the other hand, hindsight is always twenty-twenty."

"Are you suggesting that these verses were written after the fact?" He sounded amused rather than offended.

"I'm suggesting nothing, merely observing that it's possible."

He held up the book. "Our ancients," he said, "received these words from Woten himself, the father of the gods. They have been part of our people since our people *had* a people. It speaks of a twilight of humanity, in great detail, and everything that is to happen to humanity when that twilight falls. It speaks . . ." He paused, and then said, "Of how we survive. It's all here." He placed the copy of the book back into the small case, and closed it. "Understand . . . that it, and we, represent your salvation."

"How so?" she asked, intrigued but trying not to show it.

"In the book of Edda," he said, "it speaks of a bridge. A glittering bridge that serves as a connector between those who wander . . . which I take to be us . . . and Earth. The literal translation of the text is 'Rainbow Bridge.' The name the Edda accords it is 'Bifrost,' which is where the name of our vessel comes from. Our scholars believe, however, that the bridge is not necessarily a literal rainbow. It could instead be a representation of that which we understand now, but our ancestors could never have found words to frame: a wormhole, or bridge through space. Something that, should we be able to find it, would enable us to complete our journey in an instant. *Bifrost* is our way to our sanctuary . . . in more ways than one. And the Edda . . . tells us how to find it. It would bring us straight to it."

*Too good to be true. Most things that are too good to be true . . . aren't.* An old warning that her mother used to voice came back to her unbidden, but it was certainly good advice. "You're saying that your book of . . . prophecies, for lack of a better term . . . can get us to Earth?"

"That's exactly what I'm saying, yes," he assured her. "And you've no one to blame for not knowing these verses but your own church elders from centuries ago, who tried to burn all of our holy writings out of existence since they were offended by their very presence. If we'd been accepted when we should have been, then all our wise writings would be at your disposal. But we were not and, therefore, they are not. An unfortunate circumstance for you, certainly, but there's nothing to do about it now. However, give us the equality that we deserve, and you will be welcome to review all of our texts, past and future. To embrace us is to embrace the end of our voyage so that we need not wander anymore."

The offer was a fascinating one. Laura didn't quite know what to say. That in itself was irritating to her, for Laura Roslin had always prided herself on knowing just what to say in any given situation. And then, as she pondered how to respond to this startling offer, she saw something out of the corner of her eye.

It was something just out the window—"viewing port," she mentally corrected herself. Even after all this time, she was still tripping over substituting the appropriate space-going jargon for what had once been the mundane aspects of life. A window was a viewing port, a room was quarters, a wall was a bulkhead; it had taken some adjusting for her, since Laura had always regarded space vessels as merely a mode of transportation from one point to the other, never requiring more than a few hours travel time. Taking up residence in one, well, that was another matter. All of which still left her wondering just what the hell she had spotted out the window.

"Excuse me a moment," she said to Wolf, and got up from behind her desk. Wolf Gunnerson, as protocol dictated, automatically began to stand as well, but she gestured for him to remain in his seat. She went over to the window and looked out.

Sharon Valerii was looking back at her.

Laura staggered back, her mouth dropping open, her eyes wide. The sharp intake of breath naturally caught Gunnerson's attention, and Wolf stood once more, this time out of obvious concern. "Is there a problem, Madame President?"

She didn't hear him, or she heard him, but it didn't really register that someone was talking to her. It wasn't that she was seeing Sharon floating out in space. Rather, she saw her reflected in the window. The reflection exactly matched her movements, and she stared at it long and hard to make certain it wasn't some trick of the light. Slowly she reached up, and Sharon's reflection did the same. She placed her hand flat against Sharon's reflected hand, and Laura spoke softly, so softly that Wolf—sitting not more than five feet away—couldn't hear her.

"Get out of my head," she whispered, her mouth twisted into an uncharacteristic snarl. "Get . . . out . . . of my head."

Sharon's mouth moved as well, and that was when Laura realized that Sharon wasn't mouthing the same words as she was. Instead, Sharon spoke very slowly, the words she was forming easy to discern even if Laura hadn't already had them burned into her mind through what seemed endless repetition.

*Sagittarius is bleeding,* Sharon said to her.

Laura backed up and banged into a chair. She might well have stumbled over it and hit the floor, but Wolf was on his feet and righted her just before that happened. "Madame President, are you quite all right?"

*Don't you see it? How can you not see it?* She was pointing at Sharon, who was pointing back, and Laura's hand was quaking. "I . . . ?"

"Madame President?"

The door opened and Billy entered, a notepad under his arm. He was acting in his typical capacity, walking in after five minutes on a meeting that Laura didn't particularly want to attend to remind her of her next appointment. On those occasions when the meeting was going unexpectedly well, she could always tell him to rearrange the rest of her schedule to accommodate her. More likely, Billy's entrance would serve as an excuse for her to end the meeting so that she didn't have to sit and listen to someone make the same point repeatedly over the next fifteen minutes that they'd already made in the past five.

Before Billy could say anything, however, he saw the look in Laura's eyes. Wolf didn't, since her back was to him. There was a flash of concern on Billy's face, but he quickly covered it and said, as if everything was perfectly fine, "Madame President, you have that meeting with—"

"Yes, of course," she said quickly. She was anxious to get Wolf out of the office so that she could focus on what was going on in her head. "Mr. Gunnerson, this has been . . . illuminating."

Sensing the dismissal in her voice, Gunnerson frowned and said, "Madame President, I know I've given you a good deal to think about, and I did not think I would receive an immediate answer. But could you at least give me some indication of where your thoughts are on the matter we've discussed?"

"My thought," Laura said in measured tone, "is that I will most definitely consider it. You've convinced me that the Midguardians have something to offer. Now I have to determine whether there are those who are willing to take that offer. I will remind you that many on the Quorum are fervent in their beliefs, and might have some . . . difficulty . . . in accepting the notion of—"

"Elevating those who disagree with them?"

"Something like that," she admitted.

"I think it more than 'something.' I think it's exactly like that." Wolf Gunnerson didn't sound especially upset about it, more resigned than anything else. "But certainly tolerance can be embraced when mutual benefit is the prize. Although . . ."

"You'd think that tolerance could be embraced for its own sake."

Wolf smiled. The edges of his eyes crinkled when he did that; it gave him a distinctly avuncular look. "I had a feeling I would like you, Madame President. It's good to see that I was correct. I leave you to your considerations." He took a few steps back and walked out the door backwards, bowing to her in a very formal manner . . . or it might have been that it was simply the only way he could get out of the room.

The moment he was gone and Billy was certain they had privacy, he went straight to Laura with obvious concern. "What happened?" he asked.

Laura briefly considered telling him that nothing had occurred, and even scolding him for worrying after her all the time. But then she thought better of it and instead pointed at the window. "What do you see?" she asked.

He looked where she was indicating. "Space," he said slowly, as if he were being asked a trick question and didn't want to fall for whatever the catch was.

"Do you see any reflections?"

"Mine."

"Yes. What else?"

"And . . . yours." He sounded as if he wanted some

guidance as to what else he should say. "Is . . . that what you wanted to hear?"

A dozen emotions warred in her head. Slowly she sat in the nearest chair without even realizing that she was doing it. "Billy," she said as if speaking to him from very far away, "someone is in my head."

"You mean like a chip or something?"

"No. No, that would be simple." She took a deep breath and let it out. "I'm sorry, I can't burden you with this . . ." Her mind was racing. She should speak to Doctor Cottle. Or to Adama. Odd how her instinct was drawing her to confiding in him . . . the man who, nearly two months ago, would have seemed the least likely confidant in the world. But she recoiled at the idea. She had just recovered from breast cancer, a disease that had eaten away not only at her body, but at her very soul. Now she was finally regaining her footing as leader of the Colonies, and she was going to start telling the leader of the military that something was undermining her again? She was repulsed by the notion. William Adama was one of the strongest individuals she had ever known, and he had been at her bedside when she was at her most helpless. She knew he didn't think of her as a weak individual, but she simply couldn't embrace the notion of going to him with some new frailty. She had to be strong. As for Doctor Cottle, he'd start ordering up tests, restricting her from work, and sooner or later—probably sooner—the people would start questioning her ability to lead.

"Madame President, you have to talk to somebody, then," Billy insisted. "Whatever is happening—these dreams, these . . . illusions. Perhaps it's left over from the medications you were under, and it'll just work its way out of your system . . ."

"No, it's nothing like that . . . although it may well be, it's . . ." She took another breath, again let it out, trying to cleanse her mind and steady herself. "I don't want you to think I'm insane . . ."

"Never."

". . . but I think . . . Billy," she said, "I think it's the baby."

He stared at her uncomprehending. "You're pregnant?"

Laura appeared stunned for a moment, and then, despite the seriousness of the situation, she laughed aloud. "No. Not that baby . . . I mean, no. I'm not pregnant. Unless a god came down and visited me in my sleep . . ."

"Honestly, Madame President, I wouldn't put it past them."

"Yes, well . . . a valid point. But that's not what I was referring to."

"Then I don't understand what . . ."

"I think . . ." She said it all in a rush, as if the biggest challenge was just to say it and get it out there rather than dwell on it. "I think the Cylon's child has done something to me."

He stared at her. "What?"

"The child. The fetus . . . Sharon Valerii's."

She told him then of the dream she'd had, of being born, of being carried away by a Cylon soldier. The recurring imagery of blood, and the warning about Sagittaron. "I . . . suppose it's possible," he said at last.

Laura wasn't entirely sure how to respond. She was surprised, to say the least. The whole thing had seemed so far-fetched to her that she was almost thinking that simple insanity might be the most reasonable answer.

"You do?" she said with the air of a drowning woman who had had a life preserver tossed to her when she had been bracing for an anchor.

"Yes, of course," he said with increased conviction, as if just thinking about it for a moment helped clarify matters for him. "We're talking about Cylons. We're talking about unknown aspects of biology. Anything is possible." Then he said firmly, "You have to talk to—"

"No."

"Madame President . . . !" he said, clearly frustrated. "You have to—"

"I'm the president, Billy. In case you haven't forgotten, you don't get to tell me what I have to do."

As quickly as he was chastened, she regretted having said it. She patted him on the shoulder and said, "Sorry. I'm sorry about that. You're just trying to help."

"And I can't if you won't let me. The Cylon is trying to . . . to do something to you."

"That's the thing: I don't know that for sure."

"But you just said—!"

"I said I have suspicions," Laura reminded him. "Nothing more than that. Here's the thing, Billy . . . here's what I'm not sure of. That I can't be sure of. What if . . ." She knew this would sound even stranger. "What if she doesn't know?"

"She? You mean Valerii?"

"Yes. Exactly. What if this is happening without her knowledge? What if the unborn Cylon is trying to tell me something?"

It was obvious to Laura that she was starting to reach the outer limit of what Billy would and would not accept. "The *unborn Cylon* is trying to send you a message?"

"You sound skeptical."

"Can you blame me?"

With a small smile, she walked back around to the other side of her desk. "You yourself said we were dealing with Cylons, and anything was possible."

"I know, but . . ."

"If I go to Cottle," she said, as much to give herself the reasons as to convey them to Billy, "he may well come up with some treatment, some form of drugs, that will sever this . . . this connection, if that's what it is. If I tell Adama, I know him, Billy. He'll get right into Valerii's face about it, and there's no telling what might happen then. Hell, she might try to self-abort, and I'm not ready to let that happen."

"Which is somewhat ironic, considering you were ready to abort her child for her."

"Yes, well . . . life is full of little ironies, isn't it," she said ruefully.

Pressing the point, Billy said, "But you still haven't told me why? Even if it were possible, why would it be trying to communicate with you?"

"Because . . . maybe it's afraid."

Billy stood there for a moment, trying to understand the implications of what she was suggesting. "Are you . . . are you saying . . . that the unborn Cylon . . . is . . . what? Asking you for asylum?"

"I was the one who was ready to have it aborted. Perhaps . . . on some level . . . it knows that. And perhaps on some level . . . it's no happier about its heritage than we are, and it's looking to us . . . to me . . . to keep it safe from the Cylons and Cylon influence."

He processed that and then said, "Or . . . maybe it's acting the way a Cylon is supposed to act . . . and is just trying to drive you insane."

"If that's the case," she said with a heavy sigh, "then it may well be succeeding beyond its wildest hopes."

# CHAPTER 12

Gaius Baltar sat on the balcony of his former home and stared out at the setting sun. He was seated in his favorite chair with his feet propped up, and he was wearing a short white bathrobe that came down to mid-thigh. This was not the first time that he was making a visit back to the life that he'd left behind. He was never quite sure how he got there, but had learned to stop worrying about it and simply accept it for what it was: a blessing that he, and no one else in the fleet, ever had. For this alone, he was content.

There were two times of day that he had always loved: dawn and sunset. He had never wondered why that was before he had lost his home . . . his planet . . . his life as he knew it. Since then, he'd had plenty of time to ponder it, and had come to the conclusion that those were the times of day that were most in line with his personal philosophy. Others—specifically those who were far less brilliant than he, which was pretty much everyone else—saw the world in terms of absolutes. Black and white, good and bad . . . day and night. Baltar knew that things were far more complicated than that. There were no truths in absolutes. The truth lay in what was in between. The not-quite-day, not-quite-night. It was only when the two aspects of day and night merged that it was possible to discern all sides of the equation.

"So are you satisfied, Gaius?"

He knew whose voice it was, of course. There was only ever the two of them there—Baltar and the mysterious woman who had delighted in seducing and confounding him before Caprica had been bombed into oblivion by the Cylons.

She had never had a name. Even when they were together, she had never told him. It was one of the oddest aspects of their relationship: "You can have all of me," she had whispered the first time they were together, "except my name." She had been true to her word. She had never held back in the heady days of their extremely active sex life . . . but not once, not one time, had she told him her name. "A girl has to have *some* mystery about her," she had told him blithely one day when they were lying naked in bed together. It was typical male behavior, she said, that no matter how much a woman gave a man, he wanted more. "I walk down the street and I see men devouring me with their eyes," she said to Baltar one time when he had become particularly insistent. "They would kill to have just the slightest taste of what I provide you as a full banquet. And you know what?" She had leaned closer in to him, and he had trembled as her tongue slid along the nape of his neck. "They wonder what it would be like to have my legs wrapped around them. To fondle my breasts, to cup my ass in their sweaty hands. They wonder all kinds of things, and the one thing they never . . . ever . . . wonder . . . is what my name is. I leave them wondering. Names have power, Gaius, and I choose to keep my name to myself so that you do not have that power over me."

He had accepted that, for he had really had no choice. He simply wasn't strong enough of character to take a stand on something which—in the final analysis—meant a good deal to her and not much of anything to him.

He half turned in his seat and saw her standing on the stairway that led up to the bedroom, the place where dreams came true. She was wearing a diaphonous red gown, which was fluttering in response to a breeze that didn't seem to exist beyond the immediate area where she was standing. She was leaning against the wall in a posture that was simultaneously alluring and casual. "I said you must be satisfied with yourself, Gaius."

"Oh," he said in an off-hand manner. "Are you talking to me now?"

"Of course." She strolled across the room, one foot placed precisely before the next. She walked like a cat, and there was much of a feline manner about her. "I may get annoyed with you, even put out . . . but I never get so upset with you that, sooner or later, I won't forgive you."

"And what have I done, I wonder," he asked, "that requires forgiveness? Because I didn't do what you wanted me to do? I didn't incriminate an innocent young boy?"

"How do you know that's what he is?" She stood next to him for a moment, and then draped one long leg over him and sat in his lap, facing him. It was all he could do to contain a small whimper. "We both know your Cylon detection test is a sham. He might indeed be one of us."

"Yes, so you said before. Considering you've never been especially forthcoming on the identities of your agents, I'd have to think that the fact you seem determined to hang the boy out to dry reduces the odds of his being a Cylon to practically nonexistent."

"Unless, of course, I know that you'll think that, and am counting on it. Remember, Gaius, there's not a thought that goes through your head that I'm not privy to."

"You're pushing awfully hard on this . . ."

She applied downward pressure with her pelvis. "Oh?"

"On this subject!" Baltar amended quickly, and he ignored the stifled laugh from Six. "I still don't understand your obsession with—"

Abruptly she stood and stepped back away from him. She moved in the way a dancer moved, and it made him feel as if this was all some sort of strange, deluded tango between the two of them. "Because it's in my interest to protect you."

"You mean it's in your interest to control me." He rose from the chair and faced her, feeling powerful, feeling defiant. "What's the matter? Afraid that I'll have power over you now that I know your name . . . Gina?" He saw her face twist in annoyance. "Yes, you can't stand that, can you. I know your name, and that gives me power over you. Didn't you say yourself that's how it works?"

"You know *a* name," she retorted. "A name beaten out of a poor version of me. Isn't it possible that she would have lied about it?"

"It's entirely possible," Baltar admitted, but then added with a sense of smirking confidence, "because—after all—your kind is quite accomplished at lying, aren't you."

She allowed the remark to pass and then, sounding all business, she said, "You need to throw up distractions, Gaius. I think you're tragically oblivious to the amount of danger that you're in."

"And what could possibly give you that impression? Are you going to tell me again that Adama suspects? Let him. Let him suspect all he wants. He can't prove a damned thing and you know it."

"Roslin is suspicious of you as well. She believes you to be a Cylon sympathizer at best . . . a Cylon yourself at worst."

"That's ridiculous," Baltar told her, dismissing the notion out of hand.

"Is it." She circled the room, shaking her head as if he were the most pitiable individual she could ever have hoped to meet. "And how do you know it's ridiculous?"

"Because I just saved the woman's life, for gods' sake! She'd be dead of breast cancer if it weren't for me!"

"That's very true. And I'm sure she's abundantly grateful for your having saved her, isn't she. Think back, Gaius," she said with sudden impatience. "Open your eyes and think back. Did she ever, at any point, say so much as thank you?"

He didn't have to answer her, because she knew the answer as well as he: Laura Roslin had never thanked him. In fact, she had done quite the opposite. He had been there shortly after the treatment had been administered and her cancer-free status had been verified. He'd shown up in her hospital room, and he had been expecting . . . something. Some sort of thanks, some measure of gratitude. But he had gotten nothing. Oh, she had received him in her room cordially enough, and she had made small talk about impending business and how long it would take her to return to her duties. She had asked him about the expectations of reasonable recovery time.

But she had not thanked him, or given the slightest indication that she was at all appreciative of what he had done for her. Quite the opposite, in fact. She had watched him with great suspicion, jumped on any comments that could remotely be misconstrued. It seemed as if she had been looking for things to criticize, to find . . . wrong . . . with him.

Why? Why would she come out of her coma, her near-death experience, with new and increased suspicions regarding Baltar? Was there something that he had said or done that had made her think something was wrong with him?

"You still don't get it, do you?" said Six.

"Not readily, no," he admitted. "But I very much suspect you're going to tell me."

"For someone who purports to be a genius, you're not always very bright, Gaius. It comes down to something as simple as this: When someone is on the verge of death, all the detritus is stripped away from their mind.

Take it from someone who has died several times in her existence. Nothing clears the mind like impending demise, and things that may have been obscured by time and distance suddenly snap into very clear relief."

"What, are you saying that because she was going to die, she's now come to some sort of realization about me that she was blinded to before?"

"I'm saying that her behavior is not consistent with someone who damned well should have been grateful considering she would have died without your intervention."

He was about to reply to that, to again issue an automatic denial and express his complete confidence that Laura Roslin had no reason, none, to suspect him. But he didn't say that because he couldn't get the words to come out of his mouth. Finally he said, "Not everyone is skilled at giving thanks to people." He winced even as he said it, because it wasn't remotely convincing even to his own ear. That being the case, it certainly wasn't anything that Number Six was going to buy.

It was, in fact, so unconvincing that she didn't even deign to address it. Instead she said, "Something's in the air, Gaius. You can feel it. You can smell it. They think they can fool you and even hide it from you . . . but they can't. They're investigating Cylon infiltration in new and aggressive ways, and you've been targeted for suspicion. They're going to do something about it. They're going to try and find evidence."

"How do you know?"

"Because I know humans. In some ways, I know them better than you."

"I see." As far as Baltar was concerned, the entire discussion was becoming ludicrous. "All right, Gina . . . or Six . . . or whatever. Impress me with your knowledge of my people. Tell me what they're going to do to try and find evidence."

"Obviously," said Six, "they'll undertake some manner of surveillance."

"Surveillance? You mean spy on us?" Baltar snorted derisively at that. "Adama would never approve something like that. I know the man . . ."

"As well as you knew me? As well as you knew what I was capable of?" She lowered her voice to a whisper, as if somehow it was possible to spy on the deepest arenas of this thoughts. "You want to believe you're so much smarter than the rest of them, Gaius. You want to believe that you're above reproach. But we both know you live your life with one eye cocked over your shoulder to make sure that no one is watching you. You have a dark, terrible cloud hanging over you, and you're constantly aware of it. You are the betrayer of humanity, Gaius. How long do you think you're going to be able to live with that?"

"As long as it takes," he growled.

"If they want to believe they have an infiltrator, let them. Let them have the boy. At the very least, it will buy you time. Time you desperately need."

"No," he said firmly, "I won't . . ."

"Do this for me. You owe me this much."

Baltar laughed grimly at that. "I owe you? As if I haven't done enough for you already."

"Then do it for yourself. Check your lab for listening or viewing devices. Sweep your lab and come up with one. I'm sure I'm right. If I'm wrong—if I have done a disservice to the noble humans who run the *Galactica*—then I shall never make mention of it again."

"As if I'm supposed to believe that."

She hesitated, and then said with great solemnity, "If you do as I ask . . . I'll tell you my real name. Not the fake one that Gina told her captors. My real name."

"Is that so?" He sounded amused but also intrigued.

She nodded. "That's so. Just do as I ask."

Baltar, having returned to his chair, leaned back on it, tilting the front legs up a bit. "I will . . . consider it. I'm telling you, though, it's a waste of time."

He waited for her to respond. When she didn't, he turned around and saw that she was gone. That was extremely strange. It was one thing for her to disappear into nowhere when she was intruding into the real world. At such times, she delighted in spurring Baltar on into conversations that always made him appear foolish. But she had no reason to make herself scarce while inhabiting his waking dreams.

This anomaly in her behavior was the first thing in their entire encounter that actually made him start to wonder.

It hadn't been all that difficult for Baltar to obtain the equipment that he required to accomplish the task.

The result was that he was crouched in his lab, underneath his table, staring in wonderment at a small round device that he never, ever would have spotted on his own, even if he'd been looking straight at it. He needed the additional help of the detector, a small device with a wand and a helpful flashing light that blinked with greater frequency when pointed directly at what he was seeking.

"Gods," he said, except he didn't speak it aloud. Instead he mouthed it. His mind was racing over the past several days. He had no idea how long it had been there, and he racked his memory, trying to determine if he had had one of his doubtless incriminating conversations with Six while in the lab. He was reasonably sure that he had not. He had to think that if he had said anything that sounded truly treasonous, Adama wouldn't have simply stood there and traded barbs with him that other day. He'd have had him arrested and Baltar would be in a cell by this point. It was reverse logic, he knew, but it seemed sound to him. Perhaps there had been enough in Baltar's manner that had prompted Adama to start bugging him since that day, but the scientist had presented nothing sufficiently concrete for the authorities to act upon beyond that. Which meant he was safe.

*Frakking bizarre definition of "safe,"* he thought grimly.

But once he got over his initial panic, he came to a realization: As with all things, knowledge was power. His impulse had been to reach for the bug, to crush it beneath his heel as he would the device's namesake. But he paused with his hand in mid-reach and then slowly lowered it. If he destroyed the bug, they would know that he knew. The fact that he was so nervous about being eavesdropped upon would in itself be regarded as something suspicious. Now, however, he had the upper hand. They didn't know that he knew they were eavesdropping.

Which meant that they would tend to take at face value whatever they heard.

Which meant that he could throw them off the track if he said the right things.

Which meant that if they were looking for Cylon infiltraters, all he had to do to throw them off the track was give them someone else. To name names.

*Lee Adama. Give them Lee Adama. Or . . . Roslin! Even better! Two birds with one stone . . .*

The more he considered such things, though, the more he realized that he had to rein in his impulses. If he tried to point them in a direction that seemed too farfetched, they might reject it out of hand due to their damnable loyalties and instead focus even more attention on him.

Which meant that the best thing to do was point the finger of suspicion at someone whom they already had uncertainties about.

Which brought him right back to where Six had been days ago.

He started to stand and almost banged his head on the table. Slowly he eased he way out from under and sat in a chair, forcing himself to come to a conclusion that he despised . . . but that was necessary. He had his own survival to think about.

He became aware of her gaze upon him before he looked in her direction. She said nothing, but instead put a single finger to her lips in a *shhh* motion. Then she slowly, and a bit overdramatically, pointed at something. He turned his gaze to where she indicated and his gaze fell upon that which he already knew she was indicating.

It was Boxey's blood sample.

He felt a stinging in his eyes, tears welling up slightly, and just as quickly he brought an arm across his eyes and wiped them away. He hated his weakness. He despised Six for the weakness that she brought out in him.

At the same time, he picked up his portable recorder and spoke into it with a voice that was flat, even, and impressively clinical:

"Laboratory note, follow-up to test results of subject Boxman. Standard recheck of Cylon/Human veracity test indicates possible invalid results due to possible corruption of test sample because of unforeseen circumstances . . . specifically the sterile conditions of pertinent testing equipment may have been . . ." He sought the right word. ". . . breached. Reason for this suspected breach remains unknown at this time. Resolution: I will resterilize all relevant lab equipment and retest. Enough of the original sample of subject Boxman's blood remains that subject will not need to be reacquired. If results come back identical to the first, then will chalk it up to simple lab error rather than something . . . suspicious . . . and there will be no need to alert the authorities of this revised finding since it would be fundamentally unchanged. If results are different, then Admiral Adama must immediately be informed so that . . ." He gulped deeply and watched as Six nodded in slow approval. She licked her lips enticingly. ". . . So that proper defensive action can be taken.

Anastasia Dualla had no idea what to make of Billy Keikeya.

It wasn't the first time she'd felt befuddled by her on-again/off-again relationship with the presidential aide. There was no doubt that they were friends. She enjoyed spending time with him. They'd even had some serious make-out sessions. But she wasn't entirely certain where the relationship was going, or even if it was going anywhere at all.

So she had invited Billy over to share a nice home-made dinner, which was an impressive achievement considering that she couldn't cook worth a damn. That little fact had never bothered her before. She had jokingly stated on more than one occasion that she'd joined up with the military specifically so that she never had to worry about making meals for herself ever again. She would just eat her meals in whatever mess hall was on hand and that would be that.

But this night she was getting together with Billy, and she wanted it to be special. The problem was that she had no cooking facilities in her quarters. So she'd gone to the mess hall and convinced the cooks there to let her try her hand at preparing a nice dinner that she could then take out and back to her quarters. There, she told herself, she would be able to boast to Billy that she had made it with her own two hands.

Unfortunately, her cooking acumen did not magically improve as she endeavored to prepare a couple of nice steaks for the two of them. Instead she had come damned close to burning both pieces of meat and only some timely intervention by the chefs on hand had averted disaster. They managed to salvage her efforts and even provide a nice presentation of the meal, which Dualla proudly brought back to her quarters and endeavored to keep warm as Billy ran late.

And later.

And later.

Finally, a good hour and a quarter after Billy was supposed to have arrived, there was a knock at Dualla's door. The food might no longer have been warm, but Dualla was certainly seething. "Come in," she said with a tone that indicated all hope should be abandoned by those who entered.

Billy hesitated a moment and considered running in the other direction, because Dualla's voice made it clear that he was in as much trouble as he already suspected he was. But, deciding to be a man about it, he sucked it up and entered with a smile plastered on his face. He proudly held up an honest-to-gods small plant, with beautiful blue cup-shaped flowers blossoming at the top. He said, "Sorry I'm late. Things got a little . . . crazy . . ."

"For this late," Dualla said icily, "I'd expect you to be sporting at least three visible wounds." In spite of herself, she focused on the bouquet he was extending toward her. "You hang up my beautiful dinner which, by the way, I worked my ass off to prepare for you, and you think you can bribe your way back into my good graces with some flowers?"

"That was pretty much my feeble hope, yeah," he admitted.

She grunted at that and then, in spite of herself, extended a hand. He crossed the room and handed her the flowers. She brought them up to her face and inhaled deeply, and then—against all of her better impulses—moaned in pleasure. "My gods," she intoned in a voice that bordered on the orgasmic, "where did you get these? How the frak is it possible?"

"Connections," he said.

She opened her eyes narrowly and eyed him with suspicion. "You didn't get these from the black market, did you?"

"What a ridiculous question," he said quickly. "You know how the president feels about that. I can't believe you'd even ask me."

"A ridiculous question . . . and yet I can't help but notice that you've yet to answer it."

"That's because I'm astounded that you would even begin to insinuate that—"

"All right," Dualla said. She hadn't forgotten how annoyed she was with him, and yet she couldn't help but laugh. "All right, forget it. Forget I asked. Forget I said anything about it at all. Anything I should know about the care and feeding of this?"

"Well," he said, "you'll probably need to acquire a lamp that simulates sunlight. Otherwise I'm not sure it'll keep blooming."

"I see. And where do you suggest I get such a device?"

Billy paused a moment and made a great show of thinking, even though he had undoubtedly thought about it before. "I know a guy who knows a guy who knows a girl," he said after much consideration. "Not that it's anyone connected with the black market, of course, because I would never—"

She put up her hands in surrender. "Let's have dinner, you big idiot."

The steak was naturally stone cold, and she thought it was tough as boot leather. But he made a great show of loving every bite, and was so enthused about the quality of the meal that she was having trouble staying mad at him. By the time dinner was over, as much as she hated to admit it, she had more or less allowed her once-towering irritation to vanish into the lost recesses of her memory.

"So how's the investigation going?"

"Investigation?"

"You know," he prompted. "Into trying to figure out how the Cylons knew where we were going to be making our Jump."

"Oh." She shook her head wearily, then stood and proceeded to clear away the dinner dishes. "Honestly, I don't know. From what I hear, Tigh is conducting it. He grilled me up one side and down the other, and since then he's moved on. I couldn't tell you who's on the hot seat now. What a frakking prick he is."

"I honestly don't understand why Adama keeps him on as executive officer," Billy admitted. "I wonder about it from time to time . . ."

"Yeah, well, I wonder about it a lot more than that,"

said Dualla. "The man is a boozer and a frak-up, and everyone in CIC knows it. Hell, everyone on the ship knows it."

"Does he know they know it?"

"Who knows?" She cleaned off the dishes in the sink, wiping them with a towel, and said, "And how are things with Roslin?"

"Fine."

Something in the way he said it caught her attention. She continued wiping the plate but she wasn't especially paying attention to it. "What's wrong?"

"Wrong? Nothing."

"Billy," she put down the plate. "What's going on?"

"Going on?"

"Yes."

"What makes you think," he asked, "that something's going on?"

"Because I know you," said Dualla, moving across the room. She turned the chair around and sat, straddling it. "Whenever you're lying about something or trying to hide something from me, you start repeating the ends of my sentences."

"Repeating the—?" He caught himself and scowled with irritation. "That's absurd," he said, but as protests went, it sounded admittedly lame.

"It's not absurd. Is something wrong with the president?"

"Dualla," he said patiently, "even if there was something wrong—which I'm not saying there is, but even if there were—you know I couldn't tell you."

"I don't know that at all, Billy," she replied, clear irritation in her voice. "I thought we had at least some degree of trust built up, you and me."

"We do."

"Well, then—?"

"But President Roslin trusts me, too. Are you asking me to make a choice between those two levels of trust?"

"Yeah. Yeah, that's exactly what I'm . . ." Her voice

trailed off and she looked down. "No," she sighed, clearly annoyed with herself that she had said anything. "No, of course not. Especially when, y'know . . . you've obviously made the choice. Your loyalty to the president is . . . it's admirable."

"Thank you. But . . ."

She looked up. "But what . . . ?"

"But it's always going to put us on opposite sides, isn't it. Because your loyalty to Adama is always going to be more important than to me, and my loyalty to Roslin is going to be more important than you. And if we're going to have any sort of a relationship, the first thing that has to happen is that each of us is more important to each other than anything. So basically we're screwed."

Her jaw twitched, because there was so much she wanted to say in response to that. But in the end, all she could think of to say in reply was, "Seems to me like you've got it pretty worked out."

"No, I don't," he insisted, shaking his head. "I don't have anything worked out at all. Because there's still so much that I want to say, and—"

"How about this, then." Dualla was on her feet, putting up a hand to silence him. "How about you don't say it. How about we just . . . we just let this one lie here for a while."

"Dee, I still want to—"

"Want to what, Billy?" she said, trying and failing to keep the exasperation out of her voice. "Want to talk some more about how hopeless everything is, and how we should just give up?"

"I didn't say any of that!"

"Well . . . I did. Because you know what, Billy? If I can't even ask a casual question about how the president of the Colonies is without getting a whole lecture on divided loyalties, then I don't really see the point of any of this."

"Oh, come on, Dee . . ."

"I gotta go."

"What?" He was dumbfounded by her reaction. "Dee, we can still—"

"I have to go to a meeting."

"Of what?"

"Of . . . the People Under Suspicion by Tigh support group. You can let yourself out, okay?" She moved quickly toward the door and was out before Billy could say anything more.

She headed off down the hall, her mind swirling with frustration and anger that was directed both at Billy and herself. She felt that she had handled the whole thing very badly. The truth was that he hadn't said anything that hadn't already occurred to her as well. She had just wanted to believe that she was wrong, and despised the notion that matters might be as hopeless as he was indicating. What angered her in particular was that he'd been so matter-of-fact about it. At the very least, he should sound as if the entire prospect was tearing him up inside. Instead he was giving a simple, clinical analysis of their situation in the same manner that he might have presented a report on the economy to the president.

Was she being unreasonable? Maybe. But at that moment she didn't particularly care.

And what was worse, she wasn't entirely sure she cared about Billy all that much.

She hadn't wanted to admit it to herself, but although Billy had been a pleasant enough dalliance . . . and although she'd always think he was one of the sweetest guys in the world . . . lately her thoughts and attentions had been shifting elsewhere. There had been something—she wasn't sure what, but something—connecting lately between her and Lee Adama. She had no idea where it might lead. But it was sufficient to make her think there was something there worth exploring. She just couldn't do it, of course, while she was involved with Billy.

Or could she?

After all, Billy didn't know. They hadn't promised fealty to each other. There might have been a vague sort of "understanding," but nothing had been stated implicitly. Perhaps what she really needed to do was compare and contrast. See for herself how it felt being with each of them, and which brought her more . . . satisfaction.

It might not have been fair to either of them, but it was all she could think of. Because she didn't want to break Billy's heart for no reason, but she didn't want to slam the door on exploring her feelings about Lee.

Billy, meanwhile, was dwelling on the fact that he might well have had dates in the past that ended abruptly, but it was hard to recall any of them going down in flames quite this badly. He tried to imagine just how it might have gone better, what he could possibly have said to her that would have prevented their evening from dissolving into a pained discussion of loyalties and politics.

"Well, Dee," he said with a faux jovial attitude, "it's funny you should ask about President Roslin. See, she's been having such horrific dreams for a while now that she can't sleep through the night anymore. She's starting to hallucinate; she's acting erratically. She's the strongest woman I've ever known, and she's beginning to come unravelled. And . . . here's the most interesting part . . . she thinks that the reason that she's having all these dreams is because Sharon Valerii's unborn child is influencing her somehow. Maybe trying to torment her. Maybe trying to warn her. Hard to say. So . . . how's your day been?" He sat back, closed his eyes and moaned softly. "Yeah. Yeah, that would go over really well. Good way to go with that, Billy. That would have enamored her of you and kept confidence boosted in Roslin while we're at it." He was beginning to think he was going to have to resign himself to the idea that not only was his relationship with Dualla going nowhere, but he might well never have a relationship with a woman ever again.

And as he pondered the bleak landscape that represented his dating life, he was completely unaware that he had just managed to accomplish the one thing that he never would have done consciously. He had just betrayed Laura Roslin.

# CHAPTER 13

In his quarters at the end of a very long day, William Adama was coming to the realization that his day was about to get even longer.

He listened for the second time to the recording that Tigh had brought him and was still having trouble believing what he was hearing. He'd been listening via an ear piece, for Tigh—ever cautious—felt that it was best not to play back the recordings in the very, very off chance that someone might wander past and hear their own conversation coming from Adama's quarters. Now Adama removed the ear piece from his ear and looked up at Tigh in clear astonishment . . . which for Adama, who had a reputation for a stoic expression that bordered on the inscrutable, amounted to a flicker of surprise in his gaze. "Are you sure he didn't know we were listening in?"

"Obviously, I have no way of knowing for certain," Tigh replied. "But it certainly sounds like Keikeya is talking to himself, and that he has his guard down. That's he's not saying it for our ears alone."

Adama leaned back in his chair and stroked his chin thoughtfully. "Why wouldn't Roslin say anything to me about it, if she's having these sorts of concerns?"

"Who can ever understand women?" Tigh shrugged. "They have their own way of thinking. Maybe she was concerned how you'd react to it. Maybe she—"

"Was concerned I'd try to stage a coup?" Adama asked humorlessly.

Tigh's mouth twitched as he replied, "Well . . . it's not like it would be unprecedented."

"I know, Saul. I was there . . . for some of it, at least." He shook his head. "My chickens finally coming home to roost. She's afraid to come across as unstable because she's concerned I'll take steps to ensure continued, strong leadership. She doesn't trust me."

"Should she?"

Adama looked up at Tigh, and although the question irritated him, he knew that it was also a perfectly valid one. Worse, he had no answer. He wanted to feel as if she could . . . that she should . . . trust him. But based upon what had happened before, there really wasn't a reason for her *to* trust him.

He knew there was no real reason he should feel hurt about this. Yes, granted, he and Roslin had been through a lot since those early days of mistrust and accusations. He would never say it aloud, but in some perverse way, Sharon Valerii's murderous assault on him had been one of the best things that had ever happened to him. Before the incident, he had tried to transform himself into what he thought the last remnants of humanity required: a hard-edged, hard-bitten, brutal-as-necessary commander who was perfectly willing to steamroll over anyone or anything that got in the way of his very simple goal: survival. He had even bald-facedly lied to his own people, telling them that he had known the "secret location" of Earth. It was a preposterous lie, one that never would have survived even the most minimal scrutiny. But that scrutiny was never applied to him, for two reasons. First, because they all trusted him implicitly. And second, they wanted—needed—to believe in something. They had to believe that the bleak existence they had had thrust upon them was not all that was left to them. There had to be something more, and Adama had provided it for them. He'd given them hope when he himself felt none . . . and that knowledge had created a great divide between Adama and his people. He would watch them soldiering on as if from a great height looking down. It made him feel more detached than ever before.

No wonder the gods had left them to their fates. No wonder they simply stood by and let humanity be nearly annihilated by the Cylons. Legend had it that the gods sat in residence upon a mountain and looked down upon humanity. If that was the case, then they had spent ages beyond imagining becoming more and more distant, to the point where they probably didn't give a damn what happened to human beings anymore. Adama would never have been able to undersand that attitude . . . until he had created a barrier between himself and the rest of humanity that they didn't even know was there.

All that had changed after the humanizing experience of being gunned down. It had rattled his confidence about making correct decisions down to its very core. After all, he'd been in the midst of congratulating Boomer on a job well done. When she had pointed her gun at him, he had been staring straight at it but his mind was unable to process what was happening. His instinct was that there was some sort of threat directly behind him and she was acting to protect him. When the first of the bullets had thudded into his chest, he had been astonished. Before he'd lapsed into unconsciousness, it never occurred to him that she was a Cylon. All he could think was, *She missed whoever she was shooting at behind me. She's going to be so embarrassed.*

He had learned the truth of it later, of course. And the experience of being at death's door had humbled him, even humiliated him. There's nothing that makes one stop and take stock of oneself more than being face to face with one's own mortality. His decisions, and the fallout from them, had shattered the fleet. He had put it back together . . . and discovered in the process, thanks to the mule-headed determination of Laura Roslin, that the great lie wasn't that at all. There really was an Earth, and there really was a way to get there. President Roslin had removed a huge burden from him, erasing the divide in one stroke because the lie was the truth.

He owed her a debt so gargantuan that he didn't think he could ever adequately explain it to her. So he hadn't even tried. He had, however, done everything he could to support her. To be a friend and confidant to her.

And this was the result. She still didn't trust him, even though he'd been as supportive of her as he possibly could be, particularly since he'd learned of her cancer . . .

"Maybe she thought I was pitying her," Adama said softly.

Tigh looked at him in confusion, not quite understanding what it was that Adama was talking about. "Pitying her?"

"Perhaps she thought that I was simply 'pretending' to be her friend. After all, I knew she wasn't going to be around much longer. So why spend a lot of time arguing with her when time would solve my problem."

"But that's not what you were thinking," said Tigh. "Not at all. I know that."

"Maybe she doesn't."

"Well, you can tell her . . ."

"Tell her what?" Adama said bleakly. "Tell her that I know of her situation because we eavesdropped on her aide? How's that going to inspire trust, exactly?"

"Because *we* didn't do it," Tigh said.

Adama didn't follow what Tigh was saying at first, but then he saw the look in Tigh's eyes and suddenly it was clear to him. "No," he said firmly.

"I did it, unilaterally," Tigh said as if Adama hadn't spoken. "Then, when I heard the results of this, I came to you and told you. You chewed my ass—"

"Saul—"

"—and then decided that, as President Roslin's friend, you couldn't simply ignore this evidence that had been brought to your attention. So you're coming to her now, out of conscience."

"Saul, you asked my permission and I gave it."

"And no one needs to know about that except you and me," Tigh said. "What's the worst that could happen? She'll despise me? She already despises me."

"How do you know that?"

"Because she's met me. I'm a prick. Ask her. Ask Dualla. Ask anyone."

Adama snorted in amusement at that. Saul Tigh might have had weaknesses—but self-delusion certainly wasn't one of them.

And Tigh, all seriousness, said, "Bill . . . you're the one who needs to have a solid working relationship with the president. Not me. Tell her that I acted on my own initiative. She'll believe it."

"You really feel the way for me to gain her trust," Adama said in a slow, measured tone, "is to lie to her?"

"Of course," said Tigh matter-of-factly. "Have you got a better suggestion?"

He sat and waited, his hands folded on his lap, for Adama to reply.

"What else have you got?"

"Pardon?"

"What else," said Adama, "have you picked up so far in the eavesdropping?"

"Oh. Well . . . Doctor Baltar was making some sort of noise about having to recheck that boy's bloodwork."

"You mean Boxey? There's some doubt now that his original results were correct?"

Tigh shrugged. "That's the impression I was getting."

"Wonderful. Well, I suppose we'll hear about that one sooner rather than later. Find out where Boxey is, just so we have a clear idea. That way if we need to take him, we can do so with minimal effort."

"We never should have let him leave," Tigh said in annoyance. "Counting on the discretion of a teenager . . ."

"The alternative was to make him a permanent 'guest' in one of our luxurious cells," Adama pointed out. "At which point, child services was going to come sniffing around, and presto, the media announces we're arresting children for no apparent reason. Let's face it, Saul . . . sooner or later, word is going to get out about Sharon. We can delay it, but not indefinitely. And throwing anyone in the brig who knows about her and isn't military issue is just going to expedite it."

"How can you keep calling it 'Sharon'?" Tigh asked. "There is no 'Sharon.' There never was. There was just a thing pretending to be human."

Adama said nothing at first, and then finally: "Anything else?"

Shifting uncomfortably in his chair, Tigh said, "Well . . . there's one thing that I find rather disturbing personally."

"And that would be—?"

"Frankly," he said in a severe tone, "several of our junior officers spend entirely too much downtime engaged in self-frakking. Certainly there has to be something more constructive they can be doing."

Adama's face could have been carved from slate. "Get. Out."

"Yes sir," Tigh said quickly and exited Adama's quarters.

* * *

Laura slowly rose from behind her desk, her eyes widening in astonishment, and Adama could have sworn that her face paled slightly. "Listening devices?"

He nodded. "I was shocked," he deadpanned. "Not surprised. But shocked."

Her gaze never shifted from Adama's. "And Tigh just . . . just did this of his own accord? Without consulting you at all?"

Adama took a deep breath and let it out slowly, ready to hang Tigh out on the far end of the branch and then watch as Laura took a saw to it. He found, to his fascination and disappointment, that he was unable to do so. Interesting, considering how effortlessly he'd lied to far more people than one woman and done so with facility. But, as he knew all too well, that was the pre-shooting Adama. He didn't have the stomach for it anymore.

"No," sighed Adama, and he lowered his gaze. "I gave you the impression that Tigh was acting alone, but he did not. He came to me and I approved it."

She looked stunned at the admission. "Admiral," she gasped. "How . . . how could you—?"

"Because we still don't know how the Cylons acquired our Jump coordinates, and our security is at stake," said Adama, sounding far more reasonable than he thought he was under the circumstances. "We have to take a different approach to resolving that problem, and if it means that some people's rights are lost in the process, then I for one have no trouble living with that."

"And how about if *they* have trouble with it?" Laura demanded.

"Then I'll live with that. Because the bottom line is that they want me to make the hard decisions involved in protecting them. Whether they admit it to themselves or not, they want me for that. They may grumble and grouse and cry foul, but at the end of the day, they're relieved that people like Saul Tigh and myself are taking point in doing what needs to be done."

"Just tell me if it was Tigh's idea or yours."

"What difference does that make?"

"To me? It makes a great deal of difference."

He briefly considered stonewalling her on the matter, but rejected it. Once upon a time, he could have done that without hesitation. Now, it wasn't really an option. "He suggested it; I ordered him to implement it. So if you're going to blame someone—"

"I'm not interested in issuing blame, I . . ." She hesitated, and then in a rare display of anger, she slapped her palms on the desk in frustration. "Dammit, Bill! Do you have any idea what a violation this . . . this program is? I feel violated, and I wasn't even among the ones bugged!" She paused in mid-outburst and said slowly, "I'm not, am I?"

"No. Just the residents of *Galactica*. It's a military vessel, and frankly, Madame President, it's understood that when you sign up for the service, there are certain aspects of your life that you're giving up. The option to refuse to do what you're told, for one. Privacy for another."

"Not that much privacy. It's wrong, Admiral, and you know it."

"Yes. I do," Adama said evenly. "I also know it's wrong not to do everything within my power to ensure the safety of the fleet. Whenever those two imperatives come into conflict, I will always—always—err on the side of the safety of the fleet. Frankly, I would think that's a mindset you could readily understand."

"Don't act like you're taking the moral high road."

"I'm not. I'm taking the only road available to me. I don't care whether it's lofty or muddy. It's what's there. We don't live in a world of what's right and what's wrong. We live in a world of what's necessary."

"I don't believe that."

"Really," he said stonily. "With all respect, Madame President . . . where was the high road when you wanted me to kill Admiral Cain?"

"That's . . ." Obviously she was about to say that that

was completely different, but the protest died before she could complete it. Then she let out a heavy sigh and said, "I suppose I did forfeit the moral high ground on that, didn't I."

"You forfeited nothing, Madame President. I think we both concur that sometimes we have to do things that are unpleasant in pursuit of the greater good. We simply differ on the specifics of what and when."

"I suppose that's as it should be," she admitted. "If we walked in lockstep, we'd never be forcing each other to reconsider our positions. But," and she still looked none too pleased, "I still feel my privacy has been invaded."

"Not intentionally."

"A shot that goes astray and takes down an innocent is no less fatal due to lack of intent. But there's no point in harping on it. What's done is done. And . . . I suppose I should have told you."

Adama considered all the reasons that he'd come up with as to why she had felt she could not do that. As she had just said, though . . . there was no point in harping on it. "One hopes that, should the need arise in the future, you will. For now, at least, I do know." He leaned forward. "Do you truly believe that Valerii's unborn child could be having an influence on you?"

"As we've already learned, we don't know what the Cylons are truly capable of. It's one of the reasons that I wanted the pregnancy aborted. There's too many unknowns attached to its development."

"I agree." He paused and then said, as dispassionately as he could, "That option still remains."

"I know. And if I relapse . . . ?"

"We could drain the fetal blood. Keep it stored on an as-needed basis."

"Would you embrace that idea?"

Adama's face never changed, but he admitted, "It's a bit . . . parasitic . . . for me."

"Me too," said Laura. She rubbed her eyes in a manner that emphasized the lack of sleep she'd been lately experiencing. "Honestly, Admiral . . . I'm open to suggestions."

"There's one avenue you haven't pursued."

"That being."

"You could talk to Sharon Valerii."

She stared at him with a level gaze for a time.

"I could indeed," she finally said.

# CHAPTER 14

Sharon knew something major was happening when the marines came in to manacle her to her place.

Ordinarily she only spoke to visitors through the phone unit. So when the marines came in and bound her wrists, and fastened them in turn to a shackle on the floor, she was aware that meant someone was actually going to be entering her cell. Her guess was that it was Adama. Typically they made sure she couldn't move, and even then they kept guard with weapons that they would use if she made the slightest gesture toward whomever was there. She had once considered making a mocking comment such as, "Aren't you worried I'll shoot death rays out of my eyes?" but then thought better of it once she realized they'd probably clamp a metal blindfold around her just to play it safe.

She sat there with the stoic resolve of someone who was prepared to endure whatever her captors put her through. There were days when she wondered how she tolerated it, and she always kept coming around to the same answer: It wouldn't always be this way. She didn't know why she believed that. From the evidence of things, there was really no reason to. And yet she did, day after day. After all that she had been through, and with the baby growing in her belly, she had to believe that God had a greater purpose for her than to allow her to suffer and die.

She just wished she knew what it was.

Perhaps at some point the humans would come to realize that she was not a threat to them. Or perhaps the Cylons would take over *Galactica*, as Sharon suspected was inevitable, and she would be set free. Or, hell, perhaps the Cylons would wind up killing her themselves. It was always difficult to be sure.

But she was certain she knew when she'd find out. It was whenever D'anna Biers finally showed up at her cell.

She knew that if Adama ever asked her about other Cylon agents, she would never tell. Not even if it meant her death. She would keep her silence because she firmly believed that if she did betray them, then she would die of a certainty. Not only that, but it would be D'anna Biers who would pull the trigger. No one else. That was the sort of thing that D'anna would reserve for herself.

Every time she thought of D'anna, a shiver ran down her spine. She was the most formidable Cylon of all the models. The boldest, the most confident. To hide in plain sight the way she did. Other Cylon agents insinuated themselves quietly into positions where they could do damage, but not D'anna, no. She was a journalist, putting her face out there to be seen by everyone, smiling and smug and confident that none would see through her façade. Sharon envied her in many ways. There was no reason for her to have suspected at any time during her involvement with Helo, for instance, that he would have been able to determine she was a Cylon. Yet she had always worried. Every time he'd looked at her and seen only a human, she'd been concerned that somehow, against all reason, he would realize what she was. For that matter, in her previous "existence" as Boomer, she had only been able to function by being unaware of her true nature. Almost as soon as she had learned she was a Cylon, she could no longer live with herself. She couldn't put a gun to her own head and pull the trigger; Cylons were hardwired against such pointless suicide. So her subconscious needs had kicked in and she'd settled for the next best thing: shooting Adama, thus guaranteeing herself a death sentence. She wouldn't have to live with the knowledge of what she was, and wouldn't have to deal with the way that her former friends would look at her. She preferred death to the prospect of living a life that was a sham.

But Sharon's solution simply became Sharon's problem all over again.

The thing is, death would likely have held no fear for her if it weren't for the baby. But the life growing within her gave her incentive to live.

And so she remained silent. Silence might get her D'anna Biers, and D'anna Biers would in turn get her freedom.

The marines finished manacling her into place and then they walked out of the cell. She hadn't even bothered to try and strike up a conversation with them. She knew better. They never reacted to anything she said. If they glowered at her, at least that would be something. But they didn't. Instead they just sort of stared at her with dead eyes, as if she wasn't even there. As if she was a . . .

"A thing," she finished the thought aloud.

One of the marines barely glanced at her just before he walked out. He didn't know what she was referring to, of course, and the chances were that even if he had, it wouldn't have made a damned bit of difference. Actually, he probably would have agreed with her assessment.

She wondered if any of them could ever hope to understand.

"I'm not a thing," she said, thumping her fist softly on

her thigh. "I am not . . . some sort . . . of thing." The baby kicked as if responding in sympathy. Sharon raised her fist and looked at it, turning it from side to side. Then she opened it and very slowly placed her palm flat on her stomach. "Maybe," she whispered to the child within her, "you're the symbol of this hand. Maybe you're going to take the fist of the Cylons and turn it into an open hand, which the humans will take in turn. It's possible. Anything's possible, I g—"

There was a noise at the door and Sharon looked up. It opened and, not entirely to her surprise, she saw Admiral Adama enter. He stared at her with that look she'd come to know quite well: a mixture of suspicion, pity, and forced detachment.

Then Sharon's eyes widened in ill-concealed surprise as President Laura Roslin stepped in behind him. There was no mixture of anything in Roslin's expression; rather there was nothing but deep, abiding resentment.

Well, that made perfect sense, didn't it? Roslin resented her, or at least "Sharon Valerii," for the assassination attempt upon Adama. She resented the child that was growing in her belly, since Roslin believed it represented a threat to the fleet and wanted to kill it. She resented the fact that she had to let it live because it had benefited her personally. And, obviously, she resented showing up here, now, for whatever reason they'd come up with.

Nevertheless, despite the fact that she knew how much Laura Roslin despised her, Sharon stood up. She noted with some amusement that Roslin took an involuntary step back, although the look of resentment on her face never so much as twitched. Adama stopped when Roslin did and glanced back at her.

Sharon bowed slightly at the waist in acknowledgment of Roslin's presence, and it was at that point that Roslin must have realized Sharon wasn't standing out of defensiveness or even a desire to attack. She was doing so out of deference for the office of the presidency.

Sharon smiled inwardly, knowing that it probably annoyed the hell out of her. Nothing made someone who hated you more insane than responding to that hatred with patience and respect.

Roslin never changed her expression. Sharon wondered if Roslin's face would crack should a smile ever stray across it. Sharon remained standing, although she was slightly stooped thanks to the restraints of the chains on not only her wrists and ankles, but also around her throat. Previously they'd also had a strap around her waist, but her expanding belly had gone beyond the strap's capacity.

She waited to see if they'd pick up the phone, but they didn't. Instead Adama went around to the far door, tapped in the entry code, and opened it. Sharon turned slightly to face them, but otherwise stayed right where she was and made no sudden movement. Even if it had been possible for her to do so, she wouldn't have, because Adama had produced a sidearm and was aiming it directly at her heart. No, not her heart—her belly.

Suddenly a terrible notion occurred to her, but she didn't allow that to be reflected in her voice, which remained flat and even. "If you're here to execute me," she said, "I just want to tell you that I appreciate you handling it yourself instead of dispatching a subordinate."

"Sit down," said Adama, the point of his gun never wavering.

"I can't."

"Why?"

"Because," said Sharon, and she tilted her head toward Laura Roslin, "she's standing. It would be a breach of protocol."

Roslin made a sound of disbelief, and then saw in Sharon's steady gaze that she was perfectly serious. "You have my permission to sit," she said.

"Thank you." Sharon did so. She gestured toward a chair that was some feet away, out of the range of movement that Sharon's short leash permitted her. Laura's gaze flickered from Sharon's manacles to the chair and back to Sharon, as if she were mentally judging the distance between Sharon and herself. Answering Roslin's unspoken question, Sharon said quietly, "It's sufficient distance for safety concerns."

"I wasn't worried," Roslin replied, and her expression seemed confident enough. Sharon suspected it was superb dissembling. Roslin sat in the chair, smoothing the folds of her skirt.

Sharon's gaze flickered back to Adama. "Are you going to keep that pointed on me the entire time, Admiral?"

"Is that a problem?" The question sounded solicitous. The tone most definitely was not.

She shrugged. "Not for me. But your arm's going to get tired after a while. And it could start to shake slightly from muscle tension. Which could result in your accidentally shooting me. Unless that's your intent all along, in which case I suppose it's all academic."

"Your concern is appreciated," said Adama.

"I'm sure it is," replied Sharon, who was sure it wasn't. She shifted her attention to Roslin, who was watching her as if hoping that she, Sharon, would keel over and die right then and there. "If you're not here to kill me . . . are you here to say thank you?"

"Thank you?" Roslin echoed in mild confusion.

"You're welcome."

"I mean, why would I thank you?"

"Because I saved your life," Sharon said evenly. "You'd be dead if it weren't for me."

"If a doctor found a cure with the aid of a lab animal . . . would you thank the animal?" Roslin said.

Sharon stared at her and then, very softly, chuckled deep in her chest. "I appreciate you putting it that way . . . and letting me know where I stand." She could have asked what, then, Laura Roslin was doing there. Her mind raced, far faster than a human mind could have. Just one of the perks that she possessed; humans had no idea at all just how quickly she could think. It was obvious that Adama was there to serve as guard to Laura Roslin. He was taking no chance that Sharon might abruptly break her bonds and make a move on the president, try to kill her where she sat. (Now Sharon was really relieved she hadn't made the eye beam comment.) The question, of course, was why was Adama doing that rather than having a marine guard or guards on hand to serve the same function? Well, there was only one answer to that, wasn't there. Adama and Roslin wanted to discuss something of a sensitive nature . . . a nature so sensitive that they didn't even want to chance marines standing there and hearing what was to be said.

It intrigued her to wonder what it might be.

She didn't allow her expression to change or reflect the notions that were running through her head. Instead she simply waited patiently, one hand in her lap, the other resting gently on her stomach. She saw Laura Roslin notice her hand's placement. Inwardly, she smiled. Outwardly, she waited.

"Commander Adama," she said, "has informed me that, whenever he has asked you questions about anything, you've always answered them to the best of your ability. I would appreciate it if you could provide me the same courtesy."

"Of course," she said neutrally.

"Very well." She leaned forward, studying Sharon intently, looking like she wanted to try and catch Valerii in a lie no matter what Adama might have said. "I want to know if you're doing it deliberately."

Sharon stared at her and stared at her and then said, "In the name of my people . . . in the name of the one God above all . . . I have absolutely no frakking idea what you're referring to."

"The dreams."

"The dreams," Sharon repeated. "What dreams?"

"The dreams that aren't letting me sleep. The dreams that are . . ." She composed herself and said, "If you're trying to get in my head, disrupt my life, I'm here to tell you that it's working. Congratulations. And I want you to stop it or so help me I will ask Admiral Adama for his weapon and put a bullet in you myself."

"That's your prerogative," Sharon said, unfazed. "And I'll die with no more clue as to what you're talking about than I have right now."

"She doesn't know." It was Adama who had spoken. Laura Roslin looked up at him and, although he still had no intention of lowering his gun, there was still quiet conviction in his face. "She really doesn't."

"Would you bet your life on that? Or mine for that matter?" asked Laura.

"Yes," he said without hesitation.

Laura considered that, and then nodded. "All right," she said, apparently satisfied. "Which leads us to the next question of whether this might be the baby's doing."

By this point, Sharon had a clear idea of what Laura Roslin was nattering about. But a warning flashed through her consciousness. If she allowed her deductions to color the things she said, it would make it appear as if she did, in fact, have advance knowledge of what Roslin was talking to her about. Which would mean she was "in on it" or some such. Sharon didn't dare take that chance, because she was still certain that Roslin was looking for an excuse—any excuse—to stop her child from being born. She wasn't about to hand it to her. Continuing to keep her face as impassive as she possibly could, Sharon inquired, "What is the 'this' to which you're referring?"

"The dreams," Laura said after a moment, apparently realizing that refusing to answer Sharon's question would only slow matters down. "The dreams I've been having in which you're a featured player. Dreams of birth. Dreams of blood. 'Sagittarius is bleeding.' Does that mean anything to you?"

"No. None of this means anything to me. You're having bad dreams. Everyone does. Are you trying to blame them on my child?"

"I'm trying to determine what's going on."

And Sharon was suddenly on her feet. Adama had been relaxing ever so slightly, but the moment he saw Sharon even begin to make a motion, he had the gun ready to fire if need be.

"You are trying to put the blame on my baby," Sharon said frostily. "Something's going on in your head that could stem from any number of things rattling around in your subconscious, and you're trying to use it as an excuse to kill my child."

"I don't require an excuse," Laura Roslin reminded her harshly. "All I require is a piece of paper to write out and sign the order."

Sharon didn't budge from where she was standing, but she folded her arms and said firmly, "I have nothing more to say."

"This meeting," said Roslin, "is not over until I say it is."

"Fine. Then, with all respect, I have nothing more to say until my lawyer gets here."

"Your . . . ?" She mouthed "lawyer" without saying it and looked at Adama questioningly. He sighed and nodded. "How did she get a lawyer?"

"One showed up."

Laura was about to say something more, but she quickly reconsidered it. That didn't surprise Sharon. Roslin obviously felt that she and Adama should present a united front, and standing there and arguing with him about Sharon's legal rights would only serve to undermine that front. Laura turned back to Sharon. "Look," she began.

"With all respect, I have nothing more to say—"

"It will go better for you if—"

"—until my lawyer gets here."

"If you truly are concerned about your baby—"

"With all respect," and her voice got louder and her manner even colder, "I have nothing more to say until—"

Laura put up a hand, silencing her. Her eyes closed as if she were fighting a migraine. She forced a smile and said, "All right. You've made your position clear." She rose and Adama unlocked the door, still keeping his gun aimed at Sharon. Sharon remained standing even after both Adama and Roslin had exited. Roslin paused and then turned and said, "You should have cooperated."

"I've done nothing *but* cooperate," replied Sharon, and her voice grew harsh, allowing some of the anger that had been building up to bubble into visibility. "And for my cooperation I've been confined to a cell half the size of any quarters . . . I've been beaten, sexually assaulted, and nearly raped . . . I have no room to do any kind of exercise . . . I'm getting bedsores . . . I stink because I have no shower facility, I can't even go to the head without being under observation, and I'm not sure but I think there's things living in my hair. You want to solve whatever problems I present? Let me go. Someone will put me down like the dog I'm being treated like, and we can all move on to other things." And then, her fury pushing her in a direction that wouldn't even have occurred to her earlier, she turned and focused a malevolent gaze upon Laura. "You know so little about us. Who we are, how we function. Consider this little notion: Perhaps the blood coursing through your veins that you stole from my child . . . the blood responsible for your salvation . . . is *turning you into one of us.* Never occurred to you, did it? Maybe these dreams you're experiencing are the first steps on your road to becoming a Cylon yourself. How will it feel, I wonder, if you wind up going from being revered to feared. To losing your friends, your liberty, everything, in one shot. Take a good, hard look at the décor here, Madame President. You might just be sharing it before you know it. And by the way . . . I don't have another frakking thing to say until my lawyer is here."

And with that final announcement, she flipped herself back down onto her bed. In doing so, it pulled the neck chain taut and she gagged slightly before she could readjust herself so there was some slack in the chain.

She made no further moves until the president and the admiral were gone, at which point she fought desperately to keep hot tears from rolling down her cheeks, and didn't quite succeed.

# CHAPTER 15

Adama had never seen Laura Roslin as shaken as she was at that point. She was seated in his quarters and was looking shellshocked. Inwardly he cursed himself as a fool, believing he should never have taken her to see Sharon Valerii in the first place . . . particularly galling since it had been his own damned suggestion.

"Would you like a drink?" he asked her gently.

"I've never wanted one so desperately in my life."

Reaching under his desk, he pulled out a bottle of alcohol that had been a gift from Tigh. Adama was reasonably sure Tigh had acquired it from the black market, but Tigh hadn't volunteered the information and Adama felt it better not to inquire too closely. Considering Laura's state of mind, he suspected she wasn't going to ask too many questions either. He filled a glass for her and slid it over to her. She took it without even looking at it and knocked it back in one shot. Then she held the glass out again and Adama filled it without comment. This time she sipped it far more slowly.

"You're not turning into a Cylon," Adama assured her.

"How do we know that?"

"Madame President . . ."

"How do we know?" she repeated. There was no fear in her voice, no trace of panic. She was asking in what could have been an almost clinical fashion, as if they were discussing the results of some new experiment. "You can't say it's impossible. You don't know. Neither do I. Perhaps she's right. Perhaps I'm undergoing some . . . metabolic process that is slowly transforming me into one of them."

"That's absurd."

"So you say. But you don't know." She looked him square in the eye. "Do you."

The truth was that he didn't, but he wasn't about to say that to her. It wasn't what she needed to hear. "Yes. I do."

"You were the one who said," she reminded him, "that Sharon Valerii has always told you the truth."

"All she did was float a possibility. Possibilities are nothing more than that . . . and can be dismissed just as quickly."

"Possibilities can also be things to be explored."

He gestured in a you-tell-me manner. "How would you suggest we explore it?" he asked. "Dissect you?"

Adama wasn't serious, of course, but she looked thoughtful as if were actually a viable notion. "Did you dissect the previous incarnation of Valerii?"

"Yes."

"And what did you discover that readily distinguished her from being a human?"

"Nothing," Adama admitted.

"Nothing. Which leads us back to wondering how you would know in my case."

"It's more than biological."

"Is it?" she asked, one eyebrow cocked. "If we can't distinguish them from ourselves, and if we can't even tell if we're turning into one of them . . ."

"I can tell."

"You can." Roslin made no effort to hide her disbelief of the claim. "How?"

"In their eyes. They can't disguise their pure hatred for us. I see it burning in there with cold fury. That's how you tell."

"Really. And if that tell should fail?"

"Well," he paused, "getting shot is also a good tip-off."

Despite the seriousness of the situation and her bleak mood, Laura Roslin smiled at that. "I should think it would be." Then her amusement faded, to be replaced by grim apprehension. "Admiral . . . if you ever have any reason to think I've been . . . swayed . . . over to their side . . ."

"I will act accordingly."

"Even though there will be those who accuse you of treason?"

"The survival of the fleet is my overriding concern," said Adama firmly. "I'll deal with whatever consequences may result from that. But I repeat: There is no way that you could, or would, become a Cylon."

"How do you know, Admiral? How do you truly know?"

"Because," he said with conviction, "you are far too much a woman of conscience to allow that to happen. If you truly believed that you presented a threat to the fleet . . . that you had allied yourself, however against your will it was, with the Cylons, then you would come to me and ask me to put a shot through your head."

"And could you do that?" She saw the brief flicker of hesitation in his eyes. "Could you? I come to you and say, 'Admiral, it was everything I could do not to open fire on the Quorum of Twelve. Kill me before I kill someone else. That's a direct order from your commander-in-chief.' Could you do it?"

The hesitation evaporated and slowly he nodded. "Absolutely."

"Huh." She frowned. "I don't know whether to feel relieved about that, or concerned."

"Both, I suppose," said Adama.

"All right," Laura replied. "I'll have to take your word for it."

"I hesitate to mention it . . . but have you spoken with Doctor Baltar about this?"

"No," she admitted. "I have . . . concerns about him. I would not feel comfortable trusting him with this situation at this time."

"Concerns."

"You have none?"

"I didn't say that," said Adama. "Simply nothing that I can act upon. And you?"

She hesitated and then said, "The same. Or, at the very least, nothing I can put into words."

*What would I say? That I had visions of him on Caprica, locked in a passionate embrace with a known Cylon agent? There's still too much I don't know. He's the foremost expert on Cylons. If I were becoming influenced by the Cylon fetus, then wouldn't it be in the Cylons' best interests to have the man who knows most about them to fall under suspicion?*

She knew she couldn't go on like this forever. Sooner or later, she was going to have to sort this out, or resign from the presidency. That was the only option left to her if she thought that her own mind was unreliable. Until it reached that point, though, she was going to try and play things as carefully as she could.

"You should still seek medical aid," Adama said firmly.

Laura nodded in agreement. "All right," she told him, albeit with reluctance, "I'll speak to Doctor Cottle about it."

"Excellent."

Adama began to stand, clearly thinking the meeting was over, but Laura didn't move. Her gaze hardened and she said, "She has a *lawyer*?" This prompted Adama to sit back down again with an audible sigh, as if he were deflating and that was what was lowering him back into his seat.

"Yes," he said.

"And she spoke with this person?"

"Yes."

"And you allowed this?"

"I considered shooting her," Adama said, "but I was daunted by the prospect of the paperwork."

She shook her head, clearly not amused. "You should have denied her access."

"If I had, she would have gone public with the presence of the Cylon."

"You just know it's going to happen sooner or later."

"Possibly. Considering we're still trying to get a handle on what caused the Cylons to be able to anticipate our Jump, my vote is for 'later.' "

"I suppose you're right," she allowed. She shook her head and half-smiled. "I hate to admit it . . . and if asked, I would deny it . . . but I'm starting to see the advantages of martial law. Under such conditions, you could have just held her indefinitely at your whim."

"A dictatorship is also an option," he pointed out.

"In case you haven't been paying attention to the press, there are some who are under the impression that we already have one." Laura appeared to give it some consideration, and then she shook her head sadly and said, "It wouldn't work. I look ghastly in jackboots."

"Imagine my relief." He paused and then said, "She made the argument that Sharon Valerii is so indistinguishable from a human that it was inappropriate—even illegal—to treat her as anything but."

"What did you say?"

"I said she was a machine."

"What," Laura asked after a moment, "do you truly believe?"

Adama leaned back in his chair. It was a question that

he'd been wrestling with ever since he'd come out of his coma and had come face to face with the creature that had shot him. "I hate to say it, but—"

"You don't know? Admiral . . . Bill . . . one of them tried to kill you."

"And another one of them saved you," he reminded her. "I look into the face of Sharon Valerii, and I see the enemy. I see something inhuman. But . . ."

"But what?"

He tried to figure out the best way to phrase it. "The lawyer was right about one thing. It is always easier to think of an enemy as less than human, even when you know they are. So when you know they're not, how much easier to make them less than they are?"

"I'm not sure I follow."

Adama's mind rolled back to a meeting he'd had with the Cylon. The results of that encounter had never been far from him, and they continued to haunt him. "I had a talk with her . . ."

"It."

"With the Cylon, back when we first encountered the *Pegasus*. When it looked as if I was going to have Starbuck assassinate Admiral Cain. I asked her why the Cylons hated us. Why they were trying to kill us. She brought up something I'd said about humans deserving to survive . . . and suggested that maybe we weren't. That we weren't worthy to. And when she said that, there was something about her . . . she seemed . . ."

"She seemed what?" prompted Laura.

"Wise. Wiser than us. Older than us."

Laura Roslin looked as if her eyes were going to leap out of her head. "Are you saying that they're rendering judgment upon us . . . and are *worthy of doing so*?"

"No," he said flatly.

"Then what . . . ?"

"The reason Admiral Cain wasn't killed by Kara Thrace . . . was because Sharon Valerii made me feel as if I wasn't living up to the promise of humanity. I was as willing to kill the admiral . . . as the Cylons are to kill us. In that moment, she was more human than I . . . and I was more machine than she. No wonder we can't determine, even through autopsy, what the differences are between us. There are times when the line blurs so much, I'm not sure where it is anymore."

"I remind you, Admiral, that it was a Cylon who cold-bloodedly killed Admiral Cain after you, in your humanity, declined."

"I am aware of that, yes."

Laura could almost see the wheels turning within his head. "May I ask what you're thinking?"

"I'm thinking that either Sharon Valerii is one of the most brilliant actresses of her age . . . or there may be some sort of actual dissent within the ranks of the Cylons. If there's one Sharon who truly believes in humanity . . . there may be more. And it's possible that somehow down the line, we might be able to exploit that."

She arched an eyebrow in interest. "You mean foster some sort of civil war within the Cylons themselves?"

"The notion of having them invest their talent for homicide into obliterating each other rather than us is an appealing one, wouldn't you say?"

A slow smile spread across Laura's face. "Do you think it's possible?"

"As we've established, when it comes to the Cylons, anything is possible."

Laura nodded in agreement. "The bugs in the rooms," she said after some consideration. "They have to come out."

"No."

"Admiral . . ."

"It's a military matter, Madame President. A military decision. I stand by it and until we get this sorted out, they're staying where they are."

She scowled. "I want your word that they're gone once things are 'sorted out.' "

"You have it."

"And be certain to tell Colonel Tigh that I'm not happy with him at all."

There was a knock at Adama's door. "Yes?" called Adama.

"Do you have a minute, Admiral?" came Tigh's voice.

Adama's eyes flashed with amusement as he looked at Laura. "By all means," he said.

Tigh pushed the door opened, walked in and stopped when he saw Laura. "Madame President," he said in surprise. "An unexpected honor."

"We were just talking about you," Adama told him.

"Really. Nothing good, I hope," said Tigh.

"The president wished me to inform you that she's not happy with you at all."

Tigh didn't look the least bit bothered. "Then my hope was fulfilled." Before either Adama or Roslin could explain specifically what it was that Tigh had done to draw the president's ire, his voice grew serious and he continued, "Doctor Baltar has come to me with a situation."

"Is this about the matter that we heard him muttering to himself over?" When he saw Tigh's surprised gaze flicker over to Roslin, he added, "She knows about the bugs. And she knows that I knew from the start. Colonel Tigh," he said to Roslin, "suggested that I claim ignorance of the program to spare me your ire."

"Did he."

"Yes."

"Huh," she grunted. "That was very noble of you, Colonel."

"Thank you, Madame President."

"Doesn't make me any happier with you, though."

"Understood. Admiral," he continued, looking as if the president's happiness with him wasn't of particular importance, "the doctor wishes to meet with you. He believes that the boy may in fact be a Cylon."

Roslin's cheeks pinked slightly at the prospect of another Cylon being identified. "Boy? What boy?"

"Andrew Boxman. The pilots call him Boxey," said Adama. "He was caught having a private conference with Sharon Valerii."

"Naturally he was checked over to make sure he wasn't a Cylon himself," Tigh told her. "Baltar originally gave him a clean bill of health . . . but now apparently he's having second thoughts."

Laura started murmuring the name "Boxman" to herself. She frowned a moment, trying to figure out why it sounded familiar, and then she remembered. "Wasn't the officer who was killed at the meeting station when the Cylons first attacked named Boxman . . . ?"

"Boxey's father. He's orphaned."

"We know who his parents were, and we still felt it necessary to check if he was a Cylon?"

"We know that an Alex Boxman existed at some point," Tigh said. "We've no idea whether the one who came aboard *Galactica*—in the company of Sharon Valerii yet—is the original item. Alex Boxman may well be dead and this one is an imposter."

"Do they do that? Impersonate other people?"

"We don't know," Tigh said stiffly. "But it's preferable not to take chances."

"Yes. Yes, of course, you're right. Do we know where he is now?" asked Roslin.

"We've been keeping tabs on him, just in case," Adama said. He was sifting through some notes on his desk and produced one that had been delivered to him recently. "According to child protection authorities, he's taken up residence on the *Bifrost*, under the guardianship of—by astounding coincidence—Sharon Valerii's lawyer, Freya Gunnerson."

"Gunnerson . . . ?"

He noticed the uptick in her voice. "You know her?"

"I suspect I know a relative of hers. How old is she?"

The question surprised him mildly and he glanced over at Tigh. Tigh shrugged. "Mid-twenties, I'd make her out to be."

"Probably her father, then." She laid out as quickly as she could the details of her encounter with Wolf Gunnerson.

Adama took it in, considering every word she said. "Hell of a coincidence," he said finally.

"I don't like coincidences on general principle," said Tigh.

Standing up and coming around his desk, Adama said, "Let's go have a chat with Doctor Baltar and find out what the hell is going on. Madame President, would you care to join us . . . ?"

"I think it would be better if I got back to my ship," she said, rising as well.

"If I may ask, what are you going to do about the Midguardians?" asked Adama. "Are you seriously considering their request for statehood?"

"I've ruled out nothing," said Roslin. "I generally try to keep my options open until I see how things pan out."

Tigh scowled and said, "If you ask me—which you didn't, but anyway—if you ask me, elevating those heathens to parity with the Twelve Colonies, you're asking for trouble, with all respect."

"That may be, Colonel," replied Laura Roslin. "But I've noticed that trouble tends to show up, unasked for or not. So I might as well do what I feel is right and let the consequences fall as they may."

Billy Keikeya looked as if he were about to go into shock when Laura Roslin told him the outcome of her discussion with Admiral Adama. He was literally trembling with indignation, and as she sat in her office and watched his mounting mortification, she never felt quite as badly for him as she did at that moment. Billy took his responsibility as her aide and—ultimately—confidant very seriously. It was at times such as this that she remembered just how young he truly was, because his face was stricken with an expression that would have been at home on one of her students who had just been informed he'd been caught cheating. Except in this case, of course, Billy was innocent of any criminal intent.

"They had her quarters *bugged*?" he asked in disbelief. When she nodded, he demanded, "Did Dee know about this?"

"Dee . . . ? Oh. Dualla. No, I've no reason to assume she did."

"I've got to tell her . . ."

Billy started to stand but Roslin firmly gestured for him to sit. "You're to tell her nothing. You're not to tell any of them anything. You and I may find the concept repulsive, but Adama and Tigh make a convincing argument. These are difficult times, Billy, and difficult decisions have to be made to get us through them. These include decisions we don't always agree with . . . but have to live with."

"But Madame President, with all respect . . . it's wrong," he said, still looking upset but nevertheless sitting as she indicated him to do. "Shouldn't we take stands on things for no other reason than that?"

"I'm not so sure it's wrong."

"How can it not be?"

"Because we can't afford to be naïve, Billy," she said firmly. "We're dealing with an enemy that will stop at nothing to destroy us. So if extreme measures need to be taken to avoid being destroyed, then that's what we do."

Billy stared at her for a long moment, and she wasn't sure what was going through his mind. "You have something to say, Billy?" she asked.

"It's . . ." He paused, and then said, "It's not my place. I'm sorry . . ."

"Billy, your place is where I say it is. If you have something to say, then let's hear it."

"Madame President, you've been through a lot . . . it really wouldn't be fair of me to—"

Annoyance flashed across her eyes. "Billy, I don't give a damn about fairness. Tell me what's on your mind."

He studied her for a long moment, and then he said, "You never used to be the type to back down, that's all."

She felt a brief flare of temper, and she had to remind herself that she had pushed Billy into saying what he was thinking. "I don't believe I agree with your assessment."

"Yes, Madame President." He seemed suddenly anxious to get the hell out. "That . . . well, that's fine. You're right." He started to stand once more, and a single imperious gesture from her caused him to plop down yet again. She didn't say anything; she just stared at him, making no effort to prompt him, certain that the ongoing glacial look she was giving him would be more than enough to get him talking again. As it turned out, she was right. "Okay, look . . . with all respect . . . what you said just now. You 'don't believe' that you agree. It sounded less definitive. *You've* been less definitive. Less sure of yourself."

"If that's true—and I'm not saying it is, but if it were—certainly don't you think some of that can be attributed to the fact that I haven't been sleeping much lately? That might have something to do with it."

"Something. Maybe. But not all of it."

"Then what—?"

"Madame President," Billy said, shifting uncomfortably in his chair, "I really . . . really think it's inappropriate for me to be discussing this with you . . ."

"Billy," said Roslin, her voice softening sightly, "I don't know if you've noticed . . . but you and Lee Adama are the only two people I've known I could count on from the moment I became president . . . and, frankly, even Lee has been shaky every now and then, since he's got a bit of a conflict of interest."

"That's understating it," muttered Billy.

"You've seen me at my worst and at my best . . . or at least what passes for my best. You, of all people, should know you can speak honestly with me."

"All right." He lowered his head and interlaced his fingers, looking as if he were working to find the best way to put it. "I think it's more than just the dreaming . . . the sleeplessness. You've seemed more tentative in your decision making, in your attitude . . . in everything."

"Really." She maintained her pleasant tone, although it was not without effort. "And why do you think that would be?"

"Well . . . if I had to guess . . . it's because as long as you were convinced you were going to die, you had nothing to be afraid of. I mean, what's the worst that can possibly happen to someone? It's death, right? And because you had adjusted to the idea that you didn't have much time left, you were determined to do everything you could before your time ran out because you figured, you know . . . you had nothing to lose. You weren't in it for the long haul. You weren't a marathon runner; your life was boiled down to the hundred-yard dash. You just ran with everything you had, head down, arms pumping, and anything that got in your way, you ran right over it. But now . . . now you've got something to live for. A lot to live for. And you no longer have the—it'll sound weird—you don't have the 'comfort' of knowing that you won't be around for much longer. Now you can afford to take your time in trying to get humanity to Earth because you actually have a chance of seeing it yourself. Plus you're considering every single aspect of everything because you have time to think about all the ramifications, all the sides, where before you just . . . well, it seemed like you just went with your gut."

"That was never the case, Billy. I always considered every aspect."

"Maybe. But I don't think you gave everything equal consideration, the way you do now. I mean, hell," and he almost laughed, "there were times when it seemed like you were spoiling for a fight more than Adama, and he's the soldier. Lately you've been more cautious. More . . . politic."

"Well, I am a politician."

"No, Madame President," he said firmly. "You're a

leader. There's a difference. A huge difference. A politician cares what people think, and they hate her for it. A leader tells them what to think, and they love her for it."

"I think you're selling me a little short as a politician, Billy."

"And with all respect, Madame President, I think you're selling yourself short as a leader. I think you weren't afraid of dying, but now you're . . ."

"Afraid of living?"

"Not afraid. Just . . . concerned." He paused and then looked down, feeling ashamed. "I said it wasn't appropriate for me to say stuff like this."

"Billy," she said slowly, "I may be many things . . . but the one thing I remain is your president. If you, of all people, can't communicate with your president . . . what hope does any of the rest of my constituency have?"

"You're not upset then."

"No. I don't agree with what you have to say, but I respect that you said it."

"Thank you, Madame President. Is that all?"

She nodded and yet again he rose from his chair. He started to head for the door and then Roslin called, "Billy . . . I know you graduated with degrees in political science and government. But before that, did you study psychology at all?"

He smiled. "Two years, before I changed majors. You could tell, huh."

"Let's just say that it wasn't a wasted two years."

"Thank you, Madame President," he said, bowed slightly, and left.

His words stayed with her, though, long after he had gone. Her impulse really was to reject what he he'd said out of hand . . . but the more she thought about it, the more she wondered if he had a point. It wasn't that she'd resigned herself to dying, but she had accepted it. She knew how her life was going to end, and her existence had turned into a race against time. It had enabled her to focus her efforts with laserlike efficiency. Now, though, the ending was no longer certain, and her future—so clearly defined—was now murky. The focus was gone. She was still determined to get humanity to its new home, but with the time element gone, she could afford to . . . to . . .

"To be more cautious. More politic," she echoed his words. "Let's face it . . . more weak." Billy hadn't said that, but she said it. It was part of the reason she'd been content to let Adama and Tigh go talk to Baltar. She had a feeling that someone like Baltar would easily sniff out weakness. She'd come to see Adama as an ally, and even with him, she didn't want to allow anyone to see her at less than her best. But Baltar would sense her weakness and—if he was indeed a Cylon sympathizer of some sort as she was beginning to believe—she didn't want to chance letting on to the opposition that there was any diminishment in her capacity.

But she couldn't keep it up forever. She needed to pull herself together. Laura hated to admit it, but Billy might have indeed had a point. The cancer had loomed large as the final coda on her life. Now the end of her life had yet to be written—which meant that everything leading up to it needed a heavy rewrite. And she was going to have to take pen in hand and write it herself . . . before someone removed the pen from her hand and did the writing for her.

Weaker. Less of a leader. She didn't like the sound of it or the feel of it. And she was starting to think that maybe she should be doing something about it . . .

. . . provided there wasn't an unborn Cylon who was trying to drive her insane.

Saul Tigh had the sneaking suspicion that Gaius Baltar was trying to drive him insane.

Adama didn't look any happier, but as always, he was able to contain whatever annoyance he was feeling beneath his stony exterior. They were in Baltar's lab and

Baltar—as he so often did—looked slightly furtive, as if he already knew what you were going to say and was planning his next response several steps further along the projected conversation. Tigh didn't understand why anyone would feel the need to be thinking that much about something as simple as a discussion. It was as if Baltar considered it all some sort of battle of wits, and rather than communicating the way a normal person did, he was out to win a game that only he knew he was playing. Tigh felt there were only two reasons for Baltar to be thinking that way: He was so brilliant that he couldn't help but try to stay ahead of the curve . . . or he had something he was hiding and was trying to head off questions before they got uncomfortably close.

Either way, he got on Tigh's nerves with remarkable ease.

"So now you're saying," Adama asked slowly, wanting to make certain he understood what he was being told, "that Boxey *might* be a Cylon?"

"I'm saying that I've discovered anomalies in the original blood sample I drew," replied Baltar. "I make it a habit to recheck my findings . . . particularly when Cylons might be involved. Everything about them is geared towards subterfuge."

"Even their blood?"

"*Every* aspect of them, Admiral," Baltar said firmly. "In the case of young Mr. Boxman, there are some things that don't properly match up. His cell count for one. It leads me to wonder whether something went wrong with the test the first time."

"What sort of something?" asked Tigh.

"It could be any number of things," Baltar replied. He sounded annoyed that he would be required to explain something that was clearly, to him, blindingly obvious. His voice grew lower, as if he were concerned that someone was listening in. That, of course, carried with it some irony considering that he was right. It was just that the people who were listening in on him were sitting right there in his lab. "The most disturbing of those possibilities is some sort of sabotage. That someone snuck into the lab and did something to the sample I was using for testing while I wasn't around."

"Where the frak did you go, considering you know how important the test is?" demanded Tigh.

Baltar gave him a withering glance. "The test involves growing a culture, Colonel. That takes time. Simply baby-sitting it for the duration isn't really a viable option. Feel free," he added with increased sarcasm, "to refute me with your copious years of scientific training."

Tigh glared at him, hoping his scowl would be sufficiently intimidating. Baltar, tragically, didn't look intimidated in the slightest.

"That's what I thought," said Baltar when Tigh had no comeback.

Clearly wishing to move forward, Adama said quietly, "What do you need us to do?"

"Why . . . bring the boy back here, of course," Baltar said as if it were the most obvious thing in the world. "I ran tests on the blood sample that remained, and from what I could determine, he has four of the six markers that would indicate that he is a Cylon. Unfortunately, due to their close resemblance to humans, four out of six is within the margin of error. Six out of six is the only way to be sure, and that's impossible to determine with what I have on hand."

"Give us your best guess, Doctor, if you wouldn't mind," Tigh said. "Is the boy a Cylon or not?"

"I don't 'guess,' Colonel," Baltar replied with the heavy manner of the truly put-upon. "I conduct experiments and I draw conclusions. Guessing accomplishes nothing and can only lead to confusion and contradiction. I need him here to be sure."

Tigh and Adama exchanged looks, and then Adama said, "All right. We'll bring him back."

"I'll scramble a squad of marines," Tigh said, heading for the door as if the entire matter was settled.

He was halted in mid-stride by Adama's calm, collected, "That may not be necessary, Colonel."

Tigh turned and looked at him in surprise. "No?"

"We'll discuss it further. Thank you, Doctor . . ." and then he paused and added, "Or do you prefer 'Mr. Vice President'?"

"Depends on the circumstance," replied Baltar.

Adama nodded, then accompanied Tigh into the hallway. He turned back toward the lab after a moment and said, "Would you mind telling Kara Thrace to wait for me in my quarters?"

"Starbuck? Why?" But Tigh instantly thought better of what he'd just said and instead simply nodded and continued, "Yes sir."

"Thank you. I'll be along shortly."

Adama waited until Tigh was gone, then knocked once more at the lab door and let himself in before Baltar had a chance to say anything. He noted that Baltar was standing in an odd position, as if he were talking to someone. But there was no one there. Baltar jumped slightly at the intrusion and quickly smoothed his shirt . . . not because it was wrinkled, but obviously because he was endeavoring to regain his composure. "Did I interrupt a conversation?" Adama asked with a slightly bemused expression.

"I talk to myself on occasion," Baltar said. "It's how I work through complex problems. Plus I'm starved for intelligent discussion, so . . ." The last comment was clearly intended to be a joke, but Baltar had the comedy stylings of a Cylon raider, so it fell flat. Knowing that it had, he cleared his throat and said, "Is there something else, Admiral?"

"You're responsible for President Roslin's cure."

"Yes," said Baltar warily, as if worried he was being set up in some way.

"I'd like to know about the possibilities of side effects."

His eyes narrowed as if he were trying to read

Adama's mind. Caution still pervading his voice, he said, "Naturally there's the possibility of side effects. We're dealing with an entirely new branch of medicine. Using the blood of the unborn Cylon isn't exactly the sort of treatment you're liable to find in any medical textbooks. It was a desperation move."

"You didn't know it would work?"

"Of course not. I knew it *could* work, but that's not the same thing. Frankly, I wanted to keep President Roslin here for observation for a month or two, but she was insistent about getting back to work."

"She would be, yes."

Baltar now looked extremely suspicious. "Admiral . . . is there something going on that I should know about? Is President Roslin suffering from some sort of reaction? I admit, I wasn't entirely sanguine over the prospect of attempting an entirely new medical treatment on her. But since the alternative was certain death, I didn't see that she had a good deal to lose. Any negative reactions she's having, however, would certainly be helpful to know about, especially considering that others who suffer from similar illnesses might want similar treatment."

"Yes. It would." Adama paused a moment, looking to be considering possibilities, and then said as coolly as ever, "I simply wanted to know if I should be on the watch for something."

"Has there been any change in her behavior?"

"I couldn't say."

"Has she been speaking to you about any difficulties?"

"I couldn't say."

Slowly Baltar nodded, easily reading between the lines of Adama's vague response. "Couldn't say . . . or choose not to?"

Adama inclined his head slightly, acknowledging that the latter was a distinct possibility. "Thank you for your time, Doctor. If, in your further research, specific aspects of side effects occur to you, you will share them with me, won't you."

"Of course. And you would share any share specifics of negative changes in President Roslin's condition, should any of them present themselves to you?"

"You may expect me to, yes."

Baltar smiled in a way that didn't give the least appearance of amusement. "Very carefully worded. I suppose I may also expect Cylons to come flying out of my ass. But that doesn't mean it's going to happen."

"Vice President Baltar," said Adama, "in your case . . . I wouldn't rule out a single possibility." With that he headed out the door.

His exit, although naturally he didn't hear it, was accompanied by delighted laughter from Number Six. Baltar gave her a sour look as she continued to laugh and then applauded slowly and sarcastically. "Now there goes a funny, funny man," she said.

"He's the height of hilarity." He looked at her suspiciously. "What was he talking about? What 'side effects'?"

"I'm sure I don't know," said Six, the picture of wide-eyed innocence.

"Why don't I believe that?"

"Because, Gaius," she replied, "you see the world as a vast web of lies and deceit. You believe in nothing and no one."

"I believe in myself."

"You believe in yourself least of all," said Six with a giggle that sounded surprisingly girlish. "You second-guess yourself constantly and you live in perpetual fear that you're going to be found out. In so many ways, you wish you were like her."

"I don't know what you mean."

"I mean," she said, striding across the room on those legs that seemed to go on forever, "that Laura Roslin was on the brink of death and she still never showed one iota of fear. You envy her for that, because you jump at sounds and shadows. You envy her her fearlessness. You saw her cancer as a chink in her armor, and yet even staring oblivion in the face, she was unafraid. You could never look death in the face and remain unfazed."

He stepped close to her, stared directly into her eyes, and said tightly, "Oh really? I'm doing it right now."

Then he turned his back to her and strode out of his lab, leaving her behind to watch him go with her face a mask of thought.

*What the frak did I do now?*

Naturally that had been the first thing that had gone through Starbuck's mind when Tigh had approached her with a determined look on his face. Then the perpetually sour executive officer had told her, as bluntly as he could, that Adama wanted to see her in his quarters. Her initial sense of relief *(Oh, good, Tigh hasn't found some new excuse to toss me in the brig)* was immediately replaced by a sense of vague dread (*What did I do to piss off the Old Man?*).

She knew it was ridiculous for her to feel that way. It wasn't as if she had a perpetually guilty conscience. Still, she couldn't help but occasionally feel a bit besieged, and although she was reasonably sure she hadn't done anything out of line lately, well . . . there was always the stuff she'd done in the past that she'd never been caught out for. So . . . well, yes, maybe she *did* have a perpetually guilty conscience at that, always wondering when one of her idiot pranks was going to catch up with her.

Or, for that matter, it might be something of more recent vintage . . . literally. She'd been hitting the booze fairly hard lately, and had been hung over well into duty hours. Thank gods it hadn't happened during a toaster attack. She had never been at anything less than her best when it had counted, but even Kara had to admit that that was as much luck as anything else. There was always the possibility that she might be forced to leap into a cockpit with her head ringing and her vision impaired.

She liked to tell herself that if such a situation presented itself, she would automatically regain full sobriety and be ready to launch an attack at a moment's notice. But she didn't know how much of that was genuine and how much might just be wishful thinking.

She didn't want to think that anyone in her squad would have ratted her out, but she knew that was overly optimistic. It was entirely possible that someone had indeed done just that, and if she was going to be pointing fingers at anyone, it would probably be Kat. Kat had had it in for her for the longest time, and if presented with an opportunity to make Starbuck look bad, well, wouldn't she grab it immediately?

Maybe. Maybe not. Kat was determined to show Starbuck up, and to prove that she, Kat, was the best fighter pilot in the squad. But to show someone up, that person had to be around to *be* shown up. If Kat got Starbuck grounded somehow, then how would she, Kat, have the opportunity to prove to everyone that she had the goods and Starbuck didn't?

So it probably wasn't Kat.

Lee, maybe? Nah. If Lee had a bone to pick with her about drinking, or about anything, then he would just face her and tell her, not rat her out to his father. That just wasn't his style.

As she knocked on Adama's door, she came to the conclusion that she had nothing to worry about. He probably wanted to talk about duty rosters, or perhaps he had an assignment for her. But she hated the fact that she had such a checkered history that she felt compelled to run through an entire litany of possible negatives before she could finally decide that she had nothing to be concerned about. It made her think about the times that Tigh would look her in the face and practically snarl at her, "You're a screw-up, Thrace, and that's all you'll ever be." At which point she'd punched him and, well . . . that's when the fun usually started.

"Come," called Adama and she entered with no indication of anything in her mind other than being ready, willing and able to serve in whatever capacity she was required. Adama was leaning against his desk, sipping a cup of coffee, and he gestured for her to sit. She did so, folded her hands in her lap, and waited. She didn't have to wait very long. "I have a job for you," he said.

"Anything, Admiral," she replied. Outwardly her demeanor didn't change; inwardly she breathed a sigh of relief that her hyperactive imagination had been off base. Her inner big-mouth urged her to ask if she was going to be required to assassinate anyone this go-around, but she wisely managed to keep silent.

"Boxey is currently in residence on the transport *Bifrost*. I need you to go there and bring him back."

That surprised her. "How did he wind up on the *Bifrost*?"

"The Midguardians have apparently taken him under their wing."

"I see," said Kara, who didn't. "And may I ask why we need him brought back here? I mean, with all respect, Tigh had me give him the heave-ho from *Galactica*. He wasn't happy about leaving and I wasn't thrilled about sending him. So . . . ?"

Adama stared at her for a long moment, and she instinctively knew what was going through his mind: He was trying to decide whether to answer her question or not. Something was going on with Boxey that was obviously on a need-to-know basis, and he was endeavoring to determine whether she needed to know or not . . .

That was when it hit her like a lightning bolt. Her eyes widened and before Adama could speak, she said, "This isn't about the thing with him being a Cylon, is it? What, did Baltar change his mind?"

Adama was a hard individual to provoke a visible reaction from, and there were probably two people on *Galactica* who could accomplish it with facility. One was Lee Adama, and the other was looking at him at that moment. He blinked in surprise, and then looked wearily amused. "I should have known you'd figure it out," he sighed.

"I don't believe it," Kara said firmly. "I don't. Baltar's up to something. The man's a born liar."

"Really. I didn't think you knew him that well."

She flinched involuntarily at that, and she was sure that Adama had caught the subtle but telling reaction. Not a damned thing slipped past him. Covering as quickly as she could, she said, "I've played poker with him."

"I see." The words hung there, and Kara was certain that she was being paranoid. Was there any possible way that Adama could tell—from that slightest of exchanges—that she'd had a drunken one-night stand with the then future vice president? It was one of the most ill-advised encounters she'd ever experienced, attributable partly to liquor and partly to morbid curiosity over whether mental prowess translated to . . . other types of prowess. The encounter had been something of a disappointment, and even now she and Baltar endeavored to look in other directions when they chanced to cross each other's paths.

Adama continued to study her with his dissecting stare, and then said, "Then I guess you would know. The question then becomes, why would he lie about it?"

"I don't know," she admitted.

"Neither do I," Adama said. "So it's better to be safe than sorry, don't you agree?"

"Yes sir," Kara said without hesitation. "I assume you want me to go in presenting a friendly face. It's better to have me going in as a friend than storm the place with marines trying to force them to turn him over to us."

"Infinitely better," said Adama.

"You want me to go over there, tell him we miss him over here, tell him I talked to you and you've relented on him hanging out with us, and he'll return with me . . . at which point he gets tossed in a cell and poked and prodded all over again."

"Yes."

Kara kept her face carefully neutral. Inwardly, she was recoiling at the entire prospect, and there was a deep, burning rage building within her that was directed entirely at Baltar. But Adama didn't need her outrage at that moment. He needed her cooperation, and he needed her level head. Since she was at her most focused when she was behind the weapons console of a Viper, she pretended that was where she was. Mentally she conjured up a vista of space before her, and coming toward her was a Cylon raider. Except instead of the standard Cylon helmeted face upon it, the sneering face of Gaius Baltar was etched on it. She pulled the trigger and, in her mind's eye, blew it out of space.

"No problem," Kara assured him and then, as an afterthought, asked, "Mind if I bring Helo? He's the other pilot besides Sharon that Boxey associates with being rescued. So having him along will likely help."

"Be my guest," said Adama.

"I'm on it."

"Kara," said Adama, standing, "thank you. And be careful."

"Aren't I always?" she asked with a wry smile.

He didn't return the smile. "Almost never."

"Wow," she said. "I got an 'almost.' "

"I was being generous."

# CHAPTER 16

In what she had to think was the most admirable display of restraint she'd ever shown—and, sadly, no one was ever going to know it—Laura Roslin sat at her desk and watched blood pour from Sarah Porter's eyes and ears and mouth without giving the slightest indication that anything was wrong.

Porter was the representative of Gemenon, an extremely hard-nosed and intelligent dark-skinned woman who had never hesitated to get into Laura's face on any topic. Of all the members of the Quorum, she and Roslin had the most fractious history, going back to when Roslin had denied Porter's request for additional water supplies on behalf of her constituency. Porter had retaliated (or at least that was how Laura had seen it) by backing Tom Zarek as vice-presidential candidate, but she'd been outmaneuvered when Laura had brought in Gaius Baltar who had, in turn, coasted to victory.

Since then Laura had wondered whether or not Sarah had, in fact, won out in the end. It wasn't as if Baltar was any picnic as vice president. But she kept those thoughts to herself.

"The Midguardians?" Sarah Porter was making no attempt to mask her sheer disbelief that Laura Roslin was bringing up such a subject. "They're clamoring for recognition . . . and you're actually thinking of giving it to them?"

"That might be too drastic a way to put it," said Laura. Under her desk, she was jabbing her fingernails into the palm of her hand, endeavoring to keep herself steady in the face of what she was certain were more delusions. *I am awake. I am awake and this is not happening,* she kept telling herself, and it was all she could do not to scream. "More accurate to say that I'm . . . thinking about thinking about it. That's why I wanted to speak to you."

"Me?" Porter looked amused. "Do you see me as a potential ally, Madame President?"

Laura wasn't sure how to take that, plus it required all her effort not to become ill from the sight of Sarah Porter's eye slowly seeping out of her head. Behind her, Sharon Valerii was mouthing, "Sagittarius is bleeding." Laura forced a smile that bore far more resemblance to a grimace and said, "Of course it is."

"Of course what is?" said Porter.

A part of her mind heard the disconnect between what she was saying and what Porter was hearing. It sounded vaguely familiar to her for some reason, and then she realized why: It was like having a conversation with Gaius Baltar. He likewise spoke in a disjointed manner. For one wild moment she wondered if he, too, was speaking to invisible Cylons that only he could hear, and then dismissed the notion as just too crazy for words. "Of course . . . I do," Laura corrected herself with effort. "I think, if you look at the issues that we typically face, you'll find we're united on far more things than we disagree upon."

She wasn't wild about the look that Sarah was giving her, as if there was something that should have been obvious to her that wasn't. Finally Porter said, "Perhaps you've forgotten, Madame President, but I vouched for you."

"Vouched . . . ?"

"There is no one in the Quorum more conversant with the Pythian Prophecies than I am," said Porter with a clear touch of pride. "No more who is more familiar with the Sacred Scrolls."

"Ahhh," Laura said, suddenly comprehending. "I understand."

"Do you?"

Laura rubbed her eyes, partly from fatigue, and partly in hopes that when her vision cleared, Sarah Porter would look normal once more. "You verified that the Prophecies spoke of a dying leader. You stated that you believed that leader to be me." She lowered her hand and tentatively looked up at Sarah. The blood was gone and, mercifully, so was Sharon Valerii. Laura let out a sigh of relief.

"That's exactly right," Porter said stiffly. "The leader whose vision would send us toward Earth . . . but who was dying and so would not live to see us arrive in the promised land."

"You said it was me, and suddenly I'm cured."

"Yes." Porter didn't sound particularly happy about it.

"What can I say?" asked Laura Roslin with a shrug. "Pardon me for living."

"Madame President, I staked a good deal of my credibility to the notion that you were the leader of prophecy," Porter said, giving her a defiant look and tilting her chin in a pugnacious manner. "With your miraculous cure, that credibility has taken a hit. Plus we have not seen satisfactory disclosure over the manner of your cure. People are asking questions."

"They can ask all the questions they want, Councilwoman," said Roslin calmly. "My cure is a matter of doctor/patient confidentiality. A radical new treatment for which I agreed to volunteer."

"A cure that will be made available to others who may be ill?"

"If long-term observation of my recovery indicates that it would be appropriate, then yes, absolutely," Laura told her. "But it would be premature to attempt to duplicate my cure. Anyway . . . Sarah . . . that's not why I brought you here."

"A rather clumsy attempt to change the subject," Porter observed.

"I prefer to think of it as a clumsy attempt to bring us back to the original subject."

"The Midguardians." With the air of someone who not only doesn't suffer fools gladly, but would prefer to see them all roasting on a spit, Sarah Porter asked, "What do you want to know? If I will support their petition to become part of the Quorum? Absolutely not."

"Why not?"

"Because they are heretics. Because they do not worship the same gods as we."

"Should that make a difference?" asked Roslin.

"Of course," said Sarah Porter. "Of course it makes a difference. What are you suggesting?"

"That perhaps we should consider putting aside religious concerns when it comes to government. That perhaps they should be two different aspects of life, not commingled."

Porter tried to stifle a laugh and failed utterly. "You're saying there should be a separation of church and state."

"It has occurred to me."

"President Roslin," said Porter, looking at her with amazement as if seeing her for the first time, "I knew that you had many ideas others might consider . . . aggressive. But they were always steeped in tradition. The deviation came from those people who believed the traditions and writings to be sweeping cautionary tales, as opposed to others such as myself, most of the residents of Gemenon, and other more spiritual colonies who accept the divine wisdom of the Prophecies. But no one has suggested simply operating as if religious beliefs don't matter."

"I wasn't suggesting that at all," Roslin replied. "You know how deeply rooted my convictions are. I was simply suggesting that perhaps just because they're my beliefs, and your beliefs, doesn't mean they should guide our decisions in terms of the rights of others."

"With all respect, Madame President, that's absurd. Our very morality stems from our beliefs and the lessons that the gods have taught us. If we don't root our decisions in those beliefs—if we don't allow the Sacred Scrolls to guide us—then we have nothing. We might as well be soulless Cylons." She paused and then said cautiously, "Certainly you're not advocating supporting this . . . this Midguardian bid for power."

"I don't feel as if I know enough about it to advocate it one way or the other."

"They are unbelievers," said Sarah. "What more do you need to know than that?"

"Well, for starters . . . I'd like to know about their writings. This 'Edda' that one of their leaders discusses. That's really why I wanted to talk to you; because you're so knowledgeable in these matters. Do you know anything about these writings that were supposedly excluded from the Sacred Scrolls?"

"Just rumors," Porter said. "The Midguardians have always been an insular people. The Edda itself is written in an ancient language that's handed down by their leaders, and they've kept entire portions secret even from their own followers. Their followers, amazingly enough, are satisfied with that. They have that much confidence in their historic leadership."

"I'm almost envious," said Laura with a hint of jest. Porter didn't respond to the humor, and Laura opted not to press the matter. Instead she said, "Certainly in the ancient writings there was some discussion of what the Edda had to say. Some record of why it was stricken from the main prophecies."

"As I said, rumors. For starters, it celebrated gods we didn't accept. But of even greater concern . . ." She paused and Roslin waited patiently. "Of even greater concern was that the Edda supposedly focused mainly on doomsday prophecies."

"Considering what we've been through . . ."

But Sarah Porter shook her head. "As you well know, our recent . . . travails . . . were predicted in the Pythian Prophecies. As is often the problem with such prophecies, they were easier to understand in retrospect than before the fact. The Edda writings . . . they were nothing but gloom and doom. The end of humanity with no hope of survival, of redemption . . . of anything. I don't know the specifics, but from my studies, that's the general gist of it. Now I ask you, Madame President . . . why would we want such dreary portents to become public knowledge?"

"Perhaps because the people have a right to know," replied Laura. "Because they have a right to make a decision for themselves."

Porter stared wonderingly at Laura Roslin. "Do you actually believe, Madame President, that we have the wisdom to gainsay our elders? To make these prophecies of the Edda a part of our teachings? And what if the fleet embraces it? What if they decide that humanity truly is doomed, and there's no point even in trying to survive?"

"I doubt it will come to that," and she continued before Porter could interrupt her, "and so do you, Sarah. All we're talking about is the prospect of giving them something new to think about. Where's the harm in that?"

"Where else but from new ideas does harm come, Madame President?"

Laura Roslin considered that a moment, and then shook her head. "I can't accept that," she said firmly. "I cannot accept the notion that new ideas should be suffocated. Without new ideas, new thoughts . . . we have nothing. Nothing."

"Madame President . . ."

But Roslin talked right over her. "We are being tested, Sarah. You, I, humanity. We are being tested, and how we come through that test may well determine our right to continue to exist as a species. If we put a stranglehold on even discussing new concepts, what do we have left?"

"Survival," replied Sarah Porter.

"There's more to life than survival."

"Perhaps. But without survival . . . what does the rest of it matter?"

"It matters," Laura said firmly. "I know it does. And furthermore, Sarah . . . I think you do, too. As much danger as we face on a day-to-day basis, I think we wind up seeing danger in everything. And if we're seeing danger even in the simple act of talking . . . what's that going to lead us to?"

Sarah Porter didn't reply immediately. Her lips twitched a bit, and it was impossible for Laura to discern what was going through her head.

"Let me get back to you," she said finally.

Never one to miss an opening, Roslin immediately said, "When?"

"Soon. Very soon."

Laura nodded slightly and then they both rose. Laura shook her hand firmly and Sarah Porter turned and walked out of the room. The moment she was gone, Billy entered, a look of concern on his face. Displaying no interest in what had just been discussed, he said immediately, "How are you feeling?"

She turned to face him and saw blood covering his chest.

Her expression frozen, she replied, "Fine. You?"

Sarah Porter entered the shuttle that would take her back to her home ship and said, "My apologies. I didn't know it was going to take that long."

"That's quite all right," said D'anna Biers, smiling graciously. "May I ask how it went?" She did not have her cameraman with her, but a compact camera rested on the seat next to her.

"It went as well as could be expected." She paused and then said, with a hint of amusement in her voice, "Are we on or off the record?"

"Are we even talking?" asked Biers with wide-eyed innocence.

Porter then proceeded to tell Biers everything that she had discussed with Laura Roslin. When she finished, Biers did nothing to hide her interest. "So what would happen next? A gathering of the Quorum of Twelve to discuss the prospect of allowing a thirteenth member?"

"It seems a waste of time."

"You never know," replied Biers.

Sarah Porter was as openly skeptical as Biers was anticipatory. "They'd never go for it."

"Who cares?"

"What," asked Sarah, "is that supposed to mean?"

"It means that it presents an opportunity. You're a Councilwoman. I'm a reporter. And both of us are . . ." She hesitated and then smiled. ". . . Instigators. People who like to see things shaken up. Personally, I think it would be criminal to miss out on this opportunity to bring everyone together and see what happens."

Porter drummed her fingers thoughtfully on the seat next to her, and then picked up the phone that was hanging on the wall. "Patch me through to the president, please," she said. D'anna gave her a thumbs-up, a cheerful gesture which Porter returned, and then Sarah continued, "Madame President . . . yes, it's been ages." She smiled slightly at the weak but expected jest. "I was calling to say that it didn't take me much time at all to realize you were right. What are we coming to if we're faced with ideas and concepts so dangerous that we're even afraid to discuss them. You set up the day and time for the Quorum to convene, and I will make damned sure that everyone's there. Yes," she paused as Laura spoke, "yes, I'm sure there will be some resistance to the meeting once they learn of the subject matter. There are some ancient tensions with the Midguardians that go back generations. But that's why you spoke to me, isn't it. To make certain that I would convince the Quorum to at least consider it."

She chatted with the president for a few moments more, and then assured her that she would eagerly wait to hear from her. She hung up the phone then and looked challengingly at D'anna, as if daring her to say something.

All D'anna did was smile and say, "It should make a hell of a story."

# CHAPTER 17

Boxey had been going to the Midguardian sanctum on a regular basis since returning to the *Bifrost* with Freya. The sanctum had been unlike any other place of worship that he had ever attended. There were no symbols or testaments to the many gods worshipped by the Twelve Colonies. Instead there was a large upright symbol of a hammer hanging at the far end of the sanctum, right above a large double-doored cabinet wherein, Boxey had been told, the "original" Edda resided. It was securely locked in there, and although Boxey was tempted to try and crack the lock to check it out, he had resisted the impulse to do so. It didn't seem right, somehow . . . an abuse of the trust that Freya had placed upon him.

There were also no standard rows of pews as he'd seen in other temples. Instead there were long tables, rows and rows of them, and benches on either side of each table. The tables were lined with heavy mugs that appeared to be made of iron or some other heavy metal. That was because the Midguardians were big believers in drinking during services; most of their invocations of their deities consisted of raising mugs in their names and knocking back doses of alcohol.

This had become a bit more problematic since they'd been on the run from the Cylons. Alcohol wasn't in as plentiful supply as it used to be. Fortunately enough the Midguardians had considerable stores of various worshipful beverages aboard the ship and it was continuing to last them. Their attempts at building distilleries so they could produce their own home-grown booze had been uneven. Wolf had been one of the leaders in the attempt and continued to be the only one capable of swallowing and then keeping down the brew that his machine produced. Freya and other Midguardians had pronounced it fit for scrubbing down the engine coils and not much else.

The unlikely savior on that score, as it turned out, was Boxey. Several of the pilots that Boxey had been hanging out with back on *Galactica* were quite ingenious when it came to constructing such devices, and Boxey had picked up not a little knowledge from watching them at their endeavors. So Boxey had been able to spot a few flaws in Wolf's still, and Wolf was in the process of producing new batches that had been tentatively pronounced as "quite nearly potable" by his reluctant but pleasantly surprised test subjects.

The problem for Boxey was that actively participating in the salvaging of Wolf's still had only saddened him because it made him think of his friends back on *Galactica.* Or, as Freya had put it, the people who had led him to believe that they were his friends.

There was no one in the sanctum now, for it was not a prescribed time of worship. Boxey had not been allowed to participate in services since, as Freya had delicately put it, he was not quite "officially one of them." She didn't rule out the possibility that that might change in the future. In fact, she was very encouraging of it, saying it was a "definite likelihood."

Boxey stared at the hammer which, he'd been told,

represented a god of thunder, and then he said softly, "Are you guys there? Are you listening to me?" He didn't receive a response, nor was he truly expecting one. Nevertheless he eased himself down onto the nearest bench and said, "That's okay. 'Cause, frankly . . . I'm not sure any of the gods are listening to me. Or to any of us. With everything that's been going on . . ." He shook his head, discouraged.

"Why did you let it happen?" he asked finally. "I mean . . . honestly? My family dead. Millions . . . billions of people dead. I just . . . I don't get it." He stood and went to the cabinet in which the Edda was secured. "Are the answers in here?" he asked. He placed his hand against the door. "If I looked in this, and had a dictionary to help me understand it . . . would it tell me what's going on? Okay, actually, I know what. But *why* is it going on? It's almost like . . . like the gods are totally behind the Cylons. Why? Why would they be? Are the Cylons right about . . . about I don't know what. About everything? And which gods are behind them? Are any behind us? Are we alone? Really . . . alone?"

"Be kind of a shame if you were alone. Can I be alone with you?"

Startled by the unexpected voice behind him, Boxey jumped slightly as he turned and gasped in astonishment. "*Starbuck!*" he cried out joyously.

She stood in the doorway, grinning in that lopsided fashion she had, and Boxey was even more stunned to see that Helo was right behind her. Without hesitation he ran to Starbuck and threw his arms around her. "What are you doing here! I didn't think—! And Helo—! This is so—!"

"I know, I know," grinned Kara Thrace, and she riffled his hair. She glanced around the sanctum and whistled. "Well, this is . . . interesting. You a Midguardian now? Sick of the old gods?"

"Can't say I blame you," Karl Agathon, a.k.a. Helo, put in, his arms folded across his broad chest. "Between you and me, I been thinking maybe these Midguard types are smarter than we are."

"Helo!" said Kara with mock horror.

"Well, frak, Starbuck, we keep worshipping them and they let us get kicked in the teeth by the Cylons. Maybe we should start looking around for something better, is all I'm saying," and he nodded toward the large hammer that was erected at the front of the sanctum. "Make the old gods stop taking us for granted."

"Aw, shut up," snapped Kara and she thumped him on the chest as if he was speaking blasphemy . . . which, technically, he was. Although she was making a great fuss of being offended by Helo's comments, Boxey had a clear recollection that Kara herself had gotten fairly liquored up on one occasion and made some rather choice comments about the gods herself. To say the least, they were disparaging. To say the most, they seemed to indicate that she had some serious doubts—either about the existence of the gods, or that they had any generous intentions toward the remnants of humanity.

"You haven't told me! What are you guys doing here?" said Boxey.

"Isn't it obvious?" Kara told him, looking surprised that he would even have to ask. "We're bringing you home."

"Home?" Boxey was amazed. "What do you mean, home?" Then his expression fell. "You mean back to *Peacekeeper*? But . . . but I didn't want to go back there. Freya said I could stay here . . ."

Helo shook his head. "She's not talking about *Peacekeeper*, sport. She's talking about *Galactica*."

He couldn't believe what he was hearing. "*Galactica*? But . . . I thought . . . you said . . ."

"We had a talk with the Old Man," Kara told him. "We got him to change his mind; and he went to Tigh, and that was that."

"Change his mind?" Boxey sat on one of the benches, astounded. "You got him to change his mind?"

"That's right, kid," Helo said, drawing up one of the benches opposite him. "You should have seen her go. She was a dynamo. She pleaded your case and got him to realize that you should be able to come over to *Galactica* whenever you wanted to."

"Really?"

"Really," said Kara, and she looked him right in the eye and repeated, "Really."

And there was something there . . .

. . . something that didn't seem right . . .

. . . something that didn't altogether make sense.

Boxey's impulse was to trust Kara Thrace. And Helo . . . hell, he had seen Helo's bravery close-up and first-hand, when the valiant lieutenant had given up his seat on the rescue raptor to Gaius Baltar in the firm belief that Baltar was more important than a lowly raptor pilot. Kara was his friend, Helo was a hero, and friends didn't lie to you and heroes were better than other people. So every instinct of his told him that there was no reason he shouldn't just march right back to *Galactica* . . .

Except . . .

Except he had seen Kara's eyes when she had told him that he had to leave. He had seen the frustration and, most of all, the uncertainty there. She had come across as extremely sympathetic, but there had still been something there in the way she looked at him that suggested she thought maybe . . .

. . . possibly . . .

. . . that he could be one of . . .

. . . them.

Well, that was the problem with suspicion, wasn't it? Once it took hold in one's imaginings, it was difficult to blast it loose. Starbuck had been suspicious that Boxey was a Cylon, and even though he'd been cleared of it, it was always going to be in the back of her mind.

And suspicion went two ways. Just as doubts about Boxey had been planted in Kara Thrace's mind, so too was he now starting to harbor doubts about her. Not that she wasn't human; oddly, the thought that she was anything other than flesh and blood, normal, one hundred percent a spawn of humanity never entered Boxey's mind. But the notion that her intentions toward him might be something other than she was saying . . . well, now that was coming straight to the forefront of his concerns. Because as he gazed into her eyes, he was seeing some of that same concern, and that didn't seem right to him. She should be overjoyed that he was going to be coming back with her. She should be smugly triumphant that she had managed to achieve the damned-near impossible: to get Adama and Tigh to change their minds on a matter of security. None of that was present in her expression, and when Boxey shifted his gaze to Helo, he wasn't seeing it there either. Instead he saw that same kind of guarded look that roused his suspicions and made him wonder just what the hell was going on.

He glanced at the mighty hammer emblem on the wall and surprised even himself when he mentally directed a plea toward it of *Give me strength.*

"Really," he echoed once more. Boxey had long ago acquired the habit of thinking quickly, and his mind was racing faster than even Kara Thrace would have suspected or been able to adjust to. "Y'know what? How about this? How about you stay for dinner tonight. I'm eating with Freya, and she's not here right now 'cause she was heading over to *Galactica* to talk with Sharon again." He watched carefully and saw Starbuck flinch just a bit when he mentioned Sharon's name. "But I bet she'd have no problem with you guys as guests."

"I don't know that we'd be her favorite people right now, sport," Helo said. His legs were outstretched and he crossed them at the ankle. He looked casual and comfortable. Except not exactly: Instead it looked like he was trying his damnedest to look as casual and comfortable as possible, which suggested to Boxey that maybe he was neither. "This whole thing with her representing

Sharon . . . I think she'd be worried about . . . you know . . . talking to us. And things she might say . . ." He looked to Starbuck and there was a flash of desperation in his eyes as if he needed her to bail him out.

Starbuck quickly stepped in. "She'd probably be worried that she might say something she shouldn't and violate the whole, you know, client/patient confidentiality thing."

"Sharon isn't her patient."

"You know what I mean."

"Not completely, no," said Boxey, which was true enough.

"I'm just thinking," Kara said, and she patted him on the shoulder, "that we should head back to *Galactica* now. Because . . . you know . . ."

"The surprise," said Helo.

She glanced at him and made a show (too big a show, as far as Boxey was concerned) of looking annoyed with him. "You're supposed to keep that to yourself," she said. Heaving an annoyed sigh, she said to Boxey, "The guys were making a surprise party for you coming back, and big-mouth here tipped it off. Don't let on that you know, okay?"

On the surface of it, it all seemed perfectly harmless. Boxey wanted to believe her. He didn't want to overcomplicate this. She had come to him, and really he'd been dreaming that she would. He'd dreamt that exactly this moment would arrive and now that it had . . . it didn't feel right, smell right, sound right.

He remembered playing cards with Starbuck and the others, and he suddenly remembered one simple fact about her that had played to his advantage that evening when he'd thrashed her to within an inch of her chip stack: Starbuck was a lousy liar. She just stank at it. She was a little better at it when she'd had too much to drink, which was probably more often than she should have. But she wasn't much better sober, and generally speaking she was woefully deficient at it. It went against the grain, because Starbuck was much more someone who not only excelled at saying precisely what was on her mind, but reveled in whatever trouble might arise when she did so.

She wasn't telling the truth now. Or at least she was withholding part of it. So why was Helo there? Because she knew perfectly well that she stank at it and might well have been afraid that, left to her own devices, she wouldn't carry it off sufficiently to achieve her goal. So he was there to help.

But what was her goal?

The tumblers clicked with ruthless efficiency through Boxey's mind and unlocked the obvious answer. They wanted Boxey back at *Galactica*. That much was the truth, which was why she might have thought she could carry this thing through. But it wasn't for the reason she was telling Boxey now. He was almost positive of it.

There was one way to know for sure, though.

Boxey leaned back on the bench and draped his arms on the table. He looked extremely casual, maintaining the illusion that this was just a group of friends chatting away with one another.

"How about tomorrow?" he said.

"Tomorrow?" Kara looked surprised and puzzled. "Why, uh . . . why wait until tomorrow?"

"Is there any reason I can't?" He was speaking very carefully, his voice remaining noncommittal, as if he had no suspicions at all that something might be wrong.

"No," Kara said quickly, and she looked up at Agathon, who barely shrugged. "No, no reason not, except . . . y'know . . . the surprise thing . . ."

"They can do it tomorrow, right? Or next week?"

"Next week?" she repeated.

"Yeah, it's just that . . ." He thought fast. "This week is a Midguardian holiday."

"All week?"

"Yeah, all week. They do a lot of praying and celebrating and . . . stuff. And I . . . well, I kind of promised Freya that I'd be here for it. So I really feel like I should be. So maybe next week. That works better for me. Does that work for you?"

He could sense something changing in the room. Although Helo and Starbuck didn't exchange words, the tension level increased unspoken, and Boxey intuited exactly why that was. It was because he wasn't just marching back to *Galactica* with them.

"Boxey," Starbuck began, still clutching onto her shroud of affability with both hands. Then she hesitated, and then she grunted to herself, giving Boxey the impression that she had just hit the wall in terms of what she was going to be able to accomplish through simple, casual chitchat. "That . . . would work for me, but . . . look, I don't know that Admiral Adama would be okay with that . . ."

"Why not?"

Starbuck looked to Helo in what was, as far as Boxey was concerned, a silent plea for aid because she was running out of things to say.

"It's going to make us look bad," Helo said quickly. He wasn't looking casual anymore. Now he was sitting upright, his legs no longer crossed at the ankle.

"Look bad how?"

"Because we did a major selling job to the Admiral to enable you to return," said Helo. "The whole thing hinged on how important it was for you to come back. How much you meant to all of us . . . and us to you. If we go back to the Old Man now and say that you basically blew us off . . ."

"I'm not doing that."

"You pretty much are," spoke up Starbuck. "Adama didn't change his mind lightly. It's like Helo says. We go back now and tell him you just said you'd see us when you got around to it, Adama might just go back on his word again."

"Well, if that happens," Boxey said confidently, "then

you can probably talk him right back again. You're good at that, Starbuck. I believe in you."

"Boxey," she began.

"I'm not going back now, Starbuck," Boxey informed her. "You're welcome to stay here with me. Or go and tell the admiral I appreciate his changing his mind, and I'd like to take up the invitation at some future date. You can tell him that, can't you?" The problem was that he already knew the answer to it.

And Starbuck didn't disappoint him. "Yeah. I could tell him that," she said slowly. "But . . ."

It was obvious she didn't know what to say, so Helo quickly stepped in. "He'd be insulted."

"Yes," Starbuck said urgently. "He'd be incredibly insulted and, you know, we wouldn't want to do that . . ."

Boxey drew himself up. "Maybe some other time." And suddenly he was out the door before Starbuck and Helo could even react.

"Frak!" snarled Kara Thrace as she and Helo leaped up in pursuit of Boxey.

The entire thing had gone exactly according to the worst-case scenario she'd conjured in her head. The "turnaround" on Adama's part had been too abrupt. She'd done far too good a job selling Boxey on the idea that he was going to be *persona non grata* on *Galactica* for the indefinite future. So now, when she'd shown up in his new backyard and started making nice to him, it was only natural that it would arouse his suspicions.

His reactions aroused her suspicions as well. He was acting like someone who thought they might be on to him. On to him as what? As a Cylon, of course. It could well have been that they'd all been right to be suspicious of him, and now he was just trying to keep the hell away from them lest his true nature be found out.

On the other hand, he could just be a scared kid who didn't want to find himself stuck back in a cell while a mad scientist—who also happened to be the vice president—poked and prodded him and pronounced him to be an enemy of all mankind.

Either explanation made sense. The problem was that she didn't have the slightest inkling which was the right one.

She charged out of the sanctum, Helo right on her heels, and then Kara slammed into what appeared to be a bulkhead, but turned out to be a man. Under ordinary circumstances, it would have been expected that she would head one way and he the other. Instead it was solely Kara who ricocheted backward and stumbled into Helo. It was a small miracle that Helo managed to catch himself and not tumble over, righting the two of them. The man she'd collided with, in the meantime, hadn't budged from the spot at all. He'd tilted slightly but otherwise held his footing, and was now staring at the two of them with a combination of confusion and suspicion. "Who are you?" he demanded. "What were you doing in there?"

"Sir, this is military business," Kara said quickly.

"And this is my ship, making it my business."

She could have stayed to try and explain things, but Boxey had already whipped around a corridor and they were in danger of losing him. So Kara made as if she were about to stand and address the man's concerns, and suddenly she bolted right, ducking just under his outstretched arm. It was just enough distraction that Helo was able to get around him on the other side, and seconds later they were both pounding down the corridor after Boxey.

They got around the corner just in time to see Boxey vanish overhead.

It wasn't that he had disappeared into thin air. Rather he had leaped straight upward, torn off a metal grating accessing an air circulation shaft, bounded upward once more and slithered away into the narrow confines of the shaft.

"Frak!" shouted Kara. Helo took two steps in front of

her, cupped his hands, and Kara propelled herself upward and into the shaft. Or at least she attempted to do so; her head, outstretched arms and shoulders made it through, but that was as far as she got. She let out a yelp of pain.

"What's wrong?!" said Helo. "Is he hurting you?!"

"No, you muttonhead! I don't fit!"

"Are you sure?"

"Well, I *would* if I had no breasts and no hips!" her irritated voice echoed from above.

"You take a look in the mirror lately?"

Now it was Helo's turn to shout in pain as Starbuck slammed one of her feet down on the top of his head.

He stepped back, rubbing where she'd kicked him, and Starbuck dropped back down to the floor. "We gotta find him."

"And do what?" demanded an irritated Helo. "It's not like we can stuff him in a sack and sling him over our shoulders."

"Don't bet on it."

"He's *a kid*, Starbuck!"

"In case you're not paying attention, that's what we don't know for certa—"

*"Don't move!"*

Kara froze in place as she saw the large man they'd darted past standing a few feet away. He was aiming a gun at them. It looked tiny in his oversized hand, but that didn't make it any less threatening. And there were a couple of men behind him who were also holding weapons aimed straight at them.

Her peripheral vision told her that there were more men at the other end of the corridor. Starbuck and Helo had been outflanked, encircled from either side.

"What do we do now?" muttered Helo out the side of his mouth.

"For starters, we don't move." She paused and then said, in as authoritative a tone as she could muster, "This is military business!"

"And this is me not caring very much," said the large man. The business end of the gun never wavered. "I assume you have weapons on you. Now would be the time to produce them very slowly and lay them down equally slowly on the floor."

Their guns were hanging on the backs of their belts, covered by their jackets. Neither Helo nor Starbuck had been armed in the expectation that they would have to shoot Boxey or something like that. It was simply standard operating procedure for them to go armed into any situation that was not merely a social one. One never knew when one was going to stumble over a known Cylon operative, and on such occasions, Adama never wanted his people caught unprepared.

But just because they had weapons didn't mean it was always a good idea to use them. And somehow the prospect of getting into a firefight with a group of civilians didn't seem like the wisest course of action. Although it had been some time ago, feelings in the fleet were still raw over the notorious shooting incident during the period when Tigh had declared martial law. The last thing they needed to do was exacerbate matters by having anything resembling a repeat of the incident, even though the circumstances were extremely different.

Helo and Starbuck exchanged looks and then—slowly, as instructed—they reached out and removed their respective weapons. "You're making a mistake," Helo said evenly.

The big man gestured for the men on either side of him to approach and take the extended guns. "Not as big a mistake as you would have made if you'd taken a shot at any of my people."

"One of your 'people' might not be a person at all," Kara informed him, making no attempt to keep the annoyance from her voice. "That's why we're here. You may have a Cylon infiltrator."

"And would he be the one who stole our most precious possession?"

The angry question puzzled Kara. "What are you talking about?"

He took a step toward her and seemed to loom even larger than he had before. "Don't play games with me. Where is it?"

"Where . . . is what?"

"The Edda. I looked in the sanctum after you and your associate ran out of there and it was gone. Our holy book, missing. What did you do with it?"

"Us? Nothing! Boxey must have taken it."

"The boy?" growled the big man. "You would blame something like this on the boy? Why would he do such a thing?"

"Because we think he may be a Cylon, and he's trying to distract us or maybe just stir things up. Set us against each other."

He barked a skeptical laugh. "I find that . . . doubtful."

"She's telling the truth," Helo said.

"And I'm supposed to just take her word for it?" He looked hard at them. "The word of a military that's more interested in guarding its secrets than the balance of humanity. You keep information from us until someone else finds out about it, at which point you reluctantly admit it. You cause disharmony and discord."

Not at all intimidated by the fact that he could likely break her in half, Kara snapped back, "We've saved this fleet more times than I can count. When the Cylons come swooping down on us, you're safe and snug here second-guessing everything we do while it's my ass out in a Viper that's fighting to keep us alive for another day. And that's what we're trying to do now, and if you don't like it, then frak you, so get the frak out of my face, you got that?"

He glared at her, and then—to her surprise—the look he was giving her melted ever so slightly into amusement. He took a step back. "Yes, ma'am," he said coolly, and then turned to his people. "Take them to a private room. Search them thoroughly. See if they have the Edda on them. Find Boxey. I very much doubt their claims that he's a Cylon operative, but we should at least talk to him."

"He went up there," Helo said, pointing overhead. "If you've got someone small and skinny, you may want to send them up there, because if he took your Edda thing, he could stash it anywhere in there."

"I don't need your advice, thank you," said the big man. Then he paused and muttered to his nearest lieutenant, "Do as he says. Find someone. Now." The lieutenant nodded and went off as the big man turned his attention back to Helo and Starbuck. "I am Wolf Gunnerson. As I said, this is my ship. You will be my guests here until we get matters sorted out and the Edda is recovered."

"You'll search us and find we don't have it," Kara said.

"You might have hidden it somewhere. You might have an accomplice somewhere in this ship. I try never to underestimate the ability of the military to be deceitful."

"Thanks for the vote of confidence," Starbuck said sourly. "Look, Mr. Gunnerson, there's something here you have to understand . . ."

"You're here on military business."

"That's right. And you're interfering with it. That is not going to be looked upon favorably by my CO or the president. Furthermore you're holding us against our will. That's going to be viewed by some as a hostage situation. The action of terrorists. I don't think you really want that. I don't think you want a squad of heavily armed marines crashing in here."

Wolf leaned in toward her again. His breath alone was powerful enough to rock her back on her feet. "And I think that you don't have the slightest idea of what I want. A hostage situation? Fine. So be it. I have no problem with that. You show up here, you've got concealed weapons, you threaten a boy and try to drag him back to your ship against his will, tossing around accusations that he's a machine without the slightest shred of proof, and oh, by the way, our sacred book vanishes shortly after you arrive and you're seen coming out of our sanctum. And *you* accuse *me* of terrorist activities?"

"Admiral Adama is going to want us back, with the boy," Helo said.

"You throw that name around as if it's supposed to intimidate me. If he wants you back, I'll be more than happy to throw you out an airlock and you can walk back to *Galactica*. How does that sound?" When Helo made no answer, Wolf Gunnerson made a slight gesture with his head, signaling his men. They came in from all sides and took Starbuck and Helo firmly by the wrists and arms. "Be careful, men. They're colonial warriors. They likely bruise easily."

"You're going to regret this!" Starbuck called defiantly as they were led away.

"I really don't think so," replied Wolf, who really didn't.

He stood there and watched them go. And then, after a long moment, a door to the side opened and a figure emerged. "I told you that was exactly the attitude you could expect from them."

"Indeed you did. It's fortunate you happened to be by, Councilman."

Tom Zarek nodded thoughtfully and said, "She's right about one thing, though. Adama isn't going to take this well at all. He's going to want his people back, and he could make it very difficult for you if you refuse to cooperate."

"I'm sure he could. And I could make things very difficult for him."

"He has the *Galactica*, Wolf. Face facts: You can't possibly go up against him. Meantime your bid to be part of the Quorum of Twelve could be seriously hurt by this."

"I have no trouble with being both feared in my wrath . . . and admired in my generosity."

Zarek eyed him suspiciously. "Meaning . . . ?"

"Meaning the day is young." And he clapped Zarek on the back in a manner that was gentle for him and, even so, nearly dislocated Zarek's shoulder. "And I am thirsty. Let's quench that thirst together and we'll wait for matters to play out to our advantage."

# CHAPTER 18

"Animals," said Freya Gunnerson.

From within her enclosure, Sharon Valerii looked in confusion at her attorney. Pressing the phone tighter against her ear, she said, "What about animals?"

"Adama suggested it to me . . . although he didn't realize that's what he was doing," Freya said smugly. "Talking about the Cylons trying to slaughter us like animals. His whole argument to keep you cooped up in here, despite the fact that you've committed no crime, is that you're not human. But there's plenty of case law on the books about animal rights."

"But . . . I'm not an animal . . ."

"Yes, you are, in the sense that I am and Adama is as well. All humans are part of the animal kingdom. He keeps calling you a machine, but there's not a shred of proof that you are. Certainly no more so than any human who's operating with an artificial heart or a replacement knee. There's every proof, however, that you're an animal, and under our law, animals have rights."

"Animals get put in cages all the time. In zoos . . ."

"Yes, and there were laws to guard their best interests even then. Safeguards."

"I don't understand where you're going with this."

"It's very simple, Sharon. We go to precedents. That's how the law works." Freya's voice was becoming more excited, more enthused, as she contemplated what was to come. "We build case law to show that even the humblest zoo creature has more rights, has more protection under the law, than you. We—"

"Who do we do this with?"

Freya blinked. She seemed rather surprised that Sharon would interrupt her. "What do you mean?"

"I mean, who do we do this with? I don't know if you noticed, Freya, but the legal system as we know it has fallen apart somewhat." She ticked off options on her fingers. "There's Adama. There's the president. There's the Quorum. My understanding is that there's a few freelance mediators going around who are overseeing simple disputes. But people are just scrambling to survive. There's no full judicial system that I know of."

"Not at the moment."

"Moments are all I have," Sharon said fiercely, so fiercely that it startled Freya. "Don't you get that? Every day I wake up might be my last if Adama or the president decides I'm too great a risk. I don't have the option of looking at the big picture."

"And that's what I'm trying to change."

"Why? I still don't understand."

"Because," Freya said, "it's the right thing to do!"

"And do you think they'll give a damn?" Sharon started to walk around, her body giving vent to her frustration. Within moments she'd moved beyond the distance that the phone cord would allow and the receiver flew out of her hand. She grabbed for it and it thudded against the side of her cell. Sharon started to reach for it, and then let out an anguished cry of fury. "You're going to file my appeal with the same people who stuck me in here? You must be crazy! And I must be crazy for listening to you! You know they're going to reject any argument you make."

"I'm just trying to get you what you want," Freya assured her.

Her voice came over the phone receiver, and Sharon could hear it even though it wasn't to her ear. And Sharon was speaking so loudly that Freya had no trouble hearing her.

"What I want?" She thumped her chest. "You don't know what I want! You have no frakking clue!"

"Freedom for yourself! Freedom for your child!"

"*I'm not going to get freedom!* I'm a *Cylon*! I'm the frakking *enemy*! They're never going to just let me go! I don't get to live happily ever after with Helo and my baby, and we set up a nice family. You think I don't know that? You think I don't see what's coming? The only reason I'm alive is because *Galactica* needs me to keep saving their ass. The only reason my baby is alive is because they needed it to save Roslin's life. If they ever make it to Earth and find safe harbor, you know what the first thing they're gonna do is? Put a *bullet* in my *frakking brain* and turn my baby into a lab rat! If you ever convince them that they can't treat me the way they currently do, that's when I die. And they'll do it without fanfare, and without a thought, and without you. And what'll you do after I'm dead, huh? File a protest? Wag your finger and say 'Shame on you'? What do I want? What I want is, just once before I die, to walk around where there's some flowers and trees and dance on some grass in my bare feet, just for a little while. For a couple frakking hours. Then I'll be happy."

She looked as if she wanted to shout even more, but exhaustion overwhelmed her. She sagged against the side of the cell and then onto her bed. She put her hand on her stomach and just sat there, shaking her head.

"Sharon," said the frustrated Freya, "pick the phone back up. Please. Pick it up and put it to your ear."

Sharon stared at the receiver from which Freya's

voice was emerging. Then she picked up the phone but, rather than listening to it, she spoke softly, in a voice that was measured and tired but had an undercurrent of strength to it. "You know what I think?"

"Sharon, you need to listen to me—"

"I think," Sharon continued as if she hadn't spoken, "that you just wanna frak with people. With me. With Adama. With the president. The whole council. You just wanna use me to stir things up. I don't know why. I also don't care very much. Maybe something will come up to make me care but, right now . . . I don't."

With that, she turned and hung the phone up, cutting off Freya's voice as she continued to protest.

Freya thumped with her open palm on the outside of the cell, but Sharon ignored her. Then there was the heavy noise made by the outside door that led into the cell area, and Freya glanced over. She was not remotely surprised when Adama strode in.

She was surprised, however, when two colonial marines followed him in and pointed their weapons straight at her.

Adama barely kept his cold fury in check as he stared at Freya Gunnerson. His jaw was so clenched that it was difficult at first for him to utter words. "I've just been informed," he said without preamble, "that two of my people are being held on the *Bifrost*. On your father's vessel."

"Really." Freya looked as if she were feigning interest and not doing a good job of it. "Should that be of particular importance to me?"

"Considering it's going to have a very direct impact on your own liberty, I'd think it should."

Freya laughed at that. Her laughter did not sit well with Adama, who refrained from ordering the marines to shoot her in the leg in order to get her full attention. But resisting the temptation was no easy chore. "My liberty?" asked Freya when she'd sufficiently recovered herself. "Two of your soldiers got themselves into some trouble on my father's ship. How does that have anything to do with my liberty?"

"They're being held there on some trumped-up charges. Suspicion of stealing a holy book of yours."

"The Edda?" The amusement vanished from Freya's face, although Adama was sure it might be nothing more than a superb acting job. "They took the Edda?"

"They are suspected of doing so . . . except my own suspicion is that your father knows perfectly well they didn't. He's doing this to force the issue of your people, the Midguardians, becoming members of the Quorum."

She shrugged. "That's possible. I certainly wouldn't rule it out. He tends to come up with unorthodox solutions to achieve his goals. I still don't see what any of this has to do with me. Certainly you're not intending to keep me prisoner as some sort of retaliatory step."

"That is exactly my intention."

She laughed again, but this time it had a much more skeptical, even scolding tone to it. She addressed him as if the matter were already resolved and she was trying to guide him to the solution in the same way that a parent would ease a child over the span of a brook lest they wet their feet. Adama's face didn't so much as twitch. "Admiral," she said when she'd composed herself, "Perhaps you think that your feckless imprisonment of Lieutenant Valerii gives you the right to lock up anyone and everyone you want. Hell, you tossed the president of the Colonies into jail as part of a military coup. Some people believed that, since your . . . unfortunate incident . . ."

"My assassination attempt by someone who looked just like your client, you mean."

"Yes," she said dismissively as if the specifics were of no importance. "As I was saying, some believed that you had changed in your attitudes and outlook since then. It appears now that you're . . . what's the best way to put this . . . ?"

"Not frakking around." There was no trace of humor in his voice, no flicker of pity in his eyes. The absence of both finally got through to Freya Gunnerson, and she began to realize her extreme vulnerability.

However, she was almost as skilled as Adama in presenting an air of conviction and certainty. "I was going to say 'regressing.' You don't seriously think you can hold me here?"

"Unless you're packing enough weaponry to shoot your way out, I seriously think exactly that. Your father has my people. I have you. I'm thinking you might be something I can trade."

She squared her shoulders and faced him, not backing down in the slightest. "I am not a commodity. However you may choose to view Sharon Valerii, Admiral . . . I am human. I have committed no crime. I am not responsible for the actions my father has taken. I knew nothing about the theft of the Edda until I heard it from you just now. You have no grounds whatsoever upon which to hold me."

"Arrest you," he growled.

"The smartest thing you can do—frankly, the only thing you can do—is stand aside so that I can return to my vessel. If you wish, I assure you that I will talk to my father and convince him to release your people as soon as they turn over the Edda. Considering our tribal law prescribes murder as the punishment for theft of the book, I think that's rather generous on my part. This offer has a limited shelf-life, Admiral. I suggest you take me up on it."

Suddenly Adama was distracted by a loud thumping from the cell. He glanced over at Sharon. She was now holding the phone inside to her ear and was gesturing for Adama to pick it up.

His first instinct was to ignore her. To just let the phone sit there in the cradle where Freya had left it. But Adama had gradually come to the realization that his first instinct was frequently unreliable when it came to

Sharon Valerii. Without looking back at Freya, he strode over and picked up the phone.

Her voice came through low and conspiratorial. There was demand in her tone, but it was laced with pleading. "Take her outside. I want to talk to just you."

He was tempted to ask why, but saw no reason to hurry it. He turned to the marines and said, "Escort Miss Gunnerson outside and wait there for further orders."

"Admiral," said Freya angrily, "she's my client."

"And this is my ship," he reminded her grimly. "I win." He nodded confirmation of the order he'd just given, and the two marines removed Freya from the room. They kept their weapons in plain sight, but it wasn't as if she offered huge amounts of resistance as she was ushered out. As combative as she was, Freya knew better than to try and have it out with two heavily armed marines.

The moment they were alone, Sharon said briskly, "She was lying. She knows something."

The flat assertion caught Adama by surprise, although naturally there was nothing in his expression that would have confirmed that. "You were able to hear us?"

"I can lip read."

This admission startled Adama. Even more startling was that he'd never thought of that before. "All right," was all he said.

"So I wanted you to know . . . she was lying." She hesitated and for a moment even looked slightly confused. "I just . . . I wanted you to know that. I thought it might help you." Then, as if rallying from self-doubts, she said more forcefully, "Because that's what I do here. I help you. That's *all* I do," she added pointedly . . . a point that did not elude Adama.

"How do you know she was lying?"

"Because I can tell."

"That's not an answer."

"Maybe," she allowed, "but it's the best one you're going to get. I can tell. *We* can tell. There's certain ways to determine when a hu—" She caught herself and amended, "when someone . . . lies. We're trained to see them, spot them. Take advantage of them."

"Trained?"

"Maybe that's the wrong word. It's . . . hardwired into us. One of the tools of our trade, so to speak."

"And I'm supposed to believe you?"

She smiled thinly. "You're not 'supposed' to do anything, Admiral. You can do whatever you want. I'm just telling you what I know."

"In order to help."

"That's right."

He considered that for a brief time. Then he said, "Let's say . . . for the sake of argument . . . that I believe you. What do you suggest I do with this information?"

Sharon shrugged. "I don't know. Get the truth from her, I suppose."

This time the pause from Adama was far longer, his eyes studying her with calculated coldness. Two of his people were in trouble, and the reason they were in trouble was because he had sent them into the situation in the first place. So it was bad enough that he was dealing with the sense of personal responsibility over having thrust them into harm's way. He didn't feel guilty over it; putting soldiers of his, even beloved ones—hell, especially beloved ones—into jeopardy was simply another day at the office for him. He wasn't second-guessing his decision. Given the same circumstances, he'd do the exact same thing again. Nevertheless, his sense of personal involvement was even sharper since difficulties had arisen from a specific mission upon which he had dispatched two of his people, as opposed to ordering pilots into the air to defend against an unexpected Cylon assault.

He had no hesitation, none, about sending in armed troops to get them back. After all, he had been willing to throw his pilots against the *Pegasus* in order to retrieve Helo and Chief Tyrol when Admiral Cain had been ready to have them executed. But if there were ways in which to resolve the situation that didn't risk yet another incident that the press could transform into *Galactica*-against-the-fleet, he was more than willing to pursue them.

Adama was starting to think that Sharon Valerii was hinting she might serve as that means of resolution.

"Are you suggesting," he asked slowly, "that you would be capable of getting that truth from her?"

Her eyes narrowed. "I wasn't suggesting that, no."

"I see."

The seconds of silence stretched out.

And finally, Sharon said, "But if I were . . . what's in it for me?"

At that moment, things that Tigh had said to him came back to him. How it was that, despite everything that had happened, Adama still looked at Sharon Valerii and saw Boomer, the eager, ready-to-please young recruit and pilot whom Adama and Tigh couldn't help but have a fatherly enjoyment of and tolerance for. When she'd become inappropriately involved with Chief Tyrol, the bulk of their anger about such a relationship had been focused on Tyrol rather than Valerii, even though they were both equally responsible.

As insane as it sounded, despite the fact that his chest had been ripped open by several shots delivered at point-blank range by a creature who was identical to this one . . . a creature now dead, and yet here she was hale and hearty and pregnant, of all things . . . despite the fact that he knew in his heart of hearts that she was nothing more than a machine, an automaton, a damned frakking toaster . . . despite all of that, he still couldn't help but feel as if she were still good ol' Boomer, the utterly human Sharon Valerii.

But the individual who had just asked the question, "What's in it for me?" was not Sharon Valerii, nor was she Boomer. Right there, right then, was the calculation and coldness of a Cylon agent: detached, unemotional, deliberating as to what would be required in order to complete a mission that would potentially bring misfortune to a human being . . . misfortune that didn't bother Sharon in the least, because she wasn't remotely human.

He should have turned away. He should have been repulsed and revolted over the slightest notion of embarking on any endeavor in league with this . . . thing.

But he didn't. Because instead of simply surrendering to the notion that this was indeed some unemotional, calculating inhuman machine which feigned every emotion in service of its greater goal of sabotage, Adama decided to say something just to see how she would react.

"One of the people taken prisoner on the *Bifrost* is Starbuck." He hesitated for a carefully timed moment and then said, "The other is Helo."

And there it was.

The coldness of the Cylon that she was at the moment instantly dissolved into the Sharon Valerii that she once had been . . . back before Adama knew her to be anything other than Sharon Valerii. Telling her that Starbuck was in trouble gained her interest. Telling her that the father of her child was endangered engaged her heart.

So apparently . . . she had one.

Her face paled, her eyes widened, and he saw a sharp little intake of breath. Quickly she tried to cover it, but he'd seen it. More than that: She knew he'd seen it.

"Does that change things at all?" he asked, knowing the answer before he asked it.

"It . . . provides some incentive." She considered the situation carefully, obviously turning over all its aspects in her mind, and then said, "Are you interested in a deal?"

"I don't bargain with Cylons," he replied. Then, before she could say anything, he added, "But if I did . . . hypothetically . . . what sort of terms are we talking about?"

* * *

Sharon Valerii had had a lousy night's sleep.

She had been dreaming of Laura Roslin . . . and she didn't know why.

She had seen herself lying flat on her back, tied down to a bed in sickbay. Her stomach had been flat and taut, not at all the swelling lump it was now. She had struggled to free her hands and feet, but they were too well secured. She had tried shouting at the top of her lungs, but even though her mouth was wide open and she was trying to scream, nothing was emerging from her throat.

And then Laura Roslin had walked in, and Sharon had gaped at her in complete shock. Roslin's belly was swelled with pregnancy, as far along as Sharon's own. More than that: She knew without the slightest doubt that it was hers—Sharon's—child within Laura Roslin's body. She had no idea how it could possibly be that she was no longer the mother of her own child, and yet that was what had happened.

Laura had stood there, smiling, affectionately rubbing the child that she had taken from Sharon, and she cooed, "Mine now. All mine. Alllllll mine."

*Give it back! Give me back my baby!* Sharon's voice had echoed in her own mind. She felt as if she were moving in slow motion, trying to swim through heavy, viscous liquid, and Laura Roslin turned and waddled away, singing some annoying human lullaby.

Sharon had woken up at that point, her clothes soaked in cold sweat, gasping for air. A guard had charged in in response to her outcry, but he wasn't remotely concerned about her well-being. Instead it was abundantly clear that he was wary of some sort of trick on her part. "What's wrong?" he had demanded, the business end of his rifle aimed—not directly at her—but certainly in her general direction.

She had gasped out, "Nothing. Bad dream. It . . . was

nothing," and he'd glared at her for a time and then turned and walked out.

As silly as it sounded, she'd actually jostled her stomach to make sure the baby was still there. Despite the obvious distention of her belly, she wasn't taken anything for granted. That's how disturbing and confusing the dream had been. So she had shaken her stomach repeatedly until the baby—who'd presumably been asleep—offered a kick in protest. It was at that point that she gave a relieved sigh and settled back in her bunk.

But she had not fallen back to sleep.

Instead she had lain there and stewed on her situation, and although yes, it had all been a dream, she found herself being irrevocably drawn back to a grim and depressing realization: She had nothing. Anything that she possessed—even something as inviolable as the bond between mother and child—could be taken away from her at a moment's notice and a president's whim.

Ever since the first visit from Freya Gunnerson, she had nursed the notion that maybe, through some miracle, Freya could prevail. Perhaps it was possible. Perhaps she could indeed achieve for Sharon some measure of freedom, some claim upon happiness. But her thoughts in those dark hours had turned bleak and frustrated. She knew the dream itself was not, could not, be real. That didn't prevent her from connecting with the emotions and fears that were the underlying motivators for it.

Despite the fact that there was a child within her, she had never felt more alone.

Her foul mood had not dissipated during the day, and it was at that point that Freya had unfortunately chosen to show up and share with Sharon her latest views and theories on her case. When Sharon had lashed out at Freya, allowing her deep frustration with her situation to fuel her hostility, she had almost enjoyed the comic look of confusion in Freya's face.

Almost.

Part of her was still angry with herself. After all, this had been the first individual in ages who had shown herself remotely interested in Sharon's welfare. So why was she lacing into Freya, of all people?

She had to think it was because she had come to the conclusion that her situation was not only hopeless, but it was obviously hopeless, and anyone who didn't realize that . . . well, there was simply something wrong with them. They were stupid on a genetic level. That being the case, why should Sharon be wasting any time at all with them?

And then . . . then Adama had shown up.

And she'd learned of the situation that had developed on the *Bifrost*.

And she'd learned who was involved in it.

And that had focused her attentions in a new direction.

So it was that when Freya Gunnerson was escorted back into the cell area that Sharon Valerii occupied, Sharon fixed her with a level and very disconcerting gaze. Adama, to Freya's clear surprise, was no longer there. All bluster and annoyance, Freya said loudly to the marine escorting her—as if she were hard of hearing, or as if she were playing to an audience in imaginary balconies—"I don't know what you think you're doing! You have no legal right to hold me here!"

"I know," said the marine. "I'm just sick about that."

There was a second marine backing him up, and Freya looked around in confusion as the marine escorting her unlocked Sharon's cell. The second marine kept his weapon leveled on Sharon lest she, for some reason, decide to charge the door in what would certainly be a suicidal escape attempt. Sharon stayed right where she was. Freya was shoved into the cell with her and the door locked behind her.

"What's this supposed to mean?" she demanded. "What, we're *both* Adama's prisoners now? Is that it?"

Neither marine said anything. Instead they walked

out of the room, the heavy door slamming shut behind them.

"Oh, they'll fry for this," Freya told Sharon. She glanced around the cell as if seeing such an enclosure from the inside out was a huge novelty. Perhaps it was. Sharon had had plenty of time to become accustomed to it, so the "charm" had pretty much worn off. "I'm telling you, Sharon, they're going to fry, the lot of them. Adama's military-industrial complex has gone too far this time. Too far by half. They think they can silence protest or run roughshod over individual liberties, but when I get through with them—"

"Shut up."

Freya looked taken aback. "I beg your pardon?"

"Shut up . . . and listen."

There was something in Sharon's voice, a . . . deadliness . . . that completely seized Freya's attention.

Sharon took a deep breath and let it out. "You lied to the Admiral. You're not going to be allowed to lie to me. If you know what's good for you, you're going to tell me what's going on, and you're going to tell me now."

"Sharon, this is—"

"If you don't know what's good for you," Sharon continued, unfazed, "then you're going to give me grief, and you're going to stonewall . . . but you're still going to wind up telling me, because I'm going to make you do so. Do you understand what I'm saying?"

"Obviously I do. I'm not stupid. And it's perfectly clear what's happening. You think that you have to throw your lot in with Adama and his ilk because you don't have a chance when it comes to fighting for your own interests." She smiled in a way that was an odd combination of sufferance and pity. "Sharon, Sharon, Sharon . . . you're underestimating what a careful program of legal savvy and public relations manipulation is capable of producing. I didn't have a chance to show you my nine-point plan to—"

She didn't get any further. Sharon's right hand

stabbed out and seized her around the windpipe. Freya's eyes were round white orbs of shock and terror, and Sharon told her in low, measured tones, "Okay . . . obviously you didn't understand what I said, which would seem to indicate that, yes, you are stupid. Normally that would be your problem. Now I'm making it mine."

Sharon took a step forward and shoved Freya back. Even though she was a couple of heads shorter than Freya, there was no disputing who was the stronger. Freya, having no say in the matter at all, was slammed back against the cell walls, which rattled under the impact. She let out a cry. Sharon didn't care. Instead her eyes burned with fearsome intensity and her fingers worked their chokehold around Freya's windpipe. Freya tried to cry out a second time and this time around she wasn't even able to inhale the required air.

"Listen very carefully," Sharon Valerri told her, and there was no mercy in her voice and less than none in her eyes. "You need to understand your situation: You are locked in a cell with a Cylon. Do you understand that? A Cylon. Not a human. Not one of your own. A Cylon. And Cylons do not hesitate to do whatever the frak we feel like doing in order to accomplish our own ends. You are going to talk to me. If you do not . . . I am going to hurt you. I am going to hurt you in ways that you didn't know you *could* be hurt. I have a thorough and intimate knowledge of human anatomy and I am not afraid to use it. There are places on your body where applying the slightest pressure will visit agonies upon you that you will not have believed possible. And there will not be a mark on you to show an adjudicator or a Council member or the president herself. But the recollection of the pain you will suffer will stay with you forever. It will stay with you until old age, presuming you live that long, and on nights when you go to bed convinced that you've finally, finally left it behind you, on those nights you're going to wake up screaming and your old nightmares will be back to haunt you. And in those worst nightmares, you're going to see my frakking face looking at you with the most inhuman expression of detachment you've ever seen.

"I will torture you for information and I absolutely will not give a goddamn about it. I can do that, you see. Nice advantage over humans. I can just turn my emotions off and do what needs to be done.

"And I will do that to you.

"Now talk to me about what I want to know . . . and don't stop until I've told you I don't want to know any more." As a perverse afterthought, she added, "Please."

She released the pressure on Freya's throat slightly on the assumption that Freya would start talking.

Instead Freya snarled in her face, "F-frak you," and launched wad of spittle that landed squarely on Sharon's left temple. Sharon made no move to brush it away.

"And we're off," Sharon said softly.

Outside the cell, the marines heard the screams start. They weren't Sharon's. The guards stared at each other, and silently exchanged a question: *Are we going to do something about that?*

After a few long moments, they did do something about it: One of them went off to get some earplugs while the other remained at his post and whistled idle tunes softly to himself.

And he listened to the screams.

He hated to admit to himself how much he liked the sounds of them. He wondered if it made him a bad person.

Ultimately he decided that, if it did, that was okay.

He could live with that.

# CHAPTER 19

Laura Roslin was doing an admirable job of keeping her cool, which provided a sharp contrast to Tom Zarek. She sat behind her desk, her fingers steepled, her level gaze on Zarek, whose renowned cool under pressure was showing its first signs ever of melting.

"You can't be blaming me for this bloody mess," Zarek told her fiercely.

Laura tried not to flinch at his use of the word "bloody." Images from her dreams still had considerable force to her, and she was bound and determined not to let any of her haunted nights impede her ability to deal with the current situation. She couldn't remember the last time she'd slept for more than two hours straight, and inwardly she lived in fear that some new delusion was going to present itself to her and make her unable to handle whatever problem she was embroiled in.

Outwardly, she wasn't presenting the slightest hint of her inner doubts. "They're your people, Councilman."

"They're from Sagittaron, Madame President. That doesn't make them 'my people.' "

"You brought him in here. Brought him to my office,

with high-flown words of how they deserved respect and proper treatment. How they were discriminated against because of their beliefs. And now it turns out they're nothing but terrorists."

"That is not true," Zarek said forcefully. "They have a grievance . . ."

"So do terrorists."

"They're the injured parties here, Madame President. Gunnerson is asserting that members of *Galactica* are responsible for one of their most precious artifacts going missing."

"If Mr. Gunnerson had a dispute with the military, and he wanted to be treated like a civilized member of society, then he could have come to me."

"With all respect, Madame President, the last time *you* had a major dispute with the military, Adama threw your ass in a cell and nearly demolished the fleet. So in my view you don't exactly have a stainless record when it comes to such matters."

The blush of her cheeks shone a bit brighter against her makeup. "One wonders how that would have come out if you *hadn't* been speaking with all respect."

Zarek started to speak again, but then reined himself in. "I'm sorry," he said, which were two words that she certainly hadn't expected to hear him utter anytime in their relationship. "That was uncalled for. Not . . . entirely irrelevant, but uncalled for nevertheless."

She inclined her head slightly in acknowledgment of the apology, as half-hearted as it was. "The point remains, Councilman," she said evenly, "that we have an explosive situation on our hands. Adama is champing at the bit to get in there and get his people back," which wasn't entirely true. Certainly Adama was monitoring things and she'd been talking to him extensively about it. But Adama wasn't anxious to have yet another incident on his hands, and as long as his officers weren't in immediate threat of losing their lives, he was willing to hold off taking action and instead allow diplomatic efforts to proceed. There was no reason for her to tell Zarek that, though. "I want to sort this out as much as you do, Councilman. There are human lives at stake, and besides, I've currently got every reporter in the fleet packed into my press room howling for a statement."

"Let me go over to the *Bifrost*," said Zarek. When she shook her head, he said more forcefully, "I'm their representative, Madame President. I have some degree of relationship with their leader. In fact, I was over there earlier, before this business began. I'm the logical person . . ."

"You're the logical person to be an even better hostage, Mr. Zarek," Roslin reminded him. "You're not an outsider anymore. Like it or not, you're a man of influence. A member of the Quorum. That gives you a certain amount of trade value. I'm not interested in handing them yet another chip. Their ship is embargoed for the duration and that's the end of it."

"Then at least let me talk to them."

"Gladly," she said, "provided they were willing to talk to us. Our initial attempts have received no response . . ."

With timing that Laura Roslin would look back upon as being almost supernatural, Billy knocked and entered the room without being told to do so. "Wolf Gunnerson of the *Bifrost* on the line for you, Madame President," he said, clearly trying to deliver the news in as dispassionate and professional a manner as he could.

Roslin and Zarek exchanged looks. "People will surprise you," Zarek said calmly.

"Record the call," she told Billy.

He nodded. "Recorder is already on."

For a heartbeat she considered conferencing Adama in on the call. She quickly discarded the notion, not because she didn't trust him to remain cool in the situation, but because she preferred to hold him in reserve as a possible club. *I'm not sure how much longer I can hold the admiral in check* was going to play better if Adama wasn't actually in on the conversation sounding firm but reasonable.

She took a deep breath, let it out slowly, and then picked up the phone. In deference to Zarek, she pushed a button so that a speaker was activated. That way Zarek could listen to what was being said, although he couldn't be heard himself. "This is President Roslin."

"Madame President," came Wolf's voice. "Thank you for taking my call."

"Thank you for calling," she said formally.

"So . . . it appears we have a bit of a predicament on our hands."

He didn't sound especially threatening. They might just as easily have been chatting about each other's respective health. "I would categorize it as somewhat more serious than that," she said. "I hope you don't think this is some sort of game, Mr. Gunnerson."

"No, Madame President, I most certainly do not. The most obvious difference is that games have clear winners and losers. If matters spiral out of control, we will have nothing *but* losers."

Roslin wouldn't have said it aloud, but Gunnerson was sounding amazingly reasonable about it. It was hard to remember that he was the one who had set this entire fiasco into motion. Although the chances were that he would have come right back and said that Adama was the one responsible.

She knew perfectly well the reason that Adama had sent two of his people onto the *Bifrost*. Adama had been most efficient in keeping her apprised of his actions. The problem was that she had no way of knowing whether this entire issue with the Edda was some sort of trumped-up maneuver to try and distract from the business at hand. She wondered if Gunnerson even knew that they had a possible Cylon agent on board, although admittedly she was still having trouble believing that the boy was an operative. Roslin had to think that making no mention of Boxey was the best way to go, particularly if Gunnerson didn't bring him up.

Zarek, hearing what Gunnerson was saying, nodded and gave Roslin an encouraging thumbs-up. She tried not to roll her eyes at that. As if she needed moral support and pep talks from Tom Zarek, of all people. "I'm pleased to hear you say that, Mr. Gunnerson. This matter needs to be resolved immediately by the release of the colonial officers."

"I would love to comply with you, but I can't at this time. Not until I know what the status of the Edda is."

"You have my personal guarantee, sir, that the two officers had nothing to do with it."

"And my people have my personal guarantee," he replied, "that I will take every step to ensure the Edda's return. Releasing two prime suspects—whom I assure you will not be harmed—would be counterproductive, wouldn't you say?"

"I would say, Mr. Gunnerson, that if you have the slightest hope of the Midguardians becoming members of the Quorum, then you have to release Admiral Adama's people. Certainly you see that your actions won't sit well with the Quorum."

"That is only because I'm not making my case to the Quorum itself. Were I to do so, I believe I could make them understand not only why I'm being forced to take this action, but why we should be given our rightful place in the hierarchy of the colonies."

"I am making endeavors in that direction, Mr. Gunnerson, but they will be completely undone if this is allowed to continue. All we have is your word that the colonial soldiers will remain unharmed. You've no way of guaranteeing that . . ."

There was no response from the other end.

"Mr. Gunnerson?" She flashed a look of concern in Zarek's direction. He shook his head, his face blank. Obviously he had no clearer idea than Roslin of why Gunnerson had suddenly gone silent. "Mr. Gunnerson, are you still—"

"Sorry. Sorry, Madame President," his voice came back, and he quickly added, "And I'm sorry I interrupted you just then."

"It's quite all right." She kept the relief out of her voice. "Go ahead."

"I was just thinking: There's an easy solution to this, other than freeing the suspects."

"It's not readily apparent."

"Allow me to come to *Colonial One* and address the assembled Quorum."

She was startled at the notion. Zarek was quickly nodding enthusiastically, but a silent look from her stopped him. She glanced toward Billy, who shrugged noncommittally. "Mr. Gunnerson, we are not going to allow ourselves to be strong-armed into meeting with you."

"No one is strong-arming anyone, Madame President. I am volunteering myself in what could reasonably be viewed as a hostage exchange. You are asking me to place myself into a weaker position by releasing the suspects. I am instead offering to put you into a stronger position by voluntarily coming over there. Strong-arming? I would be counting on your good offices to allow me to meet with the assembled Quorum rather than, say, turn me over to Adama to be tossed into a holding cell."

"I could still do that, you know."

"Yes, but I would believe you if you said you wouldn't. I would take your word for it. I am that determined to have my chance to speak to the Quorum and make my case on behalf of my people."

Zarek gestured that she should put Gunnerson on hold a moment so that he could speak to her. Her immediate instinct was to ignore him. It wasn't as if she needed Tom Zarek to tell her what to do. On the other hand, she *had* brought him here as the Sagittaron representative, so it probably wasn't going to hurt to hear what he had to say. "Mr. Gunnerson, please hold on," she said, placed him on hold and then said brusquely, "What?"

If Zarek was put off by her tone, he didn't let it show. "What have you got to lose?" he said, trying to sound reasonable. "We both know we're on the clock. Adama may be—"

"*Admiral* . . . Adama," she corrected him. She had been the one who had given him the rank, and she found she didn't like Zarek simply referring to the fleet's CO simply by his surname. It struck her as disrespectful.

Taking it in stride, he amended, "Admiral Adama may be willing to wait, but he's not going to do so forever. If Gunnerson is here, that could well buy us more time. The longer a hostage situation goes on, the better chance there is having it ended with words instead of casualties."

"And you would know."

"Yes," he said crisply, "I would."

She tapped a thoughtful finger on the desk, and then took the call off hold. "Mr. Gunnerson, are you still there?"

"Still here, Madame President."

She realized she was rolling the dice with the Quorum. She was counting on Sarah Porter and Tom Zarek, of all men, to make this happen. As president she could call a meeting of the Quorum but she was not constitutionally empowered to force them to show up. It was part of the checks and balances built into the constitution, to guarantee that the president would always have to use tact and diplomacy in her dealings rather than strong-arming the representatives of the people. Of course, the constitution—or at least the original copies of it, preserved from its original drafting—had been blown to bits by the Cylons. Its spirit, however, lived on. "If you come here to *Colonial One*, I will ask the Quorum to assemble. You will be allowed to present your case to them. But what this will buy you, Mr. Gunnerson, is twelve hours. After twelve hours, barring credible evidence that they have committed some sort of crime, I will insist that officers Thrace and Agathon be released. And by credible evidence, I am ruling out confessions. I am not going to give anyone over there incentive to try forcing admissions of guilt out of them. If the officers are not released by that point, I will indeed turn you over to Admiral Adama, at which point, gods help us all."

There was another pause, but this time Roslin said nothing, allowing time for a response to come.

"Very well, Madame President," said Gunnerson finally. "Your terms are acceptable. I will take a transport to *Colonial One*. You will assemble the Quorum and I will speak my piece over allowing my people to be given official representation. In return I guarantee the safety of the colonial officers for twelve hours, as of which point they will then be returned, hale and hardy, to the *Galactica*."

It still didn't answer the issue of Boxey, but her priority at that point was ending the immediate situation without bloodshed. That was especially important to her. She knew to what extent Adama was willing to ensure the safety of his people. Furthermore, although she knew Adama didn't place higher priorities on some lives than others, she was aware that there was a particular bond between Adama and Kara Thrace. If anything happened to her while she was in the hands of the Midguardians, Roslin didn't even want to think what the ramifications might be. She was reasonably sure that Adama wouldn't simply turn the big guns of the *Galactica* on the *Bifrost* and blast it to pieces . . . but on the other hand, she wasn't interested in finding out.

"Very well. I will see you shortly. *Colonial One* out." She hung up the phone, looked over to Billy and said, "Send a copy of that recording to Admiral Adama immediately."

"Yes, ma'am."

Billy headed out, and Tom Zarek was promptly on his feet. "Madame President . . . we've had our differences . . . but I just want to say, I thought you handled that quite well."

"Tell me, Councilman," Roslin said, "in your honest opinion . . . what chance do you think there is that the Quorum will vote to give the Midguardians a seat on the Council?"

"There's always the chance that—"

"Honest. Opinion."

He hesitated and then admitted, "Very slim. Almost negligible."

"Yes. I agree. And do you think that Wolf Gunnerson knows that?"

"I think he's hoping otherwise, but I think he knows that, yes."

"Then why risk his personal liberty to pursue such a hopeless cause?"

"There are some people," said Zarek, "who consider the hopeless causes the only ones worth pursuing."

"Hmm. Yes," replied Roslin, sounding distant. "At the same time, pursuing a hopeless cause can mean someone feels they have nothing to lose. And people who have nothing to lose can be very . . ." She turned her attention back to Zarek.

He was bleeding out his eyeballs again.

". . . dangerous," she sighed.

# CHAPTER 20

Saul Tigh had commandeered a private room and sat there for hours upon hours, listening to the tapes that had been made by the recording devices he'd implanted in various rooms. Aside from the matter involving President Roslin that he had brought to Adama's attention, he had absolutely nothing to show for the hours of time invested. Not only that, but he had come to a depressing realization: Most people, when left to their own devices, were astoundingly boring. The amount of time they spent discussing completely trite and trivial subjects—it boggled the imagination.

It almost made him wonder what it would be like to bug get-togethers of Cylon agents. Did they spend it discussing far-reaching plans of galactic domination? Or did they just hang out discussing fashion, hair styles, and gossip? He was starting to think that scientists were wrong, and hydrogen was not in fact the most common element in the universe. No. It was banality.

The only one who seemed to spend any time at all concentrating on important matters was Mr. Gaeta, which was ironic considering he was one of the key people under suspicion. He didn't seem to have any social life at all. Instead he spent his off-duty hours in his quarters, going over calculations, making new ones, planning, always planning. He'd spend hours muttering to himself while he worked things out. Tigh might have been inclined to think that Gaeta was actually conversing with other Cylons, except that he was alone in his room. His room could have had a Cylon listening device in it, but Tigh—as he had done with every other room—had already swept it to make sure it was clean of bugs before he had placed his own in.

Tigh leaned back in his chair and removed the headset he'd been wearing to listen to the recordings. He rubbed his eyes, feeling the fatigue.

The pressure was getting to him. In trying to track down Cylons, he was starting to feel as if there were no safe haven. Cylons were invading peoples' lives, their very minds.

It made him start to wonder about . . .

"Anything?"

Tigh started slightly and looked up to see Adama standing in the doorway. He shook his head. "Nothing. Not since the earlier things we discussed."

Adama pulled up a chair and sat. "Getting to you, isn't it."

"I think it's getting to all of us." He rubbed his eyes. "If Roslin thinks she hasn't been sleeping well, she should get a load of me. How about you?"

"I sleep like a rock."

He opened his eyes narrowly and stared at Adama. "Technically, rocks don't sleep."

"There you go."

Tigh chuckled, but then grew serious. "What if . . ."

"What if what?"

"What if we find Earth . . . and it really isn't a safe haven? What if the Cylons track us there? Hell, what if the Cylons are waiting for us? What the hell is our Plan B, Bill?"

"Finding Earth *is* Plan B," said Adama. "Plan A is keeping humanity alive. Everything else is open to negotiation."

"That's a hell of a thing."

"Believe me, I know."

Tigh wrapped the wire around the headset and placed it in a drawer, along with the recorder he'd been using to listen to the recordings that were stacked neatly on the table. "Speaking of negotiations . . . what's happening with our people on the *Bifrost*?"

Adama told him what Laura Roslin had just relayed to him. Tigh's eyes widened as he heard about Gunnerson's heading over to *Colonial One*. "In fact," said Adama, glancing at his watch, "he's probably already over there."

"My gods, what are we waiting for?" Tigh demanded. "Let's go get him. Let's take charge of the bastard and start issuing some ultimatums of our own."

"Not yet," Adama said coolly. "We're going to see how it plays out on both ends."

"Both ends? What are you . . . ?" But then he understood. "Oh. You mean the Cylon and the lawyer." He shook his head, a grim smile on his face. "There's poetic justice in that, you know. A Cylon and a lawyer in a cell together. I've dealt with a lawyer or two in my time. Hard-pressed to see the difference."

Adama didn't share the amusement. Although he addressed Tigh, he seemed as if he were looking inward. "It's an evil thing I've done, Saul. Tossing Freya Gunnerson in with Sharon and looking the other way. Gunnerson is right. She broke no laws."

"She's up to something," Tigh said darkly. "Something about her interest in the Cylon stinks to high heaven, and we both know it."

"So she deserves what she gets?"

"Abso-frakking-lutely."

"I wish I were as sure as you."

"You could be," said Tigh. "You just choose not to be."

"And you don't let yourself get dragged down by uncertainty?"

"I try not to."

"You know something, Saul?" said Adama after giving him a long look. "You are more full of crap than any man I've ever met."

Tigh looked stunned a moment, as if he were wounded by the comment. But then he put his head back and laughed. Adama didn't join him, but he did allow a smile to play on his lips.

There was no hint of amusement, or annoyance, or pleasure, or any expression vaguely human on Sharon Valerii's lips. Her mouth was drawn back in a tight, tense manner, as if she were doing heavy exercise and was trying to focus.

Freya Gunnerson was lying on the floor. Sharon was standing over her, straddling her, a leg on either side. Freya was curled up in a ball, her arms encircling her head. She was whimpering, her body trembling.

There was not a mark on her body. Not anywhere.

A professional torturer would have been astounded at the quality of the job Sharon had done on Freya. To simply pound information out of people was . . . well, it was ugly. It was inelegant. It also presented the problem of being counterproductive, especially if the subject died from the questioning.

Sharon had not resorted to that. She hadn't needed to.

The truth was that she had not realized what she was capable of until she had started. It was as if she possessed certain capabilities, but hadn't accessed them until now because she simply hadn't needed them. Now that she did, though, they had come to her with as much ease as if she were to climb upon a bicycle after many years of not doing so and pedal away.

She knew every joint, every muscle, every pressure point in a human being's body. She knew just what to do with each of them, just how to play them against one another to induce mind-numbing agony. With absolute facility and efficiency, she could do something as simple as pop the gastrocnemius and soleus muscles in the calf, causing a small contusion inside. It didn't sound like much, but the agony that resulted in the recipient of the treatment was just overwhelming.

She was capable of inflicting agonizing little scenarios like that all over Freya's body. And she had been doing so.

And Freya had been screaming. Screaming and writhing and begging for mercy that seemed as if it would never come. Whenever it did—whenever Sharon appeared to be letting up—it was simply because she was working out some new thing to do to her.

Part of Sharon was repulsed by what she was doing. But another part of her was simply able to shut herself off, disconnect from it altogether. She found it vaguely disturbing that she was able to do that, but tried not to dwell on it.

She had taken a break, shaking out her hands, loosening up the fingers before she went back to work. Freya continued to lie sobbing upon the floor. Finally she managed to gasp out, "Okay."

Sharon had become so engrossed in her endeavors that she didn't have the slightest idea what Freya was saying okay to at first. Her eyebrows knit. "Okay . . . what?"

"Okay . . . I'll . . . I'll tell you," Freya managed to say. "I'll tell you what I did. I'll tell you everything. I'll do anything you want. Just stop, please . . ." She choked on the tears that ran into her mouth. "Stop . . . please . . ."

"All right," Sharon said dispassionately. "Tell me . . ."

"No," Freya was suddenly vehement, motivated by anger and fear and unbridled loathing. "I want Adama here."

"Why?" Then she answered her own question before

Freya could. "Because you're concerned that, once you've told me what I want to know, I'll kill you. So you want someone here to 'save' you from me."

Freya said nothing, but merely glowered instead.

She raised her voice slightly and called to whomever she knew was watching or listening in, "Please send Admiral Adama down. Thank you." Then she stepped back and settled down onto her bunk, her hands resting on her legs. She sat perfectly upright.

Freya managed to look up at her with pure hatred. "You're . . . you're not human."

"That's what everyone else was saying," Sharon reminded her. "Why didn't you listen?"

"Because I thought I . . . I could make a better life for you. Because I thought an injustice was being done, and I tried to fix it."

"And now?" asked Sharon, interested in spite of herself. "What do you think now?"

"I think," and a cold fury grew in her voice, "I think I wish . . . that you had a soul . . . because then it could burn in hell."

"How do you know I don't have one? How do you know it won't go to hell . . . or even heaven? Or maybe there's a different version of heaven that only allows Cylons?"

"There's not."

"You don't know that."

"There's not," Freya repeated, and suddenly, totally unexpectedly, she lunged at Sharon. Sharon's arm immediately crossed her belly to protect her unborn child as she lashed out with a boot, slamming Freya right between the eyes. Freya stumbled backwards, blood covering the lower half of her face. She fell heavily. Sharon continued to look down at her without the slightest change in expression as Freya lay there, clutching her nose, trying to stop the bleeding. After a moment, Sharon removed the flimsy pillow case from the pillow and tossed it down to Freya. It draped itself over her head. She snatched it off and applied it to her face, pressing against the bleeding, and moaning as she did so.

"That's going to leave a mark," said Sharon.

"Frak you," grunted her erstwhile attorney.

They remained that way, neither addressing the other, until Adama arrived in response to the summons. Two marines accompanied him as they came around to the door of the cell and opened it wide. The marines kept their weapons fixed on Sharon. It would have seemed ludicrous to any unknowing onlooker to see burly, heavily armed combat men aiming at the placid pregnant woman who was sitting empty-handed and seemingly harmless on her cot. What possible threat could she have posed? The problem was that they didn't really have an answer to that question, and thus they were determined to be safe rather than sorry.

Adama stared down at the woman on the floor who had previously been the arrogant, self-confident attorney. She looked like she had been through a horrible ordeal that transcended the injury to her face. She was sitting up, her back propped against the wall of the jail cell. There was a stark contrast between what she had been and what she was now. Adama hadn't especially liked her. She'd been a damned irritant and nuisance and too smugly superior by half. But he wouldn't have wished this on her.

*You are so full of crap,* he told himself. *You damned well wished this on her. You consigned her to this for convenience's sake. Don't pretend that you didn't want this. You knew this was inevitable. If you're going to walk a path, don't kid yourself that you stumbled down it by accident.*

He restrained himself from asking if she was all right because he knew he would simply get a sarcastic answer to the effect that he didn't care. That wasn't entirely true, but he wasn't about to put some sort of gloss on things. Instead, as curt and down-to-business as he could be, he said, "Well?"

Freya glared at him for a moment and then said, "I took it."

"It?"

"The Edda." She wiped blood from her nose and mouth and only succeeded in smearing it around her face. "What my father is looking for."

"Why?"

"Because," she said tersely, "I'm not stupid."

Adama waited, saying nothing.

"One of my responsibilities on my father's ship is traffic. I get the flight manifests of who's coming and who's going. The moment *Galactica* filed a flight manifest stating that two of Boxey's former cronies were coming over, I knew something was up."

"How did you know something was up?"

"Because you're a bastard," she snapped. "Because you wanted ties cut between Boxey and your precious pilots. So if they were heading to our ship, then that meant one of two things: Either you had decided that Boxey wasn't a threat, which meant you had changed your mind, which I assumed you hadn't since—"

"I'm a bastard," he said without inflection.

"—or you had decided he *was* a threat. If we'd refused entrance to them, that could have resulted in a direct attack from *Galactica* which we weren't prepared to repel. So I figured if the Edda disappeared while they were on the ship, suspicion would fall on them."

"So you took it upon yourself to try and frame my people. Show it to me."

"It's in my case. I have to take it out of there."

"Do so." And then, in acknowledgment of the marines standing near him, he added, "Slowly."

She nodded, understanding why it would be wise for her to exercise caution at every moment. Under the circumstances, any sudden motion could get her shot. The case, as it so happened, had slid under Sharon's bunk. She gestured for Sharon to give it over to her. Hooking the handle with her toe, Sharon slid it over to Freya, who flipped the snaps and—very carefully—opened it. She removed several folders filled with papers, set them aside, and then removed a false bottom to the case. Lifting it out, she was aware that the marines were watching her with fearsome intensity. Her hand trembled slightly and she didn't make another move until she was able to will it to stop. Then she lifted a small but thick volume from the briefcase and extended it toward Adama. Adama gestured for one of the marines to retrieve it. He did so, then stepped back and handed it to the admiral.

The book smelled of age, and there was an inscription on the cover in letters that Adama couldn't read. Opening it carefully, lest any of the pages fall out, he turned the pages carefully. The letters were incomprehensible, written in a language he hadn't the slightest familiarity with.

A snorted laugh from Freya caught his attention. He peered over the top of the book at her. "Do you find something amusing?"

"Other than that you're holding it upside down, you mean?"

Adama didn't bother to turn the book over. It wasn't as if it would suddenly have made sense if he had done so. Instead he closed it and then, in a calculatedly cavalier fashion, tossed it to her. She let out a gasp and lunged at it, snagging it before it hit the floor. Clearly shaken by her holy book nearly striking the ground, she clutched it to her, and then looked daggers up at Adama.

He wasn't inclined to give a damn. "Odd how you care so much about the rules of law . . . until they're inconvenient for you."

"The fleet still doesn't entirely trust you, no matter how much reporters from Fleet News Service sing your praises," said Freya. "I played on that in the name of protecting an innocent young boy from your investigations. I didn't want to see him treated the way you treated her . . ." and she glared at Sharon, ". . . although I admit at this point I don't give a damn what you do to that . . . creature."

"You decided you could use my people as a bargaining chip."

"Yes."

He took a step toward her, lancing her with a glare. The sheer hypocrisy of one who purported to be so morally superior to him, using his people in a game as if they were poker chips . . . it infuriated him. With a stoic demeanor born of long practice, he said, "It may interest you to know that your father is, as we speak, en route to *Colonial One.* He's presenting himself as a bargaining chip in order to make up for what turns out to be his daughter's subterfuge."

Her eyes widened. "He did that . . . ?"

"Yes, Miss Gunnerson. He did exactly that. Perhaps the next time you play games with people's lives, you'll want to make certain that all the pieces are in their correct place."

She didn't respond. Instead her head sank back and she closed her eyes. She had put her hand against her nose to stop the bleeding and she had more or less succeeded.

The marines were clearly waiting for their instructions. Adama didn't waste any time. "I'm going to send advance word back to your vessel that you have your book, along with a recording of this session so they'll know precisely what you did. Then marines will escort you back to your vessel. I want you off my ship."

Sharon looked up for the first time and registered surprise. "Off . . . ?"

"You heard me."

"But . . ."

She began to stand and the marines instantly tensed. Sharon froze in a half crouch and then, very slowly, sat down on the cot once more. "With all due respect, Admiral . . . are you sure that's wise?"

*No. It may be unspeakably stupid. But President Roslin is trying to defuse a delicate situation, and I want the meeting with the Quorum to have as few distractions as possible. So even though I may be throwing in a bargaining chip that I could have made good use of, I'm going to send her back to her ship with her tail between her legs in order to make sure that Wolf Gunnerson doesn't go off the deep end because his daughter's in the hands of the military.*

He made no answer. Instead he made a curt gesture with his head to the marines. They slammed the door to Sharon's cell shut with a resounding clang, and led Freya out at gunpoint. As they headed for the exit from the brig area, Sharon suddenly lumbered to her feet, cupped her hands around her mouth, and shouted, "Who's the bigger bastard, Admiral! You or me? Especially considering that I—as I'm always being reminded—am not human! We had a deal, Admiral! We had a frakking deal! And you'd better come through on your end or . . ."

He stopped, turned and faced her. He never raised his voice, which would have made it difficult to hear him. But he spoke slowly enough that the movement of his lips was unmistakable as he said, ". . . or what?"

Sharon had no answer. Nevertheless, she remained standing until Adama, Freya Gunnerson, and the marines exited the area. The last thing she saw of them was Freya making an obscene gesture in her direction. Sharon didn't return it.

Colonel Tigh would have been interested to know that he wasn't much happier than Sharon Valerii had been with Adama's decision. Adama, wisely, had chosen to apprise him of it when both of them were on CIC. He had obviously known that Tigh would never raise any kind of major fuss about it with the rest of the command personnel there, which made it ideal for Adama if he didn't feel like getting into ten rounds of "Why the frak did you do that?!" with his second in command.

So Tigh had held his tongue and his reaction, although he knew that Adama had maneuvered him into having to do so, and he made sure—with as many subtle hints and signals as he could—that Adama knew that he knew. Of course, in the end, Adama didn't *care*, which pretty much trumped the entire issue.

This left Tigh in CIC fuming over the ongoing situation that continued to leave them vulnerable to another Cylon ambush. He found that he was staring for ages and ages at every single person in CIC. Sooner or later another one of his people would realize that he was staring at them, but it wasn't as if they could complain about it. What could they possibly say? "Colonel, please stop looking at me." It would sound ridiculous.

Even more ridiculous was that he was doing it in the first place. It wasn't as if he was expecting one of them to suddenly collapse to their knees and begin sobbing, "I'm sorry! I can't stand the pressure anymore! I'm a Cylon! I confess! Shoot me now before I endanger the fleet!"

It left Tigh with a vague sense of frustration. The investigation had gone nowhere, leaving him feeling impotent and confused.

How could it possibly be? He was certain none of these people were Cylons. They were the hardest-working officers he'd ever had the privilege to have under his command. They were loyal, honest, unafraid to speak truth to power. Even though he knew the dim opinion of him that was held by many, they continued to treat him with respect, at least to his face.

Look there at Dualla. Constantly monitoring communications, staying on top of everything. Her logs were meticulous. Yes, it was possible that she was falsifying something, or perhaps sending communications to the Cylons, but he just couldn't believe it. Then again—he reminded himself—would he have thought such a thing of Boomer before it was revealed that she was a Cylon? Well . . . yeah. Yeah, truth to tell. He'd always had suspicions that something was off with her. Not that she was a Cylon necessarily because, hell, how could he have known that the Cylons looked like humans now? But she hadn't been quite right. He'd used to think his opinions of her were colored by her illicit affair with Chief Tyrol. It always seemed that when something was going wrong or something was being covered up, Sharon Valerii was in the middle of it. So when the explosive revelation had been made, through her attempt on the Old Man's life, that she was a Cylon agent, Tigh had been shocked but not *too* shocked.

But Dualla? Straight arrow all the way. Yes, he knew she and the president's aide had a thing brewing, but there was nothing untoward about that.

And then there was Gaeta.

Tigh's attention swung over to the ship's young tactical officer. He'd served Adama for three years, as officer of the watch in addition to his other duties. If Gaeta had been an enemy agent, certainly he could have brought Adama down in flames long before this. Things didn't just happen for no reason. Look at Gaeta, at his station, working hard on new coordinates, having dumped the previous ones for fear that perhaps somehow the Cylons had managed to find out about them. Standing there, muttering to himself as he developed a new escape plan should the Cylons attack, scratching away at his hand . . .

Tigh suddenly stopped. He frowned. He took a step toward Gaeta, who wasn't paying any attention to him, so lost in his work was he. Gaeta continued to mutter calculations, making certain that the coordinates would bring them to safety rather than disaster. It was at that point Tigh realized that Gaeta always did that: always spoke softly to himself to help focus his attention on whatever he happened to be doing.

*No. It couldn't be that simple.*

Waiting for his call to be put through to the *Bifrost*, Adama was watching Tigh with open curiosity. He imagined he could almost see the wheels turning in Tigh's head, but he wasn't entirely certain in what direction they were spinning.

At that moment, Dualla called out, "Admiral . . . Starbuck on the line."

Deciding that whatever was up with Tigh could wait until later, Adama picked up the phone and, said, "Starbuck? Are you and Helo all right?"

"Couldn't be better, Admiral," came her pleased voice. "We're hearing from our jailers that Freya Gunnerson is now stating she's the one who took their precious book."

"That's correct."

He knew that Starbuck would be able to tell from his tone that there was more to the story than that. He also knew that she would be well aware not to ask about it. "There's some skepticism being expressed by our captors over it."

"That should evaporate when she shows up with the book in hand. Her escorts will make sure she presents it." He paused and then said, "What's the status of your visit?"

"Well, the young fellow we came to visit appears to have gotten kind of shy." She said it lightly, as if they were discussing something of little to no consequence. "We thought we would hang out until he shows up again."

"Is the environment conducive to that?"

"I think it will be, once we've been cleared," she replied carefully. "In spite of everything that's happened, I'm still very anxious to hook up with the young man."

"All right . . . if you think you can handle it."

He knew what the answer was going to be even as he said it: a curt laugh from Kara Thrace, followed by a brisk, "No problem on this end, Admiral. We'll have the little scamp in hand before you know it."

"Very well. And Starbuck . . . be careful."

"I always am, sir."

"*Galactica* out."

He hung up the phone, knowing full well that Kara Thrace had many admirable qualities, but being careful never was, and never would be, one of them. He wanted her to be all right. He wanted her to live to a ripe old age. But he knew in his heart that that wasn't how Kara Thrace was going to exit this plane of existence. She was going to go out in a ball of fire, howling defiance and laughing in death's face the entire time.

"It's too bad she won't live," he said so softly that no one else heard him. "But then again . . . who does?"

# CHAPTER 21

Wolf Gunnerson was aghast at what Laura Roslin had just told him.

He had been given quite decent visitor's accommodations when he had arrived on *Colonial One*, considering the circumstances. Laura Roslin had come to meet with him once he was settled in, and delivered him the news that Adama had conveyed to her. She watched him carefully to see if there was the slightest hint of duplicity in his face as he reacted to what she was telling him.

She had to admit, if he was acting, he was wonderfully accomplished at it. The blood drained from his face, and he looked as if he was starting to have heart palpitations. "Freya took it? *Freya* . . . ?" He rocked back in the chair that was far too small for him and groaned under his weight. "I can't understand . . . what would possess her . . . ?"

"I couldn't begin to say," Roslin said, trying to be as diplomatic as possible. "Nevertheless, the fact remains: She has it in her possession. She is being turned over to the authorities on your vessel even as we speak. That aspect of this . . . crisis . . . appears to be settled."

"So it does." He was still looking like a man in shock. "That she could do such a thing . . . put a couple of innocent soldiers under the light of suspicion. You think you know your own child, and then . . ." He shook his head, discouraged, and then looked up at Roslin. "Do you have children of your own?"

"No."

"They bring great joy, but also great heartache. This is obviously one of the moments of heartache. What must the Quorum think of me?"

"They will think you were deceived," she said, still trying to choose as delicate phrasing as she could. "It can happen to anyone. In fact, I daresay it's happened to everyone at some time or another."

"I certainly hope they will still be willing to meet with me," said Wolf Gunnerson. "I mean, I can see how you could turn around and send me back to the *Bifrost*, dismissing me out of hand."

"That's not going to happen," she said. "In fact—believe it or not—this has had a positive effect on the meeting you requested."

"Has it?" He seemed anxious to hear some benefit from what he clearly perceived to be a gargantuan fiasco.

"Yes. There were two members of the Quorum who were still holding out, contending that they were being strong-armed into this meeting because of the hostage situation. With that no longer being a factor, they have acceded to the will of the majority and are going to be attending. In fact, everyone should be here shortly. You will receive a fair hearing."

"That is all I have ever asked," he said politely.

It was hard for her to believe that a man this large was capable of being so soft spoken. "There's been a recent development."

"Oh?" He raised a bushy eyebrow. "What now? My daughter has announced she has a bomb and intends to obliterate us all?"

"Hardly," she said. "A reporter who has been supportive of the administration has asked to have an exclusive interview with you."

"The press traditionally isn't friendly to my cause. I'm not sure of the advantage . . ."

"The advantage is that she has sworn to give you a platform to speak your mind and get your beliefs out to the populace."

Wolf still looked suspicious. "Can she be trusted?"

"She was given complete access to all levels of *Galactica* and came back with a story that was extremely even-handed. Even Admiral Adama was satisfied with it, and he's not exactly the easiest of audiences to satisfy."

Her description of the previous story caught Wolf's interest. "I believe I saw that coverage. That was . . . Diana Bears, was it?"

"D'anna Biers," she politely corrected him. "She's right outside with her cameraman, ready to talk to you if you'd be willing to permit it. By the time you're done, the Quorum should be assembled in the main conference room."

"She would follow us there as well?"

"Several members of the press will be there," said Laura Roslin. "I think you'll find the members of the Quorum are more likely to be attentive and patient if they're on camera. And that's what you want them to be."

"Yes, of course. All right," he said with more conviction, as if he were working to convince himself. "Yes, send her in."

"Very well." She went to the door and opened it. "He'll speak to you," she called.

D'anna Biers, cheerful and professional, came through, followed by her cameraman, and said graciously to Laura, "My thanks, Madame President. I appreciate your putting in a good word for me."

"I simply told him the truth. The decision was his."

"My thanks just the same."

"Well then," smiled Laura. "I'll leave you to it." She exited, closing the door behind her.

D'anna Biers sat down and faced Wolf Gunnerson.

"So," she said. "History is going to be made today."

"That," replied Wolf with a carefully neutral expression, "is exactly the best way I could have put it."

"Are you ready to do it?"

"Absolutely. Are you?"

Her smiled widened, but it wasn't an entirely pleasant one. Instead it appeared almost predatory. "Actually . . . believe it or not . . . I've been waiting for it for a long, long time now."

Laura Roslin was sitting in her office, endeavoring to collect her thoughts, when Billy stuck his head in and informed her the vice president had arrived. "Why?" she sighed.

"He's reporting to you about the possibilities of side effects or after effects that could result from the . . . from the cure you received."

"He is?" She didn't recall asking him to. "Very well, send him in."

She knew she didn't have much time to spend on Baltar. After all, the members of the Quorum were busy arriving, and things were simply moving too quickly for her to slow things down by talking to Baltar. Besides, it wasn't as if he was her favorite person to speak with in the first place.

Roslin was still going through paperwork when Baltar's voice spoke up. "Admiral Adama asked me to undertake this investigation. I thought you might be interested in the results of my studies, Madame President."

She looked up, about to say, "And they would be . . . ?" but her voice froze in her throat.

Baltar was standing a few feet away from her, and right next to Baltar was the known Cylon operative, Shelly Godfrey. Or perhaps Gina. They were the same "model," after all.

Claiming to be a Defense Ministry systems analyst, "Shelly Godfrey" had shown up claiming that Gaius Baltar was a Cylon agent. Having failed in that attempt, she had vanished into hiding somewhere in the fleet and was still out there . . . except now, she appeared to be right here, right in front of Roslin. Naturally she also looked like "Gina," the same model of Cylon who had been a prisoner aboard the *Pegasus*. Tragically she had escaped and had gone on to murder Admiral Cain before likewise going into seclusion somewhere. It was a source of continuing frustration to Roslin that they could actually know what the damned toasters looked like and still be unable to capture them.

And now she was there, right there, next to Baltar. She was wearing a tight-fitting red dress, cut high at the hem, low at the top. Smirking, she was leaning on Baltar's shoulder.

Laura felt lightheaded, as if her brain was going to splatter in all directions. *This isn't happening . . . this isn't happening . . . gods dammit, this isn't happening . . .*

Baltar was puzzled at the confused look on Laura Roslin's face, but didn't dwell on it. If something was bothering her, certainly it was her problem, not his.

"Inconclusive, I'm afraid," he was saying. "Since you are, naturally, the only human test study, the chemical examinations I've done thus far, particularly in seeing how the hemoglobin interacts with the cancer cells I culled, I can see—"

"She's looking at you strangely, Gaius," purred the blonde who was labeled as Shelly in Laura's Cylon agent file. "Do you think she suspects you?"

Reflexively, Baltar glanced in her direction and said, "No." Then he mentally chided himself for responding to her in front of a witness. It happened rarely, but if he was relaxed enough, she could still catch him off guard. It was a perverse little game she enjoyed playing with him. Fortunately he'd become deft at covering such slips. Furthermore since—as that annoying Boxey child had observed—people had become accustomed to the odd Doctor Baltar and his eccentricities, so such gaffes generally were shrugged off.

Not this time.

Laura was on her feet so fast that she banged her knees on the underside of her desk. Pain shot up and down her legs, but it barely registered with her. "What are you doing with her here!" she demanded.

"P-Pardon? There's, ah . . . there's no one here, Madame President, except you and—"

*"You looked right at her. I just saw you do it!"*

"What?" There was extreme nervousness in Baltar's face, and he was stammering very badly.

"She said something and you looked right at her!"

He felt his knees starting to give way, but kept himself on his feet with effort. "Her? What her are you referring to . . . ?"

"Shelly Godfrey! Right there!"

Six looked genuinely stunned. She clapped a hand to her bosom. Baltar slipped up again, looking directly toward her. "I . . . I . . ." he stuttered.

"You looked at her again! Don't tell me I'm just seeing her!"

"She can see me!" Shelly said through tightly clenched teeth. "Do something! Distract her!"

Responding instantly, Baltar tossed on a façade of concern and said, "You appear overwrought, Madame President. Perhaps you'd like to sit down—"

"To hell with that!" shouted Laura. "The audacity! To walk in here with your Cylon . . . what? Co-conspirator? Lover?!"

Baltar had never come as close to passing out from shock as he did at that moment.

"Madame President . . ." Baltar began, starting to come around the desk.

Then he jumped back as Laura grabbed a heavy paperweight off her desk with one hand while, with the other, she grabbed up a phone and snapped, "Billy! Get in here with two security guards! Arrest—"

As she spoke, she threw the paperweight directly at Six. Baltar lunged to one side, his head snapped around, and he saw the paperweight sail through empty air and smash into the bulkhead.

Laura swayed behind the desk, clearly stunned that the paperweight had connected with nothing and that Six had apparently vanished into thin air. At that moment, the door flew open, and Billy was there with two armed men from her personal guard. They looked around, saw no one but the president and the vice president and—through process of elimination—figured that Baltar was the threat. The guards grabbed him by either arm. The papers Baltar had brought with him flew in all directions.

"Get your damned hands off me!" Baltar shouted, his voice going up an octave.

"Madame President . . ." Billy began.

But she waved him off, her face ashen. "Let him go!" she said. When the guards hesitated, still confused over what had just happened, she repeated more firmly, "Let him go."

The guards did, backing off. "Madame President," Billy started once more, but then stopped, since he clearly had no idea what to say.

"It . . . was a misunderstanding," she said slowly. She continued to address Billy, but she was looking straight at Baltar. "I'm sorry to have summoned you like that. I was . . . it was just a misunderstanding," she told them once more, as if repetition would somehow make it more credible.

Her aide didn't leave immediately. Instead he and Roslin locked gazes, and Baltar knew that there was something more going on here, something that he wasn't privy to. What did the president have on him and if it was anything, why didn't she use it?

The personal guards backed out of the room, still

looking around suspiciously. Billy continued to look at Roslin for a short time longer, and then very stiffly he said, "Thank you, Madame President," and stepped out of the office as well.

A deathly silence descended over Baltar and Roslin. Both of them were standing. Finally Roslin eased herself into her chair and tried to arrange her hands neatly, one upon the other, as if nothing untoward had occurred. Baltar then knelt down, gathered the scattered papers, and arranged them neatly in a pile. He took a step forward, placed them on her desk, and stepped back. Still nothing was said.

"Madame President," he finally asked slowly, "is there something you'd like to tell me?"

She appeared to give the matter some thought, and then replied, "No. I don't believe there is."

Baltar squared his shoulders and, very casually, said, "Feel free to review my findings at your leisure. I assume you're busy at the moment . . ." He paused and then added, "And have a good deal on your mind."

"Thank you," she said.

"Do you require me to remain for the imminent Quorum gathering?"

"No, that shouldn't be necessary."

"As you wish. Thank you, Madame President."

"Thank you, Doctor Baltar."

He got out of the room quickly and headed down the narrow corridor outside. The security guards were a short ways away, and they both gave him extremely suspicious stares as he went past. The moment they were behind him, Number Six was in front of him. Perversely, she seemed delighted with the latest development. "She's on to you, Gaius."

He kept walking and, in a low voice, said, "How is that possible?"

"It's not. That's what makes it all the more exciting."

"I could do with a little less excitement in my life, thank you. How could she know about us?"

"She can't."

"How did she see you?"

"She couldn't."

"You're *not helping*."

Her long legs enabled her to keep pace with him easily. "Helping? I've done nothing but help you, Gaius. Helped you with information. Helped you see the future of the human race. Helped you fulfill your full potential. And you have resisted me and fought me at every turn, squandering precious time. And now your time's running out. She's on to you."

"It's impossible!"

"And yet it is." She stepped directly in his path and, even though he could have walked right through her, instead he slammed to a halt. "And you better figure out a way to fix it. Fast. Because you have even less time than you think."

"What's that supposed to mean?"

"It means exactly what I said, Gaius. Exactly what I said."

He turned away from her, feeling as if the corridor around him was tilting sideways. Composing himself, he turned back to face her once more only to see that she was gone.

"Bitch," he whispered under his breath.

# CHAPTER 22

Kara and Agathon, so bored out of their minds that they were tempted to stage a jailbreak just to get shot at and break up the monotony, looked up in mild surprise as the door to the room they were being kept in opened. Kara had thought sure that, once word had reached the ship of Freya's duplicity, they would immediately be kicked loose. She'd said as much to Adama. But to her annoyance, they'd been informed by a couple of Gunnerson's lieutenants—one named Tyr, the other Fenris, both of them large and sturdily built, albeit not quite as massive as Gunnerson—that they were going to continue to be kept right where they were until "matters were sorted out to their satisfaction."

The door opening suggested that such a time might be imminent, and the presence of Tyr standing next to Freya Gunnerson, holding her firmly by one arm, confirmed it. Standing behind Freya were two marines, corporals Jolly and Zac. Jolly, despite his name, had the most perpetually dour expression of any marine Starbuck had ever known, and Zac was a bulky woman who looked fully capable of breaking most men in half.

Clearly they had been responsible for escorting her back from *Galactica.*

"I believe," said Tyr, "that Freya has something she wishes to say to you." He nudged her forward slightly and she cast an angry glare at Tyr before looking back at Starbuck and Helo.

"I apologize for the inconvenience," she said tersely.

"Frak you," shot back Starbuck, having no patience for her apologies, and said to Tyr, "are we finally free to go?"

"Yes. Enjoy the rest of your stay on the *Bifrost.*"

"Sure we will," said Agathon, "because, y'know, it's been such a joy until now."

Freya looked as if she was about to respond, but before she could, Tyr and Fenris yanked her away. Jolly and Zac stepped forward, both of them tossing off salutes and saying, "Admiral Adama instructed us to report to you and aid you in your search for the suspect."

"It's appreciated," said Starbuck as she emerged from the room, Helo right behind her. She walked with quick, brisk steps, and they immediately fell into step behind her. The hell of it was that she didn't have the faintest idea of where they were going, but she looked as if she moving with great authority, so naturally they followed her. It made her wonder if there were times when the Old Man likewise didn't have the faintest idea what he was doing, but he made his moves with such confidence that people just naturally attended to everything he said and did.

*Nah. No way. The Old Man always knew what was best. Always. She should be so lucky to be as on top of things as Adama was.*

"We looking for Boxey?" asked Helo.

"Frakking right we're looking for Boxey," shot back Starbuck. "At this point, considering all the trouble and hassle we've had to deal with because of him, I almost don't care if he's a Cylon or not. We're hauling his ass back to *Galactica* either way."

"Where do we start, Lieutenant?" asked Jolly.

"I'm not sure," she said as they rounded a corner, "but we find him even if we have to tear this whole ship apart panel by panel."

Boxey awoke inside the crawl ducts. Confused, he started to sit up, but naturally that was impossible since he was surrounded by narrow metal confines. All he managed to do was slam his head on the metal above him, which sent noise and vibrations all up and down the ducts.

He had no idea how long he'd been there. When he'd clambered up into it, his heart had been pounding. He felt as if his entire world had been stood on its ear. Freya had been completely right about Starbuck and the others. They weren't his friends. Perhaps they never even had been. They were chasing him down as if he was the worst sort of criminal or enemy, and he hadn't done anything, not a thing. It wasn't fair. Not at all. Why, they were treating him like . . .

Like Sharon Valerii. Or even worse.

His heart turned cold and bitter, and angrily he said, "I . . . I almost wish I was a Cylon. The stuff they're doing . . . the way they look at me . . . it would serve 'em right. It would serve 'em right if I was a Cylon, because then they'd be afraid of me. That would be better than this. Anything would be better than this."

He waited for his ire to subside, but it didn't. It made him wonder if it had been like this for Sharon. If there had been a slow build up of suspicion, culminating in her self-realization and her ceasing to fight against her true nature.

He wondered if he had a true nature like that.

What if he was a . . . ?

Boxey shook it off. He didn't need to have his mind wandering in that direction right now, especially because he felt as if that direction was calling him more strongly than he'd like.

He slithered his way down the duct and found a ceiling panel that he could work loose. He listened for a long moment to make sure that there was no one around, and then gripped the grillwork and eased it up and out of place. He lay it down carefully to make sure that it didn't make a lot of noise, and then eased himself down and through into the corridor, landing so softly that no one could have heard him.

At that exact instant, Starbuck and Helo, followed by two marines, came around the corner, Starbuck saying in annoyance, "—but we find him even if we have to tear this whole ship apart panel by panel."

They stopped dead and all five stared at each other.

"Wow," said Starbuck, clearly impressed with herself.

Instantly Boxey tried to leap back up toward the shaft space, but he only got halfway up before Agathon tackled him around the legs. Boxey tried to kick, but Agathon's arms were wrapped tightly around them, making it impossible for Boxey to move them. Agathon yanked downward and the two of them hit the floor. Boxey desperately tried to squirm loose but by that point Corporals Jolly and Zac had hauled him to his feet and were holding him securely.

"Long time no see," said Starbuck dryly. "And here I was just thinking how we should catch up with you."

"I didn't do anything wrong," Boxey snapped. He tried to pull at the marines who were holding him still, but he accomplished nothing on that score. "I'm not a Cylon."

"Then why did you run?"

"Because you think I'm a Cylon!"

"How do you know that?"

"Because why else would you be here! You don't like me! You never liked me!"

Starbuck looked taken aback by the ferocity of his accusations. Automatically she said, "That's not true."

"You know it is! You know it's true! I tell you something and Baltar tells you something, and you believe him instead of me! Why?!"

"Because . . ." Starbuck started to reply, and then stopped. She and Helo looked at each other.

Helo shrugged. "Don't look at me. I just go where they tell me."

"Look, Boxey," she began again.

"Give me one good reason that I should listen to you!"

"Because," she said patiently but firmly, "I'm bigger than you. I have a couple of guys who are bigger than you, and they're making sure you don't go anywhere. So now's the time to come to terms with the fact that you're going back to *Galactica*, and yeah, you're gonna be checked out, but that's the way it goes because I have my orders and there's not a single frakking thing you can do about it."

As it happened, she could not have been more wrong.

She received her first inkling of her fundamental wrongness, however, the moment that alarms started going off all over the ship.

They were practically deafening, so much so that Boxey had to put his hands to his ears, and even the hardened marines were wincing.

"The two of you, stay here with him," Kara snapped at them, "and Helo, you're with me," and she bolted down the main corridor before any further conversation could be had. Helo promptly took off after her, leaving the two bewildered marines staring at their captive and waiting for someone to tell them what they were supposed to do.

Starbuck and Helo, meantime, were running as fast as they could. They passed frightened Midguardians who were certain that the alarm bells could only mean one thing: another Cylon attack. The same thing had occurred to Starbuck, and she was desperately looking for a viewing port to get a sense of what was going on outside.

"There!" shouted Helo, pointing ahead of them. "A viewing bay! Up there!"

She saw that he was right. A large round port window was set into the bulkhead ahead of them, which would give them a decent—if not enhanced—view of what was in front of them. Starbuck got to the port with Helo directly behind her, looking over her shoulder.

Starbuck gulped deeply when she saw what was heading their way.

"You've gotta be frakkin' kidding me," she said, her mind numb.

In *Galactica's* CIC, Tigh drifted over to Adama and muttered to him in a low voice, "I'll be right back."

This alone was unusual: Adama wasn't going to care if Tigh walked off CIC unannounced. This wasn't grade school. If nothing else, he would have assumed Tigh was going to the head, and that hardly was worth a separate declaration. The fact that Tigh was taking the time to say something to Adama about his departure spoke volumes. Adama instantly knew that something was up. He met Tigh's gaze, but saw the look in his XO's eyes, and all he said in response was, "Okay."

Tigh walked out of CIC like a man on a mission. When he returned a few minutes later, he was carrying several sheets of paper and a small wandlike device. Adama recognized it immediately for what it was, but he said nothing. Tigh's movement had caught Dualla's eye and a couple of other officers'. Like Adama, however, they simply watched in mute curiosity.

Gaeta looked up, bewildered, frowning. He stared uncomprehendingly as Tigh held up a piece of paper that read, "Don't say a word." Slowly, still not understanding but not about to do anything contrary to Tigh's explicit order—even if it was unspoken—Gaeta nodded.

He held up a second sign. It read, "Hold out your right hand."

Gaeta did so, wondering obliquely if Tigh was about to slap it or something.

Instead Tigh extended the wand device. Naturally Gaeta recognized it as a bug detector. On two previous occasions he had stepped back from his station as Tigh had run the wand over the entire area to make certain there was no eavesdropping device hidden anywhere. Tigh had even had every member of CIC stand with arms extended to either side and run the wand up and down and around their bodies to make sure their uniforms weren't bugged. Everything had come up clean. This time, though, Tigh ran it over the back of Gaeta's hand, right where he had been scratching. Tigh had turned the volume on the wand down to almost nothing, but there was still a detector light on the handle, and the light instantly went off.

Gaeta's jaw dropped in astonishment. Everyone on CIC, their attention completely engaged, also saw it, and their responses were similar. Adama's jaw simply twitched which, for him, was the equivalent of his eyes leaping out of their sockets in astonishment.

"Mr. Gaeta," Tigh said in a careful, measured, easy-to-hear voice, "verify the current emergency Jump point. *Pegasus* is reporting some uncertainty." But as he spoke, he held up yet another sign, and it read: "Plot a new Jump point and *keep your mouth shut as you're doing it.*"

Slowly Gaeta nodded and said, "Aye, sir."

Tigh nodded in approval and then turned his gaze toward Adama in unmistakeable triumph. He held up yet another sign. It read, "Not bad for an old guy, huh."

*Not bad at all*, mouthed Adama.

Even as he made new calculations, Gaeta spoke clearly—perhaps *too* clearly, but there was nothing they could do about this sudden self-consciousness—to the *Pegasus*, reverifying the Jump coordinates that were no longer relevant. He did so speaking into a dead phone, because naturally the *Pegasus* wasn't going to know what the hell he was talking about if he'd been speaking directly to them. But if someone was listening in via a subcutaneous listening device in Gaeta's hand—as Tigh obviously suspected was the case—they weren't going to know that.

And just as Adama was starting to think that perhaps maybe, just maybe, the current crisis was nearly behind them, it all went straight to hell.

"Admiral!" Dualla suddenly called out. "The *Bifrost*!"

The ship had been up on a monitor, being watched carefully, ever since Adama had sent Starbuck and Helo over there. Now he, Tigh, and everyone else looked up to see what it was that Dualla was alerting them to.

"You gotta be frakking kidding me," said Tigh.

And just when matters didn't seem as if they could possibly get worse, space exploded around them.

D'anna Biers was one of a dozen reporters crowded into the conference room on *Colonial One,* watching with great interest as Wolf Gunnerson entered. Already seated at a large round conference table were the members of the Quorum of Twelve, with President Roslin at the table's head.

Biers looked over the faces of the Quorum members when Gunnerson came in. They did not look to be an especially sympathetic bunch. Their expressions could best be described as "hardened disinterest," although several of them were unable to contain their surprise at Gunnerson's sheer mass. Even D'anna had to admit that, damn, for a human, he was pretty impressive.

For more ceremonial gatherings the Quorum convened on *Cloud Nine*, but this was a more "down and dirty" gathering, as Tom Zarek had referred to it. A handful of reporters were being permitted to attend in the interest of full disclosure; on the other hand, subsequent deliberations would likely be held in closed-door sessions. It simply wasn't *Cloud-Nine* appropriate, again as Zarek had put it.

The meeting had already been chaired to order, and some preliminary business had been attended to. Now there was nothing on the docket but to deal with the matter of Wolf Gunnerson. Laura Roslin, as president, was charged with overseeing the running of the meeting, and she did so now with her customary brisk efficiency. D'anna ruminated on the fact that Roslin was a non-voting member except in times of a tie vote, at which point she would cast the deciding ballot. That meant that, should the Quorum split on the issue of the Midguardians, then she, Laura Roslin, would be the one who held their fate in her hands. And as far as D'anna was concerned, it was a toss-up as to which way she would fall.

She smiled with the inner amusement of a scientist watching rats hustle through a maze, knowing that in the long run, it was all fruitless because—in the end—they were still just rats, not destined to be long for this world.

She glanced over toward Gunnerson. He did not look back.

"Madame President," Tom Zarek was saying, rising, from his chair.

"We recognize Tom Zarek, representative of Sagittaron."

He nodded slightly in acknowledgment of her recognition, fiddled with the lower button of his jacket for a moment, and then said, "Mr. Gunnerson first approached me about the issue of recognition for the Midguardians, so naturally I feel some responsibility in this matter. Consider this my personal request," and he gave a smile that looked forced, "that the recent unpleasantness regarding the misunderstanding of the stolen religious relic . . . not color the feelings of this Quorum in considering the request of his people."

"It is difficult to ignore it, Councilman," Robin Wenutu of Canceron replied. "It's a hell of a first impression to make."

"I can understand your trepidation," Zarek said. "Because, to be candid, it wasn't all that long ago that I had to face down the looks of distrust on all of you."

"Councilman Zarek," said Eladio Puasha of Scorpia. "I don't think that's a fair assessment of our earliest experiences . . ."

"I think it's a perfectly fair assessment," Zarek told her with a fixed expression. "One moment I'm a terrorist; the next I'm a coworker."

"You underestimate our ability to adapt, Tom," replied Puasha. "If there's one thing we've become accustomed to in months past . . . it's a constantly fluctuating status quo."

This drew nods of rueful disagreement, and surprisingly, Zarek's smile turned genuine. "Fair enough, Eladio." Then he grew serious once more. "I suppose all I'm saying is that, from my point of view—I fully understand the situation that would have driven Wolf Gunnerson to do what he did. And if Councilwoman Puasha's attitude is truly reflective of the rest of you . . . then I assume I can count on all of you to give him the fair hearing that he deserves." Zarek paused a moment for what he had said to sink in, and then sat back down in his chair.

During the entire exchange, Wolf Gunnerson had never taken a seat, even though there was an available one near him. Laura Roslin gestured for him to take it, and he calmly shook his head. "I think it more respectful to remain on my feet," he said.

"Very well," said Laura. "Then, Mr. Gunnerson, you have the fl—"

She stopped. Stopped and stared, and looked ashen, and she seemed to be whispering something. D'anna looked carefully, and Laura was apparently saying, "Not now . . . not now . . ."

Sarah, who was seated at the president's right hand, leaned forward, looking concerned. "Madame President . . . ?" she said cautiously.

"Headache . . . just . . ." Her voice sounded strangled. She looked as if she were having some sort of attack, and was fighting it off with Herculean effort that was only partly succeeding.

"Madame President?" asked Sarah again. And then, with the sort of intuition that only someone who sought religious meaning in every aspect of life could display, Sarah said with greater urgency, "Are you . . . are you having some sort of vision?"

D'anna leaned forward as well, eyebrow cocked. This was suddenly getting very interesting. She just hoped that it wouldn't take too long to play out, since time was not something the humans had in abundance.

She couldn't believe how smoothly everything was going. Here was Zarek, whose very presence continued to make her feel cold inside (and that had nothing to do with the fact that he was going to be her likeliest competition for the presidency; gods help the colonies if that happened), actually interacting like a grown-up with the other members of the Quorum. Gunnerson was patiently waiting for his moment to speak. When that moment came, Roslin started to tell him that he had the floor . . .

And Sharon Valerii was there.

She was everywhere.

No longer was she standing at one point in the room, drawing Laura's attention. Instead every member of the Quorum of Twelve had disappeared, and in their respective places was an identical Sharon Valerii. Each one pregnant, each one with an expression of dispassionate placidity. Each one looking directly at her. They were shaking their heads sadly, and they genuinely looked apologetic.

Laura knew she had to be dreaming. She absolutely had to be. But she felt awake, and this was going beyond the simple hallucinations that she'd experienced earlier. This was borderline dementia, and it was the tipping point. She couldn't take it anymore. To hell with the rest of the human race, to hell with her responsibilities. Laura Roslin was as much a fighter as any human being left alive, but it was ultimately too much, just . . . just too much. If Sharon Valerii's unborn child had somehow insinuated itself into her mind, then . . . then . . .

*Yes, that was it. That was the problem. All right, fine. I'll show that unborn saboteur who's boss. And I wouldn't leave it to Doc Cottle to do it, because who knows, he might be a Cylon as well. I'll just . . . I'll just go over there myself and cut the child out with a knife, or . . . or put a bullet in Sharon's brain, that's it, that's all, just done with it, just . . .*

Sharon Valerii was speaking to her. The voice didn't emerge from her mouth but instead went directly into Roslin's mind, and what it said was, *Now. Now. It's about to happen now. Do something. Save us. Save us all . . .*

And that was when it all became clear to Laura. Her mind leaped and everything suddenly seemed cast into a stark and new relief . . .

*Gods . . . I was right the first time . . . it's not trying to terrorize me . . . it's not trying to drive me insane . . . it's . . . it's afraid . . . it's afraid . . . it's afraid and it wants my help to save it from . . . from what . . . ? From . . . ?*

She heard another voice in her head, and it was Sarah Porter. Laura, feeling as if she were on the brink of something, pushed her way back to reality. Her teeth gritted, she said, "Mister . . . Mister Gunnerson . . . you may . . . you may go ahead . . ."

"Madame President," Sarah said, still looking concerned. "I asked if you—"

"I heard what you asked," Laura told her firmly, which was a lie since she was barely holding on to her own surroundings. "Mr. Gunnerson is here . . . we're all here . . . let's . . . move along."

There was a brief, uncomfortable silence, and then Wolf Gunnerson reached into the inside pocket of his jacket and removed a sheaf of papers covered with scribbling. "I had promised Madame President," he said, "that were I given this opportunity, I would inform you all of the truths of our sacred writings."

"*Your* sacred writings," Sarah Porter reminded him. She was still glancing every so often in Laura's direction, but she was all-business enough to want to get business matters back on track. "Your truths. Not ours."

"I would like to think," Gunnerson said mildly, "that truth is truth."

Laura knew that everyone at the table was still casting glances in her direction. She closed her eyes, opened them, and they were all still damned Sharon Valerii. Everyone in the room was . . . with, insanely, the sole exception of D'anna Biers, who was studying her closely as if dissecting her with her eyes. Laura had no idea what to make of that, and didn't try to figure it out. She closed her eyes firmly, as if battling a headache, and when she opened them, everyone had returned to themselves . . .

. . . and the words *Sagittarius is bleeding NOW* were etched on the table.

Wolf Gunnerson was smoothing the papers, and he began to read aloud:

*"The race of humans thus was ended*
*A blinding final winter done*
*The sword of demons, hot with flame*
*Assured no mortals left to run.*
*The gods were dead, had fought their last*
*Consumed by snake and wolf and blood*
*And so their last remains were gone*
*All swept away, as if by flood.*
*The rainbow bridge was all destroyed*
*It crashed and cracked and split apart*
*And in so doing did away*
*With humanity's last soul and heart.*
*Gods' worshippers were gone to dust*
*The last assault, did not survive,*
*Their final crash, their final burn*
*There was no human left alive."*

He paused, as if he was going to continue reading and then, sounding like a polite literature professor, said almost apologetically, "It goes on for several more pages, but truthfully, it's just a reiteration of what's already been said. The writers of the Edda tended to be repetitive in order to make certain their point was made."

The Quorum members looked at each other in confusion, as if trying to see if anyone knew what Gunnerson was driving at.

"I can't say that I understand, Mr. Gunnerson," said Laura Roslin.

He gave her a vaguely pitying smile. "It's all right there, Madame President. A blind man could see it: We're not supposed to be here. We were not destined to survive. The 'blinding final winter' is the nuclear winter of the Cylon attack . . . the signal that our gods are dead. And since our gods are the only ones that truly count, that means there's really no point in anything else existing. The vast majority of humanity was annihilated by the winter, as was supposed to be the case. We, the Midguardians, survived so as to make sure the final prophecies would be fulfilled, and we came close," and he brought his thumb and forefinger almost together, "this close. 'Their final crash, their final burn.' We were intended to die in the heart of that vast, all-consuming star. But that was thwarted at the last moment by Adama, displaying cleverness that Loki would have envied. But no matter, no matter. It's being attended to even as we speak."

Slowly Laura Roslin stood as the rest of the Quorum continued to shift uncomfortably in their seats, clearly not liking the sound of what they were hearing. She whispered, so softly that they had to strain to hear her, "The blood of humanity . . . on your hands . . . on the hands of Sagittaron . . . of Sagittarius . . ."

"Now wait a minute!" Zarek said. "I didn't know anything about this!"

"What this?" demanded Sarah Porter. "What's going on?"

And now the reporters, stirred up, started firing questions. Matters were spiraling completely out of control, and everything snapped into place for Laura Roslin, the final tumblers clicking in her mind. Even though she made no attempt to shout, her voice still rose above the crowd as she said, "Your precious book was never missing. You knew your daughter had it the entire time."

"Yes," Gunnerson said, looking mildly impressed.

"You did it to make an impetus for this meeting. You wanted us all together. Now."

"Yes."

Now all questioning and back talk had died out, and the silence was heavy as everyone in the room waited for this exchange to come to a conclusion that clearly only Laura Roslin and Wolf Gunnerson knew.

She took a deep breath and said, "You're planning to wipe out the entire Quorum in one shot."

He inclined his head slightly. "Yes."

"*What!*" Zarek almost exploded out of his chair, and he grabbed Gunnerson by the arm. "What the frak are you talking ab—"

Gunnerson swung his arm casually and Zarek was knocked backwards, sent crashing over his chair. Wolf made no other motion. There even seemed to be, insanely enough, sadness in his eyes.

"Billy," said Laura, without budging from her place. Billy was standing several feet away, looking shocked, uncomprehending. "Contact *Galactica* immediately. Tell them an immediate attack is very likely."

Billy started to back out of the room, but he never took his eyes off Gunnerson. But Wolf made no move toward him and Billy got out with no problem. Instead Gunnerson said calmly, with total conviction, "Call whomever you want. They can't save you."

"They can and they will," Laura Roslin replied, her chin tilted upward in defiance.

"Oh my gods!"

It was Sarah Porter. Something had caught her eye out one of the ports, and she had cried out in shock. Laura looked to see what it was that had provoked the response.

It was the *Bifrost.*

It was still a good distance away, but the ship had turned away from its customary position in the fleet. Instead it was moving crosswise across the flow, attempting to navigate its way toward *Colonial One*.

It was on a direct collision course. If its course went unaltered, it would smash *Colonial One* amidships, rupturing the hull of both vessels, and both of them would explode, fireballs snuffed out within seconds in the airless vacuum of space.

Pandemonium broke out in the conference room, which was instantly transformed into a maelstrom of accusation, fury, and fear.

And in the midst of it all, D'anna Biers—the eye of the storm—smiled wanly to herself and slowly shook her head.

*We tried,* she thought sadly. *We tried so hard. We tried our little booby trap the last time, after I shook Gaeta's hand during the making of the documentary and inserted that little listening device into it. We tried to herd you into a situation where you would have been so completely overwhelmed by our forces that you would have had no choice but to surrender. We could have extracted Sharon's baby at that point . . . perhaps even taken a percentage of you prisoner and turned you into workers. You wouldn't have been completely exterminated. A handful would have survived to serve us, and wouldn't that have been appropriate? But you had to be oh-so-clever to avoid the trap. So this time . . . this time we finish it. Or at the very least, we cripple you by destroying your entire membership and your civilian leaders.*

*We tried to be generous, but you simply weren't willing to allow it to happen. For this one, you have no one to blame but yourself.*

*We know where you're going to Jump to. If you try to get away, we're waiting for you, and we'll blow what's left of you to bits.*

*Too bad about Sharon, though. I bet the baby would have had her eyes.*

# CHAPTER 23

*"Cylon raiders!"*

The members of Adama's command crew had barely had the opportunity to register that *Colonial One* was in deep trouble when space all around them was alive with Cylon raiders spinning out of subspace and angling toward the fleet. They came out firing, and even though Adama had the pilots scrambling to their vessels, he was certain they were losing out on precious time.

"Vipers away!" called Dualla.

"Gaeta!" said Tigh with growing urgency as he crossed over toward him. "Get those coordinates for the Jump up and ready!" Despite the gravity of the situation, he was wise enough not to say anything beyond that, nor was Gaeta engaging in the standard operating procedure of getting verbal confirmation from other officers in CIC as to the specifics of the coordinates. Instead Gaeta was keeping his big mouth shut as he readied the coordinates and the fleet's Jump.

Adama's eyes were riveted, however, on the *Bifrost* as it approached *Colonial One.* Neither ship was especially speedy or maneuverable; both were outfitted with FTL drives, but that did nothing for them when they were operating in standard space and moving with the alacrity of a drunken cow.

"Fire a warning shot across their bow," said Adama. He was furious with himself for being hamstrung. Helo and Starbuck—Starbuck, for frak's sake—were on the *Bifrost* along with two of his marines. If the warning shot didn't take, he was going to have to seriously consider blowing the ship out of space. This would end the Midguardian threat, but it would also be the end of his people. Of Helo, of . . . of Starbuck . . .

A single shot from the *Galactica*'s big cannons hurtled past the *Bifrost* as it started to approach *Colonial One.* It seemed frighteningly as if the *Galactica* was firing upon the civilian fleet, but there was no helping that now.

The shot hurtled past the *Bifrost* without striking it. The civilian ship didn't slow.

Suddenly the *Galactica* was rocked by concentrated fire power from the Cylons. The big guns were needed elsewhere. If Adama didn't have the target shifted to the threat of the Cylons, there wasn't going to be a fleet to worry about, much less a single ship.

*Starbuck . . . Helo . . . do something,* Adama thought desperately.

Boxey sprinted down the corridor, dodging the confused and terrified people who were milling about, shouting that they were under attack, demanding to know what was going on. Kara, Agathon, and the two marines were right behind him, and they weren't especially gentle about shoving people out of the way in order to get where they were going.

Enough people were looking upset that Starbuck had the distinct impression what was transpiring was news to them. It wasn't as if there had been some vast group plan to try and send the *Bifrost* winging its way into *Colonial One.* It was the actions of a few people acting independently of the rest of the ship's populace. Unfortunately, those few people were in control of the ship.

"This way! It's this way!" Boxey was shouting, and he rounded another corner. The four adults were hard-pressed to keep up with him, but they managed to do so and then they suddenly skidded to a halt as Boxey stood outside a large set of double doors and started pounding on them in frustration.

"This the control room?" Starbuck demanded.

When Boxey nodded, Jolly shouted "Stay back!" and unslung his weapon. Zac followed suit, and they opened fire on the outer door. Their weapon fire bounced harmlessly off the reinforced armored door.

"Frak!" shouted Starbuck.

Jolly slammed a fist against the door, which didn't accomplish much since his fire power had already proven insufficient. "We should have packed explosives! Anyone got any?"

"I have an exploding cigar, but I left it back on *Galactica,*" Starbuck said with bleak humor. Then something prompted her to look overhead. She saw the grillwork and a desperate thought occurred to her. She glanced over at Boxey, who had automatically looked up to see what she was staring at, and then the same thought occurred to him.

"Lift me up!" he cried out.

Instantly Starbuck started to second-guess her own notion, but there wasn't any time for such concerns. "Helo, get it clear!" she shouted, nodding toward the overhead grillwork. Helo reached up, grabbed it and yanked it clear. Starbuck interlaced her hands, providing a step up for him. Boxey planted one foot in the aide and she propelled him up and into the ventilation shaft.

"Wait by the door!" he called. "I'll get it open from inside!"

Jolly turned to Starbuck, looking none too enthused about the situation. "We're counting on the kid?"

"Yeah!" replied Starbuck, her eyes fiery with the demented gamble. "We're counting on the kid!"

Lee Adama, a.k.a. Apollo, wished to the gods that he had Starbuck out there with him, guarding his tail. He'd never felt more vulnerable than now, when he was fighting for his own life and that of *Galactica* and the best damned pilot he knew wasn't there.

Worse, he knew exactly where she was, but there wasn't a thing he could do about it . . .

Despite the fact that there was hot fire from the Cylon raiders all around him, his attention drifted briefly to the *Bifrost*.

He gasped. He saw that the ship was on collision course with *Colonial One*. But he was too far away to do anything about it, and if he disengaged from the enemy to attend to it, raiders would get through and manage to jam their weapons fire right down *Galactica*'s throat.

"*Galactica*, this is Apollo! *Colonial One* in imminent danger from *Bifrost*!" he shouted over his comm unit.

There was a heartbeat of a pause, and then a voice came back—not Dualla's, but instead Lee's father. "We're monitoring the situation."

"Monitoring! If they hit—! Permission to engage *Bifrost*—!"

"Negative, focus on Cylons. Starbuck has it in hand."

Saul Tigh turned and looked in astonishment at Bill Adama as Adama point-blank lied to his son. Adama shoved the phone down and returned the look.

"She does," Adama said with simple conviction, without having the faintest idea why he knew. He turned toward Gaeta and asked, "Mr. Gaeta . . . how long until we're ready to Jump?"

Gaeta help up two fingers to indicate two minutes and said aloud, "Five minutes, sir."

Adama nodded and then looked back in bleak frustration at the *Bifrost*. Space was alive with Vipers engaging the Cylons. Even if they tried to fire directly at the *Bifrost,* they might blow their own Vipers out of the sky. And if *Colonial One* attempted evasive maneuvers, they could just as easily steer themselves directly into stray shots from either the Cylon raiders or even the Vipers. The entire area was too hot.

Plus if the entire fleet Jumped to escape the Cylons and the *Bifrost* was being commanded by hostiles, they very likely wouldn't make the Jump along with the rest of the fleet, leaving Kara and Agathon to the nonexistent mercies of the Cylons.

*Come on, Starbuck,* he thought in frustration.

Laura Roslin shoved past the members of the Quorum and went straight up to Wolf Gunnerson, who was the picture of calm. Two security guards were approaching him, and he fired them a look that was fraught with danger. "Stay back!" Laura snapped at them and they halted where they were. She looked up at Gunnerson and demanded, "Why are you doing this?"

"The Edda must be fulfilled," he said calmly. "These things don't happen by themselves."

"Yes! They do! Do you think I was trying to *make* myself ill so that I would fulfill scripture?"

"It doesn't matter," said Gunnerson. "You didn't succeed. I shall. My daughter shall. She's steering the *Bifrost*."

"And what about the Cylons!" Tom Zarek spoke up angrily. "They're crawling all over us out there! Are you working with them, too?"

Wolf Gunnerson said nothing, but merely smiled enigmatically.

The *Bifrost* drew closer.

* * *

Boxey eased his way through the duct work with confidence that he knew exactly where he was going. It wasn't all that far. He could do this. He had to do it.

*This is it. This has to prove that you're not a Cylon. That you were just making yourself crazy over it.*

*Although . . . Boomer helped blow up a lot of Cylons before she discovered what she was. Maybe . . .*

*Stop it! Stop it!*

He made his way around a curve in the duct and found himself staring down into the control room. Freya was there, along with Tyr and Fenris. They were manipulating the controls in the slightly cramped area, and Fenris was keeping a steady countdown going toward the imminent collision with *Colonial One*. "Eighteen," he was saying, "seventeen, sixteen . . ."

*No time! No time!*

Boxey brought both his hands down upon the grillwork and slammed it as hard as he could. The panel, and he, crashed through to the floor. He was up on his feet in a second, and he locked eyes with Freya Gunnerson.

She reached into her jacket and pulled out a gun.

Boxey's head snapped around and he saw the locking mechanism on the door. He lunged toward it. The first shot from Freya's gun slammed into his right shoulder and he cried out. He heard her shout "Get him!" and Tyr and Fenris were coming at him. He willed the pain away, stumbled fell toward the locking mechanism, and another shot struck him in the chest. As he fell, his fingers slammed against the lock, twisting it open, and then he hit the floor and the last thing that went through his mind was *If this doesn't prove it, nothing will,* and then everything went black.

"It's going to hit!" screamed Sarah Porter.

Laura Roslin looked out a viewing port. She could practically see the rivets in the *Bifrost*'s hull.

"It's for the best," Wolf Gunnerson said coolly.

She fired him a glance of utter contempt. "Frak you," she said, which was hardly the most eloquent of final words, but certainly as fitting as any.

The door slid open and Starbuck, her gun in her hand, shoved Jolly aside and was the first one in.

Boxey inadvertently saved her life, because Freya Gunnerson was aiming her weapon straight at Starbuck and Starbuck tripped over Boxey's prostrate body. She went down and Freya's shot went wide, glancing off Jolly's body armor. The impact staggered Jolly but didn't take him down.

Starbuck hit the ground, fired once, and her shot lifted Freya up, blew her off her feet and sent her slamming against the far bulkhead. The sheer impact held her there for a moment, and then slowly she slid down the wall, leaving a trail of blood behind her.

Tyr's gun was already out and Fenris was starting to pull his. Zac stepped out from behind Jolly and fired twice, both times with deadly accuracy. The first show sent Tyr's head exploding in a shower of blood, and Fenris was just starting to bring his weapon to bear when he was shot square in the chest, the impact spinning him around like a top. He went down looking profoundly confused.

*Colonial One* loomed before them.

"*Helo!*" she shouted.

Helo vaulted over the fallen bodies and grabbed the controls. There was no time for anything fancy. His hands flew over the controls and then angled the *Bifrost* up, up and over *Colonial One*.

"This is gonna be close," he muttered.

He was right. The underside of the *Bifrost* banged against the top of *Colonial One*, and there was an earsplitting scraping as the two ships slid against each other. It seemed to go on forever, and suddenly they were clear.

Helo grabbed the nearest phone.

Adama had been watching the inevitable collision of the *Bifrost* and *Colonial One* with his heart in his throat, and for just a split second, he thought his confidence in Starbuck had been misplaced. And then he saw the *Bifrost* suddenly change course, and the two ships slid one against the other, leaving behind a nasty scrape but nothing that appeared—at least from this distance—to structurally threaten either vessel.

"Admiral!" Dualla suddenly shouted, her headset wrapped around her ears, "Helo reports *Bifrost* in friendly hands!"

Relief pounded through Adama, and then he pointed at a screen where the Vipers could clearly be seen battling the enemy and made a "circle" gesture with his finger to indicate that the ships should be rounded up.

Nodding her understanding, Dualla immediately sent out the recall code, and the Vipers peeled off and barreled back toward the *Galactica* as fast as they could go.

Everyone in the conference room, with the exceptions of Laura Roslin and Wolf Gunnerson, shouted in fear as the two ships banged up against each other. They staggered, thrown about by the impact, and suddenly there was nothing. The vessels were clear. The hit had not been direct at all, but instead merely a glancing blow.

Laura Roslin had the distinct pleasure at that point of seeing the air appear to escape from Wolf Gunnerson. As if he'd been hit squarely in the face—something that Laura wouldn't have minded doing at that point—Wolf gasped, "What . . . happened? Where did . . . how . . . ?" He looked at Laura as if he expected her to share his sense of barely contained outrage. "This shouldn't be! The Edda . . . it was clear! It was all clear, right there!"

"Don't believe everything you read," Laura told him.

D'anna couldn't believe it.

Space twisted and turned around them and seconds later the entire fleet was free of the Cylon attack. Except that shouldn't have been the case. They should have found themselves, yet again, facing down a Cylon ambush, one that would have most likely been the final ambush they would ever have to deal with.

Instead they were free and clear. Space around them was devoid of any Cylon raiders, and a ragged cheer went up from the members of the Quorum.

*Sons of bitches,* she thought. Her mind racing, she put together what must have happened and realized that Adama's people must have discovered the bug planted in Gaeta's hand. She wasn't especially concerned that it would lead back to her: Humans were so routine in pressing the flesh of their hands against each other that there was no way Gaeta would associate it with her, especially since it hadn't gone active until some time later as a failsafe measure.

She waited for Gunnerson to make some sort of violent play. The man was, after all, twice as large as anyone there. He could easily have killed several of the Quorum members before he was apprehended. But he did no such thing; instead he surrendered meekly to the security officers who approached him, keeping their guns leveled at him. He seemed bewildered, frustrated, utterly perplexed that matters had not turned out exactly as he had expected them to. He acted as if . . . as if his gods had abandoned him, and without their support, he had no idea what he was supposed to do or how he should proceed.

*Humans,* she sighed to herself. It was a source of utter mystery to her that they could be simultaneously so strong and so weak all at the same time. It was that lack of consistency that would ultimately be their undoing, just as it was their total consistency that would assure the Cylons of their eventual triumph.

Just not today. Today, she had a story to cover. God knew it wasn't the story she'd wanted, but as Wolf Gunnerson was finding out, even the stories you thought you could count on the most didn't always come out the way you were expecting them to.

# CHAPTER 24

The botanical garden on *Cloud Nine* had been cleared out of civilians. Stern-faced soldiers had withstood the confused protests from various residents of the space-going garden who wanted to know why it was that—especially after enduring yet another harrowing encounter with the Cylons—they weren't being given the opportunity to take some rest and relaxation in what was easily the most beautiful piece of territory still in existence. The colonial marines had offered no explanations, but instead had simply apologized for the inconvenience in a way that indicated they really weren't all that sorry about it all.

None of the stragglers or complainers saw the slight woman who was whisked past, keeping her head low, wearing nondescript clothes and a wide-brimmed hat that covered her face. They were far too concerned with their own frustration.

So it was that Sharon Valerii walked through the gardens of *Cloud Nine* undisturbed and unobserved. Actually, "unobserved" might not have been the most accurate way to describe it, for there were sniper scopes aimed at her head if she engaged in the slightest untoward action. She was all too aware of the potentially fatal surveillance, and had no intention of trying any sort of stunt. If nothing else, she owed it to her baby to do everything she could to survive.

She had her shoes off, and was enjoying the sensation of grass under her bare feet. It was new for her. The time she'd spent on Caprica in Helo's company had been mostly taken up with staying on the run—or at least putting up appearances of staying on the run—and she hadn't had time to enjoy the simple pleasures that nature offered. Of all the crimes that the Cylons had committed against humanity, she had to think that banishing them from the embrace of nature had to be far greater than simply blowing them into oblivion. She was willing to allow for the notion that the humans might have disagreed on the matter.

Sharon sensed that someone was coming before she actually saw her. She stopped where she was in the vast open field and waited as the woman approached her. Even before the newcomer drew within range of her, Sharon knew that it was Laura Roslin. She felt a warning of alarm; she was concerned that this was some sort of trick and they were planning to gun her down while claiming that she was making an attempt on the life of the president. Because of that worry, she stood completely stock still, her arms at her sides, determined to make not the slightest gesture that could be misinterpreted. If they were going to shoot her down, then it wasn't going to be for anything that anyone could claim was self-defense. It would be indisputably murder. Not that she thought they would be unwilling to resort to that, but that was going to be what was required of them.

Laura Roslin drew within about ten feet of her, well out of arm's reach, and then stopped. It seemed odd to see someone dressed in such a stern suit standing there in such a natural environment.

The two of them faced each other silently for a time. Sharon knew perfectly well if she made the slightest movement toward Laura, that a sharpshooter would drop her before she covered a foot of the distance. But it wasn't as if she would have made a move on Laura even if her every gesture weren't being monitored by marksmen.

"Still having the dreams?" she asked finally.

"Not recently, no."

Her hand rested unconsciously on her swollen stomach. "You still accusing my child of trying to get into your mind?"

"Actually," Laura said slowly, "it appears it was . . . something else."

"Really."

"Toothpaste."

Sharon stared at her, not getting it. "I'm sorry . . . what?"

Laura took a deep breath and let it out slowly. "Several members of the command crew of the passenger ship *Bifrost* attempted to ram *Colonial One.*"

"Freya Gunnerson's people? Midguardians?"

"Yes. They were shot and killed in the attempt. When shown pictures of the scene, I recognized one of them—a man named Tyr—as the maintenance man who had been called in to effect repairs to pipes in my bathroom. As soon as I did, security came in and removed everything from the bathroom and had it tested for potential hazards. It turned out that, according to Doctor Baltar, there was a powerful hallucinogen in the toothpaste. Every time I would brush my teeth, it seeped in through my gums and . . ."

"Made you imagine things?"

"So it would seem."

"So all those accusations regarding my child . . . they were baseless . . . ?"

"I'm not sure," admitted Laura. "I've been . . . under the influence . . . at other times, and had dreams that contained remarkably accurate visions of the future. This may be connected to that."

"Or it may be that you simply imagined the whole thing," said Sharon.

"Yes. It may be that."

Laura walked in a slow circle around her, appearing to study her. Sharon continued to remain right where she was. "I understand you changed your mind about pursuing legal action."

"I decided it wasn't worth it. It wasn't going to go anywhere."

"Freya Gunnerson is dead."

Sharon took in this news without the slightest reaction. "Guess I made the right decision," she said finally.

"Her father was devastated. Man fell completely apart. He's in the custody of the other Midguardians who swear that he and his close associates were acting without their knowledge. That they had extremist beliefs."

"Of course they'd say that."

"You think they're lying?"

"I think it doesn't matter what I think."

Laura made a small *hmm* noise in the base of her throat. Then she said, "So . . . this was your deal with the admiral? Getting information from Freya Gunnerson in exchange for two hours in *Cloud Nine*."

"I wanted my baby to experience this."

"It's not born yet."

"I know. But I'm experiencing it, so the baby will as well. At least, that's what I like to tell myself."

"Was it worth it?" She looked at Sharon askance. "To torment a woman as you did . . . just for a few hours outside of a cell?"

"If you'd ever been stuck in a cell as long as I have, you wouldn't ask that question." She hesitated and then added, "But then again . . . there's all kinds of prisons, aren't there."

"Yes. And all kinds of prisoners."

Laura nodded and then turned and started to walk

away. She paused and then, without looking back at Sharon, said, "By the way . . . it doesn't change anything. I still think the baby presents a risk . . . as do you . . . I still think that . . ." She stopped, cleared her throat, and then said, "But I wanted to say . . . thank you for saving my life."

"You're welcome," Sharon said without hesitation.

She stood and watched in silence as Laura Roslin walked away, and when she was gone, Sharon went back to flexing her toes in the grass and smiling.

Starbuck walked slowly along the memorial wall, looking at the pictures of humans who had died in the Cylon attacks and pilots who had likewise died defending the remainder of humanity against further assaults. The pictures were tacked up in no order. When someone wanted to add a photo, they simply put it up there and it became one of the hundreds of pictures of loved ones.

Little pieces of their lives, caught and isolated and etched on paper. Lives unfulfilled, each filled with individual promise that would never be met. It was the single most depressing place on *Galactica*. It was also the most filled with hope, because as long as there was anyone alive to remember the people up on the wall, then humanity continued to have a prayer.

She pulled out a very small picture from her pocket. She held it up and looked at it. It wasn't an entire picture, exactly. It was a portion of one. It was considered bad luck to put the image of a still-living person up on the wall, so she'd had to take the time to do some serious trimming. But she'd managed it, and now she tacked the picture of Boxey up on the wall. She sighed, and she waited for her eyes to brim with tears. They didn't. It made her think that maybe she just didn't have any tears left.

* * *

"They're all out? All the bugs?"

Seated in Adama's quarters, Tigh nodded. Adama had a cup of coffee in his hand and was sipping it. "All of them," confirmed Tigh. "Also we swept the extremities of everyone else in CIC. Gaeta was the only victim."

"Do we have any idea when a Cylon agent might have slipped that under his skin, and how they did it?"

"According to Doctor Cottle, considering how miniaturized it was, it could have been anyone at any time. And Gaeta's been off ship socializing any number of occasions, so it could have been any one of a number of places as well. There's simply no way to be sure."

"All right," Adama said slowly. "We'll be instituting regular security sweeps of personnel for potential listening devices."

"Yes, sir."

"And Saul," and he smiled just slightly, "good work."

"Yeah. I know," said Saul Tigh, feeling positive about himself for the first time in a good long while.

*"Toothpaste?"*

Number Six laughed out loud as Baltar leaned against one of his lab tables and smiled serenly. "Yes. Toothpaste," he replied calmly. "I told her it was the toothpaste that was causing her . . . hallucinations. She seemed most grateful. Even apologized for our little scene in which she made some wild accusations."

"Too wild. How the hell did she see me?"

"She didn't," Baltar replied easily.

"We don't know that for sure, and we could have a serious problem. As much as you claim expertise about Cylons, there's so much about us you don't know. That you can barely begin to comprehend. We share thoughts, experiences. That which one of us knows, others learn of either directly or even through just sensing it, because we are connected and as one. By having a transfusion of blood from that baby, it's not impossible that Roslin is starting to share in that knowledge. And knowledge is power. She claimed she saw me . . ."

"She doesn't know what she saw," Baltar said with complete confidence. "Everything's scrambled up in her brain. Are you ready for this? She claimed she thought that Sharon Valerii's unborn baby was playing tricks with her mind. Can you believe that?"

"Yes. I can, as I've already made clear. Furthermore, on some level, you believe it, too. Or at least you believe it's possible, if you were willing to fabricate that nonsense about the toothpaste."

"I said it because I wanted to throw her off the track, and I succeeded."

"Did you?"

"Never underestimate the power of placebos. I gave her a reasonable explanation for her hallucinations. That alone will likely be enough for her to have night after night of blissful sleep. There's nothing to worry about."

Six shook her head. "The woman suspects you, Gaius. Suspects us. Perhaps you managed to get her to bury it for a short while . . . but it's going to resurface. She is a danger to you . . . to us . . . for as long as she's in power."

"What would you suggest I do? Assassinate her? Or—even better," he snickered, "I could run for president. Win the people's love and force her out of office."

He continued to snicker and then noticed she hadn't joined him.

"It's a thought," she told him.

"It's a stupid thought, and by the way . . . we had an arrangement."

"Did we?" she said dryly, one eyebrow raised.

"Yes, one that you've never fulfilled. You told me if I did as you asked regarding those listening devices, you'd tell me your real name."

"Did I. Oh, yes. I did."

Slowly she walked toward him, her long legs wildly alluring. She leaned in toward him and whispered something in his ear. Then she leaned back and smiled.

"Legion?" said Baltar skeptically. "What do you mean, your name is 'Legion'?"

"Work on it, my dear," she said, patting him on the cheek. "Work on it."

Minerva Greenwald sat in the promenade of the *Peacemaker* and found herself missing Boxey.

The young lady—if a thief and gadabout such as she could possibly be called a lady—had very much enjoyed hanging around with Boxey. First, he was close to her in age. Second, he had learned extremely quickly from her, picking up the fine art of everything from cards to petty thievery. She'd found him an eager student and pleasant companion. But ever since he'd gone off to live on that stupid ship with that stupid woman, Freya . . .

"Hey."

She looked up and gasped in surprise. "Hey!" she cried out. "Hey, what're you doing here?!? I thought you were living over on, whattaya call it? The *Bifrost*?"

Boxey dropped down next to her and smiled readily at her. "I was. But I decided I didn't want to stay there."

"Yeah? Why?"

"Well, for starters, Freya shot me."

"She *did*?" gasped Minerva. "Wh—why aren't you dead?"

"Had a piece of metal paneling. Shoved it under my shirt. Protected me. She didn't know."

"Frak! Why did she shoot you?"

"Because she was nuts. I mean, why else would anyone want to shoot me?"

"I should say so! And you're going to stay here now?"

"Yup. Here with you."

He draped an arm around her shoulder. He seemed to radiate a quiet confidence he didn't have before. "I'm glad you came back," she said. "It'd have been terrible if she'd killed you. Unless . . . y'know . . . you were one of those human-looking Cylons. There's this rumor going around that if you kill them, it doesn't matter, because there's bunches of them."

"Yeah. I heard that, too."

"So maybe I should be worried that you're one of them."

Boxey laughed. "That's the dumbest thing I ever heard."

"I know. It was dumb. Mad at me?"

"Never."

She nestled in closer to him, and he sat there with a distant look on his face that she didn't see, thinking about Cylons, thinking about how they were all connected, and how things were often not what they seemed . . . and most of all, he wondered why he was having the strangest dreams about stone carvings that were bleeding . . .

# About the Author

Peter David is the author of dozens of works of fiction, including novels, comics, and screenplays. He has worked with both Marvel and DC comics, and has penned many bestselling *Star Trek* books. In addition, he has written for several television series, including *Babylon 5* and *Crusades*, among others, and was the cocreator of *Space Cases*, which ran for two seasons on Nickelodeon. His novels include *Knight Life*, *One Knight Only*, *Fall of Knight*, *Howling Mad*, and the Sir Apropos of Nothing series. His most recent fantasy novel is *Darness of the Light*. He lives on Long Island.